GREED

GREED

A DEADLY SEVEN NOVEL

LANA PECHERCZYK

Prism Press, Perth Australia.
Copyright © 2019 Lana Pecherczyk
All rights reserved.

Text copyright © Lana Pecherczyk 2019
Cover design © Lana Pecherczyk 2019
Editor: Ann Harth

www.lanapecherczyk.com

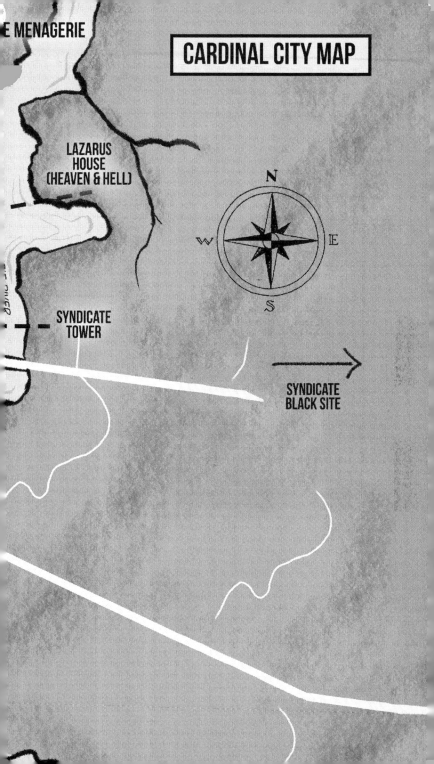

"To greed, all nature is insufficient."

SENECA

CHAPTER ONE

GRIFFIN LAZARUS

In the light of a full moon, Cardinal City glowed softly under a blanket of white dust. Griffin Lazarus slipped on a roof tile, cursing when a clump of snow thudded with a powdery explosion three levels below.

"This isn't stealth." His voice modifier made his speech deep and gravelly.

His brother Evan crashed onto the roof beside him, narrowly missing the ledge. "Stealth is my middle name."

"You don't have a middle name."

The chuckle they shared was short lived as the cold, frigid air seeped through their clothes. They wore identical black leather pants, hooded jacket, and *fukumen* face-scarves covering their noses and mouths. Except where Griffin's scarf was blue, Evan's was green.

Evan jumped to a jutting rooftop a level down, slipped and almost toppled over the edge. In a flash, he unsheathed his twin Katanas and used them like trekking poles, stabbing onto surfaces as he moved until he hopped to another ledge below, and finally down to the cobbled laneway.

Griffin winced. *So noisy in the quiet night.*

He pulled his baton from his back brace and activated the spring lever with a well-trained flick of his wrist. In an instant, each side of the baton lengthened with a metallic *shing*. The staff, now body length, was stronger than titanium and as flexible as ash wood. Griffin popped a button and a spike shot out of the end to jab through the snow at his feet. A muted thud sounded. Yes. Sturdy. Good grip. Less noise than the Katanas.

Before he went down, he pulled back his sleeve to check the status of the Yin-Yang tattoo on his inner wrist. The special ink reacted to his response to sensing greed. In short, the more greed he felt, the blacker the ink became, darkening the entire symbol in ink. Too much black and he was in danger of losing control and killing any greed signature he sensed in his proximity—*any*. It was a chaotic, deadly urge he never wanted to repeat. Using his wristwatch, he'd learned that timed exposure to sin or virtue had a sliding scale response on his tattoo ink. Seeing he was about to foil a robbery, he'd be curious to see which way the act tipped the balance—toward dark, or light.

After noting his tattoo's current status, he laboriously set the timer on his watch, tongue touching the tip of his teeth until he got the correct setting. Once satisfied he was recording, he took a deep breath and vaulted down to the ledge, and then to the next until he landed swiftly and silently next to his brother.

"About time. I'm freezing my nuts off." Evan used his Katanas to gesture around his general crotch area.

"Maybe you should have worn thermals," Griffin ground out.

A masculine chuckle came through Griffin's ear piece, reminding him that his brother Parker monitored their progress. Technically, Sloan should have been providing tech support… or at least their father Flint, but neither were available tonight.

Evan touched his earpiece. "ETA, Pride?"

When in the field, they had to address each other as their sin's code-name to avoid their true identities being exposed.

"I can't triangulate a location. I need more information. Greed?" Parker said through the earpiece.

"I told you, the sensation keeps moving. And *we* keep moving," Griffin replied, miffed.

"So stop and focus."

He clenched his jaw at Parker's authoritative tone. With a sigh, he shut his eyes and forced all street noise from his mind. The feat was an effort for him, more so than any of his brothers. Sounds seemed to drill into his bones, teasing him until they irritated, but the brutal training he'd received during his youth had also been drilled into his bones.

His breathing deepened, and his heart slowed. The hoot of the owl became a breeze, his brother's heavy puffing became a whisper, and the distant sirens became a memory. He inhaled deeply and focused on the sense of sin causing his gut to wrench. Greed coated the city like a toxic film, slowly suffocating it.

But he was after the strongest, the most grimy, the—

A cold, hard projectile hit Griffin in the face, along with a burst of gravelly laughter. Griffin tried to shake it off, and refocus, but the cold hit had shocked him out of his meditation. His knuckles whitened on his bo-staff. His teeth clenched. Every nerve in his body screamed as rage took over, and bloody memories flashed before his eyes. Broken bodies lying in the dirt. White bones poking through red flesh. Blood on his hands... Soldiers screaming for him to stand down. Stand down. *Stand down!*

He opened his eyes to find Evan packing another snowball, glee sparkling in his eyes.

Bile burned the back of Griffin's throat as he forced the bad memories to fade.

Not tonight. Not now. He was in control now. Nothing like back then.

A second snowball hurtled at his face and he deflected with his bo-staff, exploding the ice into white powder.

"What the hell?" Griffin growled, trembling with restrained violence, twitching with the need to inflict pain.

Evan shrugged. "I'm not used to feeling cold. Need to warm up. Plus, you're too uptight. We're not going to find the source of greed unless you loosen up."

"You sound like Lust." Were his family conspiring behind his back?

"Yeah, well, Lust's got a point." Evan sniffed and looked away, as if that dismissed the conversation.

Griffin kicked the bottom of his staff out and thrust it at Evan's face. Milliseconds before he struck, air crackled with electricity, and Evan dodged to the side. The staff whacked the brick wall, echoing through the dark alley. *Damn Evan, using his ability to predict and dodge the blow.*

Evan scowled. "Don't start something you can't win, bro."

Griffin struck again, flipping the staff, striking with the opposite end.

Evan caught it an inch from his face, eyes narrowing. His tone slid to ice. "Last warning."

Griffin yanked on the rod, but Evan wouldn't release.

"I dare you," Griffin shoved.

"You have a death wish."

Death would be too kind for someone like Griffin.

"What the hell is going on?" Parker's voice broke through.

"Greed's having a dummy spit because I told him to loosen up," Evan said.

"You don't want to see me unravel, brother," Griffin growled.

Electricity visibly crackled over Evan's hand as it hovered near the staff threateningly. "Maybe I do."

Evan and Griffin stared off in a battle of wills.

Griffin could almost hear the question behind his brother's eyes. It was the same question the family asked in hushed tones when they didn't think Griffin was listening.

What happened over there?

What happened during Griffin's combat training to make him the vicious, uptight fighter he was today? Or perhaps they already knew, and that's why they tip-toed around him. They were all created in the same lab to sense evil. All born as the enhanced beings they were today. All forced into a life of combat training and educated in the deadly arts. Except where they all came out of it unscathed, Griffin had been pushed to the limits. Captured during training and tortured. He'd lost control.

Never again.

"Greed?" Parker prompted.

"That way." Griffin pointed to the alley exit.

"No shit, Sherlock. It's the only way out," Evan grumbled.

Griffin wanted to thrust the staff back in his face but a sharp twinge of gut pain had him suddenly doubled over. The metal staff dropped. He clutched his middle.

Evan's hand shot out to steady him. "You okay, bro?"

"Yea—" A pained breath burst out. *"Greed."*

Bad. The sense was so powerful, he could only deduce a deadly crime was about to happen.

"Got it." Evan powered up, fists sparking. He sent a furtive glance down the alley.

The sound of glass breaking and hushed voices cut through the silent night, reminding Griffin that they hadn't exactly been quiet themselves. Anyone could be watching, or listening.

Evan caught Griffin's gaze. "You good?"

He pushed the ugly sensation of sin down and then reset the timer on his wristwatch. Fighting Evan had contaminated his experiment. Wristwatch set. Tattoo status checked. "I'm good. Let's go."

"Hostiles at the east alley exit," Evan murmured, directing his words at Parker on the comms. He crept forward.

"Roger that. Accessing street cameras now."

Moving as one, Griffin and Evan entered a cobbled retail courtyard and assessed their location. They were within the Quadrant—a popular cultural area of the city split into four districts: art, retail, food and entertainment dispersed with apartment living. Smack bang in the middle was a burglary in full swing.

Griffin sent his awareness into the jewelry store, sensing the number of greedy sin-signatures.

He held up three fingers, waggling two toward the back of the store, and one toward the front. Three perpetrators.

Evan gestured that he'd take the two, but Griffin mentally wrestled with the options. If he let Evan take the bigger battle, hence having the most fun, it could be perceived as generosity. Although, depending on the point of view, it could also signify Evan was taking the bigger risk, thus making Griffin greedy to remain safe. Once he started thinking down that path, he realized there were too many variables to predict. There was no way of knowing until after the fact. Either way, his bio-indicated tattoo would lighten or darken, marking Griffin unbalanced. The important thing was he timed the act, and recorded which direction his tattoo went, then his equilibrium was easy to rectify.

He indicated he would enter first.

Evan rolled his eyes and entered anyway.

A cry of amazement came from inside as Evan bypassed the thug on lookout and disappeared out back, no doubt where the safe was. As the panicked lookout tried to escape, Griffin clotheslined him across the throat. The man fell back and skidded across the floor, weapon flying under a cabinet.

He groaned and attempted to move, but Griffin pushed him down with his bo-staff.

"I wouldn't do that if I were you." Griffin pulled a cable tie from his belt. He secured the man's wrists then said to Parker: *"One down."*

"Copy," Parker replied. *"Now backup Envy."*

Griffin hesitated. He revealed his wrist tattoo. *Damn.* Too much white and it had only been four minutes. He clicked his tongue and reset his timer. He should've gone first like his gut told him. Now he was faced with another multitude of options on rectifying the imbalance, and he had no data to support actions relating to this specific incident. Would backing up Evan be considered greedy, or generous? It all depended on whether Evan wanted backup or not.

"Greed. You copy?"

Griffin touched his earpiece. "Yes, I copy."

"Go help Envy."

Two perpetrators were well within the scope of Evan's skill-set. Considering Griffin's tattoo was tipped toward the white, he'd make better use of his time by committing a greedy act to put him back toward balance.

"Negative. I'm heading home."

Parker argued but Griffin ignored him. He retracted his staff and secured it to his back brace. The voice in his ear became demanding, so Griffin pulled the earpiece out and left the store, swiping some costume jewelry from a rack as he went.

CHAPTER TWO

GRIFFIN LAZARUS

When Griffin returned home to Lazarus House, he entered through the secret back alley entrance of the basement headquarters. Above and reaching into the sky was a multi-level private apartment complex faced with a restaurant and a nightclub at street level. Usually upon returning from a mission, the team shucked their uniform in the communal wet area, sent it for private laundering and debriefed in the new operations room. But tonight, Griffin wanted to avoid Parker's judgement.

As quietly as he could, Griffin strode along the darkened tunnel leading from the street to their headquarters, hoping to silently bypass anyone still in the operations surveillance room. He peeled his hood back, tugged his scarf off, and breathed unhindered for the first time in hours.

The fake crystals in the necklace he'd stolen cut into his palm, but he dared not loosen his fist until he returned to the seclusion of his apartment. It made sense to release the stolen object in a dumpster somewhere, but Griffin had studied the effect of greed on his bio-indicator, and leaving something outside for anyone to pick up wasn't the same as taking it home. A twelve percent difference in change of tattoo ink color, to be precise, and tonight, he needed the extra points. He'd spent too long fighting to protect the city. He needed all the greed he could get.

Air burst from his lungs as he made it to the elevator and the doors closed behind him. Finally, he was alone. As the car lifted to his level, he tried to relax, but the cut of the necklace wouldn't let him.

It scratched and irritated, but it was necessary.

The twin elevator doors opened and Griffin stared along the long, dark corridor to where a tall, muscular shadow loomed against his doorway. He tensed and moved to grip his baton while his other fist ducked behind his back, hiding the stolen evidence. Then he recognized the shadow's brutish outline. Parker. Griffin let go of his weapon and strode toward his brother who lifted an indignant eyebrow at his approach.

"What happened, Griff?" Parker asked, pushing off the wall to stand unaided.

With his long auburn hair and golden eyes, Parker had an animalistic look he was somehow proud of. Must be pride, otherwise why would he wear the ridiculous maroon velvet smoking jacket and designer pin-striped satin pajamas. All he needed was a pipe and a girl on his arm to complete his own predatory Playboy picture.

Parker waited expectantly.

"I don't know what you mean," Griffin replied.

"Don't get fresh with me. Can we talk about this inside?" He waved toward Griffin's apartment door using a stack of folded papers in his hand.

Panic choked Griffin. "It's only Tony across the hall. We can talk out here."

Their brother Tony fought the sin of Gluttony and was an actor. He wouldn't be home. Whatever Parker needed to say, he was safe doing it there. No need to enter Griffin's place.

Parker cast an assessing eye over Griffin. "You ditched your brother in the middle of a mission."

Griffin bit the inside of his cheek. There were two ways this could go. He could lie outright and come up with an excuse, or simply state the fact that he left because of the needs of his sin. One response would tilt him toward greed, one would keep him neutral—or worse, edge him more into the light. Yet another decision to make when he was already exhausted.

Parker must have seen Griffin's gaze twitch toward his wrist because he shook his head disparagingly and lifted the stack of papers.

"For fuck's sake, Griff. I know you think you have this balance thing sorted, but you don't. We each need to find our mate, else we're going to end up our sin incarnate and become the monsters the Syndicate intended. Is that what you want?" His tone was painfully loud in the small hallway, and Griffin winced.

"You know it's not."

Finding a life partner who embodied their sin's opposing

virtue would supposedly release them from the burden of their sin, unlock special abilities, and leave them free to fight crime and make whatever decisions they wanted without consulting the tattoo. Without their mate, they would forever be prisoners to the destiny forced upon them at birth—purify half the world of sin, no matter the deadly consequences. To prevent that, Griffin would rather trust the predictability of science than some woo-woo unquantifiable *fated mate* theory. Just because Evan had found his mate, didn't mean the rest of them would. They had all searched for decades and come up dry. That was all the evidence he needed to stick to his timing protocol.

"Well," Parker continued, "while you've been obsessively managing your sin, the rest of us have come up with a plan to hasten the search for our mates. We just need your help to finish it."

"I don't need a mate when I'm handling this fine on my own."

Parker burst out laughing. It was a deep roar that tipped his head back to display perfect white teeth, and it shook the hallway. When he finished, he wiped tears from his eyes with a forearm.

"That's a good one. Handling it on your own." Then his expression deadpanned. "There's more to it than keeping your goddamned tattoo in equal parts."

"But there's not," Griffin argued. "You told me all we needed was to make sure the marking stayed equal parts black and white and we'd be fine. It's worked for years for me and I taught you all how to balance each act of sin with an equally quantifiable act of virtue. It's not my fault none of you have listened and are in danger of falling."

Griffin needed no reminder of the consequences of ignoring his balance. The blood on his hands visited him nightly in his dreams.

Parker narrowed his eyes. "That tattoo was only ever meant to be a Bandaid solution to the problem. Not a fix. Without your mate, you won't get special abilities."

"Don't need them. I win all my battles without them."

"Your pride is making my stomach hurt. It will be your downfall, Griffin."

He shrugged. Didn't care.

Parker kept at him. "You can't have children until you find your mate. You're shooting blanks. Or did you forget that? Or don't you care?"

"I don't think people like us should bring children into the world."

"Yeah, well the rest of us do, because what's the point if we're not fighting to make a world where it's safe for our children?"

"You need something, or can I get out of my gear?"

"Evan was almost captured by the police."

A beat of silence.

Griffin lowered his gaze.

"And that's not the only thing. Someone turned up and executed two of the perps."

"What?" Griffin's gaze snapped back to Parker's.

"That's right. While you were nursing your sin, some-one—we don't know who—turned up and put a bullet in the center of each head while Evan was checking on the guy you secured. He didn't get a good look at the shooter, but the only reason either of them were left alive was because they heard the cop sirens as they arrived at the shop. Evan was lucky to get out, no thanks to you."

Griffin didn't know what to say.

"If you had stayed, Griffin, two people might be alive, and the world might not blame the Deadly Seven for murder."

"Why would they blame us?"

"Because the survivor only saw you and Evan in uniform. Who do you think he's going to say killed his thieving pals?"

"Evan's okay?"

"He's fine, but you owe us." Parker slammed the stack of papers on Griffin's chest. "This is the result of an algorithm Flint and I have been working on to isolate candidates for our remaining potential mates. It crawls data on the net and narrows down any candidate who might personify any of our sin's opposing virtues. Take a look at it and give us feedback."

Griffin met Parker's eyes. "I'm not some sort of romantic matchmaker. I'm an analyst. You should know that since I work for your company."

"Well, analyze the data. And... yeah, about working at Lazarus Industries. You've been reassigned, starting Monday week."

"What?" Griffin stepped back, incredulous. "You can't fire me."

"Like I said, you owe us." He handed Griffin another

package—a folded newspaper. "And I'm not firing you. I'm transferring you to the Cardinal Copy Newsroom. A reporter has been printing defamatory articles about the Deadly Seven and we need someone on the inside to run interference and reconnaissance. Restoring our public opinion is of the utmost importance. Considering tonight you added to our bad name, you have to do this."

"Also not a journalist," Griffin said pointedly.

"Don't need a journalist."

"The answer is no." He wouldn't do it. He had a routine. He had work. He liked his work. He liked his office at Lazarus Industries. It faced the Quadrant's central park. It was private and quiet. No one bothered him there.

If he did as Parker bade, everything would be messed up.

"It wasn't a question, Griff. And it's too late. We have a contact on the inside. Grace's friend has put in a good word to get you an executive consultancy job. Officially, you'll be analyzing and providing productivity and efficiency suggestions for the paper. Unofficially, you'll be figuring out why this man is spreading false and misleading information. I want to know why, and I want it stopped."

"Why me? Why not Sloan? She's got tech skills. She does nothing but mooch around all day playing video games. I have a life. I was good at my job." *Am good at my job.*

"Greed has been called out by this reporter on numerous occasions. For you, it's personal." Parker looked at the newspaper now in Griffin's hand. "Take a look at the cover page."

Griffin couldn't adjust the packages without revealing the stolen item in his other hand, so didn't. His throat closed up. Sweat prickled his scalp. This wasn't happening.

"Whatever," Parker said. "Look now. Look later. I don't give a shit. Just look. You have an interview scheduled next week, and you'll start the following Monday at eight."

"So sure I'll get the job?"

"You're a Lazarus. Of course you'll get the job."

Parker sidestepped Griffin and made his way along the hall to the elevator, his dressing gown flapping like a royal cape as he went. Just before the doors closed, swallowing him up, he added, "I expect progress on the algorithm by family dinner Tuesday after you start work." Then he was gone.

In a week's time?

Griffin opened his apartment door, but it jammed a few inches in. He kicked. It didn't move. He squeezed his eyes shut and counted to ten. Then he counted to a hundred in multiples of ten. When he opened his eyes, he nudged the door with his shoulder until it opened enough to let him through.

The lights automatically switched on, illuminating the rubbish dump he lived in. Once a pristine neat and tidy place, stacks of stolen items teetered all over the open planned living space. Each item was taken to atone for the acts of generosity he committed in the name of fighting crime. From books and newspapers, to expensive vases and jewels. Some would call it a treasure trove. He called it his nightmare, but at least no living souls were harmed from this collection. He'd never lost control, never been out of balance, never had a situation where the darkness swallowed him and greed took over. He threw the necklace into the void and heard a clatter as it landed and sifted down between the cracks of a pile.

He unzipped his jacket and tugged it off, immediately checking on the state of his tattoo. Equal parts black and white. Then why did he feel like his world was coming apart?

CHAPTER THREE

LILO LIKEKE

It was six-thirty in the morning as Lilo Likeke rushed into the Cardinal Copy newsroom. Most other reporters made it by five-thirty to check the competitors' news reels before starting on their own day.

She hurried along the carpeted corridor in her sensible heels, popping a double wad of blueberry gum to take her mind off her hunger pangs. She'd forgotten to stock her pantry. It was her own fault for giving the last of her milk and bread to the stray cat who frequented her fire escape.

When she got to her desk, she ditched her threadbare satchel bag, waved a quick hello to Beverly Saks, the blue-haired sixty-five-year-old advice columnist, then rushed toward the break room.

Bev went on a new date every Tuesday, played poker on Thursdays, and went to Bikram Yoga with their friend Misha on Sundays. Bev was amazing. Lilo hoped she'd have the guts to live so vigorously at Bev's age because, right now, at twenty-eight, she felt like a jaded old woman. Being a criminal investigative reporter could do that to you. Being the daughter of a city mob boss could also do that to you.

Shaking thoughts of her father away, Lilo snuck into the break room before her senior editor, Fred, could spot her. He'd assigned a story yesterday, and she'd done nothing on it. Admittedly, it was about a dog who rescued his owner from severe dehydration by feeding him toilet water, only to have the owner contract Hepatitis A, and in turn attempt to sue his dog—not exactly a riveting criminal case, especially since she'd been chasing vigilante leads for weeks.

The last time she'd had a break in that direction was two months ago when she'd been with her friend Grace walking home from a restaurant. Pure luck had her at the scene to witness one of the Deadly Seven helping local enforcement detain a group of white-robed terrorists. It was a momentous occasion. Not only had a vigilante come out of hiatus, but he'd demonstrated a supernatural ability—electricity came out of his hands! The story had put the crime fighting group firmly in the superhero category, which was unheard of outside of comic books. Since then, although no more super-powers had been reported, there had been numerous Deadly Seven sightings.

Who were the Deadly Seven, and where did their powers come from? Were they even real, or some trick of the eye? What were they doing in Cardinal City?

The white-robed terrorists were also a mystery she wanted to solve, but so far, had come up with nothing. Considering the Deadly Seven were so secretive, the public knew little about them. Uncovering secrets about them, or the terrorists, would be her unicorn story and she was fast becoming obsessed.

God knew the city needed heroes. Crime was at an all-time high and climbing. Lilo couldn't help but feel partly responsible for that. Her family had a lot to answer for and she'd been trying to make up for it by being one of the good guys.

Lilo blew and popped gum while she glanced around the break room, searching for the coffee pod basket. She found it; there, shoved behind the coffee machine. *It's a miracle!* One pod left.

She could almost taste blueberry flavored coffee sliding down her throat. Her hands trembled from low blood sugar as she searched the dishwasher for an empty mug. *Success!* She pivoted to return to the pod basket and slammed face-first into hard cashmere. Her nose squished and her bubble popped. She dropped her mug and… and a thick string of purple gum hung from her mouth to the soft-knit wall in front of her.

"I'm so sorry," Lilo garbled, desperately trying to keep the remaining gum in her mouth. She picked at the edges of the flattened gum on the man's sweater. Stuck. Gummy. Going everywhere. Oh no! The purple blob kept stretching. It stuck to her fingers. Stuck to him. Strung from her mouth. Strung from his sweater to her hand. Awareness prickled over her forehead and she knew he scowled at her. Forcing her eyes open, and refusing to buckle under the pounding of her heart, she slowly tilted her head up… and up… and her heart stopped. Her jaw dropped. The last of the gum fell from her mouth and dangled heavily on the cashmere, bouncing on a perfectly flat masculine stomach.

The man in front of her was so handsome, he could have been out of the latest GQ magazine. Her gaze ran over him from top to bottom. Trim, brown hair parted and styled. Full black lashes blinked behind black-framed spectacles. Perfect five-o'clock shadow that accentuated a strong jaw. Wide lick-able lips. Sexy, strong neck. Her eyes traveled lower. White shirt. Silk tie. Cashmere sweater. Purple gum. Navy blazer tailor cut to fit his extraordinary musculature. Yep, he worked out. Gray slacks. Long legs…

He held a metal mug in one hand and her pod in the other.

Golly gosh, you're magnificent. Where on earth did they find this man? *Obviously, the gym. Silly question, Lilo.*

Wait a minute—*her pod!* She blinked rapidly. He had her pod. The last one. She snapped out of her lust-filled daze.

"What?" he asked.

Even his voice was magnificent. It melted her insides with a smooth, buttery lilt that had her licking her lips.

"What, what?" she replied, realizing she hadn't in fact pulled herself out of her daze after all.

"You said 'Golly gosh, you're magnificent'."

She'd said that out loud?

"Um." She laughed. "Don't mind me." Then shut her mouth, cheeks flaming. "I have a tendency to say the first thing on my mind. My mother says I'm too generous with my words, but… I guess that's why I'm a journalist. Plus I like reporting the truth. Facts, you know. Not fiction. Not like what some so called reporters here like to call spin." *Jeez, Lilo. Shut up.*

"Fact." He raised a brow.

"Yes, like the fact I saw that pod first, so technically it should be mine."

"I didn't see your name on it."

"Well, that's because I hadn't... you know what? Never mind. It's yours. I owe you." She winced and tried picking at the gum on his chest again. This was not going well. "Er. Sorry about the gum. If you take off your sweater, I can freeze it and then the gum should crack right off."

To prove she knew what she was talking about, she began to outline the process she'd seen on a Martha Stewart episode once, but the more she spoke, the more he seemed to pale and all she could see was the purple sticky mess on his front shuddering with his stilted breath. She had the sense that gum *never* got stuck to his shirt. He never had a hair out of place, and if anyone dared to disrupt his fastidious life plans, they'd rue the day.

"I'll just—" She picked some more and made an awkward face as the gum came off in big, long sticky streaks. "A little more."

She used two hands. Gosh, he was solid. Built like a brick house. And behind the blueberry gum, she could smell a delectable hint of a deep, rich forest that wanted to climb inside her and purr like a kitten. That sudden masculine perfume had her splaying her hand on him for balance. Now the gum was on her palm and she couldn't get it off. She'd made it worse, in fact.

But he wasn't paying that attention. Sweat dappled his

brow, and he tugged at his tie. "Why is it so hot in here?"

"Hot." Was the only stupid word that came out of her mouth while she stared at her hand on his chest.

He covered her hand, most likely to remove it, but a jolt of heat speared through her at their contact and they both flinched. He pulled away and stared at his palm. Big hands. Good God, he had big hands.

When he spoke again, his voice was rough. "You don't need to worry about cleaning it."

"Yes, I do. It's my fault."

"Statistically speaking, there's a high probability the gum has already ruined the sweater, so it's fine. Please stop."

"Do you know that statistically eighty-five percent of statistics are made up?"

The corner of his mouth twitched. "Are you mocking me?"

Heat flared up her neck. She decided to focus on the damage the gum had caused. "How about I buy you a new one?"

He glanced at his chest, wincing. "You're still touching me."

Lilo froze. Oh no. Her mother had warned her about this. She got handsy. People didn't like it. Her ex, Donald Doppenger—or Donnie Darko as she now called him behind his back—used to berate her constantly if she touched him in public. Which was very hard not to do, mind you, especially when they were allowed to touch as much as they wanted behind closed doors. She liked touching. A lot. But she shouldn't really use that relationship as a benchmark to compare other relationships. Not that this incident was a relationship. Oh for goodness sake, now she rambled in her mind.

"I'm so sorry," she murmured and stepped away, hiding her hands behind her back. This was a nightmare in need of immediate rectification. She turned away and spoke as she made two mugs of instant coffee with sticky hands. "If you send me the bill, I'll be happy to pay for the sweater damage. You can find me in the criminal investigations section. My name is Lilo Likeke."

Please God, don't let it be real cashmere.

Quick. Hurry. Make the coffee and get out of there.

The silence extended for a good few minutes while she poured steaming liquid into two mugs, then added cream and sugar. His presence burned along her back. Why wasn't he saying anything?

Something crunched behind her, like a squashed soda can.

She whirled around.

He stared at her, wide-eyed and white faced. His accusatory gaze ping-ponged between the crushed metal mug in his hand and back to her as though she had something to do with the mangled wreck.

She'd made him angry enough to crush his mug.

With another mumbled apology, she rushed out the door to the open-plan office area.

She shuffled into her cubicle and lowered into her chair until she was sure she became invisible. Only when the burning in her cheeks subsided did she look around to see if anyone noticed her flaming embarrassment. Her desk was next to an eclectic array of others. Over the partition was

Bev. A depressed investigator called Quentin sat to her left, and behind Lilo was Candy the fashion journalist.

Criminal Investigations bordered with the lifestyle section. It was a hoot.

The latter two journalists weren't in yet which made Lilo grateful. The last thing she needed was more eyes judging her embarrassing morning.

"Coffee, Bev." She put the mug on her friend's desk and ducked back into her little cubby to twiddle her hoop earrings and fade away.

"I didn't ask for a coffee, love." Beverly's husky voice carried a "do-not-fuck-with-me" vibe. It was misleading because Bev was as sweet as pie.

"Well, I made it anyway. You can have it. It's all yours."

"I drink tea," Bev mumbled. "But, thank you anyway, gorgeous."

"You're right. You like tea. I know that." Lilo put her face in her hands. "I don't know what's wrong with me this morning. First, I sleep through my alarm, then there was the bubblegum incident, and now this. Knowing my luck, I'll log on and find a police report about something that should have been uploaded to the web hours ago."

Silence from over the partition. Bev slowly stood on the other side, just long enough for Lilo to catch blue hair, arched eyebrows and blue eyeshadow before she popped back down again. She lifted. She sat.

Doing her morning squats.

"The bubblegum incident," Bev said on an up squat. "That shmendrik bothering you again? I thought you told him to stick it where the sun don't shine."

She referred to Donnie.

"No. All me this time. I—" She couldn't even picture the incident without blushing. "I totally face-planted the cashmere chest of this uber hot geek-god in the coffee room and kinda accidentally popped my bubblegum on said cashmere and then I tried to rub it off but made it worse and then I told him to take it off and oh my God I'm going to be sick." She clutched her stomach.

This time, Bev stood up and stayed, peering over the partition. Her red nails clicked on the divider as her fingers thrummed. "We don't have hot geeks working here. Only old, semi-retired schmoes."

"Yes, I know. He must be new." As the words fell out of her mouth, the world closed in on Lilo and she sat up straight, back like a rod. "Oh no. The new guy. He must be Grace's boyfriend's brother. The one I referred for the consultant job."

"You referred someone you don't know?"

"Grace knows him. I trust her."

Grace rarely asked for anything, so when she'd called for a favor to help her boyfriend, Evan Lazarus, Lilo knew she had to help. Grace had always supported Lilo and stood by her during her difficult breakup with Donnie. As it turned out, the favor was easy for Lilo to grant. All she needed to do was hand in Evan's brother's resume and the executive almost fell over their feet to book him in for an interview. Apparently he had access to some new fandangled news automation software that would triple productivity and increase sales.

The Lazarus family were synonymous with fame and

ambition in Cardinal City. The eldest, Parker Lazarus, ran a multi-million dollar—possibly billion dollar—tech company. One other brother was a movie star… Tony Lazarus, and she was sure another brother was head chef at the Michelin–starred restaurant Heaven. Wyatt Lazarus, that was his name. There were more family members, but Lilo couldn't quite remember them.

Memories flashed before her eyes and she was instantly transported back a few months to when she'd lunched with Grace at Wyatt's restaurant. Grace had been trying to sink into her seat to hide from the imposing and hard-to-miss men as they walked into the room. The Lazarus women at their table had been absolutely stunning, and the men… Parker Lazarus, Tony Lazarus and… the man she popped the gum on.

Griffin. His name was Griffin.

Even his name sounded like something imposing out of mythology. A majestic beast, part eagle and lion that protected treasure—her coffee pod—and crushed metal beneath his savage grip.

Bev's eyes widened as she took in something over Lilo's shoulder, then sat in a rush.

"Definitely not a schmoe."

Lilo turned to find the man in question standing behind her with a steaming mug of coffee and looking at her vision board with curious eyes.

He'd removed his sweater and replaced his blazer—no bubblegum in sight. The hard set of his jaw and flared nostrils hinted at the displeasure still riding him. He was about to say something confrontational. She tensed.

He calmly put the mug on her desk. "I don't want your coffee."

"Oh. Okay." That wasn't what she expected. "But it's not my coffee. You got it first. Finders keepers, remember?"

"No. You were right. You got there first."

Were they going to argue about whose coffee it was?

"But I ruined your sweater," Lilo added diplomatically. "So you should have it. I'll pay you for the sweater, of course. Just hang tight while I get my checkbook out of my bag."

Her hands trembled as she retrieved her satchel and opened the flap. Dread coated her insides. The last thing she wanted was to write a check. It meant asking her father for help, and she wanted nothing to do with him. She shouldn't even still carry her old checkbook around.

"No." Griffin's loud voice rang out in the office and people glanced over. Realizing the unwanted attention, he dropped his tone. "I don't want payment for the sweater."

He had to take payment. She wouldn't be able to look him in the eye if he refused. Every time she'd see him in the halls, she'd think about how she ruined his sweater. She owed him something.

"Consider us even," he added, then elaborated: "You also referred me for the job."

Lilo blinked. He knew who she was?

"So, I owe you nothing, and I want nothing from you. Let's leave it at that."

He shoved his hands in his pockets and strode away.

CHAPTER FOUR

GRIFFIN LAZARUS

Griffin strode into his new private office, refusing to believe what his body screamed at him: that woman was his mate.

Heat suffused his pores along with the lingering scent of blueberry gum laced with something inescapably feminine. It made every muscle, every sense, every nerve, raw in his body. His shirt scratched, and his shoes felt too small for his feet. Tugging his tie, he sat at his desk and forced his lungs to breathe at an even pace.

Even if she was—*irrelevant*—he was in perfect control.

He didn't need a mate. Especially not some bubblegum-popping, rambling woman who probably had no idea what a real statistic was, even if she did like facts. He raked his fingers through his hair, messing up the style.

Fact: Being near her screwed with his equilibrium. He didn't care if his tattoo said he was balanced. He knew how he felt, and his emotions were in turmoil. How could that be good?

Fact: He couldn't afford weakness—just touching her blocked out all sense of greed in the building.

Fact: She distracted him, and that was dangerous. When she had her hands on him, he couldn't breathe from the intensity of his irrational desire for her.

It was illogical how all sense of normalcy disappeared the moment they'd made contact. It was like he'd entered the Twilight Zone. His lungs had seized. His heart had pounded, and he'd sweated profusely. What was worse, her natural scent under that infernal bubblegum made him so aroused he went rock hard instantly. He'd never been more grateful for a woman getting flustered and fleeing in his life. He knew Evan said he'd felt something similar around Grace, but it all still sounded so ridiculous to Griffin.

But even as he thought it, another voice whispered that science was based in fact. If his biological mother created him and his siblings to recognize their sin's exact opposite, then it most certainly wasn't a mistake. There must be a reason, perhaps one that was necessary.

She was a beautiful distraction he couldn't afford. Loss of control was the first step to chaos. The piles of dead bodies in his memories were a testament to that.

Pushing thoughts of the woman from his mind, Griffin took a deep, restorative breath, adjusted the spectacles on the bridge of his nose, and peered at the collection of newspapers laid out on his desk. Arriving early that morning, he had been shown to the office by the editor's secretary and told to make himself comfortable until the meeting where he would be introduced to the rest of the staff. He wouldn't be welcome, he knew that. Nobody employed with the purpose of cutting jobs would be welcome.

He focused on his other reason for being there: the defamatory articles and the person writing them—Donald Doppenger. He'd never met the man and would have to hunt him down to investigate why he liked to publish lies about Griffin's family.

A few nights ago, Parker's assistant had supplied Griffin with a series of newspapers, all with articles by the man in question. All newspapers were now on his desk. Four columns of folded newspapers, three rows deep and displaying the cover-page, stared back at him. Each had a different headline marking the Deadly Seven as disruptive and destructive vigilantes. All written by Doppenger. Pity he wasn't one for facts—half the nonsense he wrote was sensationalist conjecture.

A headline caught his attention.

City Under Ransom; Where is Greed Now?

The story was dated three months ago and detailed a number of shocking kidnappings in the city. In one, the son of a wealthy aristocrat had been kidnapped and a ransom well within the means of the father was requested and not paid. But instead of writing about the lack of parental concern for the wellbeing of his child, the writer blamed the negligence of Greed for not responding to the mother's desperate call for help in tracking the kidnappers.

Griffin sneered in distaste. So he had to be everywhere at once, did he? He put down the paper and moved to the next.

Another story claimed the Deadly Seven were to blame for the building collapse that Wyatt's ex-fiancee, Sara, orchestrated. That story went far deeper than what the newspaper reported. In the course of the past few months, thanks to Evan's persistence, they'd discovered Sara's true sinister nature. She worked for the Syndicate—the organization that created the seven—and they wanted them back. Since they couldn't get them, they tried replicating the experiment by creating clones with supernatural biology, but failed at this as well. Their clones had a shelf-life of a few months. Didn't matter now, Evan had destroyed their lab two months ago, giving the Deadly Seven an advantage over the Syndicate.

Their only other advantage was how their biological mother locked supernatural abilities behind layers of DNA junk in their bodies, only to be revealed when they each met their mate.

Their mate.

Not a partner, or a wife, or a girlfriend or lover. A mate.

Someone they would be pair-bonded to on an intrinsic, and unescapable biological level. Someone who would trigger a pheromone response in his body to entice them to feel the same way about him. In nature, animals mated for breeding purposes and often connected monogamously for life. Nature was where their creator got all her research and ideas from, but because she was dead with only an encrypted laptop left behind with her nonsensical notes, Griffin had been forced to conduct his own study. He wanted to understand what his future held. More importantly, he wanted to know how to break free from it.

Griffin stared at his hand again, turning it over. His inner wrist tattoo had itched since he'd met Lilo in the break room.

It was impossible to tell if she had an effect on his biological balance since he was already in harmony, but it itched. Maybe the simple fact it hadn't changed an iota since he met her was a sign she was *the one*. An altercation with any other person regarding who owed what would send his tattoo scrambling. But not her. Not Lilo Likeke.

Before Evan had met his mate, Grace, his tattoo had been almost completely black. Within moments of entering Grace's orbit, his tattoo had equalized—returning to the normal Yin-Yang black-and-white pattern everyone recognized. Griffin had thought this sudden change to be cheating, but he couldn't hide the fact that the balance meant Evan was free to help anyone, anytime he desired with no consequence to his sin's dangerous internal pull.

A scar ran along the back of Griffin's hand, a byproduct from the time he was on a tour in the Middle-East with the Australian SAS. Like the rest of his family, his deadly combat training had spanned six other countries around the world. From deep covert cover, man-hunting expeditions, to Kung-Fu with the masters in Tibet. It had been a lonely, frightening time starting from the age of fifteen, and he'd come out with scars not always seen by the naked eye. If Mary knew the full extent of the training's brutality, she would never have let them go. Then again, maybe she did know. His adoptive mother was as deadly and determined as they were—except, where they grew up with loving parents, Mary grew up brainwashed into being an assassin for a secret society known as The Hildegard Sisterhood.

Mary and Flint's loving relationship had been a beacon of

hope for each of the seven. They made it seem like a normal relationship was possible for people like them.

Unbidden, Lilo's face entered Griffin's mind and the smell of bubblegum came with it. He supposed she was attractive. Quite. She had soft luminous skin. Her brown hair was a little messy, but the flush in her cheeks and the sparkle in her eyes had brought her to life. She had passion. He respected that.

Thinking of Lilo sent a wave of unseen energy rippling through him, making him dizzy. The wave crashed, and he was left reeling, only to feel the entire surge again. And again. Each time, metal objects on his desk lifted a few inches, hovered, and fell back with a clatter, throwing his desk into chaos. Paper clips, staples, scissors, and his phone; all rose as though he'd entered a zero gravity container. The stronger the wave of energy prickling through him, the higher the metal objects lifted. All items twisted and rotated in the air to point at Griffin, as though he were their true north.

His lungs seized at the reality of his new power manifesting.

First the metal mug crushing inward on its own, now this.

Flying metal?

No.

Not on his first day on the job.

Not now.

Not ever.

A knock came at the door and every metallic item dropped. He scrambled to neaten the disorder, lining up the newspapers in perfect rows and dragging the pencils into a pile.

"Mr. Lazarus."

Fred the Editor poked his head inside the office door. In order to remember his name, Griffin used the association technique. Not only was he an editor, but Fred was an older man. Judging by his white hair and wrinkled face, he neared retirement. But Fred the Elderly Editor was too much of a mouthful. Like most journalists and editors Griffin had met so far, Fred's hair was as unkempt as his clothes. He should run a comb through it every so often. Maybe people would respect him more if he took care of his appearance, and Griffin wouldn't need to be employed to consult on the department's efficiency.

"Yes?" Griffin smoothed his tie.

"It's time for the morning meeting. If you'd like to follow me, I'll take you there."

"Yes. Thank you." Griffin put his hands in his pockets, hoping to dispel the residual tingling left by the invisible magnetic pull of his new ability. He'd deal with that later.

He followed Fred the Editor through the hallway to a meeting room filled with a long, oblong board table and Cardinal Copy staff sitting in chairs. Seemed as though he was the last to arrive. He stood behind Fred at the head of the table. The sense of greed gently pulsed at him, and Griffin took a moment to acquaint himself with each person —aligning their greed signature with their face. The brunette man at the end of the table held the strongest greed. Casting his eyes over the man, Griffin couldn't see anything synonymous with strong. The man was tall, in his early forties, slim and soft. His jaw was pointed. His eyes were a shrewd washed out blue.

A light pressure on his arm made all the greed seep out of the room. The strange notion had Griffin turning in time to catch Lilo as she squeezed by. Greed filtered back as she removed her light touch. It had been mere minutes since he'd last seen her, but his body reacted as though it had been years apart and they were long lost lovers. Every hair stood to attention. The blood in his veins ignited. His body craved her, he couldn't deny it.

"Good morning everyone," she said in a sing-song voice as she placed a tray of baked goods on the table. "I picked up scones from the bakery downstairs. And, yes, Peter. I added a few donuts."

A gray-haired man with round spectacles grinned from big-ear to big-ear and immediately reached in to retrieve a chocolate covered donut.

Peter the Donut-Eater. Easy to remember.

Lilo shot Griffin a nervous sideways glance before taking the last remaining free chair at the end of the boardroom table. It was next to the tall greedy man which made Griffin curious. Why did she grimace and lean away as though there were a bad smell on his side, and why had his greed flared to new heights when she arrived?

"Right, well, if we're all here, let's get on with the meeting." Fred plucked a donut from the tray and dropped into his chair. He suddenly realized Griffin was left standing. "Is there a chair somewhere for Mr. Lazarus?" he asked the table in general.

Nobody put up their hand or offered to get a seat.

"You can have mine if you want." Lilo piped up from the end. "I'll just get a new one from the office."

Griffin flinched. Did she really think he would let a woman give up her seat for him? In fact, did everyone else? He cast a glance across the mostly male table and not one person offered their seat in Lilo's stead. Not that he needed it, but it was the principle. Chivalry was not in this building.

"No, thank you. I'll stand. It will be easier to see me while I speak."

"Great," Fred said, addressing the table. "Everyone, this is Griffin Lazarus. He has been employed to increase the efficiency of this newspaper by analyzing our productivity and working out what tasks can be mined for the new automation software coming in soon."

A few murmurs washed over the table.

"Mr. Lazarus. The floor's all yours." Fred went back to nibbling his donut, clearly not fussed about the new situation. Probably thought his job was safe.

"Thank you, Fred." Griffin opened his blazer and put his hands in his pockets. "As Fred mentioned, I'm here to assess your jobs and work out which tasks can be automated by the program. Theoretically, this will leave you all time to hunt more important stories. If you're a person whose job consists of fifty percent or more dispensable tasks, then you will be made redundant and roles will be merged. I will analyze data on record to see how your stories come into the system, how they are delegated, and the process on getting them investigated, researched, written and then put online. I will also be spending time with individuals from each department to account for data errors so I can adjust my recommendations accordingly. Any questions?"

Silence.

Tall Guy lifted his hand. "Yeah, who died and made you God?"

Griffin narrowed his eyes. "Perhaps I'll start with you first. Mr....?"

"Doppenger," he replied, still with a smug smirk on his face. "Donald Doppenger. My friends call me Don, or Donnie if you're really close."

With that, he winked at Lilo who wasn't even looking. In fact, she still seemed to want to get as far away from the man as she could.

Griffin stared at the man while he chewed the name over in his head with appropriate associations. He wore dark clothes, his greed was deep, but the easiest connection Griffin could pull was: Demanding.

"I'm not here to make friends," Griffin said.

Doppenger scowled.

Sensing the change in room dynamics, Fred stood up. "Ah… Perhaps you can start with someone else. Don prefers to work alone."

Griffin arched a brow. "No one is exempt, Donald. For your information, the CEO of your newspaper hired me directly."

"Stories can't be automated by a computer, man!" Donald growled. "It's hard, thankless work. I should know. I've been nominated twice for a Pulitzer."

"Nominated. So you didn't win." Griffin knew he shouldn't have said it the moment the words came out of his mouth. The temperature in the room dropped to arctic. He tried to recover. "This company doesn't run on nominations. It runs on dollars and cents, which are currently hemorrhaging from every department."

Doppenger raised his voice in argument, but Griffin put up his hand, stopping him.

"Fine," Griffin said. "I don't need to start with you."

"Why don't we see what stories we have today, and go from there, yeah?" Fred opened the manila file in front of him.

Inwardly, Griffin cringed. Still using paper and pen. He looked around the table and noticed many of the staff also had a notebook and pencil. Except one sitting on the opposite side of Lilo. A petite blond woman with pouty lips and round eyes. She fluttered her lashes at Griffin when their eyes met, then went back to her laptop, coyly glancing back at him now and then.

"Okay, what's come in this morning?" Fred asked. "Anyone got something new?"

One by one, the people around the table detailed what they were working on. Already, Griffin could see holes in their process. Fred relied on each individual to volunteer for stories instead of always delegating from the start. When everyone was done, Fred lifted some papers from his file, and read through each sheet.

"I've got a handful of floaters here. You know the drill. Shout out if any tickle your fancy. Robbery at Kent Street Jewelers this morning reportedly foiled by two vigilantes. Damage bill could be extreme."

Lilo raised her hand in the air, her mouth opened, but Doppenger cut her off.

"I'll take it," he said.

Lilo frowned and lowered her hand.

Dislike for the man immediately simmered in Griffin's blood.

Fred still read the data sheet. "Hold on. One of the perps is called Liota." His gaze lifted to Lilo. "Relative of yours?"

She paled. "Uh… I'm not sure. I don't really speak to any of them anymore. I haven't been a Liota for years."

Was she married? Divorced?

"Well, you can take this one, Lil. Go to the cop shop and see what you can weasel out of the fella. Familial connection might get you through the door."

"But—" Donald started.

"Any connection is a good connection, you know that, Don," Fred stated.

"Well, she can do with a helping hand getting past the cops. I can go with her."

She's sitting right next to you, Griffin thought. *She* has a name.

"I'll go with her." Griffin found himself volunteering.

All eyes swung to him.

He elaborated: "My sister works there, and it will give me a chance to assess Miss Likeke's process."

CHAPTER FIVE

LILO LIKEKE

Lilo arrived back at her desk flustered. First, she was being forced to interview her estranged cousin Nathanial. Second, because Donnie had tried to muscle his way in on her story and, third, because the uber hot geek god was coming with her and would be watching and assessing everything she did.

"You all right, hun?" Bev asked as she returned to her desk.

"Yes. All fine." She would be fine.

Lilo's gaze tracked from Bev's blue hair to the poster pinned on her side of the partition wall. It was her Deadly Seven vision board. Pictures and newspaper clippings were pinned over it. Her favorite photo was of the vigilante Greed, taken two years ago at the scene of the bombing. Having just pulled a victim from the rubble, he'd been standing in the dust, a dark masculine silhouette outlined in white cloud. The photographer had won a prize for that shot. Lilo knew the vigilantes weren't to blame for that tragedy and had been furious at Donnie for writing the story that accused them. Why would they rescue people from the rubble if they were responsible for bringing the building down?

Donnie replied that causing a tragedy so they could come to the rescue was classic psychopath behavior.

Bev had drawn a red heart around the photo, and Candy had printed and laminated a picture of Lilo making a kiss-face and stuck it next to Greed. Don't ask Lilo how Candy had sourced that image, but it made Lilo laugh, so she left it there.

Her eyes moved to a clipping she was proud of: the one where a few months ago Envy had saved the city from the white-robed terrorists in the street. She'd titled it, *Vigilante, or Superhero?* Because that was the first day any of the Deadly Seven had been seen using a supernatural ability. He'd electrocuted the terrorists with his bare hands, bringing the ring-leader down. The feature image had been taken on her camera-phone and showed Envy in full battle gear, swords out—yes he had two of them! A green mouth scarf concealed his identity. Two menacing eyes looked at the camera, burning holes right through Lilo.

Her hand fluttered to her throat at the memory. Water had sprayed from a damaged hydrant. Two vehicles had crashed. A crazy man had a gun. There was a hostage and injured bystanders. Bedlam. A police woman had tried to take control of the scene, but it was Envy who stole the show.

Seeing the deadly warrior in action made Lilo under-stand why they all had online fan-clubs. There were Instagram accounts dedicated to each of the Deadly Seven. She'd scrolled through the accounts once or twice herself. The naked man chest pictures of imagined heroes were all in the name of research, she kept telling herself. Each Instagram account speculated on the true identity of the five men and two women in the group and posted ideal specimen examples. None of them were real, of course, but it got a girl wondering.

What she wouldn't give to break that story.

Speaking of breaking a story, how was Lilo going to survive the morning working next to Griffin? Not only was she freaking from his watchful eye and possible risk to her job security, but seeing the way he took control of that meeting had been magnetic. That same kind of take-charge personality had been what initially attracted her to Donnie. That was, until he became too domineering. She shivered involuntarily, forcing her thoughts away. She wouldn't think about him right now. That relationship had taken everything she had to offer, and then some. No. It was much safer to fantasize about the unobtainable men of the Deadly Seven.

After a quick glance at her vision board, she dragged her attention back to her computer and set about finding the details for the precinct she was to visit. At least it wasn't the dog-toilet bowl story.

"How could you?" a gruff voice accused from behind.

She turned to face the man who made her ovaries shrink. "How could I what, Donnie?"

"I needed that story."

"I can't help it if Fred assigned it to me."

Donnie's brows lowered. "Using your corrupt family connection is underhanded."

"You know very well I've ex-communicated myself from that family and, besides, you didn't seem to care where the lead came from when I gave you a story last week."

"And since then? Nothing. You're only looking out for yourself."

Lilo's jaw dropped. Seriously? She gave him every single leak her father sent her way about the crime syndicates running the city. Four years' worth! From the moment she started working at Cardinal Copy, all leads from her father went to Donnie. It was how he'd been nominated for the damned Pulitzer.

She wanted nothing to do with it. Either the leaks were her father's warped way of showing he cared, or he used Lilo for his own gain—snitching on the competitors to get rid of them.

Even as the defiant thoughts ran through her brain, she knew she couldn't speak them. Donnie had a way of overriding her senses. After she left her family, she spent years starved for affection until Donnie pounced on her vulnerability. The moment he discovered her family connection, he pretended to sympathize with her. Lilo saw it clearly now. All she did in their relationship was give, give, give. She cooked the dinners, cleaned his apartment, let him have all the say in the bedroom until, finally, she couldn't function properly. Literally. The day she realized she couldn't orgasm without his help was the day she broke up with him.

You've had someone making your decisions your entire life, he'd shouted. *You'll never be fulfilled without me.*

If only he knew how true that statement was. She hated him.

Yet... Donnie leaned against her partition and gave her a smile that brightened his face into something she once thought was boyishly handsome.

"Princess," he chided. "You know you bring out the best in me."

The best? She was sure that had been the worst.

"I've not been the same since you left," he said, voice coaxing. "I need you. Come back to me."

"Donnie…"

"I still have your toothbrush in my cabinet."

Her eyes fluttered closed. She knew she was going to regret this. Somehow the man managed to get under her skin and… "Maybe you can tag along."

Donnie folded his arms. "I work alone. You know this."

Her fingers gripped her keyboard.

"Sorry to interrupt." Griffin's voice had both of them jumping. He stood glaring and imposing, holding out an assignment sheet to Donnie. "Fred asked me to give you this, Donald. It appears to be an assignment."

"You're not my boss," he growled and snatched the sheet from Griffin. With each passing second, fury mottled his complexion as he read. "This is about a man suing his dog for saving his life," he said incredulously.

"Indeed." Griffin opened his blazer and slipped his hands into his pockets. Some would have called his pose peacocking, but on him, it looked damned sexy.

Griffin cocked his head at Donnie. "Unless you have a better story to chase?"

Somehow, Griffin's confidence rubbed off. If he could stand up to Donnie with no problems, then she could too. Stuff Donnie.

"You don't though, do you Donnie?" Lilo asked, but shrunk a little when the full menace of Donnie's gaze turned her way. "I mean, you were just here asking for a lead, so I assume you have nothing else."

Her ex-lover glared at her for a moment before turning his rage toward Griffin.

The two men faced off for what seemed an age, and then strangely, out of nowhere, a stapler flew through the air and hit Donnie on the back of the head. He jerked forward from the impact. Both men gaped and looked around for the source of the throw. Obviously that was what it was—someone threw it. Must have been.

Maybe it had been Bev. She hated the *shmendrik*.

"What the hell?" Donnie rubbed his head, cheeks staining pink. "Where did that come from?"

"Maybe the wind." Griffin shrugged.

Donnie rolled the assignment sheet into a tube and pointed it at Griffin. "This isn't over."

"I know," Griffin said. "I'll be seeing you later for your assessment."

After Donnie stormed off, Lilo breathed a sigh of relief and said to Griffin, "You know you've made an enemy for life, right?"

"I'm not afraid of him. You shouldn't be either."

Those few confident words made Lilo sit up straighter. He was right. She shouldn't be. Donnie was the only person in the world who made her feel small, but he couldn't harm her now. Somehow, sitting next to the powerhouse man, Lilo felt strong—especially because none of that Lazarus fire was directed at her. If anything, Griffin seemed to be going out of his way to stand up for her. It was time to start putting Donnie in the same basket as every other dickhead in the world. Not hers.

"I've called my contact at the precinct," Griffin said. "She's ready for us."

"Thank you for that. It seems I owe you another one."

Griffin adjusted his glasses awkwardly and a pink tinge flushed his handsome cheeks. "No. I told you, I don't want you to owe me anything."

Was he blushing?

Lilo cocked her head and studied. His cheeks held a definite flush. He suddenly became occupied with looking anywhere but at her. If she didn't know better, she would have thought he was nervous to be around her. Only one reason a man became nervous around a woman. Sex.

The idea that Griffin actually desired her gave her the courage to say in a sultry tone, "That's a shame. You might have liked what I had to offer."

CHAPTER SIX

GRIFFIN LAZARUS

Griffin drove Lilo to the precinct in his black Escalade, still flustered over her last words to him.

You might have liked what I had to offer.

In the small cabin of the car, he couldn't ignore the woman. This close to her, the sense of greed took a back seat to everything else.

It was fifteen minutes of heated agony.

Bubblegum and feminine musk surrounded him, as though it pumped through the car's internal filtration system. Her presence licked at his skin, tempting him to reach out and touch, to see what she felt like.

Would he be irritated by the contact, like he was most other times he was touched? Or would it be as she said, and he liked what she offered?

No. That wasn't what she meant. It was his own irrational biological response picking up sexual tension where there was none. It took every ounce of control to keep his hands on the steering wheel.

Eventually, he dared a glance her way, and then found he had difficulty pulling back. The morning sun on her shoulder-length brown hair cast an orange halo. Every so often, she would fiddle with her gold hoop earrings, sigh and then rest her head on her palm as she gazed wistfully out the window, watching the city whiz by.

In her profile, her lashes were long and her cheekbones were high. Definitely attractive. Beautiful, even. Griffin checked the road, then went back to her. Her worn denim jacket was open enough to see olive skin from her delicate collar bone, dipping to a precious swell of breast before hiding beneath a white collared shirt. His gaze continued to where her hand tucked between the long flowing folds of her floral patterned skirt, knees squeezed together, as though she too felt the same charged energy bouncing between them.

Did that mean she was as taken as he?

The thought tripped a switch in his body. His mouth went dry, his cock stirred, and heat prickled his skin in waves. The metal in the car rattled, and he felt an intrinsic connection between his skin and the car. Taking a deep breath, he forced himself to calm. The last time his ability showed its face was with the stapler on Donnie's head. Before that, it was in his office. Each time he managed to manipulate metal, he'd been thinking about Lilo. It seemed his new ability surged when he was around her. Maybe in a protective instinct. He had to keep it together.

He loosened his tie and stifled a groan when he caught Lilo squeezing her knees together again.

This was torture.

In a desperate attempt to command his internal physiology, he tried to come up with some association words for her, but every word his mind projected made it worse. Lovely. Luscious. Luminous.

The prickling washing over him increased in intensity. He patted his cheek with the back of his hand. Yes, he was a little damp. Sweaty. Hot.

A car horn beeped. He tugged the steering wheel to veer back into the correct lane.

"Sorry," he muttered, mentally chiding himself.

He could feel her eyes on him, and needed a quick distraction, so blurted out a question.

"How did a girl like you end up working in a place like Cardinal Copy?"

"Of all the gin joints in all the towns of the world…" Lilo spoke in a strange low voice then chuckled.

It was such an odd thing to say. "No, I said Cardinal Copy. Not gin joint."

She gasped and turned to him with vivid attention. "You've never seen *Casablanca*?"

"No, I've never been there. Went to Spain once, but that's as close as I've been."

Lilo laughed. "It's an old movie with Humphrey Bogart, you silly."

So… not the place in Morocco? He shook his head, feeling more and more out of sorts.

"No, I haven't seen it."

"Wow. You're missing out. *Casablanca* is one of my favorites."

"I don't have time to watch movies."

"You don't? What do you do for fun?"

Another odd question. "Work."

"For fun? I need to take you out dancing or something."

"I don't dance, plus... I refer you to the original point. I'm usually working."

Lilo leaned Griffin's way curiously. "Surely you don't work all night too."

Her scent amplified, making him shift with unease. Her question was too personal. Keeping his nocturnal activities a secret had been difficult, he didn't like lying, but Mary had given him many tools to help with the process. One of them was to shift the focus back to the person asking the question. "So, why is *Casablanca* your favorite?"

Lilo sat back in her seat, smiling. "It's a sad love story, but also about World War Two. These people are stuck in Casablanca while waiting for America to decide if they're going to step in and fight Hitler, or stay out of it. Reminds me about the state of our own sad world."

"How's that?"

"Bogie and Bergman play characters who are desperately in love with each other, but the circumstances of war have torn them apart. I guess I like it because it explores if we can keep lasting connections when the world is falling apart around us. Whether we keep fighting the good fight when it seems like the romance is dead." She gave him a sad smile. "They don't get together in the end."

"The couple?" Griffin looked at her.

She shook her head. "They don't make it last."

"That sounds... anti-climatic."

"I guess, but when he gives up the love of his life, he

finds himself. He learns that he had a lot of bad to make up for, and the love was owed to the better man. But he didn't give up, he tries to find out what makes someone worthy of love. I'm not making sense. I think you need to see the movie to understand."

For some reason, her words sparked defiance in him. Did someone make her feel she was unworthy of love? Her sad eyes blinked at him. "Never mind. What did you mean, a girl like me?"

"You chew bubblegum. You bring in baked goods. You have posters at your desk with love hearts on them. You wear floral—"

She held up her hand, cutting him off with a dark look. "I get it. You think I'm too much of a weak woman to be a successful criminal investigative journalist."

He realized his faux pas a minute too late. "That's not what I meant."

"Sure it was."

"No, I meant you seem too nice for a place that sees a lot of bad things."

"Oh. Well, this is Cardinal City. I've seen a lot worse growing up, believe me."

Griffin thought back to what Fred said about her connection to the thief in prison and her earlier words about not being worthy for love. "Your family?"

"Yeah."

"Do you want to talk about it?"

"With you? Mr. Perfect with not a hair out of place." She huffed a laugh. "Not particularly. No thank you."

Perfect?

He ran a hand over his hair and glowered at the road ahead. His silence must have made her uncomfortable, because she quickly changed her tone.

"But if you need me to talk, I will. My mother used to say I can talk the hind legs off a donkey."

"That doesn't make sense."

"I know."

"I imagine the donkey would be extremely put out by losing his hind legs."

This earned him a laugh, although he knew not why. He was just stating the obvious.

He should have been happy she conceded, but he wasn't. He was irritated, and he didn't know why. This woman was so used to doing what other people wanted. People like Donald the Demanding. The ingrate had spoken to her like she was his lap dog, ready to roll over for him.

"No. It's fine," he said. "You can tell me if, or when you want to. Up to you."

A small sigh of gratitude was her only response.

A few minutes later they parked in the garage attached to the CCPD precinct. Griffin got out and went to open Lilo's door.

"When we get inside, you should stay close."

"Why's that?" She grinned up at him as she collected her bag at her feet.

"We're at a Cardinal City police station."

Did he really need to explain further? There would be criminals everywhere. Already the sense of greed tugged at him, testing his resilience. Like little fires lit at night, the beacons of greed shone brightly in his mind, coaxing him to come and find them and put them out of their misery. But none of the greed signatures were deadly. Not yet.

"I may be a weak woman, Griffin—"

"I told you I didn't mean that." He adjusted his glasses with frustration.

"—but I can take care of myself. I'm a criminal journalist. I know Krav Maga. I can fight my own battles. I'll be just fine inside a police station."

"Which Krav Maga?" he asked, bracing his arm on the doorframe and looking down at her.

"What do you mean?"

"Well, there are the few moves you learn in a self-defense class that help you resist an assault, or there is the real Krav Maga—developed by Israel forces and is ruthless, vicious and designed to maim and disable your opponent as quickly as possible."

She gaped. "Um. I take classes at the Y every Thursday."

So it was the useless kind, he'd bet. Some hackneyed instructor who'd learned techniques from another hackney instructor, none of them ever seeing real combat or having been a smaller person overcome by a much larger one. All it would take would be one misread situation and it could mean the end of her life.

The thought made him queasy.

Lilo stuck out her chin, lifted her skirt and slipped out a long rod from a strap attached to her thigh. "I also have this."

He blinked. "Is that a cattle prod?"

"Yes, and I'm not afraid to use it."

"Wow. Okay." He took a step back.

"Not on you! But I'm a female crime reporter in Cardinal City. I sometimes have to go to undesirable places on my own. It's for protection. The point is, I'm not as weak as I look, so you can just put that thought right out of your mind."

Griffin couldn't stop the growl rising in the back of his throat. The fact that a woman had to walk around Cardinal City with a weapon to protect herself didn't sit well. She should be able to walk the streets feeling safe. Lilo should feel safe.

"You're going to get yourself killed," he said.

"I'd be happy to give you a demonstration if you don't believe me." Her saccharine sweet smile held a hint of tease.

"So you can take care of yourself. Then why were you about to let Doppenger take your story?"

She paled and averted her gaze. "You heard that, huh?"

"It didn't seem like you were fighting your own battle then."

"We have history." She packed away her cattle prod.

"What does he have over you?"

"Pardon?"

"For you to yield to him so often."

Lilo got out of the vehicle and shut the door. "We used to date. That's all."

"But… he's older than you."

"Oh, don't look so surprised. He's not that much older. Just over ten years and, besides, true love knows no boundaries."

Griffin frowned. Lilo and that greed-monger? Together? And he still tried to worm his way into her life. "So, was it?"

"Was it what?"

"True love."

When Lilo cocked her head and contemplated Griffin, he knew he'd overstepped.

Why did he say it? It wasn't like he cared.

"Never mind," he added quickly. "It's not my place to ask. Let's go."

As they walked to the entrance, he couldn't help wondering what had happened to a girl like Lilo to make her the woman she was today. What was it about that family connection that showed her the worst of Cardinal City, yet instead of succumbing to the sin, she fought against it?

What was it she said about that movie?

What makes someone worthy of love?

Just before his palm hit the precinct door, she added: "I wouldn't touch him now with a ten-foot pole. So, no. It wasn't true love."

CHAPTER SEVEN

LILO LIKEKE

To get inside the busy precinct, Lilo dodged a toothless hobo and squeezed past a woman wearing a purple sequin mini dress who stank like alcohol and things she didn't want to consider. It seemed the police station was the place to be on a Monday morning. Lilo resisted taking hold of Griffin to avoid losing him in the buzzing crowd, especially since she'd made a big deal of being able to protect herself.

The reception desk was behind a wall at the far end of the lobby. Next to a simple red door, the desk was a hole in the wall where two male police officers processed reports behind a metal grate for protection. Between Lilo and that desk were hordes of people. Criminals in handcuffs lined wooden benches against the walls of the lobby, waiting to be processed. People stood before the reception, eager to complain or report a crime.

A body jostled into Lilo and she went careening into Griffin. He threw out a big hand to steady her and looked over her head to the offender—a small, wiry teenage boy wearing gang colors and a bandanna on his head. The teenager must have seen something in Griffin's eyes because he lifted his hands in surrender and backed away.

Still with his hand on her shoulder, Griffin directed Lilo to the side in a clear space. To the right, a woman in torn fishnet stockings, and to the left, an old man clutching his cane like a lifeline.

Griffin pulled out his phone and made a call. Two-seconds later, he spoke in a gruff tone laced with impatience. "We're here. Where are you?"

From the look of his jaw ticking and lips flattening, he wasn't happy with the response, but shortly after put his phone away. "She's on her way."

"Oh. Great." Lilo pulled out her press ID and pinned it to her denim jacket lapel. "So, normally, if I didn't have a connection like you with ties to one of the detectives, I'd stick this on and—what? Why are you looking at me like that?"

Griffin's head cocked. "Why are you telling me all this?"

"Because you're here to assess my process, right?"

Recognition dawned on his features. "Right."

"Little brother!" A feminine voice boomed across the din of the room, forcing them to break eye contact and search for the source.

Jaws dropped open in the room. Men drooled, women sighed with envy. Standing at the open red door to the back of the station was a tall brunette who looked like she ate men for breakfast. In fact, Lilo had seen her in action in the field two months ago when the white-robed terrorists attacked in the street. Lilo had tried to interview her, but she'd been too busy recovering from punching a crazy man's lights out.

This intimidating and stunning Amazonian woman must be Griffin's sister. Same wide lips, same thick lashes. She wore little makeup. No nail polish. Black army grade boots. Her long wavy hair was tied at her nape. A black gun strapped under her arm contrasted nicely against her white punk-rock T-shirt rolled to the shoulders. Impressive arms. Strong, but still feminine. The woman put her hands on her hips, jutting her curves to the side. Even from this angle, Lilo could tell she had a great butt curving under her dark jeans. The kind that powered strong legs, and if left unchecked, would expand relentlessly from excessive sweet cakes. It was obvious the woman kept herself in tip-top physical shape. Probably never seen the inside of a donut. Or outside for that matter.

Maybe Lilo should start bringing in healthy baked goods instead of donuts.

Griffin placed his palm at the small of Lilo's back and nudged her through the crowd to the woman everyone gawped at. Or maybe they gawped at Griffin. He was taller and just as impressive.

"Liza," he grunted, in way of greeting.

"That all you got?" Liza grinned and ruffled her brother's carefully styled hair, making him wince. "You're such a tight-ass." Then she turned to Lilo. "Did he tell you that? How much of a tight-ass he is? Never gives up anything. Never takes anything either. So boring."

A giggle tried to burst free from Lilo. His ass was tight, all right. Sexy. Perfect. She just wasn't sure she should say that in front of his sister. Instead something stupid came out. "Your ass is pretty tight, too."

Both Griffin and Liza stared at Lilo until she felt the heat drain from her face. "Um… That is… Nice. Rounded. Firm. It's supposed to be a compliment." Oh God she wanted to shrink. "That's what you mean by tight, right?"

Liza burst into a loud laugh. "Thanks, babe," she said, wiping the tears from her glistening eyes. "But I'm not into chicks. At the moment, anyway."

"Oh, neither am I. I just thought you had a nice butt. Um. His butt is great too, if that makes you feel better. Oh, God, I can't stop." Lilo slapped her hands over her mouth.

Griffin's mouth twitched and Lilo almost believed she'd see his first smile, but he held back, brooding expression holding firm.

"She's got no tap on her mouth apparently," Griffin explained to Liza.

Her embarrassment doubled, but he was right. To confirm, Lilo nodded, hand still covering her mouth.

"Fucking excellent. I'm the same," Liza said, appraising Lilo then back to Griffin with a jab on his arm. "I like her. She can stay."

Lilo expelled a breath of relief and dropped her hands from her mouth. The last thing she needed was to be blocked from speaking with her cousin.

Griffin's sister ruffled his hair again, and he scowled. "Stop touching me."

Liza whacked him over the top of his head with her palm. "What do you mean?"

He ducked and avoided another tap. "You know what I mean."

"Like this?" Liza slapped his stomach with the back of her hand. "Or like this?" She poked him on the chest. "Or like this?" She nabbed his glasses from his face and put them on her own.

The skin around Griffin's lips went white. His nostrils flared. His eyebrows lowered. Lilo could almost see the red blanket of fury drop behind his eyes.

"Do it one more time," he ground out. "I dare you."

Liza laughed, caught Lilo's eyes, and pointed back at her brother with the glasses she removed from her face. "His Royal Tight-Assiness needs reminders to loosen up, otherwise he'll never get to use that butt plug I bought him for his birthday."

Mortification plastered Griffin's features. "I threw that out the moment I got home."

"Ah, you're no fun. He's no fun. See? Needs reminders." The tone in Liza's voice hinted at more than simple sisterly smack talk. Her words almost felt like a message to Lilo. *Look after my brother.*

"I'll keep that in mind." Lilo grinned and looked back at a chagrinned Griffin, now smoothing his hair into pristine order. She took a moment to appreciate his face without the spectacles. Some people looked strange without their glasses, but not Griffin. He looked fierce. Majestic beast, fierce. A wildness came over him that took Lilo completely unprepared, and she loved it.

He took the frames back from Liza and put them on.

"Fucking fabulous," Liza said, clapping her hands.

"Let's go."

She stepped back and led them through the red door, shutting it and locking it once they were inside.

They went through a stone cold corridor to an open-plan chaotic detective's area. It wasn't like Lilo's office, where people sat quietly at their desks—except for Candy who usually listened to the radio streaming on her computer. The people here were shouting at phones, throwing paper balls at each other, and playing video games on their cells. Lilo couldn't believe how many of them were sitting there wasting time when a crowd waited in the reception room. Maybe detectives didn't deal with that sort of thing... or maybe the CCPD had given up.

Liza walked ahead of Lilo and Griffin. Someone wolf-whistled from the bullpen of detectives and Lilo wasn't sure if it was directed at her or Liza, or both, but Liza kept walking, unflinching. Lilo emulated her. Griffin didn't. He paused and turned to survey the office, trying to identify the offender. The bottled fury he'd contained at his sister's friendly ribbing resurfaced. His fists opened and clenched.

A tall detective with a mustache stood up at his desk a few feet away and gave Griffin a derogatory once-over. "You got something to say, Poindexter?"

Laughter broke out among the detective's overweight, unfit and saggy eyed friends.

Realizing she wasn't being followed, Liza pivoted and collected Griffin.

"Not worth it, brother. They're misogynistic ass-wipes with more blood in their pin-dicks than brains."

"That's not what you said last night," the mustached detective said, to the ribald glee of his buddies.

Griffin bared his teeth, and they flinched.

Liza took a deep breath and put her palm on her brother's chest. "I got this."

She calmly walked over to the man seated at his desk. Lilo thought she was going to punch him in the eye, or something—that's what Lilo wanted to do—but Liza slowly put her hands on the man's armrest and leaned forward until her lips were next to his ear. She whispered words only they could hear.

The detective's face went from cocky, to red, to pale and then finally finished the rainbow with a sickly green. When Liza pushed off his chair and sauntered back, the man returned to his computer, not another word said. His friends tried to speak with him, but he brushed them off.

Lilo hurried after Griffin and Liza as they continued along the corridor.

"What did you say?" Lilo asked, catching up.

Liza smirked and then shot a meaningful glance at her brother. "I threatened to reveal who he really lusted after."

"Griffin?" Lilo gasped. "How did you know?"

"Um." Liza took a moment to consider. "Maybe I've seen him looking at dude-on-dude-porn on his phone when he thought no one was looking, so took a wild guess. C'mon. This way."

Maybe?

They got to another door and entered through to the holding cells. A wide hallway with three prison cells on each side fronted by a thick door made from grubby plate glass.

Liza lifted her chin to the bulky officer standing guard at the entrance and he did the same back.

"These guys want to speak with the perp we brought in this morning." Liza indicated to the far cell on the right. She slipped a twenty into his pocket. "You need a coffee, don't you, Bobo?"

The guard scrutinized Lilo and Griffin then shrugged. "Yeah. I'm feeling thirsty."

Then he left.

Bribery. Ugh. Lilo knew it was the only way for them to get through to the cell, but it went against everything Lilo believed in. That guard didn't even blink. He should have at least mentioned their visit went against protocol, but he just shrugged it off. It was just as despicable as the detectives slacking off. Their lack of respect to uphold the law was the reason she got into crime reporting. Well, part of it.

The other part was a private vendetta against her parents and all the corrupt people in the city who believed they could buy their way through life.

She'd learned the harsh truth about money on her sixteenth birthday. Her parents had thrown her a surprise party in the backyard of their mansion. At the start of the night, she thought she had the best parents in the world. She had a gorgeous pink taffeta dress and gifts galore. Renata, her housemaid had been given the night off to enjoy the festivities. Every kid in her year at school was invited, even her best friend Misha from the mainland. Children she'd never met from down the street were invited. Extended family were invited. Strangely, her favorite History class teacher was invited and even gave her a crystal figurine of an animal. She'd loved crystal figurines and remembered being so impressed that her teacher took the time to find out.

But there were so many people, that it felt impersonal. On the surface, it seemed like a dream, like she was the most popular and loved girl in the world. Then she noticed little things. People being paid with wads of cash on the way out. Undesirables with peek-a-boo weapons, lurking in the corners. Everyone was overly friendly to her. It seemed fake. The only genuine person was Misha, but she had to leave early to work in her family restaurant. Lilo had been sad that her good friend had to leave, but then Andy, the young man who interned at the library, filled the gap. For a moment, Lilo had believed finally someone took an interest in her, not because her parents scared him or payed him, but because he genuinely liked her. They had spent hours talking about the library, connecting over their mutual interest in old newspaper stories and cold cases.

At the end of the night, she had gone to bed feeling comforted that the world was still a little honest. But before she'd gotten into bed, she remembered she'd left her new figurine on the drinks table outside and slipped back out to find it.

There had been voices coming from the garden and Lilo had thought perhaps a few guests had gotten lost in the enormous backyard hedge maze. Following the sounds of conversation through the maze, Lilo came across her father at the center water fountain, paying Andy with a wad of cash for his efforts in cheering his daughter up that night. Lilo hid behind a manicured bush, careful not to let the other men standing around see her. They were all men Lilo knew well. Uncle Bobby. Uncle Peter. Big Jo-Jo. They were all in on it.

All paid to be her friend.

Money was the root of all evil, and her parents were rolling in it. The very next morning, Lilo had begun a job at the local fast-food outlet, despite her parents disgust, and saved enough money so that by the time she was eighteen, she moved out of home and never looked back.

CHAPTER EIGHT

GRIFFIN LAZARUS

From outside the holding cell, Griffin watched Lilo stare at the skinny man on the cot and wondered what he'd done to make her clutch her bag so tight. Her other hand reached to where the cattle prod lived.

"This little turd is Nathanial Liota," Liza said as she slid open the thick, glass holding cell door. "Caught red-handed stealing from the jewelers last night. His two accomplices were DOA."

Unease itched. Two dead because Griffin had left Evan on his own.

Inside the cell, Nathanial's eyes widened when he caught sight of Lilo and he rushed to his feet. "Lilo! You came."

The criminal's greed flared in the presence of Lilo. He wanted something Lilo wasn't prepared to give, something possibly worth harming for, and that made Griffin wary.

Her brows drew together. "I'm here on behalf of the Cardinal Copy."

She didn't see the change in expression on Nathanial's

face because she rifled around in her bag for her tape recorder. Griffin saw, and he didn't like it. Nathanial's initial hope melted and flickered to something insidious— only for a second—before it was gone. Griffin stepped closer to Lilo.

"You good?" Liza asked Griffin. "I got a pile of papers on my desk I need to work through."

"Yeah, we're good." He folded his arms, staring down the man who was Lilo's cousin.

Lilo flared her eyes at Liza. "You're leaving us alone?"

"Don't worry. This tight-ass is stronger than he looks." Liza patted Griffin on the shoulder. As she left, she slid the glass door closed, locking the two of them in with the criminal.

Lilo was clearly worried. She bit her lip, her eyes darted around, and her knuckles went white on her tape recorder.

Griffin did something unexpected. He took hold of her free hand and squeezed, despite the sudden contact sending ripples of sensation up his arm. Immediately her shoulders relaxed, and she sent him a grateful smile. Seeing her tension leave because of him made his chest swell. It was uncomfortable, and he didn't like it. Made his clothes feel tighter. Made him feel hot again, and the sense of greed had dissipated, meaning he could no longer feel out what the man wanted from Lilo.

Griffin glanced at their connected hands, then turned his gaze back to Nathanial and gave him a once over. The man wore unlaundered clothes, had blond hair that looked self-cut, and broken capillaries surrounded his nostrils and sallow eyes. Possibly the same age as Lilo, but possible drug addiction made him appear older. Nathanial the Narcotics Abuser.

The man stepped toward Lilo.

Griffin intercepted and put his free palm on Nathanial's chest. "Don't."

He looked daggers at Griffin but stepped back. "I got no beef, man. Just want to talk to my cousin."

A small, polite smile flattened Lilo's mouth. "Okay, what can you tell us about the robbery this morning?"

Nathanial's eyebrow rose. "You don't know?"

"Know what?"

"About your father."

Lilo blanched. That warm feeling in Griffin's chest turned to ice.

"In case you've been living under a rock, Nathanial, he hasn't been my father in years. I've cut all ties with him."

"He's missing," Nathanial said. "Your father is missing. Don't you care?"

Lilo's grip tightened. "With his line of work, I'm not surprised. Now, back to the reason you're in this cell?"

"We were in the store this morning to gather a ransom."

Griffin's ears perked up.

"If we don't come up with the goods by noon Wednesday, your father is as good as dead. Doesn't that dig at you?" Nathanial added, sniffing.

Lilo took a deep breath and let it go slowly. "Even if it did concern me, I don't have anything to give."

"If you opened his safe, you'd have something."

"My mother can do that."

"She's not the one coded to the lock."

"What do you mean?"

He wiped his nose with his sleeve. "Your father made it so only he and you can open the lock. He didn't trust anyone else. Our plan to raise the ransom hasn't worked. You need to go and get the backup money from his safe and then take it to the rendezvous point to collect your father."

"Why didn't my mother call me?"

"Lilo. You're not actually considering this, are you?" Griffin asked.

"You stay out of this, man. This is a family matter."

After a deep breath, Griffin forced his anger down and raised a questioning eyebrow at Lilo.

"I'm not getting involved," she confirmed. "My father made his bed, he'll have to lie in it."

"Nah, you don't mean that, cuz. I know you, Lilo. We played Murder in the Dark together as kids. You're not as righteous as you think you are." His humor fled, and he frowned. "If we can't get your father back, then you know what's going to happen to the South-Side without a leader. What will happen to your mother?"

"My mother lives in a gated community far from the South-Side. She'll be fine."

"What about the South-Side kids?"

Griffin snorted. "Don't pretend this is about children."

Nathanial clenched his fists. "Last warning, man. Stay out of it."

"Let's just keep to the reason I'm here." Lilo blinked rapidly and then held out her recorder to her chin to activate the record button because the other hand was locked tight around his. After the device began recording, she held it toward her cousin. "I need to remind you that we're on the record. Anything you say can be published in the paper and incriminate you. What can you tell us about the two deaths at the robbery?"

"You wouldn't believe me if I told you." Nathanial began to pace the floor.

"Try me," Lilo said.

"I ain't telling you anything that will get me time."

"You were caught red-handed stealing from the jewelry store," Griffin added incredulously. He was already doing time.

"No. I was caught sitting in the jewelry store with my hands tied. Nuthin' more than that can be proved. I could've been in the wrong place at the wrong time."

Griffin couldn't believe the nerve. "You just said you were raising a ransom."

"Yeah, well, that could mean anything."

"Please, Nathanial. Any light you can shed on the deaths will be helpful," Lilo added.

Nathanial looked at Griffin, then back to his cousin. "If I do this, will you help your father?"

"I can't promise anything, but I can try."

Griffin closed his eyes and exhaled. Damn it, Lilo.

"We got stopped—"

"We?" Lilo interrupted.

"Yeah, me, Big Jo-Jo and Ruff-Nut."

"Big Jo-Jo's dead?" Lilo's eyes widened.

Nathanial nodded solemnly. "We were there... that's all I'm saying about that, but the fucking ninjas turned up and —well, that's how I got tied up, you feel me?"

"Go on."

"Okay, so, I'm sitting there on the floor of the store, minding my own business, and one of the ninjas—"

"Are you talking about the Deadly Seven?" Lilo asked.

"Yeah."

"Any idea which one?"

"The one in blue, and the one in green."

"Two?"

"Yeah. So, the one in blue splits, but then comes back. Except, when he's back, he's got a gun this time."

"You must be wrong," Griffin interjected. "They don't use guns."

Well, *he* didn't. Occasionally Parker did and Tony did. And Liza did, but that was in the line of duty. Guns were loud, messy, and not conducive to stealth missions in close quarters and, besides, he'd gone home after he left the jewelry store. The man must be mistaken.

"You weren't there," Nathanial accused. "I was, and I can tell you, that the blue ninja came back and shot my friends point blank in the head."

Lilo shook her head. "Griffin's right. Shooting isn't really the style of the Deadly Seven. I read the official police report and none of that was in there. Only that the Deadly Seven originally foiled a robbery and then left the secured perpetrators for police to take into custody."

A loud bang shattered the air, imploding in Griffin's eardrums.

Every nerve and sensation in his body went haywire. On instinct, he tugged Lilo close and rolled to shield her body with his as a second *bang* shook the room. Something hit him in the head, pain exploded at his temple, and everything went blurry. A rock. From somewhere. Warm blood dripped from his temple and he touched the wound. It came away sticky and red. The blurriness shifted, and the floor tilted toward him. Griffin staggered, blinking, confused. His boots crunched underneath and instead of seeing the inside of a cell, he saw red dirt. Flashes of other red, pulpy and broken things went before his eyes. Disgusting sights from when he was tortured in the Middle East. He smelled the acrid scent of petrol and a resulting burn up his left arm, and for a moment, he was lost in the panic of his memories —when they'd doused him with fuel to get him to talk. Gray haze covered his eyes. Ringing deafened him. He blinked a few more times before he understood what happened.

A bomb had gone off. The external wall had caved in.

Lilo?

"Are you okay?" he asked the trembling woman encased in his arms.

"I think so." Together they turned to face the gaping hole in the external wall. Light streamed in on dusty rays. A groaning sound came from the foot of the rubble. Nathanial was semi-covered by crumbled bricks and mortar.

"I have to help him," Griffin said to Lilo. "Stay here."

When he went to let go of her hand, she resisted.

A shadow blocked the light. He looked up at something nonsensical. Standing inside the hole in the wall was Greed, or someone dressed in his blue trimmed leather combat gear. Griffin rationally tried to come up with an explanation. Maybe someone had stolen his suit. Maybe he'd left it somewhere. But even as the thoughts formed, they dissolved with disregard.

This was something else.

Someone else.

To get a better hold on the intruder, Griffin pried his hand from Lilo's. The sense of greed bloomed in his gut until pain pierced him, begging him to double over. The sin came from the imposter and was vaguely familiar.

Lilo panicked and took hold of Griffin's hand again, washing the sin away, leaving Griffin only the sense of sight and smell to view the offender. A black hood covered a head, and a blue scarf made from stretch fabric covered a nose and mouth. Only dark, flat eyes stared at Griffin from beyond the hood's shadow. Eyes that tracked around the room until they settled on the squirming man beneath the rubble.

"There you are." A dark, lifeless voice came out of the masked man. He pointed a gun at Nathanial.

Griffin was too far away. He would have to leap over the rubble and that would push more onto to Nathanial. But then again, if he tried nothing, the fake Greed would kill Nathanial, anyway. This imposter had missed Nathanial at the jewelry store and had come to finish the job.

Griffin stepped forward. The fake Greed shifted his gun to point at Griffin and fired. Pain burst through his shoulder. Lilo screamed. Griffin slapped the wound to put pressure on and everything inside him buzzed. Warm blood pulsed at his fingertips and the imminent danger was enough to set his instincts scrambling into protection mode. His new power swelled and filled the room with magnetic energy. Power surged and tingled in his veins. The taste of copper hit his tongue. It was as though he'd stepped inside an electric field. Every metal object in the room became connected to Griffin. He felt the nuts and bolts underneath the cot. He sensed the iron in Lilo's hoop earrings, the bullet embedded in his shoulder, and the metal in the gun now aimed at his head.

Pushing further into his sixth sense, Griffin connected with the bullet in the barrel of the gun and somehow, he knew that if he concentrated, he could move that bullet any which way he wanted.

Lilo whimpered, and his concentration lapsed. All he could think was to get her to safety. She was more important than testing out some new inexplicable power. Wincing against the pain in his shoulder, he nudged her back to the glass wall.

On the other side, the police officer on duty desperately tried to unlock the door.

Seeing the cavalry, the interloper pointed his weapon back at Nathanial—his priority purpose for being there.

"No!" Lilo shouted.

Nathanial turned to Lilo. "Find your fath—"

Bang!

Nathanial went limp as a bullet ripped through his chest. Lilo flinched away to avoid seeing the bloody carnage.

Griffin had been too late. Too slow. Yet, another life lost because of his negligence, of his denial. If he'd embraced his new ability instead of running from it, perhaps Nathanial would be alive.

He pushed off the glass wall and torpedoed into the imposter. Agony shrieked in his shoulder as he hit the man in the torso. Together, they tumbled through the hole in the wall to the cold, soggy snow outside, blinded in the morning light. Griffin twisted so he landed on his good side, then rolled and recovered to face his opponent. His glasses had slipped and embedded in a pile of old snow, slowly melting under the sun.

"Who are you?" Griffin growled, crouched and ready to pounce.

The man looked at him and then turned to escape.

Unlikely.

Griffin pushed off his feet and punched toward the imposter, but he deflected with his forearm, blocking Griffin's attack.

"You should have left well alone," the attacker said, voice muffled under his face mask. "I'm only after the greedy ones."

Defiance bloomed in Griffin. That was *his* job. No one else's.

"Like hell you are." Griffin sent his magnetic awareness out and latched onto his opponent's weapon. He let his power coat the metal, cover it like a blanket, and then pulled until it tugged out of the imposter's hands and hurtled to the pavement beside them.

They both sloshed through the wet mess to get to it first, but Griffin kept amping his polarity to push the gun away. Every time the other man grabbed hold of it, the gun slipped from his fingers.

The attacker changed tactics and kicked Griffin in the chest, sending him spiraling backward. He landed with a thud on the concrete, knocking the wind from his lungs. The sun blinded Griffin and, dazed, he didn't notice the danger until the gun was pointed in his face.

For a moment, time stopped.

Then the fake vigilante stiffened and seized with a buzzing sound. The attacker's back bowed, and he crumpled to the floor, writhing in pain.

Behind him, Lilo stood like a warrior goddess, cattle prod squeezed between her two hands, wind whipping her brown hair stained gold by the sun.

People in the street had stopped and stared, and the police had finally gotten through the glass door to the cell, but in the time it took for Griffin to check on Lilo, the imposter had somehow managed to get up and run.

He should go after him.

"Oh my God, Griffin. Are you okay?" She dropped her cattle prod and crouched to put a hand on his shoulder, blocking out the sense of greed he felt receding with the criminal. "You're still bleeding. Oh my God." She repeated the mumbled words then turned back toward the hole in the wall. "We need an ambulance!"

He blinked, light headed from the blood loss, with only one thought: she saved his life.

What would he owe her for that?

CHAPTER NINE

LILO LIKEKE

When Lilo went to hospital, she was grateful Grace had time off her surgical rotation to attend to them personally—although it did little good for Griffin. He claimed the bullet only grazed him, but Lilo could have sworn the stain of blood on his shirt originated in the middle of his shoulder, not at the edge. As it was, Griffin let Grace see him privately, and then he went home.

Lilo couldn't believe it. He'd been shot. Who went home instead of staying at the hospital after a bullet wound?

By the time Lilo saw Grace, she was a mess. So much had happened in the past hour that she didn't know what to think. Her father, her cousin… Griffin getting shot, and *then* fighting… what on earth possessed him to do that? The imposter dressed as one of the Deadly Seven. He shot Nathanial.

"So," Grace said, snapping Lilo out of her daze. "Are you okay?"

Grace helped Lilo perch at the end of a bed and pulled her arms out to investigate the scratches.

Lilo looked at her friend and some of her nervous tension released.

Grace and Lilo had met two years ago when Lilo reported on the bombing that was falsely blamed on the Deadly Seven. Grace's parents had died in the tragedy, and Lilo had been tasked with interviewing some of the survivors. Since Grace was one of the few to survive the wreckage, she was Lilo's first stop. Lilo vividly remembered the day she turned up at the hospital to sneak her way past the doctors to Grace's room. Lilo had overheard Grace pleading with the police.

Strange things happened that day, and nobody believed Grace, but Lilo did. Why would the woman lie about it? They'd spent the consecutive two years trying to uncover the truth about the bombing but had come up with nothing.

They gave up until a few months ago when Grace had revisited the investigation in one last ditch effort to prove the identity of the bomber for insurance purposes. She seemed hell bent on discovering the truth, but then suddenly told Lilo not to worry about it after the insurance company overturned their claim denial. All the victims and families of victims received compensation so Grace left the rest alone.

"Lilo?" Grace said again as she swabbed Lilo's forearm and inspected the shallow wounds.

"Sorry, was just thinking about the day we met."

Grace smiled and tucked an escaped lock of hair from her ponytail. "One of the best days of my life. Apart from meeting Evan."

Lilo smirked at the swoon in Grace's eyes. She didn't blame her. Evan was a babe. A little on the messy side, but most artists were, and to be honest, Grace was super messy too. It was a match made in heaven.

"How's all that going?" Lilo asked. "I feel like I haven't seen you since forever. You're always working, or with him."

"Yeah. He's great, isn't he?" Grace sighed. "But—oh hey. We should be talking about you. How's it going working with Griffin?"

Lilo almost squeaked. "What do you mean by that?"

"Well, with him doing that consulting at your work. Thanks again for doing me the favor."

"No problems. Happy to help."

Grace waited expectantly for the answer to the rest of her question.

"Oh," Lilo bit her lip. "Um. Okay, I guess. Well, apart from what happened today."

"Mmm." Grace squinted at Lilo's forearm and plucked a tiny stone out with tweezers.

"Ow."

"Sorry. You want to talk about what happened? It was your cousin, right?"

"How did you know?"

"Griff told me," Grace added.

"Griff?"

"That's what the family call him."

"Huh. I think I like Griffin better. Much more regal and mysterious."

Grace dropped her tweezers on the metallic tray. "Oh my

God. Regal and mysterious? You have the hots for my boyfriend's brother!"

"No I don't." A flush crept up Lilo's neck.

"Well, why not?"

"What do you mean?"

"He's a lot better than Donnie."

"Don't I know it."

"So, what's the problem? I know he can be a bit stand-offish and stiff, and maybe he uses spreadsheets too much, but he's an impressive man." Grace picked up a bottle of saline and began irrigating Lilo's wound. "Very clever, loyal, reliable."

"Reliable? That's like saying a ramshackle house has 'character' in an attempt to sell it. I'm onto you, lady."

Grace laughed. "It is not. He's also assertive… brave, and well, he's a good man."

He was brave. He jumped in front of Lilo, knowing full well he could get shot. He also tried to save her cousin, despite the fact he had no conscionable reason to. Nathanial was a criminal stranger, and still Griffin had tried to help him. But…

"He's too confident. I tried that with Donnie, and look where I ended up."

"You're stronger than you give yourself credit for. You won't let another person walk all over you like he did."

"Well, Griffin doesn't want anything to do with me, so it's a moot point."

Grace assessed Lilo for a long moment. "I find that hard to believe. You're a smart, beautiful woman."

"I also ruined his cashmere sweater by accidentally popping gum on his chest."

"Naw. C'mon. It can't be that bad. Maybe it was your blueberry gum. He's a bit sensitive to strong smells."

That was an interesting point Lilo filed away for later introspection. Just another clue in the mystery that was Griffin Lazarus. And she didn't know why she was considering solving his puzzle because he didn't like her. So, stop it, Lilo. Stop fawning.

"He was so angry that he crushed his metal mug," she pointed out. No arguing that.

"Serious? That doesn't sound like Griff. He's always in control."

"Yeah, his sister Liza said he needs to loosen up." Lilo shrugged. "Well, it happened. Whatever. I have more trouble in my life than chasing a man like that, even if he does smell amazing."

"Smell amazing?"

Lilo waved her down. "Oh, it's nothing. Just this weird thing."

"Do tell."

"Always. I can't keep secrets. So, every time I'm near him all I can smell is him and it's like this musky-forest kinda smell and a hit directly to my—you know what? Never mind. You don't need to know that." Lilo shut herself down. The last thing she needed was to start mooning over Griffin's body odor when she knew there'd never be anything between them, especially since he'd been so clear about his intentions.

It was probably just a post trauma sort of fascination.

A slow smile inched up one side of Grace's face. "Magical body odor. Right. Been there, done that."

"Forget it. It's stupid."

Grace shrugged, but couldn't stop the smile on her face. "So, are you coming to the grand opening of Hell?"

"The new nightclub next to Heaven? Isn't that owned by the Lazarus family?"

"Parker I think, but yeah. So?" Grace wiggled her eyebrows.

"Isn't it invite only?"

"Do you mean to tell me Griffin hasn't invited you?"

"No. Why would he? We just met."

"Why would he indeed," Grace mumbled to herself as though she knew a secret Lilo wasn't party to. "You have to come. Maybe bring your Polish friend, what was her name again?"

"Misha."

"Yes, that's right. From what you said last time, she was having trouble with her father's business, and a night out might be good for her too. You can both be my guests."

"I don't know…"

"I heard the press have been ignored… this could be an opportunity to get the story no one else can!"

"You're dangling a carrot in front of my face. You always do this!"

"I know. C'mon, when was the last time we got to hang out together. It's only one night."

"When is it?"

"I think it's this weekend sometime. I'll have to get the

exact time and date." Grace held her breath and implored Lilo with excited eyes. "Come on. I miss you."

"Okay, fine." It wasn't like Lilo had anything more important to do. May as well give her spare time to her best friend.

"Yes!" Grace fist pumped the air and Lilo laughed because she knocked over an instrument tray.

It was good to see her friend so happy, and Evan was a big part of that. The thought made the little pang in Lilo's chest grow. It had been a while since she had someone who made her glow like that. Being with Donnie drained her. And before him, there hadn't been anyone in her life. No one since she left her family.

"Hey," Lilo said. "Do you happen to have Griffin's number?"

Grace smirked as she straightened her tray. "Sure."

"Don't look at me like that. I need to speak with him about what happened at the precinct. I want to get our story straight before I go into the office and write it up, and he left in such a rush. I should also check that he's okay. Is he on his own? Maybe he needs help getting around."

Grace stilled and hesitated. When she spoke, she lowered her voice. "When you say get your story straight, are you speaking about the person who shot your cousin?"

"Griffin told you? What did he say?"

"He said some imposter dressed in a Deadly Seven suit attacked and murdered Nathanial."

Lilo bit her lip. "I don't think it was really one of them either, and if I mention what I saw in the write up for the paper, then it could be taken the wrong way. I'm torn. I have to report the truth. You know me. I'm the first person to cry it out. But… it's only a gut feeling telling me it's a fake vigilante. I have no proof. You can't write up gut feelings, that's not how it works."

"Hey, it's okay." Grace touched Lilo on the arm and gave a gentle squeeze. "It will work out fine, don't worry."

Lilo smiled, but the turmoil inside her refused to abate. "I don't know. I have no leads. Nothing."

"No leads at all?"

"Well, the fake vigilante wanted Nathanial dead." Lilo paused and then took a deep breath. She'd been avoiding the subject since she arrived, but if she couldn't speak about it with one of her best friends, then who could she do it with? "My cousin said my father's been kidnapped, and there is a ransom involved."

Grace sat next to Lilo on the bed. "Are you okay?"

"I don't know."

Grace put her arm around Lilo's shoulders. She didn't say anything, just provided comfort.

"I don't know what to do," Lilo admitted.

"What can you do?"

"Before he died, Nathanial said there is enough in my father's safe to pay the ransom and that I'm the only one coded to the lock. I think I have to do it."

"You should take Griffin with you."

Lilo pulled back. "Why would he come with me?"

"Lilo. You put too much of yourself out there for others, and you never expect anything in return. I'm one hundred percent sure that if you ask him, he'll come with you. Maybe even tell Liza."

"No police. You know how these things go."

"And it never works out."

"As far as I'm concerned, if I do this, I just want to hand the money over, collect my father and go back to ignoring him."

Grace pulled her phone from her pocket and started typing. "I'm getting Griff's number. There. Sent. Call him."

Lilo's phone pinged with Grace's message. She'd only just met Griffin, but knowing Grace trusted him made Lilo feel the same. He'd helped her out today on numerous occasions. She knew holding her hand at the precinct had made him uncomfortable, but he never pushed her away. She appreciated that.

Perhaps Grace was right, and asking for help just this once wouldn't be too bad.

"Thanks, Grace."

"And if Griff is being obtuse, then Evan will go with you."

"Really?"

"Absolutely. You're family to me, Lilo. He'd help you in a heart beat."

Tears burned the back of Lilo's eyes. It might take a while, but she knew that if she kept surrounding herself with people who cared, she'd build herself a new family.

CHAPTER TEN

DONALD DOPPENGER

Donald Doppenger strode into his apartment, shed the Greed leather hoodie and kicked his Chesterfield couch ten times.

"Stupid, stupid, stupid!"

He tugged the mask from his face. Then on second thought, lifted it clear off his head and threw it across the room. It didn't even fly properly. It floated and flapped until it landed limp on the carpeted floor. He bit his lip until it bled, then stomped on the scarf with his boots.

"Take that you—fucking—I don't know. Aargh!" He pushed over a lamp on the side table. It crashed to the floor.

The serum he'd been given still coursed through his veins, giving him excessive energy and strength. He needed to let it out, and with nowhere else to do it, he punched a hole in the wall until his fist bled, and the frame holding his university degree fell to the ground, shattering the pane glass within. When his fist couldn't stand the hard surface of the wall, he punched his leather cushions on the couch until they split, then he threw them in the air.

Done destroying, he sat on the Chesterfield and watched the cushion feathers float to the ground.

Softly, softly.

They whispered on a silent wind, not a care in the world.

He roared at them and punched his thighs.

This was not how it was meant to go. He didn't give a fuck about shooting that stuck up Lazarus dick, but he was almost found out! If it wasn't for the serum, he'd not have recovered from the stun Lilo gave him in time to escape.

Donald frowned. If Lilo had known it was him, she would *never* have hurt him. Not his princess.

If he'd been allowed to head to the station to interview the surviving witness as he'd planned—alone—then Lilo wouldn't have been there, and neither would that jerk-off.

There were too many ifs in this scenario, and Donald was over it. He'd been swimming in if-infested waters his entire life. *If* he wrote a better piece, he'd have won the Pulitzer instead of Michael Prowler from the Times. *If* he'd been a little more forceful with Lilo, she wouldn't have left him. *If* he had been born first instead of his brother Milo the Senator, he'd have been treated like a champion. Instead, Donald had to always come second. Nominated for the Pulitzer wasn't enough in his parents eyes… so Donald was going to win it, no matter what cost.

He wanted it.

He needed it.

He would damned well get it, no matter the cost.

The power was fading in his veins, and the sense of

greed diminishing. The serum only lasted an hour or two, and the people he received it from would only give more as long as he fulfilled his end of the bargain—make the public hate the Deadly Seven. Fine with him. He could use the situation he orchestrated to write an exposé on what really went on in the minds of the Seven. Despite the public nickname for them, they'd never really been death dealers. Always preferring to wrap criminals up in a neat little bow before handing them over to the authorities. It drove Donald nuts. They had the power to kill, so why not? Why not rid the city of the sinners?

The city was over crowded, stinking, and in chaos. With the population teetering on seven million, getting rid of the gutter trash would do everyone a favor.

A few months ago, Donald had been drinking in the bar on Fitzgerald, drowning his despair in a glass of scotch. Lilo had left him. After their two-year relationship, he couldn't believe his princess left him. She'd never done anything without his approval, but that friend of hers… the doctor. She'd gotten in Lilo's ear and poisoned her against Donald. That bitch had turned his girl against him. If Lilo had been home to cook dinner when she'd said she was, instead of parading around during that attack on First, then they would never have gotten into a fight. Donald would have been the reporter to get the story, and he needed it more than her.

Vigilante or Superhero, my ass.

Well, he'd get Lilo back. She wouldn't survive long without him. Not when he'd commanded everything in her life. She wouldn't be satisfied without him. She'd come crawling back soon.

Soon he'd have the story, and the wealth to back him up.

That night in the bar was when the white-haired woman had first appeared in his life. At first he thought all his dreams had come true. Who needed Lilo when this beautiful woman was about to give him a pity fuck. He'd get over his princess. Rebound and drown his sorrows.

But the lady offered him something else. An opportunity.

She'd asked him what it would take to give him hope again, and he'd replied *to end the Deadly Seven…* as long as he was the one to cover the story.

Then he added, to have Lilo back.

And while he was fantasizing, he included fame and fortune.

Why not? If he was being honest with himself, he wanted it all.

She took him back to a warehouse just outside of town. There she changed into an all-white leather costume, the polar opposite of what the Deadly Seven wore. She wore a bird mask on the top half of her face. For a minute, he thought he'd entered some underground kinky scene, but there were others like him there. They called her Falcon behind her back. She made it clear she was an enforcer for someone else, someone important, and if any of them were having second thoughts, they should leave. When a man stepped forward to take her up on the offer to leave, she snapped his neck.

No one said a word after that.

It was in this warehouse, with the other strangers that he'd been given the serum.

His phone rang, snapping him back to the present.

Donald got up and kicked items away until he found his cell under a coffee table.

He answered it. "What?"

Silence on the other end. He checked the calling display and recognized the burner cell phone number linked to her —Falcon. *Shit*.

"Did you complete your mission?" came a hollow voice. Just hearing her tone made him cringe. He didn't know how he'd been attracted to her when she was out of her costume. The woman had a voice like nails down a chalkboard.

"Yes," he said in a clipped tone. "I killed the witness, but I didn't get the story. I almost didn't make it thanks to that Lazarus prick. I need more serum."

Silence again.

It extended so long that Donald thought maybe she'd hung up, but then she spoke. "We're under no obligation to give you anything."

"You don't, I spill. I make my award-winning story about you instead of the vigilantes."

"Did you just threaten us, Mr. Doppenger?"

He bit his lip. "I'll do whatever you want, just give me the serum. This time, I'll make it so the right people see me."

As it was, only Lilo and Griffin saw Donald kill that man in the cell. He needed public witnesses to the actual crime, not just him dressed as Greed running from the explosion. It had to be big enough, senseless enough, that the city turned against the heroes. He'd almost succeeded two years ago when he wrote the story about the Deadly Seven destroying the building that killed all those people. He didn't see a peep from the vigilantes for years after that. The city had lost their faith in them, and they lost faith in themselves. He did all that without the help of the Falcon lady and her benefactors. He could do it again.

"Mr. Doppenger? Are you still there?"

Donald snapped back to attention. "I'm sorry, I missed that."

"I asked about the Lazarus you mentioned being there. Elaborate."

"He's irrelevant. A data analyst or some shit. But because of him, I didn't get the lead for the story, and someone else did. He turned up to accompany my princess, then the asshole decided to fight me. The weapon you gave me was defective. I aimed for the head, but shot him in the shoulder and he walked away."

He would ask for a refund, except, he didn't pay anything for the serum. Strangely, they'd given it to him for free.

"Our weapons never fail. Your inexperience must be the cause."

"I don't think so. I spent most my teenage years hunting in the woods with my father and brother. I know how to use a gun. I know how to aim."

"Interesting."

Why the fuck? Donald wanted to ask, but he knew better than to pry with Falcon.

The serum was supposed to make him stronger, heal faster and sense the sin of greed in the foulest of sinners. She said she would supply a costume identical to the one the vigilante Greed wore, and then he was free to do as he wished. Kill whoever, whenever. The night Donald caught the sinners stealing from the jewelers was the first night he'd tested the serum. It worked like a charm. He felt invincible as he prowled the city streets following that gut wrenching radar to a crime. He hadn't expected the other Deadly Seven member there, and he would've shot him too, but then the sirens dragged him away. His plan only worked if he wasn't in a prison cell to write the story.

"You're sure you mortally wounded him?" Falcon said.

"Yes. Absolutely."

"And another woman was there."

"Yes." Nerves ticked Donald's jaw. He didn't like speaking about Lilo to this emotionless woman. He wanted Lilo all to himself.

"I want a full report emailed to me by the morning. You will have your serum Mr. Doppenger. You will have as much as you want, especially if you can capture a blood sample from the Lazarus man you mentioned was at the precinct. Try to be inconspicuous."

CHAPTER ELEVEN

GRIFFIN LAZARUS

Griffin stormed into the workout area in the basement headquarters of Lazarus House. He needed to let off steam and hitting an inanimate object was the safest avenue for at least three reasons he could think of: it couldn't hit back; it didn't matter if he obliterated it; and it had no feelings. Perfect for the aggression he was about to unleash.

Stripping his bloody blazer and work shirt, he rounded the corner to the fitness room and stopped short. His mother was running drills at the wooden man. Why anyone called it that was beyond him. It looked nothing like a man. Just a stump with smaller stumps jutting out from it. More like a tree. She hit each branch over and over again in a well-timed routine. Punch, hit, slap, block, kick, knee. And again until her movements blurred.

Apart from training around the world, Griffin and his siblings were also taught deadly combat skills by Mary. The one thing she instilled was repetition.

Again. Again. Again. The sound of her voice echoed from his memory.

They ran through their drills until their brains turned to mush and it became second nature for their bodies. That way, when an attack took their minds by surprise, or their emotions got the better of them, the memory in their muscles could be relied on.

That's what he needed now. Mush.

Mary noticed Griffin's entrance. Sweat plastered her dark hair around her face, and the rest was tied at her nape in a low braid. She wore black yoga attire and looked mighty fit for a woman of her age.

"Griffin," she said, halting. "What happened to your shoulder?"

He glanced at the red raw puckered wound, already closing over. "I got shot."

Obviously.

She knew what a bullet wound looked like as much as he. It even had the stitches Grace had put in there.

Mary stared. It was as though she gathered her patience. She always had that look around him. He knew he was hard to communicate with compared to the others, but she never lost her temper with him.

"How did you get shot?" she asked.

He moved toward the wooden man—tree. Wooden tree. Chopped tree. Felled tree. Something. He removed his glasses and put them on his folded pile of clothes.

"If you're finished," he said. "I need to hit something."

Mary stepped to the side. "Be my guest."

To avoid aggravating his shoulder, Griffin started slow,

but with Mary watching, he quickly became irritated and pushed too hard.

"You're dropping your left elbow."

"That's because I've been shot."

"Perfect time to train."

Was she being sarcastic? He didn't want to ask. Instead, he lifted his left elbow, stifled his wince from the shot of pain, and jabbed another branch.

After a few minutes of silence, Mary spoke. "Are you going to tell me what's got your panties in a twist?"

"By panties in a twist, you're referring to my mood."

"Naturally. What's bothering you?"

"Nothing." Jab. Knee. Jab. Knee.

Soon, sweat poured over Griffin's naked torso and soaked into his waistband. His lungs burned. His shoulder screamed. But it felt good. It felt something. It felt like control.

"Griffin."

"Mary." He punched a wooden arm, and it splintered off, landing on the rubber ground with a thud.

Damn it.

"It's not nothing. Griffin, look at me." Mary tried to turn his face with a soft touch to his jaw, but the sensation made him flinch.

"Don't!" he snapped. Unwanted touch still made him skittish.

Nobody told Mary no, so with a more forceful grip, she displayed his wrist tattoo. Usually this was the way she could tell if her children were lying to her, but with Griffin, his was always balanced.

He allowed her the look. The pressure was firm, unlike the soft feathery touch she'd used on his face. He could deal with firm.

She growled in frustration. "Talk to me."

Griffin didn't need her sympathy, her pity, or her help. She'd left him to that grueling seven year training on his own. Each of his siblings went through it a year apart. He'd hated it. He'd been beat up, tortured, and ruthlessly punished with endless nights of physical training. In the end, he also became something none of his siblings were—a cold hearted killer. This control was the only way he stopped that from happening again. No thanks to her.

"Griffin," Mary said. "Are you listening to me?"

But he wasn't. His mind was already in the past, to when he'd woken from a black haze to finding dead bodies all around him. To the foreign scenery covered in red eviscerated body parts. And he didn't even remember doing it. How could he be Lilo's mate, let alone stand next to her with that kind of monster inside him?

Right on queue, at the thought of Lilo, metal objects around the room started to shake. The dumbbells. The weights. The machines. It was as though a zero-gravity earthquake had hit, or a freight train traveled nearby. Each metal item lifted a few inches from the ground. They trembled and shook.

"Griff?" Mary gasped, eyes darting around nervously.

"There's nothing to talk about." Griffin bit his tongue and forced himself to calm. He imagined hot water streaming over his body. He imagined himself alone in the shower, at peace. The air in his lungs slowed its journey, and his heart rate steadied. The metal objects lowered to the ground and stilled, rattling becoming nothing but a memory.

Good. See? He could control himself fine when he pushed Lilo from his mind. He was in control, and he needed no help.

Mary gaped, looking around the room at the disarray of metal objects, now scattered haphazard across the room. "You're lying to yourself if you believe that."

Wooden man done. Cardio next.

Griffin stalked to the treadmill on the far side of the gymnasium. Before he got onto the conveyor, he shifted the skewiff machine back to its straightened position and then hit the program button for the most demanding workout.

The more he taxed himself, the easier it would be for him to process the events of the day. The new job. The fake Greed. Owing Lilo. Lilo. Why did he keep coming back to her? Her bubblegum scent had seared into his nostrils.

He started jogging but, before long, his sweat pants were drenched with sweat and sticking to him. He pretended he didn't care, that he was in control, but the texture of the fabric had changed. Once smooth, it was now sticky and weighty. Stubbornly, he kept running until he couldn't take it anymore, roared in frustration and stopped, stripping his pants until he sat on the gymnasium floor in his boxer shorts.

"Satisfied now?" Mary's distant voice held no smugness, only patience.

And that made him more irritated. His emotions threatened to overwhelm him, but he forced his outward countenance to calm. "Not even close."

He tried to stand, but wavered and sat back down. Just a minute, that's all he needed and he would be fine. He rested his elbows on his knees and winced at the pinch in his shoulder. After placing his head on his forearms, he slowly breathed through the gap and stared at the floor. It was a technique Mary had shown him when he was younger to help block external stimulation and focus on recovery.

"You met someone." It was a statement, not a question.

Griffin's only reply was that he didn't need anyone.

Mary clicked her tongue. "You of all people need someone."

"You of all people have no right to say that." He regretted the words the instant they came out of his mouth. He'd been doing a lot of that lately.

"Why would you say that?"

"Because you made us leave you to train with strangers." Because he'd been away from her protection, and he'd been tortured. He'd killed. "What do you know about needing someone?"

What kind of mother sent her children away?

Mary's quiet footsteps padded through the room until Griffin saw her bare feet in front of him. She crouched and waited. He inhaled a deep shuddering breath. When Griffin lifted his gaze, he found eyes glistening with unshed tears.

"Griffin, I did the best I could to prepare you for what you have to face now. The future I foretold years ago is starting to arrive, and we've only seen the beginning. I couldn't train seven gifted teenagers on my own. I had to get help."

"Sometimes the help did a terrible job."

"I'm sorry." She tried to put her hand on his arm, but he cut her down with a glare.

He knew he was being irrational, pushing his problems onto her because she was an easy target. It was unfair, but he couldn't stop. The alternative was looking at himself.

A man cleared his throat.

Griffin shifted his glare to the door where Flint stood, hands on hips. Flint was a tall man of about sixty who had kept fit and slim. He wore a flannelette shirt, buttons open to reveal a white T-shirt tainted with black grease. The baseball cap on his head was also stained and turned backward.

He probably shouldn't wear light colors with his occupation.

"I think it's about time you and I had ourselves a little chat, son. Step into my office."

Flint sent his wife a look Griffin couldn't decipher.

Mary backed off and straightened. "I just have one last thing to say to you, Griffin."

He tensed.

"You may think you can ignore finding your mate, but you can't ignore that new ability. You need to train before you hurt someone. I expect to see you here in full battle gear in one hour and then ready to hit the streets at sunset. I'll find someone to run comms for you. Maybe Evan can join you on patrol. Call me crazy, but electricity and magnetism go hand in hand."

She walked out.

Griffin shook his head. At what, he wasn't sure. Maybe himself, because he liked that Mary wasn't one to be pushed around. He liked that she kept him in line. To be honest, it was a relief.

Some things never changed.

He got up, found himself a towel to wrap around his waist, and then followed Flint out of the room.

To get to the workshop, Griffin had to pass through the operations room. It was a space filled with screens on walls monitoring CCTV and news footage around the city. In the center of the room was a strategy table laid out with maps and computers. The glass cabinets lining another wall were empty except for bare mannequins, waiting to be covered by the new battle outfit Parker worked on. Griffin looked forward to the prototype's completion.

When he entered the tech workshop, he found Flint already at his desk rearranging his tools around a metal sphere open to expose something that looked like a miniature gas chamber.

Griffin almost asked about the project, but Flint spoke up.

"I heard about what happened on patrol last night," Flint said. "You left your brother because staying would have put you out of balance. He could have gotten hurt."

"He survived."

"That's not the point, and you know it. Your control issues are impeding your effectiveness and reliability in the field. It's time to do something about it. You should talk to us about what happened during your training."

Control issues kept him from murdering every person he loved, and then some… but perhaps Flint had a small point. The stolen clutter in his apartment was getting out of hand.

The protocol he'd formed to keep him in balance was no longer optimal.

"I overheard what your mother said about your new abilities. You've met someone."

"I don't see how that is relevant to my… habits."

"You've seen how Evan and Grace are together. It's natural. It's good. And Evan doesn't need to worry about cutting time short when he's fighting crime because he's worried he'll be out of balance."

"I don't like relying on someone else to reset my equilibrium. It's unreliable."

"Life is unreliable."

"I know this," Griffin growled.

"So, what else is it? What's really putting you off?" Flint shifted a mechanical box on his desk, opened it and then rearranged the metal tools inside. "Is it… have you, I mean…" Flint cleared his throat. "You're not nervous to be with a woman, are you?"

What did he mean by that? Of course Griffin wasn't nervous to be with a woman. He was around them all the time.

Oh.

"I've been sexually involved with women before, Flint. I'm not a teenager."

"Okay. Good." He cleared his throat again and avoided Griffin's gaze. "Because, you know, I'm here if you need to talk. About anything. Girl stuff, you know. I mean, I was your age once."

Griffin stifled a smile. "I know."

"In fact, I met Mary around your age. We worked at the

same place, as you know." Flint's gaze turned wistful. "She loved it when I made her coffee. I'd turn up to the break room, and we'd spend our ten minutes together."

"Coffee," Griffin mused.

"Yep. Simple as that. I turned up like clockwork every day. Took me some time to get into her good books, but once I did, I knew there was no turning back. Is there anything about this woman you've mated that isn't quite right for you? Grace was perfect for Evan, but we haven't any understanding if everyone else will get a mate of similar age and be physically and emotionally attracted to them."

An image of Lilo's lovely face rose in Griffin's mind—it was the image he'd captured of her sitting in his car, sun casting a soft halo around her head.

"Lilo is above physical expectations, she's aesthetically attractive and of a similar age. I'd say her personality is also acceptable. Perhaps she's a little too talkative, and she likes to touch, but one can expect that from a generous person." He thought about it for a moment longer. "She chewed gum. I didn't like that. It was too fragrant."

"None of these things seem like deal-breakers. So, what's holding you back?"

"I told you. I don't like relying on something we know little about. This mate business is unpredictable and new to us all."

At least with his protocol, he had precise implications for each action he made versus the response on his tattoo marker. Steal a piece of jewelry, the marker would shift into the dark. Do something selfless, it would shift to the light. Lilo had saved his life, but he'd shielded her with his body when the explosion went off. Was that enough to equalize their debt to each other?

Griffin peered at his tattoo, still equal parts black and white, and that concerned him. It had been hours since he'd been with Lilo. If it were anyone else who had saved his life, his tattoo might have tipped toward the dark side—the selfish side. Especially if the marking believed he *let* Lilo save his life for selfish reasons. Following his current protocol for keeping balance, that would mean that Griffin had to do something equally selfless to put him back to center, but with the tattoo in its current state, he had no evidence to suggest he was out of balance.

Unreliable.

The entire protocol he'd built over countless years would be null and void if he couldn't get accurate readings from his tattoo anymore.

Without understanding his new situation, he felt as though he waited for a bomb to go off. Would he suddenly tip into the dark-side when least expected? Or did her proximity reset his internal equilibrium, as though wiping a slate clean? How much of his life would be controlled by his need to be near her? And on the flip side, how many of her feelings would be controlled by the pheromones he released around her? Both of them would be living their life according to a specific set of rules someone else had written.

"Can I make a suggestion?" Flint asked. "Do what you're good at. Gather evidence and make an informed decision before you write this woman off. In the mean time, be nice to her. You don't want her to turn off you before she's had a chance to meet the real you. Change is good, Griff."

But it wasn't easy.

"I'll think about it," Griffin said. "I have to go. Mary will be waiting for me soon."

"While you're at it, apologize to your mother. Your behavior was uncalled for earlier."

"I agree."

"Good chat." Flint clapped Griffin firmly on the shoulder and then let go. "See you at dinner tomorrow night."

CHAPTER TWELVE

LILO LIKEKE

When Lilo got back to the Cardinal Copy, she sat at her desk, staring into space, trying to decide if she trusted Griffin enough to send the message churning in her mind. He tried to save her cousin. *I have to help him*, he'd said. Not, *Get him*, or *RUN!* His first instinct had been to save the criminal. Any man who acted so selflessly must be good. With her resolve hardened, she typed into her phone:

We need to talk.

He didn't answer. Probably because he had no idea who she was.

This is Lilo, by the way, she added. *Lilo Likeke.*

Still no answer. Maybe he was freaking out because Grace gave her his number.

Grace gave me your number. Hope that's okay.
Griffin?

Lilo tapped her finger on the phone screen, waiting. Maybe he was busy. She could probably just phone him, but she was at work with a thousand prying eyes. Plus, if she didn't start work on the story soon, Fred would start to worry. Fred would come over and discuss. Then Lilo would blurt out something she shouldn't.

She turned on her computer then promptly distracted herself by ordering her old housekeeper a birthday present. It was a necklace she'd spotted in the lifestyle section that Candy had recommended. Renata had always been kind to Lilo when she grew up. Because Renata was poor, Lilo never worried her affections were paid. She didn't have to be kind to the spoiled princess Lilo, but she was. And now that Lilo had seen the truth behind her family money, she always did what she could to let Renata know she was thinking of her.

Good. Paid. Express delivery so it arrived today. God she loved same day shipping. It helped every time she forgot someone's birthday.

When it was all done, and Lilo checked her phone. Still no response from Griffin. He had left the hospital in such a rush. What if he was sitting at home bleeding, and that's why he couldn't answer the phone? She tried texting again:

Griffin?
Hello?

Just when Lilo was about to find a supply closet in which to call him privately, her phone finally pinged back.

Hello.

Thank God. I was beginning to worry you were sitting in a puddle of your own blood. We need to speak about what happened today.

No puddle.
Shall I call you?

No! I'm at work and there are too many people listening.

He didn't respond. Insufferable man. Why was it men liked to use simple sentences when texting? Would it kill him to release a little more information? Lilo kept texting.

I'm writing up the news story about this morning.
I'm saying it all happened so fast that I didn't get a good look at the perpetrator.

Okay.

I'm not ready to throw the Deadly Seven under the bus until I get some more information. I'm sorry if that offends you, but I need facts before I publish a story that could condemn them.

What kind of information?

Lilo took a deep breath. If there was a time to let him

know about her intentions to help her father, now was the time. She could ask him to come with her like Grace suggested. But, she couldn't bring herself to ask.

The kind that involves understanding why a member of the Deadly Seven would suddenly resort to murder in cold blood when they've never done it before. I'll be going out and investigating. Standard journalist stuff.

Griffin's message returned almost immediately.

Tonight?

As soon as I've finished my article.

I'll be there in fifteen. Wait for me.

Butterflies flipped in Lilo's stomach. He was coming.

Was he coming to watch her process, or was it something else? She knew having someone to watch her back was what she wanted, but suddenly she was nervous.

You've been shot. You should rest.

Griffin?

Does that mean we're on the same page about this morning?

…

Hello?

But no more messages came. After a while, she stopped trying. She guessed he wasn't a text type of guy.

To take her mind off the fact she was developing a serious crush on this man, she turned back to her computer and began typing the news article. It was the hardest story she'd ever written because, for once, she wasn't being truthful and it hurt. Those butterflies in her stomach twisted and rolled. On one hand, the truth was why she got into the industry, but on the other, being honest had the potential to hurt more people. It could also tarnish the reputation of the Deadly Seven if she was wrong, and the last time they had an incorrect story printed about them, they disappeared for a couple of years. It wasn't like they spit the dummy; it was simply that they knew the city had lost faith in them. Why fight for the city when they weren't wanted? Lilo didn't blame them. But now they were finally back, saving their city from self-destructing, and she had the power to help them, or hinder them.

But she never lied in a story.

This wasn't lying, she told herself sternly. It was withholding the truth because it could be defamatory, and misrepresented. This was the flip side of journalism, knowing your words could be misread or reinterpreted as something else. In the end, Lilo only kept out the supposed identity of the attacker, and the private conversation with her cousin. The city didn't need to know that her father had been ransomed, and they didn't need to know that the attacker looked like Greed. Not yet, anyway. She sent the article to Fred for approval.

It wasn't the best, but it would have to do.

A few minutes later, Fred called on the internal phone system wanting to speak with her in his office. When she got there, she was surprised to see Donnie sitting in the other free chair in front of Fred's desk.

"Come in, Lilo," Fred said and pointed to the only other free seat. "Shut the door behind you. Sit."

The room smelled like cigar smoke, and Lilo knew the two of them had shared a moment before she'd entered. Despite being the twenty-first century, it was still a boy's club in many ways, and the thought that she wasn't invited to their little tête-à-tête made her growly. Stuff them. It was bad enough the men in the company got paid more, but here they were discussing her behind her back.

Fred's unimpressed tone unsettled Lilo. If it was about her article, why was Donnie there? And why were his eyes tracking Lilo as she stepped into the room and took her seat?

"Is something wrong, Fred?" Lilo asked, threading her fingers together and placing her hands on her lap.

From the look of him, he'd already had a hard day. His white hair was disheveled. Round spectacles sat crooked on his nose.

"Well, Lilo." Fred's eyes flicked to his computer screen and then to Donnie. "While I appreciate you coming in after your ordeal this morning, I think perhaps you're leaving a few facts out of your story."

Lilo's muscles seized. "What?"

"Oh, don't play dumb, princess," Donnie said. "We're not fiction writers here. We're journalists."

She sat there dumbfounded. Her instant reaction was to shrink and roll over. Anytime Donnie used that tone on her in the past, she was a walking yes-girl. But… after the morning she'd had, she wasn't feeling very yes-like. She'd single handedly saved Griffin's life. Her! The cattle prod to the back of the imposter worked. The adrenaline may have worn off, but the after effects of her monumental effort hadn't. Griffin had been right. She shouldn't have to take Donnie's shit anymore.

Instead, of saying something stupid, she allowed her empowerment to sizzle inside and let a slow burn of hate leak from her eyes. She imagined them shooting lasers into his face. *Pew pew. Pew pew.*

The more distance from the end of their relationship, the more she realized his toxicity, and how she was a toy, or a play thing for him to poke around. Well, she wouldn't play his games. Not anymore.

Pew pew.

"Lilo?" Fred prompted.

Right. She turned back to him. "I still don't know what you mean."

While her outward appearance was at war, her mind scrambled back to the events at the precinct. Apart from Griffin, the only other person who saw the attacker up close was Nathanial, and he was dead. She supposed if there were cameras and Donnie had somehow received CCTV footage, he might have seen. But the police weren't in the habit of releasing that information to a journalist. Not until it was officially ready to go public.

"I understand you may be in shock from what happened, and perhaps you need to take some time at home," Fred continued, voice softening.

"You think I made up what happened?" They thought she was some hysterical woman?

Donnie scoffed under his breath. "We think you're keeping certain facts out of the story. Like, for instance, oh, I don't know, the fact the person doing the attacking was one of the Deadly Seven."

How on earth would he know? Nervous tension prickled her body.

Donnie added, "Witnesses saw him escape the scene."

"Well, I can only report on the truth, and all I remember was a person in black wearing a hoodie. It could have been anyone. Ask Griffin if you don't believe me." Saying the words twisted a knife in her heart.

Fred frowned. "How is he, by the way?"

"Relax, Fred. He won't sue." Donnie rolled his eyes.

Lilo wanted to strangle him. What's wrong with asking how someone else was doing for once? Maybe Fred was just concerned about the new employee.

"He's doing okay. He was very brave and protected me." Saying the words made the fact hit home. For a moment, Lilo lost all sense of surroundings and was taken back to the attack. She'd been terrified, but Griffin had held her hand. He'd jumped in front of her, and when he'd had a gun pointed in his face, he hadn't run away. He'd run forward. Griffin had put himself in harm's way to either stop the criminal, or to save Lilo. Maybe both.

Her eyes cut razors down Donnie's foul body. When was the last time he'd ever done anything selfless?

"Foolish," Donnie muttered. "Now look at him. He should have stayed out of it."

What a jerk. Lilo already knew there wasn't a chivalrous bone in his body, but to take it one step further and put another man down for being brave? Lilo wanted to tell him Griffin was twice the man he was, but held her tongue. No. You know what? "Griffin tried to stop the man, Donnie. If he hadn't, who knows what might have happened, or how many other people were going to die. It could have been me next. I could be dead." Your little princess, she wanted to add. The one you claim to want back.

"Instead, he almost died. Doesn't sound very smart to me."

"No, it wouldn't, would it Donnie?"

"Okay then," Fred said. "So perhaps add the details about the witness testimony to your story, then we're done, Lilo."

"No problem. If you could supply me with the names of the witnesses, I'd be happy to get the fact-checker to follow up with them."

"That will take too long, and you know it," Donnie argued. "Another paper will have the story written by then."

"I'm sorry, I'm not sure why you're here, Donnie." She was at her limits. "Were you there? Were you assigned the story?"

She turned back to Fred who sighed and waved his hand at Donnie.

"Donnie, do you have the witness information?"

"No, they refused to give me their contact details."

"You were there?" Lilo couldn't believe it. He'd followed her. "Didn't you trust me to investigate the story, Donnie? And you, Fred. You allowed this blatant waste of resources?"

Stuff Donnie and his meddling.

For once, Fred came through. "No, I didn't. Lilo is correct, Donald. You shouldn't have been anywhere near the precinct unless it involved the story you were assigned. You're not freelance. You're a full-time employee of the newspaper which means your hours need to be justified. And if you don't have the witness information for Lilo to corroborate, then unfortunately, we won't be printing it. You know this. We're not fiction writers here. We're journalists."

Ha! Lilo scowled at Donnie. *Pew pew.*

He stood up. "Fine. You want to print fake news, that's up to you."

Then he left.

Lilo slumped back into her chair, all empowerment gone, hands trembling from the confrontation. What on earth was up Donnie's butt?

Fred fixed his spectacles and turned to his computer. "Thank you, Lilo. I will have the article proofed then we can upload it. Now, as far as working with Mr. Lazarus goes, did everything work out fine? Apart from the shooting business, of course."

"Yes. All fine."

"Good." He removed his glasses again and peered at Lilo. "Are you sure you're okay?"

She nodded.

"Well, just remember, sometimes these things hit you unexpectedly later. If you need to take some time, I'd understand."

"I think if Mr. Lazarus can come in after getting shot, then I can keep working."

"He's coming in?" Fred blanched. "He can't. We'll get sued. He needs to take the correct time to recover. The lawyers are already breathing down our necks."

"If it's any consolation, he insisted the bullet only grazed him."

"Still. There's the mental health component. You should probably take time off too." Fred rubbed the bridge between his nose. "On his first day at work, he gets shot. Not good."

"I'm fine, Fred. Really. I have balls of steel."

"Always about the cojones, isn't it?"

She smirked. If they didn't see her as an equal to men, she just had to speak in a language they understood, and he was right. It all came back to the cojones, and she was fast learning she had big ones. All she had to do was remember that around Donnie.

Lilo shifted in her seat in silence, waiting to be dismissed. When Fred didn't raise his head, she asked, "May I leave?"

A nod was all she received.

Hoping Griffin was already in his office, she detoured there on the way back to her desk. With Donnie already disputing the facts of her story, it was imperative that she confirm with Griffin a unified version of events. There was no reason to believe that he would lie for her, but if he didn't corroborate with Lilo, then she could be fired. Her heart beat faster. Maybe she was fired anyway. Maybe he was rushing in because he was going to head straight to Fred's office and tell him the truth about what happened this morning. Maybe she'd made a terrible error with her judgment of character. It wouldn't be the first time.

CHAPTER THIRTEEN

GRIFFIN LAZARUS

Having spent the afternoon training with Mary, Griffin arrived at the Cardinal Copy newsroom, sore and drained. Working his new ability had taken a surprising amount of mental energy, and combined with his recent injury, he felt altogether lethargic. His shoulder was stiff, and he knew he should have rested it, but he couldn't sit still at home.

Lilo's messages were unsettling, and both he and Mary agreed he should forgo his patrolling tonight in favor of assisting Lilo with her investigation of the fake vigilante. Mary would also conduct her own investigation and discuss the incident with the rest of the family at their weekly dinner tomorrow night.

It presented the perfect opportunity to gather evidence in relation to Lilo and her effect on his internal balance.

He entered his office and found Lilo waiting, staring out the window to the city below. Excellent. He could start his study immediately.

Quickly, he checked his tattoo, then his watch. First, he

would measure how long it took for his equilibrium to equalize after touching her. After spending the afternoon away from her, his tattoo had begun to tilt off balance. Letting Mary train his magnetic skills had been a generous act on his behalf because he had done it to appease her. Now his tattoo was more white than black.

Lilo hugged her denim jacket tight across her front as though it were as cold inside as out. But that was not true. Outside it snowed gently. Inside the building's internal heating kept the temperature at a cozy ambience no matter what room you walked into. If anything, she should have her jacket removed. That would make it easier for him to find a spot of skin to touch.

His tongue pressed against his teeth and he fiddled with his watch until he set the timer. A loud beep announced his arrival.

"Hello, Lilo," he said.

"Griffin." Lilo slipped off the desk and came over to him, stopping just a foot away.

He inhaled and wished he hadn't. Common sense fled, and he had to close his eyes to rein in his emotions, but all he could smell was her and it was more intoxicating than ever. No bubblegum this time—just raw, pure woman.

"I'm so glad I caught you." She sounded strained.

"Is something wrong?" Griffin opened his eyes.

"Donnie was there this morning. He claimed people witnessed the attacker's costume and confirmed it was Greed."

"Doppenger was there?"

Something sparked within Griffin, recollections almost

fitting together. It was a fleeting feeling, as though he almost remembered, but it remained out of reach. He shook it off. Usually thoughts like that resolved themselves when he otherwise occupied himself.

"Yes," she continued, "but I told them I only saw a man wearing a black hoodie. I'm sorry if that puts you in a terrible position. I hate lying, and I just want you to know that if you feel you have to tell the truth, then that's okay. Well, it's not okay really, but I respect your opinion, but if you hold off for a wee bit, we can investigate properly." She gasped as though she hadn't taken breath the entire time she spoke.

Hopeful brown eyes blinked up at him.

This was clearly causing her anxiety. She wrung her hands together until her knuckles whitened. Chagrined, she noticed what she did and shook them out at her side.

Perhaps this was a good opportunity to make contact. He took hold of her left hand and squeezed firmly, mentally counting the seconds. He figured five would count for prolonged contact, then he could check his tattoo.

"I only saw a man in a black hoodie too," he confirmed.

"Oh, thank God." She sighed and covered his hand with her right.

But it was a light touch. He flinched.

"I'm sorry." Lilo let go and looked pointedly at his hands. "You're sensitive, aren't you?"

In those few short words, he felt exposed. Open. As though she'd cut into his mind and pried out his innermost secret. It even felt more of an intrusion than if she'd discovered he were one of the Deadly Seven. She saw straight through to his vulnerability. Lilo didn't look at him as though he were some odd creature, or with pity, she noticed the ropy scar on the back of his hand and stared at him with all-seeing eyes, smiling gently.

Sensitive.

His mouth went dry. "Correct."

"Again, I'm sorry." She shook her head, admonishing herself. "I can be so handsy sometimes. I will be careful not to touch you in the future."

That he would never again feel the warmth of her skin was not a thought he enjoyed entertaining, and it had nothing to do with his study. Her heat echoed on his hand, a ghost of her touch. He was sensitive, yes, but not immune to wanting that human connection. In fact, he felt it more acutely than most people.

"I hope that's not true." He swallowed. "It's just, some-times firm is better than soft. Like this." Griffin kept his eyes locked with hers and lifted his hand toward her neck. He paused, realizing that earlier he too had touched her without permission. "May I?"

She tipped her chin in consent.

As his hand lifted toward her, he hesitated. Every fiber in his body wanted to reach out to her. It was so natural and, yet, it was unlike anything he'd experienced before. After his tactile trauma, he'd hand picked his sexual experiences to be brief encounters, wary of what would happen if he exposed his vulnerabilities to the wrong person. But Lilo watched patiently. She waited for him. He knew that she'd never call him weird, freak or anything else.

His fingers slid around her neck to grasp her nape while

his thumb brushed her jaw in a single sweep that stopped firmly at her cheekbone. He fought the tingles now drilling into his body. His muscles locked tight in anticipation and he waited for the surge of anxiety to hit him.

Two glazed eyes stared back at him, pupils dilating, as she turned her awareness inwards.

Her lips opened, and she inhaled.

"Like this?" She lifted her own hand to slide around his neck in a firm grasp.

He tensed as the touch hit him. More sensations shot along his spine. But where he usually felt anxiety, this was different. He wanted it. His body reacted with heat and longing.

His lids shuttered as he immersed himself in the moment. It had been so long since he'd simply been like this with another person. With a woman. He dipped his forehead until it met hers and exhaled, letting his breath take away his discomposure, replacing it with peace.

"Yes," he murmured. "Perfect."

While icy gusts blew against the windows of his office, they stood leaning into each other for what felt like minutes. Minutes filled with steady breathing and heat soaking through his palm, slowly melting away the tension that often held him hostage. He sensed movement as flurries of wind hit the pane. Light flickered with the fading light outside.

Slowly he opened his eyes; her own were shuttered. The wrinkles between her forehead had smoothed, and her pink lips tipped up one side, happy. He'd done that, given her a smile... made her feel good just like she'd eased him through touch. That revelation battered against the logical preconceptions he'd held so dear. She shouldn't make him feel so good simply by being there, but she did, and he didn't want to let go.

He disengaged and stepped back.

"I apologize Lilo. That was inappropriate." Clearly he wasn't thinking straight. He was at work. He cleared his throat and tucked his shirt which had somehow pulled clear of his pants when he stretched. "Please forgive me."

She flashed a brief smile. "Believe me, nothing to forgive. It was nice. In fact, I'd be open to doing that again. Any time. I mean." Her eyes widened. "I don't know what I'm talking about. I'm embarrassing myself, aren't I? Oh goodness, this is as bad as your butt. I mean, your butt wasn't bad, it was good. I'm talking about it being nice. And your sister's." She clapped her hands over her mouth. "I'm sorry."

A small smile touched his lips. He liked it when she couldn't hide her thoughts. It was refreshing to have someone so open in a world ruled by lies and greed. He had a sudden urge to kiss that honest mouth and his emotions frightened him. He wasn't the kind of man to spontaneously kiss a woman. He was planned and prepared.

The metal objects on his desk began rattling and Lilo looked over, confused. *Shit*. He turned away and calmed his beating heart. God, he was awful at controlling his urges around her. Until he was, she wouldn't be safe near him.

"We should probably get back to work before the day is done." He gestured at the closed door leading to the rest of the office.

"Yes. Right. You're right. I need to get back to my desk." She sidestepped Griffin and went to open the door.

"Wait," he blurted.

She stopped.

"In your message, you mentioned another investigation."

Lilo turned, paling. "Yes."

"Do you have a lead?"

"Maybe. I think speaking with my mother is a good start."

"I'll come with you."

A blush tinged her cheeks. "You will?"

She stepped forward. He wanted to kiss her again. And that was wrong. So wrong. He wasn't in control around her. This couldn't be about him wanting to be near her, it had to be about work.

"It would all be part of your process and something I should learn to understand before I move onto the next employee."

"Oh. The process. Of course." Her demeanor changed from relaxed to tense. The mood in the room darkened. She opened the door stiffly. "Thank you for the offer, but this is personal. I'll manage on my own."

Griffin followed her through the door and frowned as she walked along the corridor. He must have said something wrong, or maybe he'd overstepped personal boundaries when he'd touched her.

To make matters worse, in all the confusion, he'd failed to check his bio-indicator for a control marker and neglected to stop his timer. Frustrated, he flicked out his arm to reveal his wrist and viewed the tattoo. Completely balanced after skin-on-skin contact. It had only been a few minutes, but when writing a new protocol, seconds could make the world of difference. Now, the question was whether to do something selfish or generous and record the effect, or to start over. He should probably start a spreadsheet.

Sitting at his desk, he moved the newspapers he'd been looking at earlier to the side and stacked them in a neat pile.

A woman's choking scream curdled through the corridor. It echoed in his battered ears, chilling him to the bone.

Lilo.

Adrenaline surged through his veins and he ran toward the source, taking the corridor corner so fast he nearly crashed into a group of people running in the same direction. When he ended in the open plan office, a crowd of workers had gathered around a desk. Griffin's gaze flicked to the wall where the break room was, and then to the commotion in an effort to orientate himself. It was Lilo's desk.

"Somebody call the police," came a male voice over the crowd.

"On it," someone else replied.

Griffin locked onto the sense of greed in the room. He recognized a few signatures, but most of all, he zeroed in on Doppenger standing in close proximity to Lilo's desk. Every protective urge in his body stormed to the surface, and he shot toward Lilo as though his life depended on it.

"Out of my way," Griffin barked as he pushed through. "Move." He didn't care who he shoved, because nearest to Lilo's desk was that tall, grimy sensation of greed clawing his gut, and feeling it now for the third time, Griffin knew it was the same one he'd picked up emanating from the imposter this morning.

Doppenger was the fake Greed.

Griffin elbowed someone out of the way to find Lilo sitting at her desk, sobbing with Donald towering over her, a possessive hand on her shoulder.

Griffin zeroed in on that connection and fire erupted behind his eyelids. The rest of his thoughts weren't coherent because all he could see was the touch of that slimy man on his mate.

Magnetic energy swelled in his blood, in the atmosphere, and Griffin's awareness expanded in the room. Suddenly, he knew where each and every piece of metal alloy was. The bolts in the cabinets, the paperclips on the desk, the hard casing of the computer, and the heating vent in the ceiling. On a breath, his world became exponentially larger. He breathed hard, counting in his head until he slowly came back to his senses.

Lilo was alive. She wasn't hurt… she was upset over something in that box.

Catching his approach, Doppenger swiveled his head in a smooth, unhurried motion to lock eyes. Something tangible came across that connection, a battle of wills, a challenge. Vitriolic thoughts collided behind Donald's irises. There were secrets and turmoil and evil things lurking there, and all Griffin could think was that the sinner had his hand on Lilo, that he'd had his hands on her many times in the past. The notion violated the peace she'd previously gifted him.

The metal heating grate in the ceiling fell on Doppenger's head.

"Damn it," Doppenger exclaimed as he shielded himself, deflecting the grate to the side.

Perhaps Griffin needed more training after all.

"Lilo?" Griffin cut out, ignoring Donald's cursing.

She uncovered her eyes and looked up with two orbs of glistening desperation. "Griffin?"

"I'm here," he said.

The words sounded easy, so natural, yet they fit between them like they'd always been there.

Her face screwed up, and she launched out of her seat, away from Doppenger, and into his arms.

"It's so terrible. It's his, I know it."

He glanced at the box and went cold. It was a severed ear. Someone she knew.

"Shh." He held her tightly, applying firm pressure. It always made him feel better, safe. He wanted to cocoon her and protect her from the world.

Over her head, Griffin glared at Doppenger, wanting to tear the man into pieces and feed him to the rest of his deadly family. Impersonating one of them, murdering in cold blood, defaming their name. It had always been Donald Doppenger the Demanding, the greedy, writing those slanderous articles. He'd had a vendetta against the Deadly Seven for years, and now somehow, he'd taken it to the next level. Griffin just didn't know why.

Griffin wouldn't be surprised if the severed ear had something to do with him and he'd orchestrated the entire thing. He probably got some sick pleasure in seeing Lilo in pain.

Doppenger squinted at Griffin with disgust. "You two look awfully cozy for people who've just met."

"I don't see how that's relevant," Griffin replied.

"You knew each other from before. That's how you got the job, isn't it?"

"I got the job because of my proven skill set, and it's none of your business how long I've known Lilo," he fired back. "This isn't the time, nor place for such a conversation."

Lilo's body shook in his arms as she gasped in shuddering breaths.

"It's his ear," she sobbed, gingerly pointing at a box on her desk. "It's my father's."

The simple black glossy box looked like a gift. A red satin ribbon had secured the lid, but now lay in a discarded stream. Inside the box, sitting on white tissue paper stained with old blood was a jagged carved human ear. A single crystal animal hanging from it.

"Hun, are you sure? How can you tell?" An older woman with blue hair asked.

Lilo pulled back enough from Griffin so she could look at the blue-haired lady, but kept herself cocooned in his arms.

"It's the figurine. It used to be mine, but I threw it at my father when I left them. Bev, it's his, I know it."

"*Oy vey*," Bev replied under her breath. "Who would send that here?"

Even though it pinched his healing wound, Griffin's grip around Lilo tightened, as if he could keep her from falling apart with the strength of his arms.

"There's a note," Griffin said, eyeing off the small hard square of card poking out from behind the tissue paper.

"What's it say?" someone asked.

Increasingly aware of too many eyes watching, Griffin turned to the gawping co-workers. "Show's over. Every one take a break," he growled and made a shoo sign with his hand. "Go home early. We've got this."

Most of the workers reluctantly left, slowly filtering back to their desks or leaving the office completely. Griffin wished Doppenger had followed suit, but he hung around like a bad smell. Bev was also there, clutching what looked like a dumb-bell as though it were a security blanket.

"Where's Fred?" Griffin asked.

"Gone home for the day," Bev replied. "Should I call him back?"

"No. I'll sort it out."

"I can't." Lilo clutched Griffin and refused to look back at the box. He moved to collect the note, but Doppenger got there first.

"If you want to see your father alive," Doppenger read, "deliver the contents of his safe by seven Wednesday night. No police, or the next gift will be a head."

Under the instructions was an address. Somewhere in the industrial center in the South-Side.

"This is my fault," Lilo cried. "I should have tried to save them a long time ago, but I left. Instead I wanted nothing to do with them. If I had stayed and tried to make them see how bad their choices were, this wouldn't be happening. I'm a coward. This is all my fault."

"Someone else's greed is never your fault, Lilo." Griffin flexed his grip on Lilo.

"You should take the money to them, Lilo." Doppenger pointed at the note. "It's how these things work."

"No. You should leave this to the authorities," Griffin replied. It would also mean Liza could intercept and stall the investigation while he went to the rendezvous as Greed. He'd have better luck rescuing Lilo's father on his own. Without the police, without rules, and without Lilo there to see if things went sideways.

Doppenger scoffed. "When do the police ever do anything on time?"

"I have to do it." Lilo pulled away from Griffin and took the note. "Besides, it says no police. I know I can do this. I can get what they need, then give it to them. That's all they want. It should be simple."

"Dealing with criminals is never simple," Griffin pointed out.

"I'll go with you, Lilo." Doppenger lifted the lid on the black box and reset it to cover the gruesome sight. "I'm not afraid of a little ransom situation."

"I vote police," Bev added.

"No. I have to do this," Lilo insisted. "It's the best option."

"Lilo." Griffin pulled Lilo a few meters from Doppenger to whisper, "It's not safe."

"I have my cattle prod. I have my spy camera. I'm doing this, I can blow the whistle on them," she replied, wiping her eyes. "The pen is mightier than the sword. Thank you for your concern, really, I-I can't tell you how much it means to me. But I need to do this. I have to see it through."

"I'll go with you then."

"Griff, you've been shot already today because of me. I can't put you in danger again."

He almost laughed. He'd faced far worse than a soft man playing deadly dress ups. This morning's injury won't happen again. He'd been distracted because he denied his biology. Not anymore. Tomorrow, he would return to training with his new ability. He would involve Parker this time. The man had a mind for battle.

"How about we start with your family home," he suggested. "Check on your mother, just you and I. No one else"—his gaze snapped to where Doppenger watched nearby at her desk—"I don't trust him."

He couldn't reveal what he knew about Donald's extracurricular activities without exposing himself.

"I don't want him there either."

As if knowing they spoke about him, Doppenger stormed over. He palmed Griffin between his pec and shoulder—right where he got shot. "That's enough of you whispering in her ear."

The hit sent a stab of crippling pain through Griffin's body.

"Donnie," Lilo cried. "He was shot! Be careful."

"I thought it was only a graze," Doppenger sneered.

"You dickhead!" Lilo shouted, but she hadn't caught the clue that confirmed Griffin's suspicions. Doppenger hit Griffin in the exact spot he was shot, and the only way he knew that was if he did the shooting himself.

Griffin's smile was slow as it spread. The man didn't know he'd just signed his own death warrant. But he would deal with him later. For now, he had Lilo to worry about.

"Touch me again, and you'll lose an arm." Griffin turned his back on the man to face Lilo. "We'll go to your parents' house tonight, then you can decide whether to involve the police."

"No," Doppenger bit out. "You've known her for seconds. I've known her for years. If there's anyone going with her, it's me."

"You only want to go with her because you think it's a story," Griffin fired back, unable to help himself.

Donald's eyebrows lifted. "Oh really? Well, you're only going with her because you want to get in her pants. Or have you already been there?"

"Donnie!" Lilo exclaimed, mortified.

"Step back, Lazarus." Doppenger pushed Griffin again, aiming for the same spot, the same injury.

This time, Griffin blocked. Idiot. Did he not see he was no match for him? It was clear Griffin's physique was more robust than his. Anyone with eyes could see that.

When Doppenger's next strike bounced off Griffin's forearm, the man growled and struck with his left. Griffin blocked effortlessly again. He could stop this with a finger to the man's eye, but anything Griffin did would compromise his identity. His body was a deadly weapon, and if his background got out, the court judge would be unforgiving.

"Stop before you hurt yourself," Griffin said, but Doppenger doubled his efforts.

"What's so important about you, huh?" he hissed under

his breath on a second lunge. "Why does everyone want you?"

He punched.

Griffin dodged.

The shock of what he said froze Griffin. Why everyone?

Doppenger's fist connected with Griffin's shoulder, tearing the wound open. Blood seeped through his shirt and blazer, and then Doppenger's body collided with Griffin, taking them to the floor.

"Get off him!" Lilo yelled. "You asshole!"

"I've called security," Bev shouted.

"Never mind." Doppenger rolled off Griffin and stood inspecting his hand, now covered in Griffin's blood. "I got what I came for. I'm done."

Got what he came for?

The greedy man walked away, cradling his fist as though it were precious cargo.

Griffin had to contact his family. They needed to know about this. Too many clues pointed to Donald working for the Syndicate. Why else would he want a sample of blood?

"Shit. What an asshole! Oh shit, Griffin, are you okay?" Lilo kneeled next to him. "What can I do—shall I call the hospital? Grace? Anyone?"

"No." He sat up and peered under the collar of his shirt to the wound below. "I'm fine. The bleeding's almost stopped."

He wasn't fine. And the bleeding was worse. He should have rested this afternoon instead of sparring and training. He might heal faster than normal, but he wasn't invincible. The sense of Doppenger's greed signature got weaker as the man left the building. *Damn it.* Griffin should run after him, but he would risk tearing the wound more. Resting a few minutes and notifying the family would be better.

Lilo whimpered. "Can I help?"

She needed to do something, so he took her hand and used it to apply pressure to his shoulder. "Please hold that firmly while I send a message."

She pushed her palm to his wound despite the sticky blood. "Okay. I got it."

Careful not to show Lilo the screen, Griffin shot a text to Parker.

Identity of the imposter is Donald Doppenger. Works at Cardinal Copy. Potential link to the Syndicate. Just collected a sample of my blood. Someone needs to track him immediately. I'm wounded, but not critical.

When he put his phone away, he noticed Lilo's hand trembling on his shoulder. For a minute he thought she'd seen his message, but her eyes were locked firmly where her hands covered his wound.

"Lilo," he said. "Lilo, look at me." He slid his fingers around her neck and grasped, much like he had in his office. "I'm here."

A smile caught between pain and relief tipped her lips. "You're here," she repeated.

But the scary thing was, those words and that connection calmed him more than it did her.

CHAPTER FOURTEEN

LILO LIKEKE

After grabbing a quick bite to eat, Lilo drove with Griffin to her parents' house on the east side of town.

Home to the city's elite and exuberant, The Eyrie was a fortress of protection with cliffs facing Menagerie River on one side, and a highway on another. Guarded by security guards day and night, it had a wall so high and thick that even birds had trouble getting over. The crime rate inside was virtually zero and offenders were limited to recalcitrant teenagers out for a little midnight fun. Any real criminal daring to show their face was never seen again. If the residents knew the reason they slept so soundly was because mafiosi lived inside its walls, they'd probably think twice about residing there.

But Lilo knew. She'd seen the evil behind the designer clothes and polished silver. She'd seen the blood behind the fake plastic smiles in her own enormous backyard. Nothing was as it seemed in The Eyrie, and she'd been smack bang in the middle of it.

"Thank you again," Lilo said as the car turned into the driveway leading into the complex. "I can't tell you how much I appreciate you doing this."

"Lilo." Griffin rolled down his driver side window. "That's the fifth time you've thanked me since we left Cardinal Copy."

"Yeah, but, I know we only met this morning, so I understand this is a big deal. And after the day you've had. Being shot, then having a douche like Donnie purposefully hit your injury, I think you're being incredibly generous. I still think you should be home resting."

"It's not a big deal. I've been hurt worse."

"You have?"

He shifted the glasses on the bridge of his nose. "Plus, Grace said you're family to her. Grace is my family."

A warmth followed his words as she let them sink in and she turned in her seat to inspect him. Everything about him oozed manliness, from the cut of his jaw to the thick column of his neck, from the way his elbow rested on the window to the way his hips sprawled forward in the seat. Why was it men always looked so damned sexy when they drove?

Or maybe it was just her hormones. That neck had been so warm and inviting when she'd touched it. She wanted more and bit her finger to stop drooling all over him.

Griffin looked out his window, inspecting the security booth coming up, and the guard checking the ID of the vehicle in front of them.

"Do you have clearance to enter?" he asked Lilo.

She was still imagining indecent and insane thoughts

about this neck. What was wrong with her? She fanned her face.

"Lilo?"

"Yes. Sorry. What?"

"Do you have clearance to get through the gate?"

"I left, but my parents have always had an open door policy for me."

"But you've never taken it?"

"No. I can't forgive what they did." Fake—even with her. She could never trust them.

Griffin hesitated, but kept darting back to Lilo. She almost smiled at his transparency. "It's okay if you want to know what they did."

"Only if you want to share."

"They paid for my love." Seeing his confusion, she elaborated and told him all about her discovery on her sixteenth birthday. "After that, they weren't so careful hiding their criminal activities. I once saw my father torture some poor guy in my basement, all because the man owed him some money." She shook her head, lost in the memory. "When he caught me watching, he bought me a new diamond bracelet. As if that was enough to excuse his deeds. So you see, not only are they criminals, but they never once showed me an ounce of honest affection. I was just another transaction to them. I was too weak to go to the police back then, but now I'm doing this job, uncovering criminal activity, and putting murderers behind bars. It's my way of making up for never doing the right thing back then."

Two intense eyes bored into her, then the car in front of

them moved and Griffin put the vehicle into gear, shifting them forward.

"Name?" The security guard leaned into the window and eyed them.

"Lilo Likeke—I mean, Liota—here to see the Liotas on Parkham Way."

"And you are?" The man shifted his attention to Griffin.

Lilo covered his thigh with her hand. "My fiancé, Griffin Lazarus."

Griffin tensed, but smiled briefly at the guard.

"Right. ID please."

Both handed over their cards.

"I'll be a moment." The man went back to his booth and picked up the phone, most likely calling Lilo's mother for confirmation.

She looked at where her hand rested. He didn't complain, and she made sure to keep her pressure firm. It was a nice, solid thigh. Sturdy and warm.

"Fiancé," Griffin eventually said.

"Sorry. It's the easiest way to get you in."

Reluctantly, Lilo removed her palm and placed it in her lap. "My parents are very suspicious of strangers. Fiancé was the first thing I could think of."

Within minutes, the guard was back, holding out their cards. "You're free to go, Miss. Welcome back to The Eyrie."

Lilo's stomach churned as they drove away and wished she'd kept her connection to her rock beside her, but stared out the window instead. The neighborhood had only grown more extravagant, with Lilo's parents' house the icing on the cake. The monolith structure sat high on a hill overlooking the rest of the community like a king over his subjects, and the snow covering it sparkled like diamonds under the moon. Three-stories high, the federation style home sat behind a white picket fence and sprawling front lawns. Powdered rose bushes lined the boundaries and a single frozen oak tree sat in the middle, a ghostly swing swaying in the breeze. It was a suburban home turned into a luxury mansion. Lilo reached into the back of the Escalade to get her jacket and scarf. The walk from the road was long and cold.

Griffin parked and got out to wait by the picket fence. She tried to maneuver herself in the confines of the car to put her coat on. It took some time, but she managed it, then surrounded her neck with a woolen scarf, and put her beanie on her head. A few minutes later, she realized she was procrastinating.

Come, on, Lilo. You can do this.

The passenger door opened and Griffin stood there blowing hot air on his hands. "Everything okay?"

She smiled up at him. "Just a little nervous. It's been a few years."

He held out his hand.

I'm here, his eyes seemed to say.

A rush of raw emotion flowed over her. The shadows of the street lamp cast his handsome structure into hard angles as he watched her patiently. No pressure, no demands. Not like Donnie at all. She slipped her hand into his, appreciating it for what it was.

"Thank you."

"Not a problem. We're about to be married, after all, what's a little holding hands?"

He was amused at his own joke, and that made her laugh.

They walked through the picket gate and along the cobbled path up to her old front door. The internal house lights were on behind the frosted glass, indicating someone was well and truly home.

Still holding Griffin's hand, Lilo rang the doorbell. A few seconds later, a shadow darkened the glass at the door, and it opened.

"Hello Renata," Lilo said to the housekeeper, and then held her breath. Logically, she knew she wouldn't be turned away—they'd let her in at the gate after all— but her heart couldn't help being afraid they'd refuse her.

Renata was a short, portly woman in a maroon dress. Her brown hair had been cut close to her scalp, and she had fire engine red lipstick on. Lilo couldn't say exactly why she thought it, but it never seemed like Renata enjoyed her job at the Liota household, despite her working without complaint. Perhaps she'd seen too much like Lilo and was too afraid to leave. Whatever the case, Renata's eyes lit up upon landing on Lilo and she touched the pendant she wore around her neck.

Oh great! It was delivered in time.

"Miss Lilo. Is good to see you." Renata swept her judgmental gaze over Griffin, taking the time to stop at way points over his body: his broad shoulders, his strong arms, his face. She pouted and turned back to Lilo with a pleased flash to her eyes. "And this tall man is fiancé? Will he come to coffee date next week?"

"My name is Griffin Lazarus, ma'am. Pleased to meet you." Griffin held out his hand. "I'd be happy to come along to a coffee date with you."

Lilo smiled at Griffin. She knew he was probably acting and had no intention of coming to a coffee date with her old housekeeper, but she kind of wished he wasn't. It felt good to imagine all of them together.

Renata lifted a brow at Griffin, unimpressed. "I will know if I be pleased after I meet you. Come. I take you to the Mrs. She is packing for trip to vacation house on Menagerie Island, and well, you will see. She make big mess. Guess who will have to clean."

Her abrupt manner came from a good place. Renata was more of a mother to Lilo than her own kin, often being the one who did all the hard parenting like helping her with her homework, teaching her to bake, and make her own bed. If Renata hadn't spent the time to ensure Lilo grew to be a capable young woman, Lilo would probably still be living there, hopelessly under her rich parents' thumbs. And it cost Renata nothing more than time.

They walked through the overly wide hallway, passing the gallery wall of photographs, still portraying the happy family before Lilo left. Griffin tugged her hand as they came to a large picture of Lilo and her parents. It had been taken on her sixteenth birthday, the night everything went dark for Lilo, yet they hung it in a place of pride. She couldn't tell if they were delusional, or deranged.

"This is your father?" Griffin's brows lowered.

"Yes. Dad and mom and… I don't know who that girl in the meringue is."

"That's you, clearly."

She tried to hide her blush by turning her head. That dress was hideous, but so were her parents' outfits. Her father wore a cerulean blue polo shirt with a camel colored sweater wrapped around his shoulders. Being an Islander, his skin was already on the brown side, but somehow he'd managed to make it look tinted orange with fake tan. Next to him stood her mother with her trifecta of plastic. Fake bobble breasts, botox face, pouty pink lips. Her olive Italian skin turned a complimentary shade of orange to her father's. To be honest, there were more fake things about her mother than she could count. Lilo wasn't even sure which features she inherited from her mother's side. No, that wasn't true. They had the same brown eyes.

Griffin moved to another photograph. Ridiculously, it was of Lilo in her room, surrounded by her crystal animal figurine collection. Looking at the obscene materialism she was brainwashed with made her sick. To think there were people in the world—in their own city!—too poor to find their next meal, yet there she was surrounded by thousands of dollars of shiny rock.

"I can't believe I used to be impressed by that sort of thing," she murmured.

"What impresses you now?" he asked quietly, focused intently on her.

"None of this, that's for sure." She waved around at the expensive decor lining the tables in the hallway. Some of it looked terrible, but it had a price tag, so her mother had wanted it. "I guess, I'm more of an actions speak louder than dollars kind of girl."

He stared at her.

It made her uncomfortable. "Can we go?"

She tugged his hand, and they continued along the hallway into another room.

Now it was Lilo's turn to stop. The room had been ransacked. Torn cushions were turned from couches, all with the stuffing pulled out. Side tables had tipped over. Drawers were out, exposing bits and pieces of paper and clutter. Everything had been pulled apart, and it wasn't the only room. The designer kitchen was in pieces with cutlery and pots and pans everywhere, and as they continued to follow Renata, they learned the rest of the house wasn't far behind. Surely this mess couldn't all be from her mother packing for a trip.

"Renata, have you been robbed?" Lilo asked. It didn't make sense, not with the extensive security at the complex. Unless it was someone who lived inside the community.

Renata made a sound deep in her throat that suggested her resignation. "You will see."

They ended down some stairs at the back of the house leading toward the area where Lilo knew her father's den was… and where the safe was.

CHAPTER FIFTEEN

GRIFFIN LAZARUS

Griffin could honestly say he'd not expected what they found upon entering Lilo's father's private den, or vault, or whatever it was. After following Renata inside, he'd been so surprised that he let go of Lilo's hand and stood there with his jaw open, tasting the gunmetal in the air.

His magnetic ability buzzed, pushing at his skin in a way that tempted him to reach out and take hold in order to shut it off. Having never been in a room with so much metal since he'd developed his ability, his senses went haywire.

It was a war room filled with a wall-to-wall arsenal of weapons. Machine guns, automatic rifles, pistols, revolvers, close range missiles, grenades. Abhorrent. And standing in the middle of it all was the blond, skinny and big-breasted woman Griffin recognized from the photograph in the hall. She wore a hot pink stretch jumper with a logo of a black poodle over her right breast. Black pants were tucked into leather boots reaching to her calves.

Lilo's mother packed items from her artillery into two

open suitcases as though she were going on a vacation to the Third World War instead of The Menagerie up-state.

"Mom?" Lilo's voice wavered as she stepped down into the sunken room. Her face twisted in a way that made Griffin regret letting go of her hand. She needed him.

Everything in the room went against what Griffin knew to be the north of Lilo's moral compass. She was brave to continue.

"Sugar?" Lilo's mother looked up from her chore. "Oh goodness. When I heard it was you, I almost couldn't believe my ears. Is it true, are you back? And is this…" She knocked over a glass of wine in her haste to get to Lilo. Or was it Griffin she rushed to?

The woman stopped in front of him, a sly eye raking over his body. "My, my, hasn't my daughter done well."

"Mother," Lilo warned. She tried to pull her back, but was refused.

"Well, sugar, aren't you going to introduce us?"

"Mother, this is Griffin Lazarus. Griff, this is my mom." Lilo's lack-luster tone betrayed her reticence.

"Pleased to meet you."

"Oh none of that." She swatted Griffin's outstretched hand. "Please, call me Janet."

Janet with the Jugs immediately came to mind. It was a good association, but not quite appropriate to speak aloud. He'd have to make sure to—

Janet cupped Griffin's face and kissed him squarely on the lips, making sure to press her breasts against him.

He jerked back, but the woman kept her grip tight. He paused, not wanting to offend, but even without opening his mouth, he tasted sour wine. The sensation made his heart rate gallop and the queasiness in his stomach drop.

"Mom! Stop. You're embarrassing yourself." Lilo unceremoniously removed Janet's offensive lips from Griffin's face, much to Janet's enjoyment.

Wipe your mouth. Wipe your mouth.

But he didn't. He resisted for the sake of propriety, and it killed him.

"I'm so sorry, Griffin," Lilo said.

He couldn't speak. Still processing.

She sighed, resigned. "Mom, why are you packing guns into a suitcase?"

"Two suitcases, sugar." Janet winked at Griffin, then wiped her mouth suggestively before swaying back to her task.

If the taste of the wine hadn't tipped him off, the sway in her movement indicated she was well on her way to inebriation.

"And I'm damn well taking everything he left behind because you know what that bastard did. Thirty years of marriage and he still hides his most precious items from me."

"What do you mean?"

"What do I mean," Janet scoffed, then pointed a manicured finger at Lilo. "You know what I mean or else you wouldn't be here, now would you? Well, go on. Don't dillydaddle. Take what you want. He's not here. And then I suggest you do what I'm doing and get the hell out of town."

Griffin rubbed his face. *Unbelievable.*

His heart wrenched for Lilo. To come from a family like this. To grow up in a house filled with so much stuff at the expense of love. He slanted a look at her—and for her to come out of it all the strong woman she was. It was inspiring.

"This is Dad's safe?" Lilo ignored her mother and began a slow walk around the room. "The one Nathanial told me to raid and hand over to Dad's kidnappers?"

"You'll do no such thing." Janet slammed her suitcases shut, as if that could protect her stash from Lilo's prying eyes.

Janet's sense of greed flared until it consumed Griffin's mind and he was ready to do something about it. She boarded on deadly.

"And no, this isn't a safe. It's a room, or is your righteous head too far up your ass to see that?"

The fuming rage that ripped through Griffin made his vision blur. This woman spoke to her own flesh and blood like she was worthless. What a piece of work.

"I was just asking," Lilo mumbled and searched underneath her father's desk.

"Janet," Griffin said, tone as sharp as a knife. He was done with propriety. "Where are you going with those weapons?"

"Leaving town, like I said. Now, out of my way."

"No." He planted himself firmly before her. "I don't think so. Besides, you're not leaving town, are you? You're going to attempt to rescue Lilo's father on your own."

The whites of Janet's eyes showed. "How could you possibly know that?"

"Mom, really?" Lilo was at a small shelf loaded with grenades, searching idly. "What do you intend to do, exchange the suitcases for Dad?"

"Oh, don't be silly. I plan on using the guns, not giving them away."

"To get Dad."

Janet's eyes shuttered as her brows lifted in a smug sort of way. "If that's what you want to believe, then that's up to you."

"You're not going to rescue him," Griffin said slowly, as the realization came to him. She'd boasted before about taking everything since the father was gone. The woman obviously held some deep-seated grudge against the man. "You're going to kill him."

Janet slammed her palms on her wobbly suitcase. "He should have been dead already."

"Mom?" Lilo's hand fluttered to her throat. "Did you set this up? Did you have Dad kidnapped? All so you could get me to open his private safe?"

Janet paled. "Don't be ridiculous. If I wanted to plan your father's murder, I would have done it with a little more style."

"She didn't do it, Lilo," Griffin stated. "But she's prepared to capitalize on the opportunity, aren't you Janet? Is it the insurance?"

Janet glowered at him.

"Mom. Do you know where Dad's safe is?"

"He has a secret safe?" Hysteria had leached into Janet's voice and her eyes became manic. "Where? Where is it?" She rushed her daughter and shook her violently, repeating her questions.

"Get off me!" Lilo cried.

Griffin went to Lilo, intending to help, but she surprised him with a self-defense move. She flicked her mother's wrist and twisted it behind her body. In a few seconds, Janet was on the floor, winded and gasping for air as she stared at the ceiling.

He barely bit back the grin.

"Get a hold of yourself, mom."

"I... I just... I can't live without him. I need money. I need to support myself."

"So you're going to kill him anyway and take the insurance money? You're insane." Lilo clicked her tongue in disgust. "Look around you. This is what your precious money has given you. Violence, maniacal tendencies and an empty home."

"And a lot of guns," Griffin added absently.

Janet clawed herself upright by using the wall covered in empty gun racks. "You have no idea what it's like living with a man like that."

"Oh, I think I do."

"You were only a child! You knew nothing."

"So you're not going to help him. You're going to murder him?"

"Maybe. At least then maybe I'd get his insurance money and something good will come out of this."

"Do I need to remind you that if you get caught, you'll get nothing and go to jail? And I'm not defending you. I can't believe I'm related to you."

Griffin cleared his throat loudly. "This conversation isn't going anywhere. Should we continue our search?"

"Let's just give the kidnappers what they want. Dad comes home. You don't have to go and kill him at the exchange. I can't believe I just said that. Calm down. Have another drink. Do you know where the safe is, mom?"

She snorted. "I didn't know he had one. He hid it from me on purpose, that bastard. There are probably jewels and diamonds and emeralds. He knows I like emeralds." Janet zipped up her suitcase, pulling out bits and pieces of ill-fitting artillery as she went. "Good luck to you both. I hope you choke on his safe."

Then she heaved the suitcase up the small staircase and left the room. The suffocating sense of greed receded and Griffin could breathe unhindered again.

"Do you want me to go after her?" Griffin offered.

"No. She won't do it. She'll probably stop by the kitchen, have a few more glasses of wine, and then pass out before she gets anywhere near the car. She might not even know where the kidnappers set up the exchange." Lilo huffed and put her hands on her hips, staring up at the ceiling, shaking her head and blinking wetness from her eyes. "You see what I have to deal with?"

"I do."

"How are we related?"

"You can't choose your family."

Lilo's face grew determined. "Yes I can. And she's not part of it. God!" She screamed in frustration. "I want nothing more than to leave them all to the disaster they made for themselves. They don't deserve help when they've done nothing apart from helping themselves."

"Didn't you say they threw you a party for your sixteenth birthday?"

She shot him a look that made him feel as though he'd betrayed her, but then her expression softened. "You're right. Of course you're right."

"I'm not excusing their behavior," he added and walked up to her.

She was a trembling mess, hands scrubbing her face, all jittery. And the worst part was that after being drenched in greed and sour wine, he just wanted to nuzzle her neck and breathe her natural feminine scent.

Lilo took a few deep breaths. "You're so cool and calm all the time. I'm glad you're here to remind me of what's important."

Cool and calm? Griffin blinked. They were not words he used to describe himself. Restrained, maybe. But with her, he didn't need to be.

He put a hand on her shoulder, and rubbed his thumb on her neck until she looked up at him, meeting his eyes.

"You're incredibly brave to stay so morally incorrupt with them around," he said.

"Do you think my mother will truly go there to kill him?" Her small voice trembled.

He didn't want to admit it, but Janet was so greedy, what else could she intend?

Lilo exhaled. "Then we have no choice. I have to beat her to it. I'll have to find this safe and take whatever is in there before she—I can't believe I'm saying this—before my mother goes to kill my father."

Griffin let go of Lilo and surveyed room. The weapons weren't the kind you purchased down a dark alley somewhere, they were the type you purchased on the Black Market and smuggled illegally into the city.

"Why does your father have so many weapons?"

"He's homicidal like my mother?" She threw her hands in the air. "Who knows?"

He walked along the wall and touched the remaining weapons, letting his finger trail along the cold hard surfaces, letting his ability soak it all up. He learned what different kinds of metal felt like to his sense. Steel, aluminum, and other alloys he couldn't name. He came to the corner where two wooden panels on the wall intersected. An awareness tickled his mind as he approached. More metal behind the panels. Thick sheet metal.

"Here," he said and pulled one of the panels. It swung open like a door to reveal a metal safe embedded in the wall. "This must be what your cousin spoke about."

Lilo came to his side.

The safe was a few feet wide and slightly less high. Big enough to cram a body in. There didn't seem to be a handle, but a glass panel about the size of a hand was stuck to the front.

"Must be biometric," he mused.

Lilo raised her palm to the surface, then flinched back. "I don't know if I want this."

"Whatever is in there can be used to rescue your father." And perhaps provide clues as to why someone was interested in Nathanial enough to kill him. "That's what you want, isn't it?"

Her lip twitched. "I don't want him to die, I know that. Despite the terrible things he's done, he is still my father. Sending him to prison would be a better form of justice. He doesn't deserve to die."

"Then open the safe."

She pushed her palm on the panel and the door clicked open. He helped her pull the heavy door to the side.

Inside, sitting on a red velvet shelf was a yellow manila envelope. Lilo's fists were stuck to her side, so Griffin took the envelope and peeked inside.

His stomach dropped.

"Griffin?" Lilo's voice trembled. "Are you okay?"

He pulled out the pictures and quickly filed through them.

"Why would my father have photographs of your family?"

"That's it?" Janet's voice screeched behind them. "That's what was so precious your father had to hide it from his wife?"

Griffin turned in time to see Janet storm back up the stairs and slam the den door closed.

"I don't know." Griffin stuffed them back into the envelope. "But we have to go."

Lilo paused, contemplating something. Perhaps weighing up whether she believed his lie.

"If it's just a few photographs of you and your family, then you won't mind if I take them to exchange for my father's life. Unless of course you're hiding something."

"No. I forbid it."

"Excuse me?"

"You won't be going to the meeting. Not after what we've learned today."

Lilo wrapped her jacket across her chest. "And what exactly have we learned today? Please tell me."

He couldn't.

"Just exactly what does your family do, Griffin? I know Parker is one of the richest men around. Is he into some shady business deals?"

"No, it's nothing like that. I don't know why your father is taking pictures of us, but I intend to find out. Until then, this is not the time for such discussions." Griffin shot a meaningful look toward the den door where Janet had gone. "These pictures are none of your concern. Let's go."

"You can't tell me what to do, Griffin. This is the twenty-first century. If I want to go, I will. If I want to look into the origin of the pictures, I will. You're the one who told me to stand up for myself. Well, this is me, standing up for myself."

"I'll take these to the police and they can deal with it. End of discussion." After meeting her mother and sensing her greedy intensions, he'd already made up his mind to stop Lilo from attending the meeting. It was too dangerous, too volatile, and now that he knew his family were mixed in it all, he was even more certain she needed to be protected.

Lilo hadn't seen all the surveillance pictures incriminating his family. The ones that captured Evan and Parker tugging their Deadly Seven hoods from their faces. Whoever had their hands on these photographs had the potential to extort a lot of money from the Lazarus family, or to put them behind bars. Or worse, to blackmail them.

The question was, what was Lilo's father intending to do with them, or more accurately, what did his kidnappers want with them?

A ping sounded and Lilo took her phone from her pocket. From the way her face crumpled, it was not good news. He expected more of an argument from her over the kidnapping, but she did nothing.

"What is it?"

She wiped her eyes and sniffed. "Doesn't matter. I'm done with this place. I'm done with men, and as soon as you give me the pictures, I'm done with you."

Couldn't she see he was doing this for her own good? Nobody needed to be involved with extortion and blackmail.

"You're not getting the pictures, Lilo. They're going to the police. You're a reporter. I'm not comfortable with them in your hands."

"You don't trust me."

"Like you said on the way here, we've only just met."

"How am I supposed to get my father back?"

"The police will handle it."

"Trust is a two-way street, Griffin." Lilo glared at him.

"What are you doing?" he asked after she continued to flare her eyes at him.

"I'm shooting lasers at you with my eyes. *Pew pew*." And then she gave the envelope in his hand an intense look before checking her phone, shaking her head, and leaving the room. "I'm so done."

CHAPTER SIXTEEN

GRIFFIN LAZARUS

The following night Griffin arrived at Heaven, the restaurant below his apartment complex. Parker owned it, Wyatt used to be the head chef, and since re-committing to their crime fighting mantle, they convened once a week to discuss their operations in the privacy of a secluded dining room reserved for VIP guests.

He was the last to arrive at a frosty six-thirty in the evening. The snow had abated for most of the day, but the temperature remained frigid, just like his mood. Despite her insistence that she was done with him, he'd delivered Lilo to her home the previous night, and had been brooding ever since. He could still vividly picture her stomping outside her parents' house and into the snow to stand on the soggy front lawn, shivering despite her large coat and scarf. She'd stubbornly called a cab and ignored him to the point of agony.

He guessed the flip side of being his greedy sin's opposite was help wasn't easy for her to accept. More of a giver than a receiver. She'd spent her years since leaving her family giving every inch of herself for the benefit of other people. Whether it was to uncover criminal secrets, investigate cold-cases no one wanted to touch, or physically give when she had little herself. It was clear she spent her last dollars on those donuts for staff. Her clothes and accessories were old and worn. She lived in an affordable area of town. He wondered when was the last time she accepted a gift, or received help without offering something in return. She didn't have a greedy or selfish bone in her body. It must have taken a lot from her to ask him to go to her parents' house.

On the car ride back to her mid-town apartment, he'd learned the upsetting message she'd received on her phone had to do with her recent article written for the paper. It had been published with Doppenger's name under the byline and included the content she'd fought to have redacted regarding the attacker's appearance. Griffin could see why she would be angry at Donald, but not at him.

He was only trying to prevent more violence. He just couldn't fathom how she thought she'd be safe going to an exchange with criminals.

She'd ignored him all day at work and Griffin had little chance to record data pertaining to her proximity, touch, and effect on his biometric marker. He'd spent the time working with other employees and going over Parker's algorithm to find the rest of the family's mates.

To say he was out of sorts by the time he sat in the private dining room was an understatement. At the head of the table he had a good view of the family, including the new addition, Evan's mate Grace. Parker, Sloan, Liza, Tony and their parents Mary and Flint were all there. However, Wyatt was still absent, leaving Griffin to wonder how long his brother's self imposed sabbatical would last. Wyatt may be a hot head sometimes, but he was pragmatic and Griffin missed that. He'd been a voice of reason... that was, until toward the end, then wrath had blinded him to common sense.

The danger in their lives wasn't only physical.

"About time, bro," Evan grumbled from the chair next to Griffin. "I'm starving."

"Nothing was stopping you from eating."

"But that would be rude, and I'm not. Am I, Doc?" He nudged Grace with his elbow. "Except, maybe I had a spring roll already."

"Don't ever let Wyatt catch you saying these are spring rolls," Liza said from across the table. There was a beat of silence as everyone no doubt felt the same longing for their missing family member. "They're deconstructed... I don't know. What do you call these, Parks?"

Sitting next to Griffin on the other side, Parker arched an eyebrow. "Vietnamese gỏi cuốn."

"See?" Evan picked up one and put it in his mouth, humming in appreciation. "Spring rolls."

Grace leaned forward to peer around Evan. "How are you, Griffin? How's that shoulder going?"

He rotated it. "Good. Almost healed."

"That's good to hear. I was a bit apprehensive when Lilo told me Donnie had reopened it."

"Lilo spoke with you?" But not him?

Evan choked on a laugh, almost losing his mouthful, then

pointed at Griffin with a fork. "Look at your face, bro. You got it bad."

"You make it sound like a venereal disease." Grace screwed up her nose.

"Well, if he feels anything like I did when I first met you" —he paused for dramatic effect, then pointed again at Griffin with a smirk—"you got no chance."

"Did you bring the paperwork?" Parker asked gruffly.

Wearing a tailored suit, Parker looked every bit the CEO he was. His long auburn hair brushed his expensive collar and was impeccably styled, just like his designer stubble. *I'm waiting*, his eyes said.

Griffin pulled a folded stack of paper from his blazer pocket and handed it to Parker.

It was hard to miss Tony at the end of the table, already finished dinner and sprawled back with a drunken lilt to his puffy eyes. Having wrapped up filming on the set of his latest movie, he appeared exhausted. His usually styled short hair was scruffy, his five-o'clock shadow looked days old, and if he'd portrayed a hobo in the movie, Griffin would have believed it. Sometimes Tony liked to dress down to avoid raving fans accosting him, however, he still looked like his multi-million dollar pay-check.

"So, what did you think?" Parker inspected Griffin's notes.

"About the mating algorithm?"

Liza snorted.

Wearing a standard plain-clothed detective uniform, she must have come straight from work. She flicked her dark braid over her shoulder and leaned toward Parker to read Griffin's notes.

"Do you mind?" Parker lifted his brows at her. "There is such as thing as personal space."

"Not in this family." Another snort from her and she kept reading. "Mating algorithm. What a whacked name."

"Well, that's what it is, isn't it?" Griffin shook out his napkin and placed it on his lap. He smoothed it until the edges folded over his thighs.

"Who cares what it's called? What's the verdict? Will it work?" Parker asked.

"Just to be clear, the algorithm, I can't comment on. I don't know how to code, but as to the accuracy of the data pool…" He paused.

Liza leaned forward expectantly. Sloan stopped playing idly with her spring rolls and popped the end of her pigtail into her mouth, chewing as she stared at Griffin.

Everyone around the table hushed. Waited.

He didn't want to disappoint them.

Thanks to the success of the Evan and Grace partnership, they were all eager to begin a life unburdened by their sin. Part of Griffin rebelled at that. He'd given them all a viable alternative—his timing protocol—but even he could see Evan's mental health had improved dramatically. He had to admit the protocol took up valuable time in his schedule.

Griffin frowned at where his brother's hand rested on Grace's thigh under the table. They didn't think anyone noticed, or didn't care, but the two of them were constantly touching. It wasn't a position Griffin could ever see himself in, especially now Lilo wouldn't talk to him, but for once in his life, he considered he might have liked it. Those few moments he'd shared with Lilo in his office were… altering.

"So, not good." Parker shook his head, already making his own conclusions based on Griffin's extended pause.

"Well, it's not ideal," Griffin confirmed. His stomach grumbled, and he collected the last remaining spring roll from the center of the table to add to his plate. "The quality of the data you're sampling isn't accurate. People lie on social media all the time, plus, if you take Grace into account, you'll notice she doesn't have an online presence. So, this algorithm would have missed her entirely."

"So it's a big, fat waste of time," Liza snapped.

"Don't say that." Mary reached across the table to her daughter.

Liza shook her head. "I'll be the last one, I swear. Who the fuck has no lust in their system?"

Griffin shifted uncomfortably. "I didn't say it was useless, but in my opinion, it's not something easily quantified."

"It's better than nothing." Parker dropped the papers on the table.

Most of the Lazarus family sat back in their chairs morosely.

The waitress came and took their orders—since Tony ate early, he went straight onto dessert and mumbled about the lack of good mousse since Wyatt left. As they waited for their meals to arrive, the conversation turned to an acceptable topic while the dining-room door was open. Soft sounds of chatter filtered through from the public area of the restaurant.

"Has anyone heard from Wyatt?" Evan asked hopefully.

A few months ago, Wyatt had taken off, leaving only a letter behind and no forwarding address. The family felt his absence acutely, now more than ever because it had been months with no word. He would be alone out there, angry, and full of guilt and self loathing for not listening to Evan's warning about Sara.

"Nothing directly," Mary stated, shaking out her napkin.

"What about indirectly?" Evan smiled briefly at the waitress placing his meal in front of him, waited for her to leave, then continued. "We put a tracker on his bike, right? Can AIMI find him?"

AIMI was their artificial intelligence management interface. Designed as a joint venture between Parker, Sloan and Flint, she'd been in her final prototype stages at the time of Wyatt's disappearance.

"You know as well as anyone else at this table that AIMI can be deactivated manually," Parker replied. "But, she hasn't been. He's in town. I just don't understand why he doesn't come home."

"There've been reports in the South-Side of a rider in black interrupting gangland meetings and—" Flint hesitated and glanced at his wife.

"He's being Wyatt," Mary finished for him.

"Being Wyatt meaning he's wailing on them, right?" Liza asked. "He's not wearing his suit is he? We don't need more bad press for the family if he's recognized."

"He's not wearing the suit. Just his helmet to cover his face."

"That's not the point." Flint wiped his hands on his napkin. "The body count is growing. I'm not sure how long we can leave him to his own devices before he slips into his sin entirely."

The stunned silence around the room grated as much as noise.

Griffin's pulse beat loudly in his ears, and he swallowed, tugging at his collar. Wyatt shouldn't be out there on his own. It was dangerous to him, and everyone else. Griffin knew better than all of them what happened when you slipped into a sin psychosis… people died. All of them. Not just the sinners. He stared at the plate before him, contemplating. It was time he told the family.

"We need to bring him back," he said. "If his sin takes hold of him, he'll black out and kill anyone nearby. Mothers, children… anyone."

Parker stopped eating and zeroed in on him. The look they shared conveyed Griffin's urgency.

"You're speaking from experience," Parker said. It was a statement, not a question.

"I am."

He expected questions. Maybe a few comments. Something like, *That's what's wrong with you*. But Mary only covered Flint's hand on the table and held it tight.

"I'm sorry that happened to you while you were on your own, Griffin," she said. "But you're not alone anymore."

"I know." He turned to Evan. "What about your dreams? Can we find Wyatt that way?"

Evan blushed and looked at Grace. "I'm not seeing much other than my relationship at the moment. It seems my dreams are connected to what I'm thinking about most during my waking hours."

It was Grace's turn to blush as she dipped her gaze to her table setting.

The waitress came back and was almost finished placing meals at each setting, including Tony's dessert which he accepted with a flirty wink.

When the waitress left again, Parker shot Tony a dirty look. "Don't shit where you eat, Tony."

"Relax, I'm not going to do anything." Tony glared back, lifting his palms in mock surrender. Ignoring Parker's bold stare, he spooned some chocolate mousse into his mouth.

That man put away so much food without putting on weight. It was commendable. Although his strict exercise regime was built to keep him solid and sculptured, and his personal trainers never let him miss a session at the gym.

"I mean it," Parker added. "We can't afford to keep hiring new staff every time you get a hankering for one of them."

"Whatever. Hey, I've got something more appropriate to talk about," Tony challenged. "Did anyone stop to wonder if Wyatt actually wrote the note? I mean, what if it was a fake?"

"It was his handwriting," Mary disagreed. "I'd know his chicken scratch scrawl anywhere."

"But we're not a hundred percent sure, are we?" Tony countered.

Silence fell into an expanding pool of uncertainty.

"I think we should find him," Griffin offered. "If he wants to remain secluded, then that is fine, but we need eyes on him. I don't like not knowing specifically where he is. It's a risk, to us and to him." Especially because someone was out there with a camera, looking to capture evidence of their true identities.

"I agree," Evan added.

A chorus of agreement rolled over the table.

"Okay, then." Parker stood up and shut the dining door after the waitress had left for the final time. "It's settled. We find Wyatt. Sloan, can you do some of your magic tomorrow and start the process?"

"Huh?" Sloan looked up from her untouched meal.

"Pay attention, Sloan," Parker quipped. "This moping of yours has to end."

She pulled her hair out of her mouth long enough to scowl and say, "Screw you, Parker."

"Give her a break." Tony threw his napkin at Parker. "She probs lost all her V-bucks in Fortnite, or some shit. Don't worry, sis"—he winked at Sloan—"I got your back."

"You're an asshole too." Sloan threw her fork at Tony. "You don't know what you're talking about."

"That's enough." Mary tapped her palm on the table. "You're acting like a bunch of teenagers."

"What's a V-buck?" Grace whispered to Evan.

He shrugged. "Probably something to do with one of her games."

They joked, but Sloan was in serious danger of falling deep under the influence of her sin, sloth. Just because it was based around negligence, didn't mean it wasn't dangerous. She'd put on weight in the past, but now he noticed she barely touched her food and slept a lot. She rarely left her gaming console, and Griffin couldn't remember the last time he'd seen her in battle gear, out on the streets. Her body mass index was rapidly falling back down, and not in a healthy way.

Griffin took a bite of his steak, and chewed, trying to remember.

Two years ago.

It had been two years ago, after the bombing. He shot a worried glance her way. That was about the time she'd been all excited to meet one of her virtual gamer friends in real life. He didn't know exactly what went on, but knew the man didn't turn up. She hadn't been the same since. Perhaps Griffin's balance protocol would work for her. He made a mental note to visit her and coach her when he had the chance.

"We have more important things to discuss tonight. Griffin"—Mary looked him in the eye—"Tell us about the pictures you found yesterday."

He lowered his fork, supposing he'd better start at the beginning. "Yesterday, we discovered a link between the murdered thieves at the jewelers and Lilo's kidnapped father. I'm led to believe he's a Mafia boss in control of the South-Side district and parts of The Eyrie gated community."

"This is your friend, Doc?" Evan balked.

"Oh, don't worry"—she waved her partner down—"She excommunicated herself from her parents years ago. She's really very nice."

"Right." Evan didn't look convinced.

"As I was saying, her father was kidnapped and a ransom note sent. Yesterday, Lilo received a bloody ear delivered to the Cardinal Copy newsroom instructing her to bring the contents of her father's private safe to a predetermined location tomorrow night. I went with Lilo—"

Tony held up his hand. "Sorry, who the fuck is Lilo again?"

Griffin eyeballed him for a long time, imagining all the things he would do to make him hurt. The fork Sloan had thrown levitated until it hovered in front of Tony's eye, prongs first.

Tony lifted his palms in surrender. "What the forking-fuck?"

Griffin let go of the metal and it clattered to a plate.

"Jesus. I was just asking," Tony simpered. "I'm guessing she's the reason you're all metal-head right now."

Grace saved him from answering. "She's a friend of mine who also works at the Cardinal Copy."

"She's obviously more than a friend. What have I missed?" Tony searched all eyes at the table.

Griffin didn't want to talk about Lilo.

Parker cleared his throat. "Since when?"

Mary and Flint had kept his ability to themselves, allowing him to come to terms with the change, but there was no denying it now. "Since Monday."

"Are we going to meet this woman?"

"No. As I was saying, before I was rudely interrupted. When I went to her parents' house and investigated the contents of the safe, we discovered nothing but surveillance photographs of us."

"All of us?" Evan asked.

"Most of us. In battle gear, out of it, half out of it. Whoever had taken the shots had been following us for a while, and obviously intended to blackmail us, or to turn us in."

"It doesn't make sense. Why would Lilo's father have them and not use them?" Liza asked.

"I don't know," Griffin replied. "But I intend to find out tomorrow night when I intercept the kidnappers before the exchange."

"You going as Greed?"

"Naturally."

"Take someone with you." Parker looked around the table. "Volunteers?"

No one responded, except for Evan who waved his tattooed arm in the air like a school boy.

"Anyone besides Evan?" Parker gave daggers to the rest of his siblings. "Liza?"

"When did you say, tomorrow night? I got a hot date."

"When don't you have a hot date?" Tony taunted.

She shrugged. "Still haven't caught up to you, babes, besides, can't help it if I'm beautiful. Don't be jealous."

"He is," Evan confirmed.

Griffin supposed Evan would know, he sensed envy after all.

Tony used his spoon to point at Liza. "More like you can't help it if—"

"Shut it," Liza threatened. "You're the man-whore here, not me."

"Keep telling yourself that, Lize." Tony raised an indignant eyebrow.

"I'll make you hurt." Liza feinted a punch, pulling at the last second so her hand hovered an inch from Tony's face.

Tony's lids lowered halfway, unruffled.

"Tony. Liza." Parker cut into his meal. "Enough with the bickering. Our meals are getting cold. Tony, why don't you help Griff? Don't tell me you're filming late. You said you'd wrapped it all up."

Tony's brow furrowed. "What about Sloan? When was the last time she went out?"

It was at this point Parker pinched the bridge over his nose and sighed exuberantly.

"It doesn't matter. I'm going by myself," Griffin said. "Now, the second item on the agenda—the imposter. Most of you know he attacked me yesterday at the newsroom and ensured he received a sample of my blood. Have you gathered any information on him since I sent you his details?"

It was Flint who answered. "Donald Doppenger has been working for the Cardinal Copy for fifteen years. In that time he'd been nominated for the Pulitzer twice but no award. His brother is a Senator. His father is a retired Supreme Court judge, and his mother died a few years ago, but she was a standout surgeon who invented a new spray on membrane that could be used internally."

"Yes, I remember that name," Grace added. "Ruth Doppenger."

"As you can see, Donald came from a family of high achievers. He also dated Lilo Likeke for a few years, but that relationship is over. That's about the extent of the information we could pull, nothing to explain why he would be going out of his way to get a sample of your blood, Griff. Are you sure you have the right man?"

Hearing Lilo's and Donald's name in the same sentence

made him feel ill, but she was their closest connection to him. The thought had crossed his mind to question Lilo about Doppenger's motives, but he couldn't bring himself to involve her further.

"I'm one hundred percent certain. Doppenger's greed signature matched the imposter. He wasn't at the newsroom today for me to investigate further."

"Hold up." Tony lifted his palm. "Now, don't throw flying-forks at me, but who's to say this woman isn't still involved with him? It all sounds a little too connected to me."

Griffin stabbed his steak with his knife. "She broke up with him months ago."

"So she tells you. I'm just playing devil's advocate. Her family are mafiosi. No need to look at me like that."

"No," Grace added with a sympathetic look to Griffin. "There's no chance she's with Donnie."

"How can you be sure, Doc?" Evan asked softly.

"I shouldn't be saying this because it's a breach of trust, but I want you to know she is one of the best people I know. There's no chance she's in league with him because… it was an abusive relationship."

Abusive?

No sound, no thought, nothing moved in Griffin's mind except that word, over and over, and with each repetition, his muscles locked tighter. He couldn't get it out of his mind.

Abusive.

What had Doppenger done to her? How? When? Where?

I wouldn't touch him with a ten-foot pole.

It wasn't until Parker said, "Chill out, Griff," that Griffin realized he'd let his control slip and metal utensils hovered an inch from the surface of the table. Forks, knives and spoons whirled at face level, spinning faster and faster with Griffin's elevating stress.

"This is awesome!" Evan grinned. "I can't wait until we spar, bro. Finally on the same level with someone. Although, you know metal conducts electricity, maybe we can team up and—"

"Evan." Grace put her palm gently on his arm. "Not the time."

"Right. Sorry."

In a panic, Griffin looked to Mary. She wasn't worried. He shouldn't be worried.

Focus on your breathing.

Griffin reined in his ability, slowly and smoothly. The items lowered softly to the ground.

"You're getting better at that," Mary noted. "Keep flexing those supernatural muscles."

He wanted to dab the sweat on his brow, but resisted. The effort to keep his emotions in check when thinking about Lilo was hard, but not impossible.

Knowing Doppenger abused her, he wanted her nowhere near him, and he didn't want to ask her about him. Anything Griffin could do to avoid her pain, he would.

"Doppenger will need to be questioned. I should be the one to do it," he stated.

"No." Parker re-organized his cutlery. "You're too close to this. I'll do it. Sloan will come."

"What?" Sloan whined. "But—"

"But what? Do you have more pressing things to do?"

"I don't fit my gear."

"That excuse is getting old. Get new gear made, or wear something else, or get your ass into the gym. We have a new suit prototype coming soon, and when that happens, you'll have no excuse, so get used to it. For now, all you need is your mask to hide your face and a hood or a hat."

She groaned. "Fine."

An expression of accomplishment flittered over Parker. "Good. I think it's clear to everyone that if this is another Syndicate stunt—and let's be honest, blood sampling is their MO—then we're in some deep shit. We're getting stalked, photographed, and set up. We need to take the offensive while we still have the chance. We've lost a lot of advantage over the years we fell apart. Our identities are at stake, and if we're exposed, then losing our freedom might not be the worst we have to face."

"I hate to say it," Mary added grimly, "but it could be the Hildegard Sisterhood."

Flint frowned at his wife and lowered his voice, but they all heard him speak. "They've left you alone all this time. Why bother now?"

"Because we stole these children from them."

"We stole them from the Syndicate. The Sisterhood were only another group trying to steal them."

"Exactly."

"No," Parker added. "I don't think it's them. But we will remain wary. It's the Syndicate who have us on their radar at the moment, and none of us are safe."

Griffin looked at his plate, thinking on the ramifications of his brother's words.

It was Evan who finished the train of thought. "The Syndicate tried to kidnap me once, now the attention is on Griffin so soon after he's unlocked his DNA. That can't be a coincidence. You have to protect Lilo at all costs. If they discover the link between her and you, she's not safe."

He was right. Griffin's heart tripped, and although Lilo was angry at him for forbidding her to go to the meeting, he was convinced he did the right thing. She had to stay safe.

"They're not done with us," Evan continued. "And by the looks of it, they're roping in more people to do their dirty work."

I'm only after the greedy ones.

The memory slammed into Griffin. When dressed as the imposter, Doppenger mentioned he was hunting sinners of greed. At the time Griffin had been defiantly furious because greed was his sin, and he'd be damned if someone else thought they could hunt better than him. But he'd escaped the fact that no one else should have the capability to sense greed at all.

"Doppenger could sense greed, like me," he said.

"That's not possible," Parker replied.

Mary added, "Nothing in the intel we sourced said anything about him being manufactured in a lab, like you all were. In fact, he led a very boring and mundane life until we all turned up in town and gave him something to write about."

"Then how did he have the skill to sense greed?"

"Maybe it was a misnomer."

"Maybe he's working with the Syndicate."

"They must have given him something, altered him somehow."

Everyone spoke at once until Parker stood, towering over them all. The feral glint in his eye was enough to silence them all. "This is unacceptable. We're elite specimens, manufactured soldiers, yet, somehow this organization has all this information about us and we have nothing on them. I want everyone on this. Your lives depend on it."

CHAPTER SEVENTEEN

LILO LIKEKE

After visiting her parents' house, Lilo spent a few days keeping to herself, working quietly, and processing her feelings. It hadn't been easy as Griffin always seemed near. He wandered past her desk, loitered in her periphery and tried to strike up conversations. Once, he'd given her a mug of hot coffee which she politely declined. Nevertheless, his relentless efforts of attention let her know he was there.

She looked at her hero vision board and remembered why she'd put it there in the first place—to remind herself there were good men out there. That there was hope.

I forbid it.

End of discussion.

Those had been Griffin's unbending words.

Sitting at her desk and staring at her screen, she felt so stupid. She'd allowed herself to be taken in by him; she'd been blind to trust him completely. From the moment she collided with him in the break room, she'd been head over heels for his confidence, strong jaw, kissable lips… *God!* She slammed the heel of her palm into her eye socket and grimaced. She still couldn't stop thinking about how attracted she was to him. Had she really been so desperate for affection that she'd not seen his stubborn and rigid personality for what it was? Controlling, possessive and the opposite of what she wanted in a partner. Donnie had given her plenty of that and it almost broke her. It still messed with her brain. The very thought of getting intimate with another man gave her heart palpitations, and not for a good reason.

You'll never be fulfilled without me.

What if Donnie was right? What if she couldn't get any satisfaction because he wasn't there, telling her what to do, or how to feel? He'd always been dominant in the bedroom, and for a while it worked. She never had to worry about making the wrong decision, or disappointing him.

Enough thinking about disappointing men.

She turned to her computer screen and opened the file she'd started on the Lazarus family. Despite what Donnie or Griffin thought, she knew she could make her own decisions. She wouldn't be at the Cardinal Copy if she wasn't a decent investigator, so it was time to do what she knew best. Time to work out why Griffin had avoided giving her the pictures. He'd coveted them. Had been a little too protective.

Alarm bells had been ringing in her head since, and they sparked an unquenchable curiosity that had Lilo roaming the internet for information about the Lazarus family. On her notepad next to her keyboard, she wrote all the names down, including Mary and Flint—Griffin's parents. For hours she was lost in news article over news article. She found plenty online about Parker, Tony, Wyatt and even

Evan, but rarely any Liza or Sloan. Griffin was virtually invisible. No other family was mentioned. No cousins, no social media accounts. All of their history only started a few years ago. It was like their digital blueprint before ten years ago was a ghost.

Her journalist instincts were buzzing.

There was something about the family. Possibly something big.

Lilo tapped her notebook with her pencil and doodled next to each name. For such a large family, they were blissfully free from run-ins with the law. It was almost too clean.

She jolted as her phone alarm went off and she glanced at the clock. Four-fifty. The meeting with the kidnappers was scheduled at six, and the location was deep in the South-Side district where crime ran rampant, and even the police feared to tread. She'd have to pass through the slums by the river to get there, but she had her trusty cattle prod strapped to her thigh under her skirt. The other thigh holster held a small pistol. She also had her trusty spy-phone in her bag to help capture evidence.

Most people would be indoors because of the cold.

She would be safe.

She could do this.

It wouldn't be the first time she'd ventured to the South-Side alone at night. Once, she'd followed a lead to uncover the source of EZ-m, a new drug made from bath salts. It was snorted by many impressionable youth who missed out on a buzz, but got free trips to the Emergency Department. Lilo's father had sent her coordinates of the suspected dealers, but she couldn't take him at his word. She vetted the information herself before handing it over to Donnie for an exposé. She'd trekked deep into the district on her own, staked out a house for twelve hours, and took incriminating photographs, all without being discovered. If she could do that, she could meet her father's kidnappers and negotiate.

And she could write the story herself. This time, she would see it published in her name, no matter what boy's club strings Donnie tried to pull.

There were too many things about the kidnapping that didn't add up. Her mother's erratic behavior for one. Lilo had the sense her mother knew something about it. Janet had a greedy heart, but never before had she talked about killing her own husband. Seeing her mother's true colors made Lilo believe her father shielded her from the brunt of the psychopathic behavior, and if he'd done that, then what else had he protected her from?

A flash of her sixteenth party, of her father spending most of the evening indoors with her mother came to mind. Was there more to it? Had her father been keeping her crazy mother away from the revelers for Lilo's sake?

No.

She'd seen her father's corrupt ways with her own eyes. Nobody made him pay all those people to lie to her. Nobody made him sell weapons of mass destruction from his den. He was as bad as her mother.

Still, something didn't sit well.

A sneaky, terrible thought unfurled from the edges of her mind. What if he'd become the way he was because of her mother's irrational demands? Lilo knew as well as any abusive relationship refugee that sometimes the abuse wasn't obvious. Sometimes it silently wore you down until one day you found yourself in a situation you couldn't escape.

Lilo rubbed her eyes until they felt raw. Her brain hurt. She was tired of lies and cover-ups. She was tired of being managed by men. First her father, then Donnie, now Griffin.

Her eyes drifted to her hero vision board with a longing.

"Home time," Bev said from her side of the partition.

"Yes." Candy fist pumped the air, and launched from her seat, leaving without another word.

"Five o'clock," Lilo whispered, heart racing.

It was time.

She put on her coat, wrapped her scarf around her neck and tugged her woolen beanie over her head and ears. After waving goodbye to Bev, she collected her hand bag and made her way toward the exit. As she waited for the elevator, nervous tension crept up her spine, so when someone called her name, she jumped.

"Lilo." His voice cut through her heart to its aching center.

She turned. Griffin stood behind her, hands in his pockets, blue eyes attentive and focused on her. She'd rarely spoken to him the past couple of days, but had watched from the corner of her eye every time he entered the room, turning beet red with awareness. She'd felt his heat from across the distance and through the walls as though he'd stood next to her desk all day. It had been torture to shut down his every attempt at conversation, but she had pride and dignity. Now he stood there, looking all broad shouldered and manly in his tight black sweater, completely unaware of his effect on her.

He used a finger to adjust his spectacles at the bridge. "Do you need a lift home?"

She blinked and turned back to the elevator, now opening its doors. "No. Thank you."

He followed her in. "You are going home, aren't you?"

Oh, she saw where this was going, and fire snapped in her vision. "It's none of your business where I go."

A tall man wearing a Fedora came into the lift. Griffin growled and pushed him out. "Catch the next one."

"Griffin!" she exclaimed and then mouthed an apology to the hat man.

Griffin punched the ground button then rounded on her, eyes blazing. "I don't have time for games, Lilo."

And here comes the real Griffin, she thought bitterly, hating that she'd been right.

The doors closed, shutting them in together, but she was damned if she acquiesced to such bossy orchestrations. She stuck out her chin and stared at the doors.

"Just tell me you're going home and I'll leave you alone."

"I'm going home." At some point.

He exhaled. "Good."

The doors opened, and she strode out knowing full well his intense eyes were glued to her back, watching the entire way it took her to cross the lobby and exit the glass rotating doors into the night. She deliberately turned right, letting him think she was going to catch a cab from the bay. When she rounded the corner, she doubled back and made her way to the subway.

Until she'd bumped into Griffin at the elevator, she'd been on edge, but seeing him try yet again to sway her actions gave her the motivation to stick to her principles and continue her journey.

Half an hour later, she exited the South-Side subway station.

But by the time she walked deep into the district, her nerve began to falter.

It was an older area of town and the desperation of residents dripped from the crumbling and stained brownstone. Walls with broken windows loomed on all sides, and as she hurried through the darkened streets, loaded stares pummeled her—mostly from men wondering how long the lone woman would remain untouched. She shivered and hugged her coat tight. They weren't thinking that. It was her own paranoia trying to make her retreat.

A sense of dread settled in suffocating waves as she neared her destination. When she approached a line of homeless people huddled in the alcove of an old church, a baby's cry pierced the air, bringing her attention to a crouched woman wearing only a saggy sweater and dress. Her boots were old with holes in the toes. Hugged under her arm was a small bundle.

Lilo stopped. It was so cold out there, and people lived in squalor. That baby wouldn't survive the night.

With her current plight forgotten, Lilo walked up to the woman. She had long, stringy light brown hair that stuck to her shoulders from the dampening night. The mother noticed Lilo and hugged her baby tighter.

"What do you want?" said a grizzly man to the right.

"I just want to give you something," Lilo said to the woman.

Wary eyes watched her as she slipped out of her coat and held it out. "You need this more than me."

"I got no money, Missus," said the woman.

"I don't want any money. I have another coat at home. Please take it." God, please take it. Lilo couldn't live with a baby death on her conscience.

The woman reached out, but the man snatched it.

"No!" Lilo growled and used her bag to hit him. "This is not for you. Don't you dare take this away from the woman and her baby."

The man hissed at Lilo. "I'm the boss around here."

"I don't think so, buddy." Lilo reached under her long skirt and retrieved her pistol. She pointed it at the man. "Do I need to repeat myself?"

He slowly handed the woman the coat.

With a conflicted glance at Lilo, she dressed herself in the warm coat.

"Take this too." Lilo unwound the scarf from her neck. "For the baby."

Only when it was wrapped around the baby did Lilo reset the hammer on the gun, twist it, and give it handle first to the woman.

"For protection," she said. "So you can hold on to your warm clothes."

"Oh, thank you, Missus." The woman slipped the pistol into her pocket, then gave the man an evil eye before retreating to her corner of the stoop on the abandoned church.

A cold breeze brushed past Lilo's face and she wrapped her denim jacket tight. She'd be fine. A few hours in the cold wasn't the same as spending a night in it. It hadn't snowed for days, and the night was one of the warmest it had been all month. Cold enough to hurt if you had to sleep out all night, but not enough to harm her for a few hours. She'd be fine.

With a mutual nod, Lilo left the woman, ensuring her strides remained uniform and confident even though her heart pounded erratically. By the time she arrived at the meeting location, she was so cold, her toes and fingers were numb. Thank goodness for the beanie holding in whatever body heat her skirt and denim jacket couldn't.

She refocused on her surroundings.

Let's do this.

The warehouse was an old packing plant. Wooden crates stacked outside had been pulled apart, most likely scavenged for makeshift furniture or building supplies. The doors to the place were boarded up, all except one.

Trembling from the cold, she pulled the heavy metal sliding door to the side, cringing as it screeched from rusty rollers and debris in the tracks. Inside was dark, but the air was crisp and a breeze pushed at her face. Looking up, she located the source of the wind and the reason no one took shelter inside. Except a few steel beams, the roof was missing, leaving the warehouse completely exposed to the elements.

She pulled her phone from her bag and checked the time. *Half an hour early.*

"Hello," she called into the darkness, just to be sure.

When her voice finished echoing off the walls, she strained to locate movement, but only silence greeted her.

Rather than wait in the cold, she turned on her phone's torch function and pointed the light around the perimeter of the warehouse. May as well get familiar with her surroundings to avoid being taken by surprise. She also had to scout for a location for her second spy-phone.

Columns of stone pillars reached for a roof that wasn't there. Metal stairs rose to a platform that lead nowhere. Graffiti covered the walls and broken bricks and crates littered the floors. Nuts and bolts crunched underfoot. An abandoned fire pit sat alone in a corner with broken crate beds around it. Maybe in the warmer weather people actually used the place for refuge. It broke her heart to see such poverty in her city, while others choked on their wealth. Others like her mother and father.

Not long now.

She quickly propped her spy-phone on a crate next to the wall and set a timer on the camera. It wasn't a fancy gadget or anything, just a normal smart phone with an app she'd downloaded that promised to take continuous photographs at random intervals. If all went well, then by the end of the meeting, she should have incriminating evidence to publish in tomorrow's paper. After making sure the phone looked inconspicuous by putting a few scattered baked beans tins near, she kept moving around the darkened room, using her phone-torch to light the way.

She searched for improvised weapons to replace her pistol and mentally recited Krav Maga moves to keep her mind sharp. If she was attacked with a knife, she imagined blocking and then using the knife arm against them. If it was a tire iron, she would need to take control of the weapon. Protect her face with one hand, move forward instead of back, dodge and…

A sudden sound made the hairs on her arms lift. She swung her light toward the source somewhere behind her.

"Who's there?" Her voice echoed.

Shadows emerged from the darkness. One, two, three men. And a fourth shoved into the area by another tall shape. How did they get in? She'd been watching the entrance. Her eyes darted around for another entrance, but found nothing. She must have missed something.

Straightening her spine, she tracked their approach.

"I'm Lilo Likeke," she said, voice loud and proud.

"No pumpkin," came the raw sound of her father. "You weren't supposed to come."

Pushed into her circle of light, her father appeared haggard and dirty. Dried blood streaked from a wound where his left ear used to be and down his thin polo shirt. Once some pale pastel color, it was now almost brown. Despite his condition, her father held onto an air of self-respect she knew came from years of ordering people around. Once, she had been impressed with his strength and importance. She'd felt safe with him.

Probably why she had a penchant for confident men. God, she was hopeless.

"I'm here," she said. The same words had been a show of solidarity when Griffin spoke them, but here in the cold warehouse, they sounded empty.

Lilo glanced around, stupidly hoping to see police, even

impossibly yearning to see Griffin. But she'd spurned him and lied to him. He thought she was home.

The other men moved into a formation, surrounding her.

Coming into the light, she took note of their appearance. They wore clean leather jackets—some long and brown, some short and black. None of them seemed feral which led her to believe they were part of an organized crime syndicate. Caucasian looking, she noted, trying to memorize facts for her article. She pretended to swing her phone their way so she could see better, but quickly took stealthy shots of their faces in case her spy-phone failed.

"Did you bring the contents of the safe?" Asked a barrel chested man with a round face. He had an Irish accent, pale skin, and dark ear-length hair. His eyes were round and far apart.

Lilo patted her bag. "First, tell me what you want it for."

A burst of laughter came from the man. "Girlie, I don't think you're in the position to be asking the questions."

"Lilo, turn around and run," her father barked.

The brute restraining him punched him in the side of the head, making him stagger and Lilo cry out.

Seeing him like this, she knew she couldn't leave, no matter what he'd done.

Tears burned her eyes and resolve steeled her spine.

"I'm a reporter for the Cardinal Copy news," she said. "I've taken photographs of you and uploaded them to our cloud facility. If you don't let him go, or if I don't get out of here alive, they'll automatically publish."

Not a peep from any of them.

Then the leader laughed in a squealing sort of way. He indicated with his Glock for the men to advance on her.

"Oh, love. Do you really think we care if our faces are published? We've got friends in high places. We've done much worse than this."

Lilo froze. It would be difficult to extract her cattle prod without being noticed, but she had to try. She began scrunching the side of her skirt, gathering its folds, but before she got far, the cold press of a gun nudged her in the temple.

"Now," said the leader, as he grinned while his pierced comrade threatened Lilo. "This is the last time I'm going to ask. Did you bring the contents of the safe?"

Before she could scream, before she could breathe, a shot fired, and the man in front of her collapsed in a pool of expanding blood.

The phone fell from her numb fingers in slow motion.

The torch beam sliced through the air, hitting on random sights that burned into her retinas: a pigeon sitting on the ridge of the open roof; the desperation in her father's eyes as he met her gaze; the dark menacing approach of a hooded, blue-scarfed, leather clad body pointing his recently fired weapon at her head.

CHAPTER EIGHTEEN

GRIFFIN LAZARUS

When Griffin dressed in his combat gear that night, he strapped light. Feeling more confident with his new ability, he'd removed all knives and daggers, all throwing stars, darts, picks and iron claws. They weighed on him. He'd kept his retractable metal bo-staff, and secured a grappling hook with a strong, thin rope to his belt. Finally, he'd strapped each fist with boxer's tape, leaving his fingers free and tactile.

Walking out of the weapons room in the basement headquarters of Lazarus House, he tried not to pay attention to how the leather creaked. He hoped the new prototype was creak free.

Parker, Sloan and Evan were inspecting an enormous computer monitor under a glass table-like apparatus. It was a computer system hooked up to AIMI. Currently, they perused a map. All were dressed in their battle gear, except Sloan. She wore black sweats and a hoodie, dark hair tucked into her collar.

Two walls of the room were covered in ceiling-to-floor screens and flashed different video footage from CCTV cameras around town. There were computers and desks lining the third wall. Flint was seated at one, engrossed in something on the screen. Mary stood behind him with her palm on his shoulder.

"Did you locate Doppenger?" Griffin asked as he flexed his fists, testing the support of the tape.

Parker looked up. "Negative. He wasn't in his apartment or workplace."

His hair had been tied at the nape, his face scarf gathered around his neck along with the lowered hood. Hanging from his belt were two metal claws, ready to slip onto his fists and slice his opponents. Coming to stand next to him, Griffin felt slightly dwarfed. Not only was Parker the tallest of them, but the most robust and muscular. Griffin and Wyatt were next in body mass, then Evan. Sloan stood at a modest five foot seven. He hoped Parker would take it easy on her given this was her first time in the field for years.

"Doppenger wasn't at the Cardinal Copy yesterday or today," he added.

"We've set alerts and virtual traps around the city. If his face pops up on anything, we'll know, and we'll be ready."

"I'm heading out now to the kidnapper's rendezvous."

"I'm coming with you." Evan broke away. "We can take the Mustang."

"We agreed on me doing this on my own."

"No," Parker added. "You agreed on you doing it alone."

"Dude," Sloan sighed. "Just let him come. Then he's not pestering us when we go to find Doppenger."

Evan pushed her playfully. "I know you're hurting because we dragged you from your game, so I'll pretend to ignore that."

She gave a tight-lipped smile.

"C'mon, Sloanie. Cheer up." Evan patted her back.

"Evan's going with you because you need back up," Parker continued. "You're on the Syndicate's radar now, so no more of this lone wolf shit."

"Fine." Griffin grit his teeth and turned to Evan. "I hope you put your thermals on."

Evan winked. "Thermals and double tighty-whities for extra insulation. These nuts are staying toasty tonight."

Sloan made a vomit sound while sticking her finger down her throat.

Evan grinned and followed Parker to the glowing blue table screen.

"This is a representation of the location you're headed," Parker said, making a swiping movement on the computerized table. Satellite imagery of a warehouse came up. "Seems abandoned."

"Shouldn't be any trouble then." Evan lifted his hood. "Let's go."

"We'll head out in search of the imposter. Catch us on comms if you need anything." Parker swiped again, turning the table-screen off.

Guess they were done.

Parker and Sloan ended up taking the Mustang which suited Griffin fine. The motorcycles had better maneuverability. Chances were by the time anyone recognized their leather combat gear, they'd be long gone. The bulletproof black helmets would conceal their identities, so they were safe enough.

FIFTEEN MINUTES LATER, Evan and Griffin cut the engine on their bikes and coasted into an alley a block from the warehouse. They removed their helmets and lifted their face scarfs over their noses. Hoods went up. Voice modifiers activated, and after a final weapons check, Griffin turned on his watch's timer.

Half hidden under the shadow of his hood, Evan's eyes were unmistakably condescending. "Still timing this shit?"

"It works." Sort of.

"But you don't need to be so anal anymore. You can relax a little."

Griffin unsheathed his baton and flexed the length until it expanded into the bo-staff. "I'll relax when I'm dead."

They crept through a dirty snow-littered alley and glided through a side street, trying not to squelch in the puddles. When they got near the warehouse in question, and realized there were too many people around, they scaled the adjacent two-level building and hit the rooftop. Crouching low, they approached the lip of the building and peered over, careful not to dislodge the crest of snow.

"How many you got?" Evan asked, voice low and gravelly.

Anticipation filled the air.

He sent out his sense of greed and tracked the signatures emanating from individuals. Down in the alley separating them from the warehouse, he sensed five loitering around a parked car. Metal coated his tongue as his ability brushed upon their concealed weapons. Three of them carried big assault rifles, another a smaller gun he postulated as Uzi-like from its shape and size, and the fourth and fifth carried something like pistols. He relayed the information to his brother and was rewarded with a muttered curse, then: "That's a lot of bang-bang."

"More inside." Griffin shifted uncomfortably. If only one of those bullets went astray, it could mean trouble.

"How are you with that much metal, bro?"

"You're referring to my new skill?"

"Yeah."

"I don't know. Haven't tested that much. When I pulled the imposter's pistol, it was the only one I focused on."

"What about high speed projectiles?"

"Mary threw shuriken at me during training. I was able to stop them all before they got to me. Two at a time. Six in total."

"Good enough for me. Shouldn't happen, but worst-case scenario they pop a few off, that's your responsibility, got it?"

Griffin's stomach twinged.

Greed.

Coming in fast.

Further along the alley, near the exit at the street he felt another group of people silently approaching with the sense of sin pulsing gently from their cores. Four in total. Possibly not related to the mob in the alley, maybe even a group of waylaid homeless people. Inside the warehouse, out of sight, was a further five.

"I've got fourteen," he murmured.

"Really? I've got fifteen. You must be going soft, brother."

Griffin counted again. "No. Definitely fourteen."

"Shit." Evan went silent while his pointed finger bobbed methodically as he recounted. "Fifteen. Six in the warehouse. Five in the alley. Four approaching."

Why would they have a discrepancy? Evan sensed envy, he sensed greed. Most people always felt something. Why would one person have no greed?

The floor tilted and Griffin had to sit back from the edge. "That's not possible," he breathed. "She said she'd stay home."

"Aww, dog. Your girl's got guts."

Griffin couldn't respond, his mind was stuck on the woman inside the warehouse surrounded by all that sin. His girl, his balance, his… she wasn't his anything… *yet*.

"What are the odds," Evan whispered.

Griffin's gut churned, thinking the worst before his rational mind caught up.

"You got those smoke bombs from Flint?" he asked.

Evan pulled two metal orbs from his cargo pocket.

"Good." Griffin took one and rolled the icy ball in his palm. The sense of metal connected with him on a molecular level. The round item buzzed in his palm and he could feel the object's construction. An inch in diameter, etched on the outside, hollow in the middle. On second thought. "Give me both."

He could use them. He could control them.

"We disarm the men outside first, then go in the warehouse over the roof, drop the bombs, then get the rest. I'll get Lilo. You get her father. You cool with that?"

"As a cucumber." Evan pressed his finger to his ear. "Ground control to Major Tom." He hesitated, then updated Flint on their situation, requesting backup.

Two-seconds later, a slice of pain pierced Griffin's gut, and he doubled over with a grunt, hand splayed on the roof for support.

"What's wrong?" Evan paused.

"It's another signature. Deadly. It's Doppenger."

A shot fired from inside the warehouse and Griffin's heart leaped into his throat.

"Shot fired," Evan said into his comms. "Doppenger is here."

Lethal intent washed over Griffin, and he threw the metal orbs over the edge to hover with his power. He took a running jump and launched before Evan could speak.

Suddenly, in that airborne moment, he knew with all certainty that a life without Lilo wasn't something he dreamed of.

That was his mate down there, surrounded with deadly greed, and she had no idea what she was up against.

Two levels of air whooshed by before Griffin's boots slammed into the pavement. He tucked and rolled automatically to lessen the impact. In a fluid motion, he found his feet, checked his hold on the metal orbs and hurtled them at the heads of two gun-toting men swinging their weapons his way.

They had no chance.

The smoke bombs orbited their heads, struck temples, and then went onto the next. Round and round the little silver orbs went, one by one knocking men out like a brutal tornado. It all happened in the space of seconds and then he was creeping into the warehouse, signaling for Evan to follow.

The instant he got inside, his heart stopped.

Lilo stood at the middle of the open space with a dead body at her feet. To her right, Doppenger pointed a gun at her head—once again dressed as Greed. To her left, a cluster of men drew their weapons.

She was going to get caught in the crossfire.

Before his mind registered his movement, he pushed forward with an almighty grunt. His legs surged, his arms pumped. Had to get to Lilo.

Still a few feet away, the first shot was fired. And the second. And the third. And then a rapid percussion surrounded them, almost throwing his senses into hyper-drive and shutting him down.

But he forced the panic away. He threw his ability out to surround them with a magnetic net. Still running, he skidded to a halt in front of Lilo, enveloped her, and turned his back to the majority of the peppered bullets, just in case. Sound continued to jackhammer the atmosphere in a fire-work finale of explosion, but his ability remained strong as metal projectiles headed their way. Sweat beaded at his temples, but he held, catching each bullet in his net. The rushing roar begged him to travel back in time to when he was on tour, back when he was tortured. For Lilo's sake, he stayed present. He couldn't afford to slip into the past. Not now.

Beyond her shoulder, the imposter's eyes widened over his face scarf with the realization of what Griffin was doing. In slow motion, Griffin watched him shift the angle of his gun from the mob behind Griffin to point at the back of Lilo's trembling head.

Doppenger fired until the magazine clicked empty. Within seconds, the mob also ended their shooting. A wall of floating bullets separated them on all sides. He let go of Lilo and all the greed in the room seeped back in, allowing him to supernaturally reengage his opponents' position. Four with the mob, some approaching from outside, and still one in front of him, the slimiest sense of all, Doppenger.

"*Legendary*," came Evan's voice over the comms. "*My turn.*"

A black shadow flashed at the corner of Griffin's vision as Evan raced in. He skidded to his knees across a puddle where two of the mob stood, took hold of a leg on each man, and let rip a blue flash of arcing power. The electricity fried their nervous systems, and they dropped. Evan was up before they hit the ground, moving on to the next two.

That was Griffin's cue. He sidestepped Lilo, ran toward the imposter, planted his bo-staff on the ground and vaulted feet first to hit the man's chest, propelling him into a pile of wooden crates.

He prowled up to the writhing body and scrutinized the man, feeling his temper rise. His bo-staff clattered to the ground as he picked Doppenger up by the scruff and punched him in the face. And again. And again. Doppenger's head snapped back each time. He punched until a wet feeling bled through his face mask to coat Griffin's fist. Somewhere far away in his mind, he knew he should stop. He knew Doppenger was just a greedy man playing superhero dress ups, that he couldn't help his addiction, but he'd threatened Lilo. He'd tried to kill her.

Griffin wanted him to pay, and his red, uncontrolled rage wanted to keep hitting.

But movement niggled in his periphery. More sin. More greed. He shoved Doppenger's limp body back into the crates and whirled to survey the warehouse.

More people were coming in. Some looked like homeless people, others were fallen soldiers from the alley.

"What is this, a free for all?" Evan's voice came over his ear-comms.

A groan behind him.

Doppenger tried to rise, so Griffin side-kicked him.

Stay down.

But he kept rising, twisting, fighting back. Unnaturally so. For a sheer second of doubt, Griffin considered the man behind the mask wasn't Doppenger, but his greed signature was identical.

Lilo's yelp drew his attention.

She stabbed her cattle prod into one of the hoboes approaching her, then in a slick move he didn't think she had, she sideswiped a man's knee, and went straight for his throat, in a punch that took no quarter.

Griffin hesitated, impressed. The imposter took advantage of his distraction, got hold of his staff, and swung it against Griffin's head. Pain exploded at his temple and he staggered back.

Panic compounded in his body as sounds in the room amplified, and the tactile sensations he'd stifled roared to the surface. It was all too much. He had to protect Lilo. Had to get out of there.

With too many variables, he had only one option. Deploy the smoke bombs.

CHAPTER NINETEEN

LILO LIKEKE

Lilo couldn't believe it. The hobo who'd tried to steal her jacket from the woman and baby had come after her! And he brought friends.

Of all the nerve and greedy cheek, to attack her after she'd already been attacked, and while a battle still took place. Years of weekly self-defense training kicked in, and her body moved on instinct. She rounded on the men coming her way and released the cattle prod's fury. One went down, seizing and urinating his pants. The second came after her with a knee to her stomach, but she'd practiced that scenario many times. She deflected with a window-washer swipe, stepped in and went for his soft spots—punch to the throat, kick to the junk, fingers to the eyes and then... and then...

She looked around. Where was the smoke coming from?

White cloud surrounded her, creating a screen that blocked her vision. She stilled. With her sight compromised, the sounds grew louder, echoing around her. Men grunting, hitting, fighting and echoing off the walls. A man screamed. Oh God. That was closer than she thought.

Lilo's heart rate picked up, and her nerves sparked, wanting to breathe faster, but she choked. She covered her mouth with her sleeve. The chemicals made her eyes water.

Someone yanked her. She tumbled to the side, tripped, and fell into powerful leather clad arms. Horror seized her as she looked into the face of one of the Deadly Seven.

Blue face mask.

She'd seen two of them fighting. Two Greeds. One good, one evil. Which one was this?

Holy mother of mercy.

With barely time to register blue stern eyes, she was hauled over a shoulder and moving, bouncing through the smoke at an alarmingly fast pace.

"Let me go!" She thumped him on his back as they burst out of the warehouse and into the alley.

He kept jogging.

But there was no way she'd go down without a fight. She still had her cattle prod and shoved it into his leg, aiming for behind his knee. A buzzing sound exploded. He staggered, let loose a strangled growl that set her hairs on edge, but didn't let go.

He kept jogging.

She screamed and thumped as they bounced along. She thrashed and writhed. She went for his thigh again, but the prod whipped out of her hand and skittered to the floor. It was as though someone had pulled it on a string. No! She could cry. It got smaller as the distance grew between them.

That was her last weapon.

Her last line of defense.

No, that wasn't entirely true, she still had her fists. She twisted to use them on him, aiming for the head.

"Stop," he growled, but his voice was wrong, all distorted and computerized.

"I'll stop when you let me go." Her punches glanced off his hard back, butt and thighs. What the hell was this guy made of, granite? She was more likely to break her fists than him.

But she wouldn't give up.

She tried to pinch. Surely there had to be some soft skin somewhere.

Nope.

Another guttural growl, a grunt, and then they shouldered through a door and into a dark, dank smelling room.

No! No, no, no.

She would not be locked in a room with this man. He killed her cousin, he shot Griffin, he was a murderer. She knew this with all certainty because the real Greed wouldn't kidnap her, would he? Surely he'd be back there fighting. The real Deadly Seven were good. She'd stake her unicorn story on it.

Her brain shot into her stomach as he flipped her from his shoulder and pushed her into a wall. Oh, God. The room swayed. She almost vomited.

"Stop fighting me."

"Never," she gasped and swung wide, but it was like one of those childish games when they turn you around and around and then you have to try to walk a straight line. She couldn't do anything. The man in front of her swirled.

"Relax." A hand steadied her.

No! "Don't touch me," she slurred.

Her kidnapper watched patiently as her dizziness abated, and she became aware of a buzzing, flickering light behind him, a globe dangling from a cord.

When she brought her attention back to the man, cold, hard eyes peered back at her. Killer! He grappled her flying fists and flattened her against the wall with his body.

So warm.

She hated that her body rejoiced in his heat because she was cold. She pushed against him.

"I'm not him," came the deep voice as he leaned into her, nose hitting hers—only a thin layer of fabric separating their skin. "I'm the real Greed."

Stupid man stood with his legs apart. She kneed upward. "I don't believe you."

He took the hit in the groin and bit out, "I swear it's me."

"Your bo-staff is missing."

"There were more important things to carry."

"Oh sure, a likely story." He was sounding remarkably non-psycho and she didn't like it. Too much anger and aggression had built inside her with her fight-or-flight reaction. Fight, dammit, she wanted to fight.

Never again would she be tied up like Donnie tied her.

She pushed at him, but it was like being stuck between two unforgiving walls. A frustrated cry ripped from her lungs as helplessness washed over her. He was too strong.

Too powerful. As if sensing her sudden turn of emotions, he let go and stood back.

The light continued to flicker and they must have hit it because now it swung behind him with a squeak. Without breaking eye contact, he caught the cable, halting the globe. When he let go, he held up his palms in surrender.

"I'm not going to hurt you, I swear, but I need you to remove that weapon strapped to your thigh before you use it against me."

She didn't have a weapon. She'd given it away, and the stupid hobo man must have stolen it from the poor woman, and how the fuck did he know she'd had a weapon strapped to her thigh?

She pointed at him. "Stay back."

"I can sense the metal. It's small, but it's there." He frowned, cocking his head. "It's... u-shaped. A pin?"

Sense the metal? Just what the fudging fork?

"Don't you think I'd use the weapon if I had it?" She bit her lip and, knowing it was hopeless, went for his eyes, but her steam had run out. He caught her wrists, twisted and pushed her face first against the wall with the length of his body, arms trapped behind her in his grip. The cold wall on her cheek broke her composure.

"Please," she sobbed. "Please don't."

She'd exhausted her adrenal glands until nothing was left. If he truly was the bad Greed, this was it for her. But if he was telling the truth...

The hard wall behind her softened. "So... it's not a weapon?"

"No. I swear. I mean, like I said, there is no weapon. I gave it away to this woman in the street, to protect herself because I gave her my jacket and then there was a baby, and, oh my God, you can check if you like. Just check for God's sake."

The instant her rambling words finished, she froze. Did she just say that?

You can check if you like.

Idiot. Complete idiot.

"He used a gun. I abhor guns and have never used them. *You* can check *me*."

He wanted her to frisk him? That was almost as frightening a prospect.

"You saw how I stopped those bullets, correct?" His grip on her loosened, allowing her arms some lag, but he kept her facing the wall.

Who didn't see that?

When the pelting of bullets sprayed the room, she'd thought she was a goner for sure, but then Greed had arrived. He took her in his steady arms and held her tight while the world shattered around them. The real Greed could manipulate metal. The real Envy could use electricity. Those were the facts.

Focus on the facts, Lilo. She nodded.

"Okay, so if I was the imposter, would I be able to do this?"

The metal buckle on her thigh holster wobbled, tickling her skin, sending shivers up her spine from the intimate touch. She gasped. Second by second, her apprehension melted.

"I don't know how else to prove it to you." He turned her around to face him. "Honestly, you can check me for a gun if that will help convince you."

He held his arms wide, leaving himself vulnerable to an attack. Not that she had anything left to attack with.

"Check me."

If she frisked him and found no weapons, would it matter?

Would she feel safe?

The questions tumbled in her mind as she looked him over. He was a full head taller than her, broad shouldered and buff. Strength incarnate.

Even with a man as soft as Donnie, she knew her limits when he decided to force her in the bedroom. He never followed through with his threats, but he liked to remind her that he was stronger. There were times he'd tied or held her down and delighted in her struggles, saying that the excitement made the sex better.

There were times she'd felt terrified and helpless.

She had no doubt that underneath Greed's leather was a body made for war. There were many straps and pockets on his suit. Places weapons could hide. But the more she looked at him, the more reason pushed her fears away. This man before her wasn't the man who shot Nathanial, nor the one who killed in the warehouse. He was a hero who put himself in danger, for no pay, no regard, and constant attacks from the media.

And there he was, protecting her, keeping her safe. Still, she'd feel better if he wasn't hiding behind that scarf and hood. If he wanted her trust then he had to reciprocate.

"Show me your face," she demanded.

"You're a reporter. I can't do that."

"You know who I am?"

After a beat of stern scrutiny, he said, "I've read your articles."

"Oh." A blush hit her cheeks and suddenly, she remembered something. She'd left her spy-phone in there, and… "Oh shit. My father!"

Greed dipped his head and touched his finger to his ear. "Status update on the hostage." His eyes locked onto her as he listened to the relay. "Copy that. I'm with… the woman. I'll see her home safely." He dropped his hand and stared.

Well, that confirmed it. The imposter worked alone. This man had friends. As soon as the notion hit her, excitement skipped up her spine, and she saw embarrassing flashes of her vision board with the kissy-hearts. Thank goodness he'd never seen it.

"Is my father okay?" she asked.

"He is alive."

"Where is he?"

"My colleagues have the situation under control. The imposter is in our custody, and your father will be handed to police."

She fell back against the wall. At least he wasn't about to be murdered. She should feel relieved, but she wasn't. Something nagged at the edges of her mind and she couldn't quite pick it up. Her journalist instincts were telling her to keep pushing, keep investigating her father, the pictures, and those men out there. The imposter Greed turned up for the second time in relation to her family. She could have died.

All those bullets firing at her.

The weight of realization hit her and made her legs wobble.

Greed caught her by the elbows, steadying her.

She should open her eyes. *Open your eyes, Lilo.* But she couldn't. He was there. The heat of him enveloped her like a comforting blanket.

"You saved my life," she breathed.

She owed him everything.

When no answer came back, she lifted her lids to the full impact of his attention. Those eyes betrayed his thoughts—two dark blue orbs burned with intensity—at her.

He frowned and slowly, his hands slid up her arms to her shoulders, as if he couldn't help himself.

She tensed.

Okay, that definitely wasn't platonic.

It was a caress, she realized with a jolt. The moment the thought sank in, her perception changed. It was almost a click in her brain. No longer did she feel like he was a stranger, but someone she trusted. This man saved her life. Overcome with awe, she looked up at him. He could stop a rain of bullets midair and he put her above all else in that room.

He wanted her.

Inch by inch, she lifted her palms until they flattened against his front. Her simple touch through his thick leather made his pupils blacken. He made a sound as though he bit back a groan.

They stared at each other, waiting for the other to halt the direction they were headed.

No one spoke, but their eyes said enough.

She slid her hands up and over his broad shoulders.

He cupped her face, rough warrior fingers rasping along her jaw.

Now's your chance, his eyes challenged. *Tell me to let go.*

Instead, she blurted: "Kiss me."

His lids hooded with a sultry gaze and she could almost feel the heat of his breath as he exhaled.

Yes, that was a red blooded man under there, and he wanted to kiss her too. Slowly, she tugged at his face scarf, but in a snap, he captured her wrists and held them over her head against the wall.

Shock sparked a thrill.

"No," he growled, strained. "You can't see my face."

Disappointment flooded her, and she knew it was irrational. He was a stranger. A frickin' hero. He could probably get any woman he wanted... but he was there, looking at her with those sex filled eyes. Eyes now filling with the same frustration she felt.

He wanted the same things. But he held back.

"Touch me," she whispered, begged. "Kiss me."

He transferred her captive wrists to one hand, and then achingly tugged the beanie lower until it covered her eyes and darkness swallowed her whole. For a moment, panic jarred her senses and took her back to Donnie. Her heart galloped, her body tensed.

He'd covered her eyes but left her mouth free to breathe... and maybe free for something else.

"Tell me to stop if you don't want this," he murmured

hotly near her ear. His voice was deep, husky, and unmasked. He'd removed the voice modifier, trusting her.

She licked her lips in anticipation at what *this* might entail, and did she? Did she want this? Yes. Hell yes. Small blurred flashes of light came through the knitted gaps in her beanie. He was her fantasy man, no strings attached. Her vision board come to life. No ordering her around, or trying to control her. He wasn't lying, he was upfront about his identity needing to remain secret. Underneath that leather was a strong, lethal man who put her before anyone else this night. Now he was asking for permission.

"I want this," she confessed.

She waited.

Nothing happened.

Then hot lips landed on her neck, kissing and licking with ferocity. Oh, *God*. Her legs weakened as desire zipped through her body, but he held her up. Strong. Steady. With the light out, her senses amplified. He smelled like sex— musky and male. She focused on the touch of his soft, wet mouth. On her throat, her ear, her jaw. He was voracious in his appetite for her and it aroused her.

She was taken. Smitten.

Drowning in another world of heat, hard limbs, wet lips…

A moan escaped her and she writhed, sensitized nipples hardening against his body. She wanted to reach for him—to touch him beneath his leather—to feel that power rippling beneath her fingertips, to relish in his silky skin… but he wouldn't let go.

A flicker of doubt flashed again, but she pushed it away.

He wasn't Donnie. He was a hero.

She wanted this, *right?*

Those lips hit her own and his salty tongue pushed in, drugging her with his taste. All reason fled as they kissed as though the world was on fire.

CHAPTER TWENTY

GRIFFIN LAZARUS

From the moment Griffin tasted Lilo's sweet mouth, he was utterly gone, intoxicated. She was safe in his arms. Better than safe. Alive, responsive, moaning and kissing him back. God, she tasted nothing like bubblegum today. She tasted like some exquisite delight made just for him.

Everything tingled. It was almost too much. Almost painful.

What had he been thinking to deny this?

"You taste like you were made for me," he murmured into her mouth.

She sighed and tugged on her wrists, but he couldn't let her free.

It was more than his sensitivities. With her, he knew he could work through that, but he couldn't let his secret out. Evan and Grace made it work through honesty, but Grace wasn't a reporter. Griffin didn't know Lilo well enough to trust she wouldn't share that information with the world.

The collage-board at her desk had question marks over some of their photos. Question marks, and hearts, and kisses.

Somewhere, deep inside, he also knew that she had no idea it was him, yet she was giving herself to a stranger… he felt betrayed, and it made no sense.

But he wanted her.

She whined in frustration. "Let me touch you."

He kissed her again, and trailed a finger along her cheek, over her jaw, and the line of a vein in her neck. When she shivered, he knew he'd found an erogenous zone, so dipped to explore with his tongue, licking and tasting, still not believing what a fool he'd been to keep her at arm's length.

When he was done with that zone, he hunted for another, relishing in her mewling sounds of desire. She tasted like woman. Pure and raw and it hit him in the groin every time he licked, making him hard with hunger. His tongue went lower, under her collar, edging toward the soft pillows of her breasts.

He needed more access.

As if reading his mind, she arched toward him and for a moment, his mind emptied. The knit top clung to her shape like an erotic embrace. It would bend if he wanted, or it would shift to make way for his fingers, and then it would hold the two of them together—hand on breast, fingers to pink nipple. His erection pulsed painfully, wanting more, so he thrust, and the sensation rode over him like a wave.

She moaned and he may have too, but his mind was befuddled. He had to process. He stood back and let go.

"Why have you stopped?" she asked, panting, impatient.

"Because I'm looking at you."

"Do you like what you see?"

He saw a woman sculptured from perfection.

A low, heated rumble was all he could manage, and then: "How could I not? You have the shape of a goddess."

He must have said the right thing because she lunged forward.

"No," his raspy voice whispered as he held her once again firm against the wall. "No touching."

A frustrated moan whined from her.

"Let me do this for you." He kissed her. "Let me make you feel good."

He stretched her top at the neck to reveal a dark, lacy bra. He pulled that aside, releasing her from the lacy confines.

"But I want to," she started. "Oh, sweet lord. What are you…"

He released a single breast, pale and bouncing and then took its weight into his mouth. He swirled her bud around and suckled.

She gasped, hooked a leg around his waist and pushed her hips forward, grinding into him. The resulting clash of their most intimate parts had him weak with euphoria. He groaned around her flesh. She yanked on his hold again, whimpering, begging.

"Please… let me touch you."

No.

He kept suckling, tasting, experiencing.

But then her body stiffened beneath him, no longer compliant. Her leg dropped, and she made a pained sound.

"Stop," she said, voice tight, struggling. "I'm sorry. Please stop."

But he could do this for her. She'd saved his life. He'd saved hers. Now he could get ahead of the balance protocol and…

She whimpered and made a sobbing sound.

It broke something inside him.

He jerked back, horrified at himself. She was truly distressed, and he was ignoring her. What was he thinking?

"I'm sorry," he whispered and lifted her top to cover her nakedness.

She wrapped herself with her denim jacket. "No, it's my fault. I'm sorry… I can't." She trembled, honestly afraid. How did they get here? "It's the bondage."

You know her, but she doesn't know you.

"My last relationship"—she swallowed—"he tied me up, and… I mean. I thought I wanted it, and I wanted to please him, but it wasn't quite… God, you don't need to know this."

His horror took on a new edge.

Doppenger had *forced* himself on her? And she thought it was because she wanted it. And Griffin almost did the same thing.

Fuck. Shit. He hit himself in the head. What was wrong with him?

There were signs. She'd asked, plenty of times. *Let me touch you.*

Grace had told him. She had been in an abusive relationship.

But he'd ignored it because he wanted to get ahead of his biology. He wanted to be in control, but he wasn't, was he?

All this time he thought he managed his habits with an iron fist. He thought he was better than his siblings. He thought losing control was like how he was back when he'd killed those men in his past, but the truth was, he'd been out of control for a long time.

And she still stood there with her beanie over her eyes, waiting for permission.

Fuck!

He was no good for her.

Before he could change his mind, he slammed out of the room and into the alley, running as fast as his guilt laden legs could carry him, making as much distance as he could.

It wasn't until he'd turned on his bike that he realized he'd left her there, still waiting for permission. He couldn't breathe. He messed up, and he knew no way of fixing it.

Flashes before his eyes.

Another time he'd so helplessly lost control. Was this... was this like that?

When he woke from darkness to find blood on his hands. When he woke to find he'd murdered so many people? Was he somehow...

The sound of irrational water dripping reminded him of blood. The sirens wailing in the distance reminded him of people screaming. A chopper in the sky...

He couldn't see straight. He couldn't breathe.

All he could think to do was return her cattle prod and leave it at the door so when she exited, she'd see it. If he offered to take her home, he'd only make it worse. He'd put himself in the same basket as Doppenger. So he left.

NOT LONG AFTER, Griffin stormed into his apartment, crashing through the door and shedding his leathers, gasping for air. During the ride home, he'd suffocated on his own behavior. He'd left her on her own because he was a coward. Left her in that neighborhood, cold and alone, and what was worse, his erection wouldn't leave. His body didn't pick up the message his brain sent...

Because he was a monster.

With the room spiraling around him, and on the way to his bathroom, he tripped over junk on the floor and landed hard on his knees. He rolled and kicked his boots off, frantically pulling his pants to free his legs. They smothered him. When he scrambled to his feet, left only in his thermals, he ran to the shower. Not waiting for it to heat up, he entered the stream, still clothed and soaked, all the while listening to the nasty voice inside his head calling him a coward.

Monster. Freak. Loser.

Those were the kinds of words hurled at him during his training from his drill sergeant, his company, and other recruits. It had taken everything he had to get past that year from hell. The following years in other countries, with other strangers, weren't much better. He was a little different, he knew it. He never tried to hide it, but at the same time, he was never openly okay with it. Every time he felt himself reaching this level of panic, the only place of privacy he could get anywhere while training was in a shower, and even then, sometimes it was a communal block.

The water weighed his thermals, and he stripped them off, heedless of the painful situation between his legs. When the fabric rubbed over his erection, it felt good. He bit his lip and squeezed his eyes shut, but that was a bad idea. All he could see was Lilo's long delicate neck as she arched into him, her breast in his palm and her pert wet nipple begging for him to suckle it again. He took himself in hand and pumped roughly, trying to satisfy his need so it would go away. But all he could see was her willing body writhing under his touch turned sour. He squeezed painfully. The pictures wouldn't go away. There had been a single wet streak running down her cheek.

Or had he imagined it.

He roared in anguish and punched the tiles, again and again despite the splintering pain in his fist, and the red blood splattering the wall. Power exploded from him and reached for every metal object in the room and beyond. Copper pipes shuddered and groaned in the walls. The faucet trembled. He hit the wall on repeat until pain reached its limit and became his friend. Until it didn't scare him, but embraced him. Until it choked everything out—the power he couldn't keep locked away, the painful desire that wouldn't release, and the idea that control was a fairytale.

He'd been so afraid of losing it with his fists, that he never stopped to think the imbalance affected something worse—his heart. And at the end of the day, it wasn't even the sin at all. It was all him. He knew that, because as he looked at his wrist, the Yin-Yang tattoo stared back at him, in perfect harmony. It had no right to be. Not after leaving her vulnerable like that.

But his biology wasn't fussy. It was just like a toxin—you get exposed, you get poisoned. This was the same thing except in reverse. Exposure to Lilo kept him balanced for a period of time after his contact with her. She was his drug. His medicine. And he'd treated her like dirt.

Eventually the wet warmth running down his back suffused into his muscles and worked his tension. He stopped hitting and braced himself, forehead to the tiles, palms to the wall.

He counted. One, two, three... and kept going, focusing on the rhythm in his head, the logic, and the reason. It would be okay. He was alive, and she was alive, hurt, but alive. Hopefully. It was okay.

It had to be okay.

He would fix it.

He'd call someone to check on her.

Twenty-six, twenty-seven... and on and on, until finally exhausted, he turned the faucet off and, dripping, stumbled to his bedroom, wrapped himself tightly in a sheet and fell onto his bed.

His room was a simple room, and unlike the main living area, it was clutter free—the way it began all those years ago when he'd first arrived home from training. A haven with nothing but a bed, a few books, and a rarely used flat screen television on the far wall. He turned it on and searched for something that would make things right, something that would take his mind and debilitating anxiety away.

That's what normal people did, and he desperately wanted to feel normal.

He found the next best thing on demand, the movie Lilo loved… *Casablanca*.

He cast his mind back to why she said she liked it. What was it again? Something about connections in times of war, and… he conjured the memory of her face, the bubblegum scent in his car… *If we can keep lasting connections when the world is falling apart.*

CHAPTER TWENTY-ONE

LILO LIKEKE

When Lilo arrived at number three Partridge Way not long after ten that night, she didn't know what to expect, but didn't care. She needed a friend. Grace was working the night shift at the hospital, and Misha Minksi was the only one she knew who might be home.

Lilo had cried the entire subway ride, cursing the integrity of men one minute, cursing her own stupidity the next. No wonder no one dared to approach her, she'd sounded like a madwoman.

All because of him.

She stayed in that darkened stairwell with the wool literally over her eyes until her toes went numb before realizing Greed had left. At one point, the door had opened; she remembered hearing that. But never did it occur to her that he'd abandoned her, just like her ex used to. Donnie never beat her, neither did Greed. But when she'd said no, that she'd had enough, they'd both bailed. Like she wasn't worth anything if she didn't put out.

Donnie used to get infuriated and snarky, then he'd come back, all sweetness and sugar the next time he wanted something, he always did. It took her a long time to understand that was another form of abuse.

Before knocking on Misha's door, Lilo opened her big satchel bag and pulled her bottle of recently bought vodka out, careful not to knock her spy phone. She'd gone back for it after she was left in the stairwell and was eager to upload the photographs the following day. The police had been at the warehouse, but she'd managed to retrieve the phone before anyone noticed. She didn't, however, manage to get out before she was noticed and had to give her statement. In the end, it wasn't all bad. One of the uniformed officers drove her to the subway, and she safely got herself out of the city.

And there she was. In suburbia. Lilo knocked on the door to the pleasant home. It had a white picket fence, blue walls and white trim. The garden was full of flowering roses and sunflowers that had accidentally bloomed to face the house. The sun must shine from over the other side. A little dog yapped, and the light came on inside. The door opened and a man the same age as her father came hurtling out with a baseball bat.

"Who are you? What you want?" His Polish accent was thick and disjointed.

"It's me, Vooyek." It was how she said uncle in Polish, and she'd known the man for years, so had been firmly asked to use it anytime she was invited to the Minksi home. It was spelled Wujek, but she still couldn't pronounce it correctly, and he never minded. She held out the bottle of vodka she'd bought on the way and flinched. "I'm so sorry it's late, but is Misha home? I know she's not at her city apartment this week."

He shielded his eyes from the glaring street lamps. "Lilo, that you? What you doing here so late?"

"I…" she choked up.

He glanced at the bottle in her hand, frowned, and then put his bat down. Vooyek was a short man with a round face. He'd lost his wife when his youngest son, Alek was born. A sadness to his eyes had never left.

"Come." He took her by the shoulder. "*Nieszczęścia chodzą parami.* Misery loves company tonight. She is inside with the rest."

"What happened?" Lilo wiped her nose and stepped into the warm house, instantly thawing out.

"Restaurant was attacked again."

"Again! She wasn't hurt?"

"*Nye*, but her pride. You know my daughter, she try to reason with them and they throw back in her face. Next time, will be more than my shop they break if we do not pay the crook their monies."

Lilo had come looking for a shoulder to cry on, and a friend to help drown her sorrows, but instead, she'd found a family in need.

"Lilo?" Misha's blond, curly head popped around from the kitchen, along with other members of her family. Her aunt Ciocia, her twenty-year-old sister Roksana, and both grandparents were awake.

"Hi Misha. I hope I've not woken anyone else." She glanced around to check.

Misha snorted, coming to meet her in the living area and giving her a big hug. "It's only Alek asleep and he's deaf. He can't hear a thing."

Lilo enjoyed the embrace and tried not to cry.

Misha pulled back and eyed her suspiciously. "To what do I owe this pleasure so late in the evening?"

"Um." She bit her lip.

"I mean, usually it's me knocking on your door at all hours to get you to come and party."

Misha was the lovable black sheep of the family. Her motto in life was, *If it feels good, do it.* Even if it felt good at three in the morning, and even if that meant waking the entire neighborhood in the process, but despite her devil-may-care attitude, she was loyal to a fault and protective of her friends.

Lilo glanced over Misha's shoulder to where the family pretended not to listen from their kitchen table. They all sat around a pine round table, playing a game of cards. Canasta if Lilo's memory served correct. Vooyek had opened the vodka and was pouring little shot glasses for everyone.

"Come and sit on the couch." Misha sat on the two seater floral monstrosity and patted the space next to her.

The rest of the room was decorated in old seventies decor. Wooden bowls and vases were on the mantle, and macrame tapestries hung on the walls. The cream and brown wallpaper behind the macrame peeled a little, but still looked very retro chic. A fire crackled in the fireplace with a glossy wooden mantle that held portraits of the family, plus one big one of Misha's deceased mother at the center, next to a golden Madonna—the religious kind, not the pop star kind. It all smelled a little musty, but homey and warm. In fact, so warm and safe that when Lilo was stuck in that cold, desolate alley South-Side, she couldn't think of a nicer place to be—even if it was across the bridge and onto the mainland.

Lilo sat, feeling a little foolish that she'd come all that way.

"I… uh."

Misha caught the tears in Lilo's eyes. "*Siostra*, whatever it is, you can tell me."

Hearing Misha call her sister, was the tipping point. An ache as big as a chasm grew in her chest as she yearned for the big family she knew she'd never have. Not with her father and mother, not with any man. They were all lost causes.

At least she had friends.

Vooyek came in at that moment with three vodka shots on a tray. "Here we go. I think we all need the liquid courage tonight, yes?"

Along with Vooyek and Misha, Lilo took a shooter.

"*Na Zdrowie.*" Vooyek chinked his crystal glass shooter against theirs and then downed his drink.

Misha wiggled her eyebrows at Lilo and did the same. The burn of the liquid went straight to Lilo's heart and spread outward. He was right. It was some liquid courage.

Lilo spent the next twenty minutes pouring her heart out to her friend. She told her about her father, Donnie and their break up, meeting Griffin, the Deadly Seven, the incident in the alley with Greed… all of it! Misha informed her about the never ending harassment their family business was suffering under the hands of a street gang. It had been hard for Misha. She had a yoga business and an apartment in the city, and she wasn't the kind of girl to get bogged down, but having to cancel her classes to help in the family restaurant had taken a hit on her income. She was considering supplementing it by working in a Russian bar at night time.

A couple of shots, a few tears, and a few laughs later, Lilo found herself at the family kitchen table, dealing herself into the game of Canasta—because it felt good.

What didn't feel good was the hangover the next morning, and when the eternally chirpy Misha woke her at dawn to drag her onto her balcony to do her yoga sun-salutations, Lilo almost threw her pillow in her face. But at least she was with family, and she'd come away from it all thinking that she wasn't alone.

WHEN LILO ARRIVED at work the next morning, she was surprised to find Griffin leaning his hip against the partition that separated her desk from Bev's. She halted at the hallway before entering the main office area so she could watch from a distance. He spoke with Candy and Bev, who in turn, batted their eyelashes at him.

Was Candy leaning into him?

Was she rubbing him on the shoulder?

Lilo smirked at Candy as Griffin flinched awkwardly from her touch and had some stupid satisfaction that she knew Griffin better than Candy. Ridiculous. What did she care? She'd woken up rejuvenated and refreshed—she wasn't alone. But in her heart, she knew the company she received from a friend just wasn't the same as a romantic partner.

Candy leaned in some more. Couldn't that girl take a hint?

Lilo left her hiding spot and strode over.

"Morning," she said and dumped her bag on her desk.

For a quick second, she had the impression of the box with her father's ear on there and froze, eyes glued to the now vacant spot.

It was fine. Her father was in prison. Alive.

Her mother was… who the hell knew?

And, she'd been dying to go through the shots from her spy phone to see if anything of value had been captured. Fat chance of doing that with everyone standing around.

"Lilo." Griffin's smooth voice was almost next to her ear as he put his steaming hot coffee mug on her desk, right in her line of sight. Curls of white steam rose from the liquid. "This is for you."

She turned to him, frowning. "You brought me a coffee. Why?"

"I-ah…" He glanced over at Candy and Bev who returned to their desks and shuffled around, collecting themselves before they started work. If he was looking for privacy, he wouldn't get it. This was the Cardinal Copy. Everything was newsworthy here, especially the gossip.

"It was an excuse to see you," he admitted.

Her co-workers' paper shuffling stopped.

Oh, this was getting awkward. Lilo took her coat off and sat. "And why would you need an excuse to see me?"

She started her computer, failing dreadfully at keeping her eyes glued to the screen and not on him. She was still irked at the way he'd ordered her around, and after her situation with Greed, she'd come to realize that she needed time apart from men to sort herself out. The past week had turned her life upside down. It was a life that she'd carefully constructed the way she liked. She'd gotten herself away from her toxic parents, and she'd begun to build herself a career. Somehow, she'd gone from being In-Charge-Lilo to a Give-Me-Orders-Lilo. Donnie had messed with her brain. This past week, her parents had messed with her, and now Griffin was everywhere too. It was all too much. She needed fewer complications in her life, not more.

"I wanted to make sure you were safe," he said.

It was an odd thing to say if he'd thought she'd gone home last night instead of the rendezvous with the kidnappers. She glanced up at him and wished she hadn't.

The look in his eyes cut her down. It was hope. Maybe humility. Maybe something else. All she knew was that she got the impression he was truly concerned about her.

"I'm fine, thank you."

"I heard about the incident with your father in the South-Side."

"Oh?"

"Liza told me. Her unit were among the first responders. She said she saw you there giving your statement and asked an officer to take you to the station. I just wanted to make sure you got home okay, and that"—he rubbed his neck—"ah… that you weren't hurt in the exchange and I'm sorry. About your father, that is."

She cast a wary eye at him. "You're not angry that I lied to you about going?"

"I can't change the past, and I understand why you wanted to go. It was wrong of me to make demands of you." He took a deep breath. "I'm just glad you got home okay."

"Thank you."

He shrugged. "I didn't do much in the end."

Not sure how to respond to that, she gave him a small smile and turned back to her screen. When she noticed he hadn't moved, she turned back to him. "Was there something else you need?"

He flinched. He fidgeted at his side, and to cover it, he smoothed his tie. He really didn't look comfortable.

"Griffin?"

"Would you like to go to Hell with me this weekend?"

"Pardon?"

"That didn't come out right. I meant the nightclub Hell. For the grand opening. Not the real hell."

Oh. She blinked at him while she tried to understand. Was he asking her on a date? How did she feel about that? She didn't know.

On one hand, she had literally just sworn off men.

On the other hand, maybe she'd been overreacting where he was concerned. He brought her coffee, he apologized for his demanding behavior, and he seemed genuinely concerned for her.

But did that excuse him? Did that mean he wasn't going to do it again?

"I'm already going," she ended up saying.

"You are?"

"Yes, Grace invited me and another friend."

"Oh. Okay. I suppose I will see you there."

She turned her eyes back to her screen and kept them there as he left. When he was gone, she took a sip of the coffee he'd left. It was made just the way she liked it. Two sugars and cream.

Bev's blue hair popped up over the partition. "Hun, what the hell was that?"

Lilo took another sip and avoided her friend's eyes. "I don't know what you're talking about."

"Now who's the shmendrik." Bev came around to her side of the cubicle and perched her yoga pant bottom on Lilo's desk. "There's something you're not telling me. Spill."

"Um."

"The uber hot geek god just asked you out, and you shut him down. Call me crazy, but wasn't that exactly what you wanted just a few days ago?"

Lilo sighed into her coffee, now cupped between her hands. "I know but after spending some time with him, I didn't like the way he ordered me around."

Bev was one of the few people, apart from Grace and Misha, who knew the extent of her toxic relationship with Donnie. So when Lilo mentioned Griffin's bossiness, she knew exactly why it ruffled her.

"What did he do?" Bev asked.

"He forbade me to go to the kidnapping exchange."

Bev arched a brow at Lilo. "And?"

"I went anyway."

"So, you're telling me you got upset because the man asked you *not* to go and jump into danger when only that morning, he saw your life threatened. And he was shot himself, mind you."

Lilo dragged her lip through her teeth. "Well, when you say it like that…"

"Is it possible you're overacting a little?"

She frowned at her friend who'd echoed her earlier thoughts. Bev had never been so harsh with her before. "You're supposed to be on my side."

"I am, hun, I am. It's just that I don't want to see you blow off a potentially good relationship because of a lost cause like Donnie. I don't want you to think that all men are like that."

"Griffin ordered me not to go." Lilo knew how she felt, and she hadn't liked it.

"For good reason. I tried to order you not to go too, and that was because I love you and I don't want to see you hurt. And if the Deadly Seven hadn't turned up, you would have been hurt, right? You'd be in a body bag." Bev pushed away from Lilo's desk. "All I'm saying is that he's not Donnie. I've seen enough of him to know that. Maybe you should give him another chance and get to know him better."

A FEW HOURS LATER, Lilo was sitting in Fred's office, going over the proof of the article she'd just written. Amazingly, she'd discovered the best photographs on her spyphone. Not only had she caught a dramatic shot of the two Greeds fighting, but she'd nabbed a few blurry night shots of members of the Deadly Seven after she'd left—after the real

Greed had stolen her from the scene. All the members were in their crime-fighting costumes, except one woman. She wore a generic black hood and sweat pants, but still had a mask over her mouth and nose. You couldn't tell who she was and Lilo hardly remembered seeing them in the chaos. The only reason Lilo knew she was a woman was because of her curvy body shape.

There was also a picture of Lilo's father being taken away by the police.

Griffin hadn't lied when he mentioned Liza being involved. She was the arresting officer which could be a good thing. She might agree to speak to Lilo about it and give an official statement. If Lilo hadn't been in such a rush to leave after returning that night, she might have put her big girls pants on and worked the scene with the police. She might even have had a chance to see Liza there.

Something Griffin had said sparked in her mind. He said Liza had asked the officer to take her to the station. It was nice to think Griffin's sister was looking out for Lilo.

"These are great shots, Lilo." Fred held the printed photos from his face, squinting to see better. "You know I have to officially say that we don't condone this kind of risky behavior to get a story, but off the books—well done." He whistled through his teeth at some of the more violent photographs. "I'm amazed you came out of that unscathed."

She bit her lip. The only reason she did was because of Greed. He'd gotten her out of there. She would be dead if he hadn't turned up. "I'm very lucky," she agreed.

"And this shot. Is it really two of them fighting against each other?"

"I have reason to believe that one of them is an imposter. You read my story, right?"

He looked at her over his glasses as if she were stupid.

"Sorry. Of course you did."

"We can't put opinions in there, you know that."

She chewed on his words. He was right. Some of what she wrote was jumping to conclusions. She would have to go back and check over her words. But she wanted to paint the heroes in the best light that she could.

"Do you have any hard evidence that one of them was the imposter?"

"What about the fact that the fake one used a gun, and the Deadly Seven don't normally use them?"

"But they have in the past."

She slumped. That was true. A sighting a few months back showed a hostage situation on the freeway. Not much information had leaked out of that disturbance, but she knew the Deadly Seven were involved.

"What about the fact one of them tried to save me, the other one tried to kill me?"

He cocked his head, considering. "It's all conjecture and one person's eye witness account, but I'd approve that. Just keep it factual."

"I just know someone is impersonating one of the Deadly Seven. I just know it." She turned to Fred. "How do I write a story like that?"

"You're a good journalist, Lilo, and you've got good instincts. If you feel there's a story there, then keep following it. I think your eye witness account will be a very strong story. If you need to, get more facts. Do a follow up. Interview anyone else present there to see if they corroborate your story. Two eyewitness accounts saying the same thing are better than one. Put all of them together so it supports your claim. That's how you do it."

She accepted the draft paper back from him. "Thanks, Fred."

"Now, do you want your name kept out of this?"

"No. I think I'm okay with it in there."

"Good. Because writing it with a personal spin would be great. Include your history with your father and his business —but stick to the public facts." He sat back and stared at the article. "It would be nice for people to see you don't have to choose the life you're born into. You're a pillar of the city, Lilo. I hope you know that."

She blushed furiously. "Thank you, Fred."

"It's a pleasure." His expression flattened back to boss mode. "Please revise the article to remove anything regarded as opinion and have it back to me in time for the late edition."

She got up to leave.

"Lilo?"

"Yes?"

He scratched the white scruff on his chin and looked at her with pained eyes. "Like I said, you have great instincts, and a nose for smelling out a story, but don't let this job be everything. What you did last night was way beyond risky. You deserve a life, too."

CHAPTER TWENTY-TWO

GRIFFIN LAZARUS

On the night of Hell's grand opening, Griffin dressed in his favorite custom made Prussian Blue cotton-poplin shirt that fit snuggly, sleeves quarter rolled. Black pants, no belt. No tie, but he'd kept his black-framed glasses and his Garmin watch. Nerves skittered in his stomach. There would be a lot of people there, a lot of noise, and of course, Lilo.

After she turned him down, he spent half a day in his office trying to come to terms with it. When he first met her, he wanted nothing to do with her. Now she wanted nothing to do with him. He hated it.

He'd watched *Casablanca* another two times and tried to understand what she loved about the movie, but each time, he came up with nothing. It was beyond his scope of understanding. It just seemed like a black and white movie about a war, a woman who cheated on her husband, and a man who liked to drink a lot.

Maybe he was reading too much into it. Maybe she just liked the way the actor looked.

When Griffin traveled in the Lazarus Building elevator, he activated the timer on his watch. Technically, he was going to Hell because his brother requested the presence of the entire family, not for Griffin's own gain. But then again, Lilo would be there.

In the end, he turned the timer off.

The doors opened to the ground floor lobby with Heaven on one side, and Hell on the other. Because it was the Lazarus's apartment private entrance, they constructed each side of the hallway out of two-way mirrors. They could see into the establishments, but the patrons couldn't see into the lobby. Not that it helped much where Hell was concerned. The interior was dark with glowing red lights. There were a few people in there, but he couldn't make out faces, only greedy sin-signatures.

Griffin exited the apartment lobby to the street.

Paparazzi blocked his path into Hell. He'd have to go around the photographers to where a red carpet led from the street curb to Hell's gate. At the door, a big, burly bouncer stood guard. Griffin hadn't met him yet, but he was vigilant and didn't slouch. Along one side of the building was a bollard that separated the paparazzi from the red carpet, and on the other side of the building, a line a mile long held back the enthusiastic wannabe patrons, dressed in designer clothes and sparkly jewels. They wouldn't get in. It was well known the event was invite only. Considering it was still officially winter for another few weeks, he didn't know why they bothered, but then again, the irrational desires of the everyman were often misunderstood by him. If they wanted to shiver in the cold on the off chance of getting in, who was he to complain?

He walked around the line of paparazzi to the street, then walked back along the red carpet toward the gate where a woman he recognized waited with a clipboard, ready to sign off the invited guests.

The tall, buxom red-head was the Lazarus Industries publicist, Amelia the Amorous. Amorous because she was also a woman he briefly dated and was a little over excited in the bedroom. She would scrape her nails over his back, to be precise. Needless to say, he didn't enjoy the sensations.

The moment she saw him, she grinned.

A hundred cameras and questions pointed his way. Bulbs flashed, words were hurtled.

"Who are you?"

"Are you important?"

"Who are you wearing?"

Griffin put his hands in his pockets. Outwardly, he had a blank face, but on the inside, he smiled. He liked that he was one of the more anonymous members of the Lazarus family. He ignored them all and walked up to Amelia.

"Griffin, babe, you made it." She leaned in to kiss him on the cheek, then rubbed her thumb to wipe her lipstick stain off. The residue felt thick on his skin. *Irritating*.

Lilo rarely wore makeup.

"Sorry about that," she said with a wink. "Couldn't help myself. It's been too long since I put my lips on that gorgeous face. Had to do it."

"It's fine." Griffin used his hand to finish rubbing his cheek.

"The rest of your family are inside. Except Sloan. She's late."

"Not surprised."

Amelia looked him over. "Wow, Griff. You're looking good."

He surveyed her in return. She wore a red, tight dress that accentuated her curves, and flashed a long leg along the front split. "You look good too."

"Stop it." She waved him down and batted her eyelashes.

Griffin had learned that when women said one thing, they often meant another. And this felt like such an occasion, so he offered a second compliment. "Your lips are very red."

She laughed. "Oh, Griff. Still not with it on the lady-talk, are you?"

He wasn't? He thought he did rather well.

The paparazzi relentlessly fired off questions about his identity, and being the publicist she was, Amelia slid him a coy smile. "Come on. You have to pose for a photo, Parker insisted." She waved to a banner with the Lazarus Industries logo stamped over it. "Just tilt your head to the left and no one will see the lipstick stain. Show off that hot bod of yours and give the cameras a smile they'll never forget."

As he stood there, awkwardly with his face tilted to the left, he couldn't help but wish for Lilo's reassuring presence. He had hoped she'd be here with him, holding his hand, keeping him sane and grounded. He didn't want to be alone. He didn't want to end up like the main character in *Casablanca*, bitter and lonely and watching another man go off to save the world with the woman he loved.

Lucky for him, Lilo hadn't met another man… yet. There'd be no other man taking her. It wasn't too late.

Griffin counted to ten in his head, then to ninety-nine in multiples of three. When he calculated enough time had passed to be considered appropriate, he said his goodbye to Amelia and entered the club. The pounding base was already vibrating the walls, and he checked his pockets for the earplugs he put in earlier. If the sound got too much, they were his back up. And failing that, he'd slip out the back, or out the secret door in the upstairs office.

When he crested past the cloak-room, he stood on a dais that overlooked the club. It was truly magnificent inside. Parker had designed the interior extremely well.

Hell was an amphitheater with a circular sunken dance-pit in the middle of the room. The floor glowed red. Each shallow step up from the dance floor was a few meters deep and contained either booths, dancing poles, or a bar on the level. A cage hung from the ceiling with a DJ inside. Glowing red, orange and yellow stalactite chandelier lights dangled from the roof as though they were in a cave dripping with flames.

Griffin checked his watch. Officially the invite said to arrive in thirty minutes time, but he preferred to make his appearance early. The rest of his family had similar thoughts because they were already at the bar on the lowest level, except Sloan of course. She would probably arrive sometime later in the night, if at all.

Evan sat on a bar stool with Grace perched on his knee. She wore a black, tight dress that Evan obviously appreci-ated because he couldn't keep his hands off her. Mary and

Flint stood to the end looking a little uncomfortable but deep in conversation with each other. Griffin didn't think they'd stay long before retiring to the basement, or their upstairs apartment. Liza was in her standard designer jeans, blouse and heels, and next to her was Parker, wearing a navy suit with a T-shirt that stretched precariously over his muscular frame. He'd grown a short, trimmed beard for the event, and his hair had been tied back in one of those modern ways—half in a bun, half down.

The last of the family, Tony, was sprawled leaning with his back to the bar, arms stretched out on either side, staring at the red dance floor with disinterest, no doubt waiting for the party to begin. The two resident Lazarus wild boys, Tony and Parker, would be on the dance floor later, jackets off and sweating up a storm with the ladies, and then Liza would probably intervene at some point and scare the ladies away —because she liked causing a scene.

Dancing was the very last thing Griffin wanted to do.

"Griffin," Grace hopped off her manmade seat and walked over. "You're looking snazzy tonight. I love that color on you."

She took him by the shoulders and kissed him on the cheek, the same cheek Amelia had earlier, most likely adding another layer of lipstick stain. He smiled back at her, all the while feeling the stickiness of what she'd left, wondering when it was acceptable for him to find a napkin and wipe it off. Amelia didn't seem to care that he did it immediately. He gingerly lifted his finger to wipe.

"Thank you, Grace. You look beautiful yourself." In fact, she was a vision. Out of her usual casual attire, or doctor's uniform, he was completely taken. The black halter dress suited her smaller frame and accentuated her smooth shoulders and graceful neck.

Evan came up behind her and slipped his hand around her back to rest on her rear, then growled at Griffin. "Keep your mitts off my girl."

"I barely touched her."

"Evan!" Grace slapped him lightly on the arm. "That's no way to talk to your brother."

"I sensed your envy," Evan insisted. "Don't pretend."

"It's not what you think," he explained.

Evan arched an eyebrow. "Oh, really?"

But he didn't need to explain. Grace leaned over to Evan and whispered something in his ear. The resulting look of pity in his brother's eyes wasn't missed.

"Sorry, bro. This mating bond kinda makes me go caveman." Evan clamped Griffin on the shoulder. "Let me get a drink to make up for it. You want the usual?"

Griffin nodded and when Evan left, he turned to Grace. "What did you say to him?"

"That you miss Lilo, and seeing us together reminded you of that."

It was true. He must be completely transparent. He looked away, and slipped his hands in his pockets, fumbling for those earplugs wondering if anyone would notice if he put them in early.

"Not going well, is it?" she asked.

"No." He didn't elaborate. Didn't want to. Especially not to the couple who made it look so easy. Griffin had the powers now, but he didn't feel powerful.

"You know you can talk to me about it, Griff. I've been in Lilo's shoes, literally and figuratively." She laughed. "But what I meant was that I might be able to provide some insight. Does she know about your secret yet?"

His secret… the one filling his apartment with expensive junk, or the one where they all dressed in leather and fought the city's worst at night, or the one where he was terrified of losing control and killing everyone he loved. Any of them would probably do, and the answer was no. Lilo didn't know anything about the real Griffin. He was virtually a stranger to her.

"How did you feel when you discovered the truth about Evan?" he asked, swallowing.

"It took me a while to adjust, but Evan answered my questions honestly, so I learned to trust him." She smiled gently. "So, she knows nothing yet?"

He shook his head.

"And how do you feel about her?"

At that moment, Evan returned with two glasses of champagne and handed one to Griffin, and one to Grace. He'd caught the end of Grace's question and scoffed. "Doc, that's a silly question. Of course he's in love with her. You can't fight it."

"My feelings aren't the problem," Griffin confirmed.

Evan was right. He'd tried to tell Griffin months ago what it felt like to have that mating bond triggered, but Griffin had been unprepared for how much space Lilo occupied in his heart. If he had accepted it from the start, he wouldn't be in this mess.

"Well, Griff, the only advice I have is to give her time,

and to be honest with her. It's not like she's just some woman you've met off the street—she's someone your biology has recognized as your perfect partner."

"Can we talk about something else?" It was all getting too personal.

Parker came over at that moment and clapped him on the back, grinning from ear to ear. "Griff."

"Parker."

"I'm glad you could make it."

"You said I had no choice."

His brother smirked smugly. "I know."

Parker wore his favorite expression tonight. It was the *You're welcome, ladies* look. This was the playboy persona he'd crafted for his public figure. The world saw him as a handsome and reckless billionaire who liked to splurge on risky business ventures and glamorous establishments like Heaven and Hell. A man who loved his hair, took pride in his appearance and knew he was the smartest man in the room but pretended he wasn't.

"Did you catch the meaning behind the interior design, little brother?" Parker's eyes sparkled as he scoped the room.

"It's hell. Obviously."

"Nah, come on. I thought if anyone were to get the layout, it would be you."

"Not in the mood tonight, Parker."

"Of course you haven't figured it out, so I'll just tell you. It's the nine rings of hell." Parker pointed at the pit. "Ring one, Limbo. Next step up is Lust. Notice the hidden alcoves there for some privacy for our guests. You can thank me later. Third ring is where the bar is." He looked at Griffin expectantly.

"Gluttony?" he offered.

"Good man. What about the fourth ring." He surveyed the group. "Seriously, am I the only one who's read *Dante's Inferno*?" He didn't wait for an answer, but continued. "Fourth is Greed. That level has a few poker games going on. Fifth is Wrath. I wouldn't head into any dark nooks up there unless you want to be punished."

"Ooh. Do tell." Tony materialized from somewhere and looked up the steps. "Fifth you say?"

"I knew you'd be into that," Evan laughed.

Tony's shrug of acceptance made Parker happy. "Then, Tony, you might also like to check out seven: Violence. But that's where a lot of the bouncers are watching over the club, so maybe… you know what? Stay away from that level. I don't want any trouble tonight."

"What's six?" Liza asked, also arriving.

"That's boring: Heresy. I left that ring just a vacant step because we had limited space."

"I count only seven rings," Griffin said.

"That's because the eighth and ninth are up behind the mirrored ceiling. Fraud and Treachery."

Tony took a swig of his glass. "You do love your mirrors, don't you, Parks?"

"Absolutely. Why not? We can see out, they can't see in. We've got security up there keeping an eye on things, so behave yourself." Parker rubbed his hands together, looking all together gleeful. "Saying that, you're all here to have fun, and that's why I prohibited the press. Let your hair down. Have a few drinks, Griff, find your girl. I'd love to meet her at some point, and maybe I'll even see you two on the dance floor."

He flinched. The entire family assumed because he'd triggered his bond, that being in a relationship with her was the natural progression.

But what if it wasn't?

Griffin took a sip of his bubbly, wet his lips, and then lowered the glass. He wasn't a drinker, but the champagne did well to make others believe he was.

"Oh, and one more thing," Parker said, leaning in close. "Just quickly before more people get here. You should know we let the imposter go."

"What?" A jolt of panic went through Griffin. "Why?"

"Before you get all worked up, there was a reason."

Griffin's hand clenched around the glass as he forced himself to leash his wrath. If Wyatt were there, he'd be giving Griffin the evil eye. *They let Doppenger go.* Why?

The sound level in the place picked up as more guests filed in. Parker glanced at a few people he knew, smiled and held up a finger to indicate he'd be with them in a moment. When he turned back to Griffin, his expression had gone dark. That man was almost as good an actor as Tony.

"We questioned him," Parker said, voice low, "and he wouldn't give up much so we released him so he'll go back to the Syndicate."

"He's bait," Evan elaborated.

Grace smiled and excused herself. "While you're all talking work, I'm going to welcome the ladies."

Evan kissed her before he relinquished her and Griffin

couldn't help the stab of jealousy that rode him again. Griffin's gaze followed Grace to where Lilo had arrived at the bar, only meters away. He barely noticed the leggy blond with her because Lilo looked incredible. She wore a blue gown that flowed over her hips to kiss her ankles. The neckline was V-shaped and plunged from her shoulders to below her breasts, giving him plenty of skin to appreciate. The skin reminded him of her taste. His mouth watered.

She turned and their eyes clashed across the distance.

They held each other's gaze for a long, hot minute, then Lilo smiled and turned back to her friends.

Was that a good sign?

"Does Doppenger know who held him captive?" Griffin asked, without taking his eyes from Lilo.

"It wasn't my first interrogation, Griff. Of course he never discovered our true identities. As far as he's concerned, the Deadly Seven took him, and that's all he knows." Parker indicated for the rest of the family to head up to a booth on one of the higher levels that overshadowed the red dance-pit. "I'll explain when we're all seated on the fourth level."

Griffin had no choice but to follow. He cut across the room, stepping down the steps to the dance-pit, then went up the levels on the other side until he hit the fourth floor and slid into a booth marked VIP with a sign on the table. From his vantage point, he could see to where Lilo laughed at the bar with her friends.

Griffin plucked his collar from his neck. How was he going to last the night with her looking so enticing? Scratch that, how was he going to handle other men looking at her all night, because they already were…

"Just fucking ask her out, already." Liza slid into the booth next to him. "Your lust is killing me."

He opened his mouth to disagree, but knew it was impossible to lie about that. No use denying it now.

"I already asked her out," he said as Tony, Mary, Flint, and Evan arrived at the table, and sat on the other side.

"She said no?" Liza's brows lifted. "Dude, that's harsh."

"I don't know where to go from here."

"Well, what the fuck have you been doing? Because when I see her looking at you, her lust makes me all hot inside."

"Really?"

"Yeah. Look. It's like this: girls need to be asked a few times. We can have entire conversations with ourselves in our heads about why or why not we should date a guy. Your job is to keep showing up. Keep wooing her. But be respectful, you know?"

"I thought I was already. I've been making her coffee every morning at work. I brought in breakfast for her yesterday. I apologized for bossing her around."

Liza sighed. "You need to up your game. And for the record, apologizing for being a dickwad is not considered wooing."

"So, what is?"

"Oh my Gawd, you're so clueless. But I love you." She ruffled his hair to his eternal annoyance, then added: "Give her a compliment. Buy her flowers. Ask her to dance, or buy her a drink. Look after her. Treat her like there's no one more important to you than her. She comes first, and by that, I don't mean you go all caveman and protect her like she's your fucking precious. I mean, ask her what she wants, and listen to her."

Griffin rubbed his chin. "I don't know how to dance."

"Sometimes you need to do something you're not comfortable with because she likes it. It's called being in a relationship."

"Can we focus, here?" Parker tapped his finger on the table.

Right. They were up there to discuss what happened to Doppenger.

"As you know," Parker began, "We questioned the imposter, he gave up little except that he was given a serum in exchange to put sinners of greed out of their misery. This serum allowed him to actually sense sin like we all do, plus it temporarily mimicked our enhanced strength and healing. We decided the best course of action would be to release him, but not before we planted a tracker. He hasn't left his apartment all day, but from what we know, we expect him to go chasing the Syndicate for more of his special juice. He exhibited classic symptoms of a junkie going through withdrawals."

Liza shot Griffin a wry look. "Probably hasn't moved because he's still recovering from the beating you gave him."

"Was it that bad?" he asked.

"I think you broke his nose, but we reset it before we sent him back."

"Dude deserved it *not* to be reset," Tony said. "Thinking he could impersonate us."

"That's not why we do this," Mary reminded him. "We're not in the torture or revenge business."

Parker ignored the two of them. "Sloan is keeping an eye on the tracker as we speak."

"So she's not coming?" Liza asked.

"I figure at least she's helping out with something, so let her out of this one." Parker stood up and gave them all his Hollywood smile. He rolled his shoulders as though psyching himself up for something. "You got your plugs, Griff?"

Griffin patted them in his pocket. "Yes, why?"

"Because shit's about to get real in here." Parker signaled for the DJ in the cage to wind up the music. A fresh electronic beat started thumping. Base vibrated the walls, the floors and the table, making Griffin's teeth tingle.

"Now," Parker shouted over the music, looking impish. "Tonight is going to be hard on some of you with all the sin in the air, so have the night off and enjoy yourself. That's an order."

With that, he stepped from the booth with grace that belied his size, entered the dance pit and slotted himself between two women he knew.

An hour later, Griffin still hadn't moved. He'd held off with his plugs so he could hear the conversation at his table. But then Flint and Mary excused themselves, and Liza and Tony joined Parker on the dance floor. They came back once or twice to hydrate. Evan sat with him for a while, but seeing his girl down in the pit with the other beautiful women, and a growing circle of ogling men had him eager to get there.

"You sure you don't want to come?" Evan asked.

Griffin shook his head. "Not yet."

"Your loss." Evan bounded down the steps, merging into the crowd, leaving Griffin alone.

Easy for Parker to say—*have the night off*—but greed was always there, niggling at Griffin's periphery. Tony and Liza had it worst. Every club patron wanted a drink, to consume. Tony had already begun to dull his pain with alcohol and God knew what else. Liza, on the other hand, seemed to be affected by lust in a different way. He'd long suspected she felt her sin differently to the rest of them. They got a sick feeling in their gut when near sin, Liza… he caught sight of her grinding suggestively up against some tall, handsome man. She looked fine.

The music pounded, and he felt awkward sitting on his own. Perhaps if he put his earplugs in, it wouldn't be so bad. After another ten minutes of psyching himself up, he decided to visit the restroom. When he finished with that, he would walk right up to Lilo and ask her to dance—just like Liza had suggested. He didn't exactly know how he was going to dance, but he figured, there were many people around, so he could just go with the flow.

The restroom was the modern, unisex type with stalls on the outskirts and mirrors and basins in the middle. Naturally, it seemed as though the women shifted to one side, and the men the other. A bouncer stood watch at the door, making sure that everyone behaved themselves. Griffin quickly saw to his needs, sidestepped a few handsy drunk women and went straight to the center of the dance pit where he'd seen the girls last.

When he got there, he found only Grace and their blond friend. No Lilo.

He shouted in Grace's ear. "Where's Lilo?"

Smiling and red-faced, Grace replied: "Maybe she went to the restroom."

A dark, insidious doubt crept into Griffin's mind.

He'd just been in the restroom. He'd seen the girls, and not one of them looked like Lilo. Perhaps she'd been in one of the stalls. He rushed back to speak with the bouncer.

"Have you seen a woman wearing a long blue dress come in here?"

"Buddy, I get hundreds of women coming through here."

"Short brown hair. Olive skin. She's got a BMI of about twenty-one."

The bouncer shook his head. "Still can't help you. Take a look if you want."

Griffin went into the communal restroom.

"Lilo?" he asked and banged on each closed stall door. His voice echoed off the tiled walls. "Are you in here?"

"I can be Lilo if you want," a female replied. A woman at the mirror laughed and winked at him suggestively.

This was not helping.

Maybe she was having a drink, or maybe he'd passed her on her way back from the restroom. Maybe she was on another level…

For the next five minutes, Griffin searched the crowded nightclub and came up with nothing. It wasn't until he went behind the bar that he felt a flare of greed prickle in his gut. It was stronger than the club's mob. It stood out. He stood up straight to focus on it, rotating, trying to get a better sense of direction. It twisted and gnawed until the feeling became a cramp. The sensation grew as he approached the backdoor exit. By the time he pushed through to the cold alley outside, the sin raking his gut was an insatiable beast.

Lilo's trembling voice stopped him in his tracks. "I told you, I don't have your pictures."

CHAPTER TWENTY-THREE

LILO LIKEKE

Lilo squeezed her eyes shut, trying to block out the disaster unfurling in front of her. Only minutes ago she was having the time of her life, letting loose and dancing with her two best friends in the whole world. She'd only gone to the bar for a quick drink of water and had suddenly found herself accosted by a man. He'd painfully pressed a gun into her lower back and urged her outside, past the bar staff, and through the rear exit that led to a deserted alley.

It was one of the men from the warehouse, the ones who'd kidnapped her father. She recognized the brown leather jacket. Not the same face, but his Irish accent made it too easy to assume he belonged to the same gang. When the man asked for the pictures that were in her father's safe, her suspicions were confirmed.

He shoved her into the cold alley wall hidden in between two red dumpsters overflowing with trash. Three men glared at her from across the way, and the muffled thumping base of the nightclub reminded her that no one would hear her scream.

"We're getting paid the big bucks to collect that envelope, girly," said the man with the gun to her head. He had a row of hoop piercings along his ears, a ring in the septum of his nose, and one through his tongue. When he spoke, it glinted, reflecting the flickering fluorescent tube somewhere above them.

His friends watched casually, lounging against the opposite wall. One had a cigar in his mouth, blazing away. Another wore a Baker Boy cap, and the third chewed on a toothpick. All were rusty-haired and wearing the same brown, shapeless leather jacket that the kidnappers had worn.

"Look at me, girly," said Piercings.

Lilo met eyes that reflected violence and pain.

"Not going to say it again. Where is the package?"

"I told you, I don't have your pictures." She wanted her voice to be steady, but it betrayed her fear and wobbled.

"I have them."

Griffin.

She'd never been more happy to hear his voice as he walked from the direction of the nightclub. His hands were in his pockets, but he looked tense, tight, and furious.

A nod from the pierced man pushed the three men off the wall. The one with the Baker Boy hat flipped open the switch-blade in his hands. His friends went straight for their guns inside their jackets.

Griffin never took his eyes from the pierced man. "Get your hands off her."

"I don't think you're in a position to be telling me what to do," he replied, nonchalant.

"There's four of us. Only one of you." Baker Boy laughed, flashing the metal grill on his teeth.

Griffin calmly assessed the situation, taking note of the men and their weapons, the surrounding alley, and then his eyes landed on Lilo. "Are you okay?"

"Yeah." But her heart slammed against her rib cage.

"So, unless you have the pictures," the pierced man said. "This is between us, and the girl. Push off before you're hurt, ya tool."

"I don't think so. You see, I know things."

The sound of guns shifting, aiming, getting into position was the most horrifying sound Lilo ever heard.

"Griffin, just go," she begged. She couldn't believe she was dragging him into her mess again.

"I'm not going anywhere," he said calmly, looking into her eyes, then he turned to the man with the Baker Boy hat. "As I was saying, I know things. Like, for instance, that grill in your mouth is a cheap one. It looks like silver, but on the inside, its stainless steel cast with iron."

"He's insane," Baker Boy joked with his friends. "Why the fuck does it matter what it's made of, tosser?"

"And you." Griffin cocked his head to the side as he inspected the pierced man. "It's the same for your jewelry. Cheap knockoffs instead of the surgical stainless it should be."

"For fuck's sake. Get rid of him." The pierced man lost his patience, waved with his gun at Griffin, and then turned his back, dismissing him.

Bad idea.

It all happened so fast after that. Lilo barely registered what happened. The man with the grill in his mouth suddenly jerked toward the wall as though an invisible hand gripped him from the teeth and smashed him face-first into the red bricks. He lowered, bloody faced, moaning and groaning.

His friends lost their guns—the weapons flew along the alley as though they had wings—just like the way her cattle prod had gone flying when Greed carried her the other night.

Something inside her grew unsettled. She looked around for Greed, but no one else was in the alley except them. Except a savage-eyed Griffin running toward the two men, arm extended, reaching for each throat. When his fingers closed around their thick necks, Griffin used his momentum to push the men back against the wall until their heads hit bricks and bounced.

Damn, he was strong.

They fought back with dirty, street-style moves. A kick to Griffin's groin, a punch in the kidney, but no matter what they did, the two men weren't enough to escape his fury. He sliced and jabbed with his fists, punching in maneuvers too fast to decipher. Suddenly Griffin stood back, glowering at them. His fingers splayed apart. He gripped invisible air. As he clenched his fists, the fire-escape platform above their heads rattled and rumbled and shook, and then Griffin stepped back again. The platform came free from its supports and fell.

No. It didn't fall. It glided, as though being controlled—

Lilo gasped.

He was controlling it.

Griffin was moving the metal… just like… just like…

Her vision swam.

Griffin was Greed. The real one.

It had been him all along.

The platform spun and pinned the two men against the wall, trapping them in its iron grasp.

Griffin faced Lilo's pierced attacker, eyes wild behind his spectacles.

Did he even need those glasses?

A vein pulsed in his forehead, his nostrils flared, and a low growl erupted from the base of his throat, scaring the shit out of Lilo.

"Let. Her. Go," he bit out.

The man nudged Lilo's chin with his gun, but when cold metal hit her skin, the gun soared across the alley to skid across the floor, splashing through the puddles of old snow.

"What the fuck?" The guy still didn't get it. He still hadn't made the same connection Lilo had.

The man with the business-like blue shirt and black-framed spectacles was dangerous and deadly. He was the majestic beast come to life. He was a mythical warrior who had no scruples or ethics. He was the bastard who'd left Lilo alone in that dark stairwell…

She held her breath, wanting to close her eyes but too afraid to look away.

The piercings in the man's face began to rattle.

"If you don't back away from her, I will pull those from your face, one by one."

As Griffin advanced, he made a grabbing motion above his head. More metal pried loose from the rusty fire-escapes —ladders, pipes, gutters…. Long metal bits creaked and arched into the alley, as though being drawn by a magnetic force.

How was he doing this?

The Irish gang-leader hesitated. He glanced at his pinned and groaning friends, then back at Griffin's rage.

Her attacker's piercings dangled out—presumably gripped by Griffin's unseen power—hovering away from his body, and the man hastily moved with them to avoid having them ripped from his flesh. He stepped away from Lilo until he pushed up against the opposite wall with his friends.

"What the fuck are you?" The pierced man cried, wincing at the pain of his piercings being pulled to the limits. "What do you want?"

"I want to know why you want the pictures so badly." Griffin's hands were like claws in the air. The metal above him creaked menacingly for effect. "I want to know who you work for."

The pierced man held up his hands in surrender. "Fine. I don't care. We're not getting paid enough for this. I don't know why they want the pictures, but I can tell you it was a woman with white hair and that's all I know."

Griffin's eyes narrowed. He was silent for so long, Lilo almost said something, but then he let go of his metaphysical hold on the metal above him, and pulled the fire-escape from the wall where it pinned two of the men.

"Get out of here before I change my mind."

The pierced man helped his Baker Boy hat friend from

the ground, and all of them scrambled away. Their footsteps splashed loudly through puddles and echoed against the walls.

When Griffin turned to Lilo, all menace melted and was replaced with pure misery.

"Please." He held his hands up. "Let me explain."

"You!" She hugged herself. "You humiliated me."

Tears burned her eyes. She didn't know what to think. He'd saved her life. He was Griffin. He was Greed. He was someone she knew nothing about, clearly.

"I can explain."

"You can explain?" she hissed. "How? What possible explanation can excuse you leaving me in that stairwell like that?"

Anguish twisted his features and he reached for her, but pulled back and fisted his hand. "I'm sorry I left you. It was the worst moment of my life. I hate myself for making you feel like that, and I want to tell you everything. Will you let me?"

Frustrated, Lilo's gaze darted around the alley.

What the fuck should she do?

Was he safe to be around? The man could bend metal to his will. He could shake the world with his incredible power. She looked at the nightclub backdoor exit, heard the thumping base, and knew Grace was in there dancing... with Evan. If Griffin was Greed, then Evan would be one of them too. And the rest of his family. Parker, the billionaire... Tony, the fricking movie star!

"Oh my God, I feel sick." She patted her clammy forehead.

"I won't hurt you, Lilo, but I can't keep this a secret from you anymore. You're very special to me. Come inside, and I'll explain everything. I'll tell you about me, about my family. Everything. Please."

Shit. Fucking shit! She bit her lip.

He was one of them.

Clearly.

He had morals, she knew that. He wasn't a murderer like the fake Greed.

If he said he'd not hurt her… was that enough?

The Deadly Seven.

She had to go. This was the story of a lifetime. It was her unicorn—the one she never thought she'd actually find. Stamping down her fluttering heart and rolling nausea, Lilo agreed. "I will give you ten minutes."

Griffin exhaled. "Good."

She walked back to the nightclub exit. She'd need a stiff drink to get through this.

"This way," he said behind her.

When she turned around, he'd opened a cast-iron door she'd not noticed before. A glance inside showed her steps leading into a dark space. It reminded her too much of the dark stairwell he'd left her in the other night. A glance back at him showed him hopeful, and sincere.

She had to decide right now if she trusted him.

"It's a direct path to"—he bit his lip, pausing—"our headquarters. It's safe."

His words echoed in her mind.

Safe.

Holy crap, she was doing this? He was one of them, and

he was going to show her everything. Every journalistic instinct inside her wanted to uncover the truth, but every human instinct in her was fearful of finding the truth. Then again, could she really use what she found to write an exposé that outed the deadly heroes?

Not only would it hurt Grace, but the truth would hurt the heroes, and the city would be without them again. As if to punctuate her point, she heard a police siren wail in the distance.

All she knew was that she was a strong woman, a proud reporter, and she wasn't going to let him win by showing her fear. Get the information, then decide what to do with it later. Without hesitation, she stepped through the door, and down the deadly rabbit hole.

CHAPTER TWENTY-FOUR

GRIFFIN LAZARUS

He didn't speak while he led Lilo into the headquarters basement. Sensing his arrival, the ceiling halogen lights illuminated as he walked, casting the walkway into light. AIMI would be watching from cameras, cataloging the new intruder, filing away information for later use. That's the way she was designed, to take the lead from the seven. To watch, record, and leave it up to them to discern.

The magnetic build up in his body still thrummed, and he couldn't shut it down. Each day since he'd developed powers, he'd felt it in his bloodstream, in his organs, and in his mind, changing him on a molecular level. He hadn't trained enough with it, like his family suggested. He could control his power well enough during battle, but afterwards… it still rode his system like a drug. It made him edgy, wired, and in need of release—as though the magnetism bottled in his blood and wanted out. But he didn't have time for that now. Lilo walked beside him.

He stopped at an intersection of hallways where four

doors led to different rooms. "This is the workout room." He pointed to a room on the right. "That's the tech workshop. Med room is there and—"

All the lights and computers flickered, a byproduct of his overworked magnetic biology. He flinched and looked at her with guilty eyes. "Sorry, that's me."

"Griffin," Lilo said calmly. "While I appreciate the grand tour, I said I would give you ten minutes, and I meant it."

She was an angry goddess in a blue dress, and he ached to make everything right, but how could he explain this passion burning him up inside, this ache to be near her, and the fear that he'd stuff it up, just like everything else. How could he tell her she was everything to him? That she was the very thing stopping him from going insane, just by being near?

"Okay," he breathed. Grace said to be honest, and it was all he could do. After that, it would be up to Lilo. "I need to show you my room."

She arched an eyebrow. "Is that some kind of line?"

"Line?"

"Pick-up line."

"No! I swear I'm not... Lilo." His fists opened and closed at his sides. "I swear, I just need to show you something. It will help explain."

But, didn't he want more?

Yes. He wanted everything she had to give, and that made him the greediest man of them all, because he wasn't sorry.

The internal battle must have reflected in his eyes, because her own softened. "Okay. Take me there."

And with her words, he felt like the wolf who ate Red Riding Hood.

A few minutes later, they walked down the hallway leading to his apartment. Try as he might, he couldn't dispel the anxiety creeping up his spine. Would she call him a freak, a weirdo? Would she take one look at the mess which so reflected the state of his mind, and would she run… or—

"Griffin," she murmured. "Are you okay?"

Eyes wide, he caught her gaze. "No."

"It's okay. Whatever it is in there, I can deal with it… unless it's a dead body. Yeah, look. I'm not up for that, I'll tell you right now. You know what? I don't even think I'd like to see a place that used to hold dead bodies. You know, the kind that serial killers do their work in. You're not a secret serial killer, are you? Oh my god, you wouldn't even tell me if you were!" She bit her lip to stop the flow of words.

"It's not a dead body. I'm not a serial killer."

"Okay." She relaxed. "Okay, I think I'm good then."

He grimaced, hesitating.

"Griff," she said. "You know the worst about me, don't you?"

She must mean her family history. "Yes."

"And?" she urged.

"And what?"

"Do you hate me for it?"

"No." He shoved his hands in his pockets. "Not even close. You're perfect. I trust you completely, it just took me a while to get out of my own head long enough to realize that.

The only person who deserves hate is me, for leaving you in that stairwell."

"Yeah, that was a pretty shitty thing to do, and I'm looking forward to the explanation."

"I need to start at the beginning."

He held out his wrist tattoo and told her everything. How his birth mother was able to isolate the genome sequence for greed and program his body to sense deadly levels in other people. How the sensing of the sin affected him mentally. How he'd tried to curb his greedy desires with his balance protocol, and how he was the only one of his siblings to keep the sin in check, and then finally, how she came into all of it. Her calming effect on his psyche, the confusion she brought, the power she triggered in him… When he was done, she stood there with eyes so wide and glazed, he thought maybe he'd broken her.

"Lilo?" he asked, afraid, because for once, he was the one rambling with no control over his words.

"I'm just… that's a lot to take in."

"There's more."

She blinked. "More?"

Here goes nothing.

"We trained for seven years around the world in the art of war," he said, unlocking his apartment door. "It began when I was fifteen. It was brutal, humiliating, and exhausting. It pushed me to the limits of human capacity, and then some. They wanted to see me break, and… I almost made it the full seven years without breaking. I almost showed them, but I failed. I failed enough that I was lucky to get out of there alive." He wanted to elaborate, to explain why he failed… his most shameful secret, but… *not yet*. "After I got home from the training, I created a protocol to keep my balance in check so my failure wouldn't happen again. It worked perfectly, at least, I thought it did. So when I met you, I was rude because you threw my logical process into chaos. I was afraid of failing again. It took me hurting you in that stairwell to realize I was already failing, I was already broken."

"Griff," she said, emotion burning in her eyes. It looked like pity and Griffin hated it. She stepped closer. "You didn't *hurt* me, hurt me. I mean, you hurt my feelings, but before that you were completely the opposite. You saved my life and… what do you mean, I threw your process into chaos?"

"Being in the same room as you, and breathing the same air, affects me. Touching you… sends my insides into chaos."

"Um. In a good way?"

"It took me a while to see, but yes. In a very good way."

Still confused, she rubbed her temples, eyes far too round for Griffin's liking. He shoved open the door to his apartment, using his weight to push the fallen hoarded items out of the door's trajectory.

When she followed inside, and the light came on, she stood still, staring at his collected junk. Piles and piles of teetering towers and spilled items filled his living room. Beyond, the kitchen was clean and bare, and through a far door he could see into his tidy bedroom. At least he'd had the presence of mind to keep those areas neat.

"I don't understand. What am I looking at, Griffin?"

He swallowed. "Before I met you, my internal equilibrium would shift into the light if I went out and fought crime. It was a selfless act, you see, but the downside is that it ate away at my sanity. I learned many years ago that an unbalanced person with my combat skills would could be deadly."

"Deadly." She said the word as though testing it for taste.

"Yes." Okay. Here goes. It's now or never. She's either going to run for the hills, or… Griffin took a deep breath. *Time to spill my secrets.* "Once, when I was on a mission with the SAS, I failed at being human." Saying it out loud, the memories crashed back. He was back in that sandy camp in Afghanistan, laying on the hill cresting the enemy camp, surveilling the area with his comrade, James. James ribbed Griffin for the entire year block of his time with the unit. The soldier had it in for Griffin since they went through the selection course. James made snide sideways comments about Griffin's sensitivity tendencies. He was an asshole, but James didn't deserve to die.

To this day, Griffin believed he'd only gotten through the course because of his training in meditation thanks to his *Shifu* master in Kung Fu. Outwardly, it had seemed like he was calm and collected, but inside he'd been boiling.

He'd gotten through it because he'd had no choice, but it hadn't been easy. Each of James's insults built in pressure until that day on the hill. Griffin was fussing about, making sure they had all their equipment just right. Checking his sniper rifle, checking the wind, checking his uniform, his backup equipment.

Fucking weirdo, you checked that five times.

Because he was concerned it wouldn't be enough.

His crew mate had picked at him the entire night. Griffin

was nervous. He didn't belong. He worried his one rifle wouldn't be enough. He was out of balance. He knew it. All he could think while sitting up on that hill, watching the enemy, was that the man next to him had a better gun. A newer one that was more reliable, and more likely to shoot true. The greedy urge to take the weapon had bordered on obsessive. So when his friend opened his mouth to give him shit for the fifth time in a row, Griffin reached across and snapped his neck. Just like that. Then he'd calmly switched rifles.

His sudden movement had notified the enemy, and before he knew it, they were upon him. Griffin couldn't remember what happened after that. He'd blacked out completely. When he came too, he was covered in blood and gore and surrounded by dead bodies—both enemy and friendly.

Stand down. Stand down.

He could still hear his team shouting in his ears. But that wasn't where the horror ended. His own team had questioned him… interrogated him. Tortured him. He still had the scars to prove it. They wanted to know if Griffin worked for the enemy. *Did you kill our own?* In the end, nobody could explain what happened. There was no proof. Nothing but the blood on Griffin's hands. They put his blacking out to some kind of post traumatic stress, but he knew the truth. He was unbalanced.

Griffin tugged at his collar as he relayed the story to her, watching her grow increasingly wary with every word. "When I got back, I swore I'd never lose control again—that I'd keep my sin balanced, no matter what. I created a protocol to ensure that every time I did a deed of generosity, I'd commit an act of greed of equal weighting. As you can see, I stole to fulfill the greed portion of the protocol. It worked for a while, but then... well, this is the result." He waved his hand at his mess. "I've told no one about this. Not even my family."

"You've been carrying this burden alone for years?"

"It is a burden no one else should share."

She stared at him for a moment, then lifted her brows and looked to the kitchen. "Do you have any alcohol in there?"

It was such a sudden change of pace that he jerked. "Um. Maybe something really old Tony left. Some vodka, I think. I don't really drink."

"Great." She strode past him and began opening cupboards methodically until she found the glasses. "A little help here, Griff? Where's the vodka?"

"Third cupboard on the bottom."

She poured two big glasses and handed him one. "Drink it."

He tipped the glass to look inside and flinched. The fumes burned his nostrils.

"I gave you a drink. Drink it," she ordered, hands on hips. "It will help calm your nerves."

So he shot it back and let it burn the back of his throat, forcing himself to hold the spasm down. When it was done, he found she'd done the same, except where his muscles were locking with tension, hers were melting and relaxing.

"Okay. I feel better now." She shook her hands at her side. "Hang on. One more."

She refilled their glasses and gave him eyes until he drank his, and she drank hers.

"I'm still confused, and my brain is going a million miles an hour." She leaned against the kitchen island. She cast her eye over his living room. "But from where I'm standing, I don't see stolen items. All I can see is how many people you've helped."

He went to lean next to her. "But I took things that didn't belong to me."

"To balance out the fact you were saving lives."

They stared at his modern metallic fridge. He could feel the iron atoms reach for him, but he ignored them, instead turning his attention to her at his side.

"I'm sorry," he said.

She shifted to face him side-on. Their eyes were inches apart.

Her body heat mixed with his and felt just as warming as the vodka. Her feminine scent climbed into his body and set hooks into him. There was a hint of soap, but that was all. It was enough to trigger his own body's reaction, sending a surge of endorphins rushing through his system. He felt relaxed and aroused at the same time.

Wanting to get close to her, but not wanting to hurt her again, he gripped the stone bench.

"When I left you in that stairwell, I was afraid I'd already tipped my balance somehow. It was… a low point of my life. I was so ashamed for my actions. After doing so well to put your past behind you, you deserve someone better than me."

"Do you really think that?"

"My life is forever steeped in crime. Being near me will always put you in danger."

"But is that what you want? For me to not be with you?"

"Lilo." His eyes fluttered from the force of his emotions. "I want you. All of you. Any way I can have you."

She stared at her feet for a while, thinking.

"I get it," she whispered. "Don't get me wrong, I'm upset that you left me, but I get it. You didn't want to hurt me intentionally, and… I forgive you. Just don't do it again." She added, pouting playfully, but then with a self-deprecating smile, dipped her head and shook it. "I'm an idiot. That was me trying to lighten the mood. Just tell me to shut up."

He took a shuddering breath. "Thank you."

"For shutting up?"

He laughed. "For forgiving me. And I will never do it again. I promise."

At his laughter, she froze and stared at him until silence pounded between them.

"Lilo?" he tested, unsure.

"You're beautiful when you laugh," she murmured, and tugged his glasses from his face. "You don't really need these, do you?"

He shook his head.

"I still have so many questions. Like, is Griffin your real name, and do all of your family have powers, and how come you got the metal moving ability, and where did it come from? Is it like an alien invention sort of thing, or are you from the future, or something crazy like that, and also, most of all"—she turned serious, eyes intense as her hand moved swiftly to the back of his neck in a firm grip—"what happens now… between us?"

He licked his lips and saw her do the same. He wanted so badly to kiss her, but was afraid… "Only one answer can take care of all our questions."

She gasped and stepped back.

"You watched *Casablanca*," she exclaimed.

"Three times."

"Three times!"

"Correct."

"Because of me?" Her hand fluttered to her throat.

"Yes. I want to know everything about you. I want to understand you."

"Why?"

He thought back to that movie—to the main character and how he'd desperately wanted the woman to love him above all else, even if he wasn't worthy. "Because I want you to love me."

Lilo moved to stand in front of him. Her eyes were languid and heavy as she nudged his long legs apart to make room for her curvy body, and then she leaned into him until their foreheads met. Soft breasts pillowed against his chest, causing his heart rate to spike.

"I love how you're being honest with me right now," she whispered against his lips, "and I have to confess something in return. I want all of you too."

But she didn't kiss him. She rolled her face so their cheeks pressed.

Griffin tensed against the sensation, held his breath, shut his eyes, and focused on their connection, on his breathing.

In. Out. In. His every awareness sky-rocketed. He groaned against the euphoria building in his system. The follicles on his scalp goose-bumped, his tongue buzzed, and out of everything she could have done to connect with him, this was the most arousing. With only her hand on his neck, her cheek against his, and her soft body leaning quietly against his front... she undid him.

CHAPTER TWENTY-FIVE

LILO LIKEKE

The low rumble coming from Griffin sounded pained and bursting with need. When Lilo felt the hard press of his desire against her stomach, she pushed back into him. God, he smelled good. Like everything manly all rolled into one. Better than blueberry bubblegum or the smell of baked cookies. She could rub herself all over him if he'd let her. She could breathe him in and it would hit her like warm whiskey. She could lick him to see if he tasted the same. Up that hard column of neck, along that square stubbly jaw, across to his hopeful lips.

Maybe she voiced her fantasies because tension locked his muscles tight.

It was then she realized he gripped the bench as though his life depended on it, and the crease between his brows was a deep canyon. A sheen of sweat pebbled his top lip.

She pulled away, and his long lashes lifted to reveal eyes so dilated and black and full of yearning that her heart stuttered.

"I want you," he rasped, voice low and heady.

"But…"

"It's a process for me. Increased feelings and sensations make me unpredictable, and I don't want you uncomfortable, or to put you in a position like last time"—he swallowed—"but I don't want this to stop."

"Make me uncomfortable… You mean like when you wouldn't let me touch or see you."

"And it frightened you."

"You're right; I was afraid. But that's because I didn't know you enough. I couldn't see you, and I wasn't in control. It reminded me of someone who treated me badly. I don't like being told what to do. Not anymore."

"Do you know me enough now?"

"You bared your soul to me." It was the most obvious thing she could say. She trailed her finger over his scarred hand and arm. It broke her heart to think of him being tortured… by his own people. Of course she knew him. "I know you better than anyone else in your life knows you… and I'm honored by it."

He bit his lip, and the bench creaked under his grip. "What if you're in control?"

She smiled. He was determined all right. "That's a big sacrifice for you to make."

"You could take the lead," he insisted. "I trust you. I want you to trust me too."

A spear of hot desire arrowed between her legs as visions of him beneath her, naked and submitting, flashed before her eyes. It thrilled her, excited her, and scared her.

You'll never be satisfied without me.

Donnie's voice was as loud and clear as it had ever been, but she couldn't let him rule her forever, not when this strong, beautiful hero had just laid his vulnerable heart on the line.

"How will I know what you like?" she mumbled. "I don't want to hurt you either."

"You're what I like," he rasped.

Shit. She was in love. Hopelessly falling in love like a complete idiot. Her eyes dropped to where his erection strained his pants, and her mouth went dry and her heart galloped. She looked to where he gripped the bench, wounded knuckles pinched white with strain. He was a warrior, despite his sensitivity. Despite this, and despite his dark urges, he still went out and saved lives even though it cost him a little of his soul each time. Even though he knew what deadly consequences ignoring his balance could do, he worked through it.

So could she.

With that small powerful thought, a slow grin spread. Her carnal desires must have leaked through her body language because an emboldened smile curved his lips. His reaction gave her the confidence to pry his fingers from the bench and whisper, "Let's go to your bedroom."

She'd seen the open doorway when they entered the apartment and tugged him after her as she walked there. When they arrived, she stopped and let go of his hand. He came up behind her, not quite touching but close enough she could feel the heat of his aura caressing her spine.

His bedroom was sparsely decorated and lit gently by the secondhand kitchen light shining through. The king-sized bed pushed against the far wall was draped in a white comforter, copious pillows, and navy linen sheets. Two metal bed-side tables had books stacked strategically next to lamps. The floor was wooden and smooth, the walls white and unassuming, and a balcony window with soft billowing curtains revealed the night-lit Quadrant park below. She could hear a siren, traffic and even the faint thumping coming from the nightclub, levels below.

That wouldn't do. She crossed the room and shut the window, blocking out all sound. When she turned back, he hadn't moved from the doorway.

Wow. He was magnificent. Tall, cut, tense.

And he was serious about his promise to let her lead. It made her bold.

"Sit on the bed," she ordered.

It came out curt and she flinched, but he did as told. He glided to the bed, sat on the edge and faced her, fists on his thighs. She stood between his knees and looked at him. His yearning held her captivated.

Where to begin?

He was a carved smorgasbord of perfection, and she wanted all of him at once, but she needed to take it slow. To relish him.

"Remove your shirt," she whispered.

Without breaking eye contact, he popped his buttons, one by one until the shirt gaped open, giving her a sinful peek at his sculptured chest. Exactly how she'd imagined it. Hard. Smooth. Bunched with perfect abdominals and a dusting of dark hair that led beyond his waistband. He went to take off his shirt.

"Stop," she said, voice husky.

He stopped.

"I want to do it."

Slowly, he lowered his hands.

Lilo slipped one side of his shirt from his shoulder, taking special care to keep the pressure over his skin steady. But that simple touch made his eyes smokey, wanting more, and it made her sweat with impatience. Her nipples hardened. Her sex heated. *Slow, Lilo. Slow.* She slid the shirt off the other shoulder and it hit the mattress, trapping his wrists.

She could tie him up. Force him to keep his hands from her, force him to keep his promise to let her lead. But the minute she entertained the thought, she knew it wasn't how she wanted their relationship to start, and that's what this was—a new relationship. It was more than a simple one-night stand, or a meeting of the bodies. It was a connection that ran deeper than any she'd known.

He trusted her.

She untangled his hands from his sleeves and threw the shirt across the room. It hit the wall and slid to the floor. When she looked back at Griffin, she grinned.

"I like doing this. Do you?"

"Yes," he breathed, eyes drinking her in.

She stepped back to give herself a better view. The blue light from the window blended with the warm kitchen light, and danced across his hard features, creating deep shadows cut from stone. They held each other's gaze and with each passing second, she could see his chest lift and fall rapidly. Her own breath rasped as her body swelled with need.

"Now take off the rest." She pointed to his pants.

Perhaps she should have told him to take his time because his shoes and pants were off in seconds, and then he sat there in his boxer shorts, waiting for her.

"All of it." Her grin turned wicked as she glared at his boxers. "Slowly this time."

With heavy lids, and an exhaled shuddering breath of impatience, he did as he was told, hooking his thumbs into his waistband, drawing them low, releasing his impressive erection, and sitting back down, arms at his side, waiting. It was a pose that had his granite-like stomach muscles contract deliciously. Damn her, because she was the one who would lose control in a minute, not the other way around.

"Shit, Griffin," she mumbled and lifted her hands to her aching breasts. He watched with ardent eyes, tracking her movement as her fingers teased her nipples through her dress. She was so ready for him. Already wet. Aching to lose herself in his touch.

Slow.

She inhaled and trailed her touch from her breasts to the back of her neck and plucked the clasp. The dress released and dropped, slithering along her naked skin, erupting goosebumps of pleasure all over. She was left in a strapless bra and matching underwear and, from the look of his kid-in-a-candy-store expression, he loved every inch of it.

"Lilo," he begged.

"I'm going to touch you first," she said, looking between his legs. "And then I'm going to ride you."

"What about you? When will you let me touch you?"

"Later. First, I want to give you this moment, make it

pleasurable for you. Tell me how you like it. Tell me how you want it."

"It has to be about you, too. Please let it be about you." He couldn't stop staring at her breasts and she knew from the heat in his eyes, and the way his tongue touched his lips, that he wanted to taste her there.

She wanted that too. God, she wanted it. Her plans were swiftly unraveling with her urge to have him touch her. That look in his eyes. Primal. Hungry. Pure want. She stepped closer. He widened his knees to make room for her. Every nerve ending in her body throbbed with awareness. She was ready for him.

"Take off my bra," she demanded breathlessly. "Then my panties. Then I want you to lick me."

He popped her bra off, releasing her heavy breasts, and hovered his lips near them, hesitating, waiting for permission. His tender breath hit her sensitized skin and made her cry out with need.

"Yes," she breathed. "Start there."

His mouth landed around her nipple and she moaned in ecstasy as he twirled and sucked and licked and laved. She barely noticed her panties had been removed because her mind was a pure haze of craving. His rough hands slid up her backside to land behind her ribs and tugged her closer with a growl of restraint. That sound was enough to have her fingers spearing into his hair. His mouth popped off and he stared up at her, eyes dazed, jaw unlocked.

"I'm sorry," she panted and relaxed her grip. "Was that too hard?"

"It's okay," he murmured. "I'm good."

"Sit back on the bed," she ordered, but reminded herself to keep it slow. His scars were a reminder of the bad experiences he'd had with touch. She wanted to give him better ones. Heavenly ones. "Back until you hit the headboard."

She watched with burning eyes as he shuffled and sat patiently. Despite his calm exterior, his insides must be turmoil. She could tell from the way his skin pulled hard over every ropy muscle, as though he used every reserve to hold back. Her heart melted. He was being so good with her.

On her hands and knees, she crawled to him, reveling in the way he squirmed as she inched closer and closer to the proud jut of his cock, sitting upright against his abs.

"I want that in my mouth," she said.

"I want you in my mouth," he countered.

"Can we have both?"

"At the same time?" He looked conflicted. "I don't know."

The sensations might be too much for him. "How about we save that for next time?"

She circled his shaft with her fingers and squeezed gently, then lowered her lips to touch the crown. She held herself there while he adjusted to his rush of awareness. When his twitching subsided, she opened her mouth and took him inside, groaning as the taste hit her. He canted his hips, pushing into her mouth. It drew another moan from deep within her throat and she increased her efforts.

"Too much," he breathed.

She came off him, concerned, and his eyes were squeezed tight, so vulnerable right now. "Griffin?"

She didn't want to hurt him.

"Condom," he bit out. "Side-table."

In the drawer of the metal side-table, she found what she needed and ripped the foil packet open.

She rolled it onto him. "You feel everything intensely, don't you?"

"It's a curse and a blessing," he laughed painfully. "First time sex is the hardest. The next is easier. Better."

"The next?" she grinned wickedly. She liked he was thinking the same things. "Already imagining more?"

"Absolutely." Eyes like lava pinned her and melted everything inside.

She straddled him and positioned his length beneath her sex, then gradually slid lower, keeping her eyes locked onto him, satisfied as his own rolled heavenward in bliss. He dropped his head back to the headboard, Adam's apple bobbing on that magnificent neck. When he filled her, she paused, letting them both process the new flood of feeling. Tingles and sparks zip-lined to the rest of her body, to her nipples, to her eyes, to her heart.

Lilo put a finger on his chin and brought his gaze back to hers. "You okay?"

His response was to lurch forward, lick her lower lip, and then hold it firmly between his teeth.

"Move," he growled against her lips.

She began a languid rocking, driving herself while they continued to lock lips. His smell made her heady and impatient, and soon her rhythm picked up in urgency. Their kisses became wild and desperate and somewhere between that, their hands were on each other, touching, learning, testing. But it wasn't fast enough. She needed more.

"Help me," she begged, panting, thighs burning.

His strong grip landed on her hips where he pinned her while he drove in from beneath. The sight of his muscles contracting relentlessly made her dizzy with desire.

"Faster, Griffin," she moaned. "Harder."

He increased his pace until sweat coated both their bodies with a misty sheen. She gripped the headboard and held on, and he moved the attention of his mouth to her breast, sucking it hard. Each time he slammed underneath, the pressure built inside, edging her toward insanity, and when she felt her insides tightening and nerves bubbling, she cried out soundlessly and broke around him.

Even after she'd come, he pounded harder and faster, insatiably. When she was too languid and weak to help him finish, he switched their positions, so she was on the bottom and he was on top. And then she tasted his loss of control in the most delicious way until he grunted his release and crumbled, breaking around her—collapsing heavily, face buried deep into her throat. He lay so still for a while that she would have thought he'd died, except his heart pounded against hers.

"Griff?" she whispered and placed her palm on his head.

He groaned lazily.

"You okay?"

"That was…" he rolled off her to lay on his back with his hands behind his head. "Intense," he finished, looking up at the ceiling, dazed.

"Good intense?"

"The best." He turned to her with a blush staining his cheeks and a brightness to his eyes. "That's a fact."

His smile hit her all over, inside, outside, brain pleasure centers, curling toes… and she rested on her elbow to watch him and soak him up. "You mentioned a second time. So, when can we do it again?"

He chuckled. "I think I need a minute."

"So… only a minute?" she joked.

"Two," he countered with lust filled eyes. "Maybe three."

He wasn't wrong. They made love all night, until she was exhausted and drifted to the sound of his heart beating under her ear, and his hand wrapped around her bare back, dreaming already about the next time and always forever.

———

LILO WOKE to the golden sun shining gently on her face, and the sight of Griffin sitting in a chair on his balcony, drinking coffee and reading the paper. Already showered and dressed for the day in a fitted white cotton shirt and khaki chinos, she wondered how long he'd been awake.

To think that a day ago she'd been as lonely as ever, and now here was a hero who had cut out his own vulnerable heart, and given it to her before anyone else in his life.

He said she was his generous opposite, but he'd given her the biggest gift she'd ever received. The trust, the hope, the love.

I want you to love me, he'd said.

Well, buddy, she had news for him… she did.

A glance out the open bedroom showed the mess in his living area, and her gut clenched. It was so contrary to how he cared for himself, and his bedroom. It must be hell for him.

This was Griffin in here: the neat edges, the straight and clean surfaces, the no frills decor. Out there was like taking a peek into the dark corners of his mind, the side no one else but she knew about. It was his future if she didn't help him, but she would. With everything she had, she would. As if a weight landed on her chest, the anguish he would have felt when he thieved almost suffocated her. He didn't want to. He hated it, but there had been no other way to keep himself balanced enough to save the people in this city. How lonely he must have felt. And she was the one person in the world who could save him.

But she was born for this.

If he couldn't give up those items, then she would do it for him. She'd go through every single piece if it took all day and then find a home for it. There were shelters south of her mid-town apartment, and there were people in her building who needed help. That woman and her baby in the South-Side won't be the only needy mother on the streets.

She supposed she could hand the items back to the police anonymously, but—she glanced back at Griffin taking a sip from his blue mug, the gentle breeze trying to ruffle his styled hair, but failing—something good had to come out of this. He wouldn't need to steal with her, he'd said so. She gave him peace, and he did the same for her.

She was so full of love for him in that moment that her chest hurt.

As if connected to her very heart, he looked over and their eyes clashed. He paused, mug hovering mid-air, and then she smiled tentatively. He unfolded his long body and replaced his coffee with another mug before he padded over, barefoot.

"Hi." His voice was deliciously low in the morning.

"You were up early."

"I like to get my workout and meditation in before eight."

He shook himself, as if to remind himself of the mug in his hand, and then handed it to her. "This is for you. I wasn't sure how long you'd sleep, so if it's cold I can heat it up."

She took a sip of the hot, creamy coffee and moaned in delight. Perfect temperature, just the way she liked it. "I could get used to this, you know."

"I hope so."

His words brought a blush to her cheeks, and after lowering her mug, she found he had a matching stain in his expression. She glanced down. She was naked with only a sheet gathered around her hips.

"Sorry," she apologized, thinking how Donnie used to require her to cover up, even in her own home. *It's not proper for a lady to flaunt herself,* he'd said. But she'd done it when he wasn't there. She couldn't help herself. "I've always been a bit free with myself around the home. Does it bother you?"

"No," he said, a little too fast. "I'm good."

Her lips curved in a smile. She patted a spot next to her. "Excellent. Now, come and sit next to me."

He put one knee on the bed, but half way, his gaze snagged on the scene in the living area and he frowned.

"Oh, no," she said, and tugged him gently. "You don't have to worry about that anymore."

As he landed next to her, she pushed him back against the headboard to sit. She shifted the sheet away from her and straddled him, much like she had the previous night.

Naturally, his hands shifted to support her rear.

"Lilo, I'm—"

She put her finger on his lip. "Shh. I'm going to help you get rid of it all, okay?"

Her simple touch flipped a switch inside him, and just like last night, she knew he was reacting hard and fast to her. His skin flushed, his eyes blackened, and he flexed his grip on her backside. He was self-conscious about his sensitivity needs, but she loved taking things leisurely, loved building up their experience, one stroke at a time. Even a well-timed look could have him shuddering in pleasure. This was how she affected him, and it made her pulse rabbit and her body heavy with need.

"Kiss me, Griffin," she said. "Kiss me and know it's going to be all right."

He tentatively touched his lips to hers and moaned, rolling his hips underneath her. "Lilo, look what you do to me" he murmured. "Look how you make me lose control."

His words were a shot of dopamine to her brain. She unzipped him, and pulled his heavy length out, and then she made love with him fully clothed, and her completely naked, and maybe it was that extra layer of protection around him, or maybe it was the fact he knew she was his, but this time, his passion drove her to new dizzying heights.

When they were done and sated and recovering next to each other, she outlined her plan to help him give away the clutter in his home. He didn't respond at first, only drew her to his side. She hooked a leg over him and placed her head and palm on his chest, toying with the buttons on his shirt.

"So that's what we're going to do today, okay?" she said. "Box by box, and none of your family will know if you don't want them to. I can keep a secret." He was silent, and she wasn't sure if it was her bossiness. She leaned back so she could see his face. "Or we could stay in bed all day. Whatever you want, my little mythical beast."

He shot her a quizzical look. "Mythical beast?"

"Because a griffin is this magical animal from folklore that protects treasure and prized possessions."

"Like you," he said with lidded eyes.

That made her go all warm and fuzzy, but then he turned quiet.

"What is it?" she asked, returning her head to his chest. She liked hearing his heart pound.

"There's something else I need to tell you."

This had her sitting up, dragging the sheet to her chest. A slash of panic slid through her. "More secrets?"

"Not to do with me. You know everything there is to know about me. It's about someone else you know."

"Okay." Where was this going? "Who?"

He hesitated. "Your father."

"I don't need to speak about him anymore. He's alive, that's all I need to know."

"Would your feelings be different if you knew the deadly sin I sensed wasn't coming from him, but your mother?"

"What do you mean?"

"When we intercepted the kidnappers, I realized his greed was rather small in comparison to other criminals I've met. For a mafia boss, it didn't make sense. The only possible explanation is that your mother influenced him to become the man he is today. I feel like, maybe he was coerced."

She thought about it, and while her heart ached to understand, her head pointed out the facts. "He still did many bad things. He's murdered people. Stole from them. Put guns in the hands of teenagers. He should go to jail. There's no coming back from murder."

Griffin turned away, and she realized her mistake too soon. "No, Griffin. Don't ever think you're in the same league as him. Please, baby, believe me."

"I don't know. Sometimes I wonder about the point of all of this. Are we making a difference, or drawing out the pain…"

"You sound like Humphrey Bogart from *Casablanca*."

"Maybe he had a point."

"Griffin. I believe in you," she said, teary eyed, and it earned her a small smile.

"Your father turned himself in," he said. "He's already in prison."

"He did?"

"He confessed to a lot of crimes. He wants to pay for his sins."

Lilo's heart cracked a little, because now she was thinking of questions like: can a person change; can he earn forgiveness; and, how long do you hold a grudge?

"I can go with you to see him, if you would like some closure." Griffin's hand landed on hers.

"I suppose it would be a good opportunity to ask him

about the pictures. I now understand why they're so valuable, and why you didn't want to show them to me."

"I should have trusted you from the start."

"Well, there goes my unicorn." She slapped herself in the face, only now realizing she could never write an exposé about Griffin and his family. Not now. Not ever.

"Unicorn?"

"Yeah, I… God, this is embarrassing." She flushed. "I've wanted to write about the Deadly Seven for years. Wanted to be the journalist who cracked your identity, or at the very least uncovered your purpose. Anything, really. It was going to be my big break. I can't do that now. I was completely ignorant to think writing a story like that wouldn't be harmful. I see how much pain and suffering you all go through to help out those who don't deserve it."

He took her hands in his. "You can still help."

"How?"

"Control the narrative. Don't let Doppenger write his lies."

She bit her lip. *Going up against Donnie?* Yes. Damn him. She was so done with that overpowering greedy jerk. Fred had loved her story. She could do this.

"I will fight for you, Griffin," she said. "I promise you this. People like Donnie won't get to write rubbish about your family again. Not while I'm at the Copy."

He brought her hand to his lips and kissed her knuckles. "He won't stand a chance."

A small smile tickled her face, and then her stomach rumbled. "Um. Do you have any flour and baking supplies here?"

A worried tick appeared next to his eye.

"Actually, don't answer that, you look like you bench-lift bakers for fun."

He blinked. "I just use normal weights."

That made her laugh and she slapped him playfully. "Any other food?"

"Not suitable for breakfast."

"No problem." She hopped out of bed, all energized and ready for the day. "Let me take a shower, and then I'm taking you to breakfast."

She'd just had to pick somewhere cheap.

As she crossed the room, she felt his heated gaze on her back as she opened his bathroom door, then just as she entered, he shouted, "Wait!"

But she'd seen the damage to the tiles in his shower. The wall under the faucet and spray nozzle had been shattered and dented as though someone had taken a mallet to it. "What happened?"

He came up behind her, hands in his pockets. "I was angry."

For the first time since being with him, she was a little concerned he had a temper she needed to be aware of, and a sliver of doubt reminded her that Donnie was an angel when they first started dating too.

"It was after I left you in that stairwell," he uttered. "I was angry at myself."

Angry at himself. Not her. The opposite of what Donnie was like. She had nothing to worry about. He needed her.

CHAPTER TWENTY-SIX

GRIFFIN LAZARUS

A day later, Griffin was in a booth at Heaven, watching Lilo from across the room as she spoke with the waitress at her station about a special order she wanted made. He had mentioned that he wasn't a fan of garlic, and she took it upon herself to ensure his order was made without. She liked doing things for him, and he liked doing them back.

He also liked doing things to her.

The memory of how they'd spent the previous two nights had him heating up, tugging at his collar, and shifting his legs. He attempted to think of something else, but it was as though the more he tried to move his mind away, the more he envisioned her naked body beneath him. Above him. In his arms. In the shower. On his newly uncovered living room couch...

They'd spent the prior day at his place, surreptitiously removing the stolen items from his living room. She'd kept her promise and made sure to hold his secret close to her heart. The mass exodus hadn't been too hard in the end, as most of the family were recovering from the opening night of Hell.

Lilo had helped him sift through his apartment. She approached the mess like it was a house renovating project. She helped him sort every stolen object into categoric piles. Jewelry, knick-knacks, clothing... Not once did she frown, or chastise him. In fact, she enthusiastically spoke about how much it would help those less fortunate than them. Together they'd delivered the items to shelters and goodwill centers around the city. She came alive with the project and still held the same glow in her cheeks today. He was grateful that he could see his living room furniture again. Very grateful.

His gaze flicked back to where she chatted with the waitress. She tried to pay for the meal, but he told staff that anything either of them ate would go on his tab. She'd been so used to being so generous in her past relationship, it made him edgy. On the other hand, he was happy to show her what being with someone who cared for her truly felt like.

She wouldn't want for anything while he was around, and he hoped that would be for a long time.

"This seat taken?" Tony slid into the booth on the opposite side to Griffin, pulling his Hollywood sunglasses and ball cap disguise off.

He looked disheveled, but energized. The man twitched and buzzed like he had ants in his pants. His fingers thrummed on the leather. His hair was smoothed back as though he'd run his fingers through it a million times, and his pupils were dilated as they darted around, no doubt checking for misguided paparazzi who might catch him looking so out of sorts.

Griffin stiffened. "As a matter of fact—"

Tony ignored him with a sniff and rested his arm lengthwise on the top of the booth, staring around the restaurant. "What's up, my man?"

"When was the last time you slept, Tony?" Griffin frowned at him.

"What?" Tony's gaze came back to Griffin.

"For an actor, you're pretty terrible at hiding the fact you're wired."

"Fine," Tony simpered. "Haven't slept since Thursday. And before you go all righteous Griffin on me, give me a break. Shooting wrapped up, and it's a few months before the next one, I'm winding down."

"Looks as though you're winding up to me."

"Yeah, speaking of that." He gave Griffin serious eyes. "I need to work off this energy. How about we spar?"

"You want to fight me in your condition?" Griffin asked incredulously. The man was obviously still high.

Tony shrugged and whined in an entitled way. "I've been waiting for hours for anyone to be awake. I wanna see what this new ability of yours has. Come on. It will be fun."

"What will be fun?" Lilo said as she slipped back into the booth, on Griffin's side this time. "Hello Tony. Nice to see you again."

Tony gave Lilo a sly smile. "I'm actually surprised to see either of you out with all that gluttony I've been sensing."

"What?" Lilo blushed. "I don't eat that much. Okay,

maybe I've had a few muffins lately. And that donut last night after dinner. And—I like baked goods, okay?"

Tony laughed until his eyes watered, and it made Griffin testy.

"People always think gluttony is to do with food," Tony added, "but there're other things we can't stop indulging in." His new gaze was loaded with innuendo.

"That's enough, Tony." Griffin then turned to Lilo. "You'll have to excuse my brother, he's a few days old."

"A few days?"

"Still partying from Friday."

"Yeah, bo-oy." Tony whooped then faced Lilo with a look Griffin was sure melted many female panties. "I apologize for my rudeness, Lilo. It is good to see you again."

She gave a small smile, but shuffled closer to Griffin.

"Your friend was fun, by the way," he winked at Lilo and she blanched.

"You mean Misha?"

He nodded. "She knows how to party. You can invite her anytime."

"Did you two… um… you know."

Tony arched an eyebrow. "I don't kiss and tell."

Griffin gestured at his brother. "He does kiss and tell which means if he's not saying anything now, then nothing happened."

"You're no fun." Tony threw a napkin at him.

Lilo relaxed beside him in a way that suggested she wasn't pleased with the idea of his brother and her friend hooking up. He wouldn't be happy either. At least not until Tony cleaned up his act.

Perhaps a good sparring session would be good for him —put him in his place and remind him of the dangers of indulging in that pastime for someone like them.

"I do need to work on my new ability," Griffin murmured, conceding.

Tony clapped his hands together. "Excellent. Let's go now."

"You're not hungry?" Lilo asked.

"Nope."

"Well, I am," Griffin said.

Tony looked immediately put out. "You're going to make me wait?"

"I had plans before you arrived. I'm not changing them because you snap your fingers at me."

"Ugh. Fine." Tony slid back out of the booth. "Prepare for an epic battle, my brother. I'm going to see who else I can rustle up."

"That's a good idea," Griffin agreed. "I need to apprise Parker about the poor club security." He darted a glance at Lilo. "If I hadn't been vigilant, Lilo might not be here."

A flicker of a frown danced over Tony's expression, but he stamped it down immediately. Probably didn't want anything serious to ruin his buzz.

"Right," Tony said, rubbing his hands. "I'm off to gather the troops."

He slid his sunglasses and ball cap on, and then all but jumped out of the booth. As he passed them on the way to the exit, he flashed them a grin and clapped them both on the shoulders with way too much verve. "Laters."

Griffin turned to Lilo. "I'm worried about him."

"Yeah, I'm not surprised." She lowered her voice in a conspiratorial way. "Does Parker know about his... ah, special diet?"

"Probably. Tony thinks he can hide it, but he can't. We know him too well."

CHAPTER TWENTY-SEVEN

LILO LIKEKE

Lilo followed Griffin along the basement hallway leading to the workout room. Griffin said she didn't have to come, but she was thrilled to watch—to get an insider's look at this talented family in action. It appealed to every journalistic instinct she had. It also made her extremely nervous.

Dressed in sweatpants and a simple cotton T-shirt, Griffin looked no less imposing. The relaxing past few days had done much to soften his almost permanent scowl, and put some color into his cheeks, but when he entered the room, he became quietly serious.

"Are you sure it's okay for me to be here?" she asked, wiping her sweaty palms on her skirt. "I mean, I know you trust me not to go blabbing, but I've only just met your family and—"

He pressed his lips to hers. The touch was small and gentle, but it was as loud as a shout. He was there for her, and he was in her corner. It was as simple as that.

He threw his hand towel over his shoulder and then took her hand.

The room was a simple gym. A padded mat in the middle, various electrical machines and weights around the edges. Mirrors on one side, and a few chairs on the other. Two people were on the mat already, training with boxing gloves and pads.

Tony and Evan. Tony had his shirt off and wore jeans of all things. Designer dark denim hung low on his hips, giving Lilo an uninhibited view of his perfect movie star torso. Tanned and already slick with sweat. Evan wore sweats and was also shirtless, but where Tony was flawless, Evan was all dark lines and twisted tattoos, except for the one over his heart that clearly said *Grace*. Lilo smiled at that.

"Lilo!" Speak of the devil.

"Grace!" Lilo grinned. "You have a day off?"

Grace lifted her medical kit and pulled a face. "Well, I thought I did, until these meatheads decided to hold an impromptu tournament."

"Tournament?" Griffin scratched his head. "Since when?"

"Since your sister is going to kick all y'all lazy asses." Liza walked in, followed by Griffin's parents, a tall man in a check shirt and a short woman wearing yoga attire.

They all stopped and stared at Lilo. Her skin burned.

Liza's gaze ping-ponged between Lilo and Griffin. She finally punched him in the arm. "Nice to see you loosened up, bro."

His scowl deepened. "Why do you have to hit me all the time?"

"Why not?" She flared her eyes, challenging.

When Griffin huffed and went to wrap his knuckles with tape, Liza's surprised gaze whipped to Lilo. "Wow. He's… yeah, wow. Not even a comeback. He's very loose."

"We didn't officially meet on Friday night." Griffin's mother came up and held out her hand. "I'm Mary, Griffin's mother."

"Oh—" Lilo shook her hand. "Nice to meet you. I'm Lilo."

The woman's shrewd eyes gave Lilo an assessing once over, then she smiled suddenly and it was like looking into the eyes of a lioness. Lilo sensed that she could be as deadly as her children. Mary indicated the tall older man next to her. "This is Flint, my husband and the father of these *niños estupidos*."

"Hey." His hand hit his chest, as though he'd been shot to the heart. "Why am I the father when they're stupid?"

With a shrug, she smirked and walked toward the mat. "Because I am the mother when they are not."

"Welcome to the family." Flint flashed a quick grin and went to join his wife.

"Um. Welcome to the family?" Lilo squeaked to Grace.

"I hope you didn't have other ideas, because you're in deep now. There's no escaping."

"Or else what? They hunt me down if I try to leave?"

"Nope. You're just in. You belong." That knowing smile spread on her face until she swung her medical bag and made her way to the chairs, saying over her shoulder. "I couldn't be happier."

"Me too." Griffin came up behind Lilo and placed his taped hands on her shoulders. He nuzzled into her neck and inhaled deeply then tensed behind her. From the way he breathed deeply, she knew he was assimilating to the stimulation of her scent and touch. She patiently let him hold her, locked in his embrace until he worked through his visceral feelings. It made her weak at the knees and warm in the heart to know she was helping him with his sensitivity response. She knew him better than anyone else, and this was a way she could protect him—let him use her body to adjust to everything around him. She rotated and slipped her arms around his waist, looking up at him fondly.

"You mean that?" she asked quietly. "That you're happy?"

"Hey," shouted Tony from the mat. "If you two love birds are finished, we can get started."

Griffin grinned, and it lit up his face. For some reason, he seemed very smug.

A deep cough sounded at the door. Parker stood there, dressed in a black business shirt and suit pants.

"I have arrived," he said. "Now you can start."

"All right, let's get this lesson over with." Griffin strode to the mat. "Who wants to be schooled first?"

Lilo made her way to the seats where Grace and Flint sat. To Lilo's surprise, Mary had joined her children on the mat. Parker took Mary's vacant seat and handed a clipboard to Grace.

"Do you mind recording?" Parker pointed at the clipboard.

Flint took it from Grace with a disparaging look. "She's not your staff member, Parker."

"What?" he looked offended. "She's medically trained."

"Exactly, she should be on standby."

"It's no big deal," Grace offered.

"No, it's fine, Grace. Parker can do it himself." Flint handed the clipboard back to Parker.

"I'm the one running this thing," he said. "Despite what they're calling this, it's serving a purpose—to test out Griff's limits."

"I'll do it." Lilo put up her hand. "Just tell me what to do."

Parker scrutinized her. "Lilo, right?"

She nodded.

"Didn't get a chance to be properly introduced on Friday."

"Um, no," she said with a nervous laugh—the man was intimidating—as she took the clipboard. "You were busy being the owner, and I was busy being dragged into the alley and attacked."

It was meant to be a joke, but Parker's expression went from bored to downright murderous. The next word barely made it out of his clenched teeth. "What?"

"Um. Griffin didn't tell you?"

"Griff!" he bellowed then got up to join his siblings on the mat. The glares and clenched jaws were punctuated by the loaded stares they sent Lilo's way.

She bit her lip. "Why are they so angry at me? I was the one attacked."

"Not at you. They're angry because you were attacked in his club," Flint said with a furious frown. "Honestly, you can't hire good security these days."

"I didn't know." Grace patted Lilo on the leg. "Are you okay?"

"Yes. I mean, it was scary, but Griffin was there." Thinking back had her mind reeling. "In fact, he wiped the floor with those four men. I'm sure it won't happen again."

"No it won't," Parker said. "I'll be hiring security I trust." He paused, watching his family spar on the mat intently. "You said four against one?"

"Yeah, he pulled gutters with his power and pinned them to the wall. It was incredible to watch. Even the fire-escape came off."

Parker's jaw moved from side to side as though he were chewing on his thoughts. "This room won't do then." He clapped his hands. "Everybody out."

Liza protested. "But we were just getting started!"

"Into the alley," he elaborated. "This room is too small for Griffin's power."

Tony's eyes brightened. "Weapons?"

"I wouldn't bring anything metal, unless you want your ass handed to you," Mary noted.

"I got all the weapons I need right here." Evan's fists crackled and sparked with blue lights.

Grace snorted. "Show off."

Lilo couldn't hide the smile on her face. "If Misha were here, she'd be placing bets."

"Great idea!" Liza pointed at Lilo.

"Don't encourage her," Parker threw over his shoulder before leading them all outside.

CHAPTER TWENTY-EIGHT

GRIFFIN LAZARUS

Griffin stood before three of his siblings in the very alley he almost lost Lilo in. It only served to rile him up, not give them a sporting chance against his new power. It was just before midday, and most of the snow had melted. The cold snap was over—he glanced at the blue sky—possibly for good. Spring was on its way.

"Come on," Tony shouted, bouncing on his toes, fists in front of him. "We don't have all day."

Griffin glanced to the alley exit, just to be sure. Mary and Flint both stood, blocking any passersby from entering. Still —it was broad daylight, and not the sort of thing he wanted to be doing in a public alley, even if the only access was blocked, and all windows were boarded up on the opposite building. On second thought, he let his power fill his body until he buzzed from toes to head and connected with metal as though it were a phantom limb. He used that limb to shove a big red dumpster, dragging it from its space near the wall. Rubbish tumbled from the bin, and papers flew into the air, twirling. Mary watched it coming toward her with a wary eye until it stopped feet before her.

Much better. Good luck seeing over that.

Griffin turned back to where Parker, Lilo and Grace watched from the open doorway of headquarters. Parker rubbed his chin, deep in thought as he eyed the metal destruction littered around the alley, evidence of Griffin's last venture there.

"You're so going win this, baby," Lilo grinned.

He ground his bo-staff into the dirty floor. He just wanted it over with.

"Right, new plan." Parker walked over, eyeing the fallen fire escape behind Griffin. He pulled out a small handheld device in the shape of a rectangle. "It's clear you already have some control over your ability. This is a magnetometer. It's going the measure the strength of your magnetic force. Someone throw something metal at Griffin."

Tony looked deflated. "I thought we were going to spar."

"You think you can beat him?" Parker baited.

"Duh."

Parker's lips flattened. "Fine. But when this all goes pear shaped, remember you asked for it." He turned to Griffin. "Teach him a quick lesson, then we'll move onto measuring your output."

"I heard that!" Tony shouted.

Teach him a quick lesson. Right. Griffin turned his focus to his brother bouncing around, jabbing his fists in the air. He stalked to the center of the alley until they were only a few feet apart.

Tony glared at him, and a calm, lethal intent crept into his eyes. The man stopped bouncing and smoothly circled Griffin. Any well trained warrior could see that Tony wasn't as erratic and foolhardy as he led onlookers to believe. He was dangerous and deadly.

But no match for Griffin.

Make it quick.

Right.

Griffin searched Tony for a metal source. When his power connected, he almost felt bad for his brother. If he'd kept his wits about him, he might have remembered to remove his belt buckle. As it happened, the belt secured around his waist, sturdily weighted through his jeans belt loops.

Seeing Griffin unmoving, Tony launched—and jerked back as though being pulled by a string.

It wasn't a string. It was Griffin pulling him in the opposite direction by the force of his power.

Tony's face grew confused. He looked away, frowned, and then rallied. Anger swarmed over his features and he braced, boots against the ground, muscles straining against the unseen force of magnetism. Like a man staying staunch against a strong wind, Tony planted his boots and leaned forward. He stopped moving and just strained against the power. Impressive.

Still not enough. Griffin sensed metal supports buried within the soles of Tony's boots, and he added his power to those, swiftly dislodging Tony's feet until they kicked from underneath him and he went flying backward. When he landed with a thud on his back, stunned and staring up at the sky, Griffin spoke. "Anyone else?"

Liza frowned and glanced at her shoes, lifting them to peer under the souls. "You little fucker."

He shrugged.

"Good." Parker strode back to where Griffin stood. "Let's just accept that Griffin's better than you."

"You didn't give me a chance!" Evan whined.

"Me neither." Liza pouted.

Parker sighed. "You'll get your chance."

He pointed the magnetometer at Griffin. "Amp up."

Griffin flexed his fists. "Just fill with power?"

"Yeah."

Okay. Griffin did. He focused inwards, closed his eyes and concentrated on the building energy his body produced. All the while, Parker narrated to those who watched what he knew about magnetic fields.

Griffin kept going until Parker whistled in awe. "One Tesla."

He opened his eyes. "Is that good?"

"For comparison, a junkyard magnet that lifts a car is about two Tesla. Try lifting something."

Griffin lifted his palms and pumped out more power and levitated a second dumpster toward the dark part of the alley. The big, beat up red structure lifted a few inches from the ground, creaking and moaning with protest.

"Shit. Two Tesla. How do you feel?"

"Fine." He trembled and sweat formed. His insides began to cramp, but it wasn't anything he couldn't handle. He kept the dumpster levitating.

"Don't lie, Griff."

"It hurts a little," he confessed. "But I can handle it."

A small gasp from the peanut gallery. It was Lilo. The instant he made the connection, his hold on his power wobbled.

"Interesting," Parker noted. "Distraction weakens you. Do you need your hands out to lift it?"

"It helps me focus, but I guess not."

As if that were their cue to tear him down, Parker shot a look at his siblings and they attacked. One by one, they launched toward Griffin, and he defended by any means possible. Liza round-housed him. He jumped to avoid her swiping leg. Tony jabbed, and Griffin used his bo-staff to block. When Evan joined in, Griffin had no choice but to divert some of his power from the floating dumpster to his staff and use it to swing against Evan while his hands blocked the other two. Like a flurry of steel and leather, all four of them battled in a fast paced exchange of fists and boots.

Griffin held them at bay, until Evan got past his defense and locked his hand around Griffin's wrist. Electricity soared through him, seizing, cramping, tingling his teeth. His bones vibrated, and the dumpster shot meters into the sky. Griffin screamed in agony as his molecules tore apart, but Evan wouldn't release. The electricity did something to him—like being plugged into a power socket—he amped up. Got stronger.

"Three Tesla!" Parker barked. "Don't let go, Evan."

But just as quickly as the power rushed, it collapsed. Unable to speak from the torment, Griffin dropped to one knee, a horrendous crash sounded, and Lilo's distant voice screamed for them to stop, Evan let go.

White dots swam before his eyes. Everything hurt. His body felt like he'd been fried in a lightning storm. Griffin didn't realize he'd fallen until faces peered over him, blocking the blue sky in his vision.

"Griffin?" Grace waved her hand in front of his face. Pressure at his neck told him she checked his pulse. "Good lord, his heart is racing—200 bps."

"Griff?" Lilo was there.

He still couldn't speak. Could hardly swallow.

"You good, bro?" That was Evan.

He tried to nod. Must have worked because a collective sigh of relief surrounded him.

"Pulse is dropping."

He groaned. "That hurt."

Mary and Flint had jogged over.

"What happened, Parker?" Mary asked.

"My guess is Evan gave too much. Griffin's body couldn't handle it."

"It's too dangerous."

"I'm fine." He tried to sit, but only managed to prop himself up on his elbows. Lilo sat behind him and rested his head on her thighs.

Parker rubbed his stubbled jaw, a frown on his face. "I think it's best we avoid powering you up with Evan in the future. You might be fine this time, but the next, it could kill you."

CHAPTER TWENTY-NINE

DONALD DOPPENGER

In his small apartment, Donald had been accosted by Falcon and a handsome man in his fifties, wearing a suit. From the way he ordered Falcon around, it became apparent the tall man was her superior.

"Tell him what happened to you earlier," Falcon ordered Donald as she crowded him, edging him toward his ruined Chesterfield.

"I was taken and tortured by the Deadly Seven," he answered, sitting down. "Those bastards kept me in a locked room and threw water at my face, over and over until I answered their questions."

"Yet here you are. What were their questions?" The boss's voice was deep, thick and smooth as he loomed over Donald. It was the kind of voice that never wasted or minced words. He was a man people listened to. Reminded Donald of his asshole Senator brother. He hated him already. Fuck him.

"They asked how I was able to sense the sin of greed.

They asked where I got my temporary strength, and they asked something about a syndicate."

That last word stilled the man until Donald thought perhaps he was a cardboard cutout, and nothing more.

"So they're finally catching up." His voice was cold and dissonant. He left Donald and moved to the window overlooking the city.

Falcon followed. "I don't know why you haven't just killed them all. We know where they are, we know who they are. Get rid of them and be done with it."

The man breathed heavily through his nose. "Do you remember when we lost them, all those years ago."

"How could I forget?"

"We'd had such high hopes for them all." He sighed. "For a few years, I truly thought we'd lost them, but when they started popping up in this city, playing at comic book heroes, I knew all was not lost."

"We don't need them."

The man tilted his head marginally Donald's way. When he spoke to Falcon, a layer of disgust rolled off his tongue. "He's nothing like them. A poor carbon copy, no more."

"What do you want me to do with him?"

They spoke about Donald as though he wasn't there, as though he was a piece of trash to be thrown out.

"Keep the project online. While we wait for the originals to fall, we keep running contingencies."

"Agreed."

"Sin never sleeps."

"We chip away until the cracks become a chasm."

"Yes, my darling. Yes." His piercing blue eyes locked

onto Donald. "They asked you questions. What were your answers?"

Donald blinked. "I didn't tell them anything."

"So, they just let you go."

"Yes."

The boss let out a gust of air, muttering under his breath, "And you led us straight into this building, like lambs to the slaughter."

"Well—"

"Enough." Falcon was there before Donald could finish, threatening him with her closeness.

The boss looked to Falcon. "Your thoughts?"

"They will be tracking him, waiting for him to come to us. I don't think they'll actually be watching the building. We should be safe."

"Good." The boss relaxed and linked his hands behind his back. He turned to Donald. "What are you going to do about it?"

"About what?"

"Well, they humiliated you. They took everything from you. Are you the new Greed, or are you a coward?"

"I eradicated over ten greedy sinners already."

"Ten. Is that all?"

"I want more serum."

"Too much and you risk organ failure."

"I'll be fine."

The boss indicated to Falcon, and she left the room to return with a zip-lock leather satchel. She opened it and showed four syringes filled with glossy liquid. "You know the dose. One at a time."

But Donald's eyes were as greedy as his mind. The more he took, the stronger he would be, and fuck anyone who tried to get in his way this time.

"Eradicate more sinners, and you will get more of the serum." Falcon snapped the satchel shut and zipped it closed.

Donald nodded in a daze as he accepted the package from her.

The boss came forward to stand before Donald. "You know the real Greed is Griffin Lazarus, don't you?"

Every furious bone in Donald's body swelled. *Fucking Lazarus.* Should have known. Well, Donald knew exactly how to deal with him. He knew how to deal with them all.

"So, what will you do?" the boss asked. "Think big, Donald."

Donald's gaze spanned the city outside his window. There were thousands of greedy sinners out there. The more he removed, the more serum he got, the more powerful he became. No more vulnerability or humiliation from the Deadly Seven, he'd be serving it up instead, and as his benefactors went to leave his apartment, he thought, he'd see the last of them too.

"Whatever you choose." The boss paused in the doorway. "Just don't kill Griffin Lazarus. We want him alive."

And that made Donald the most furious of all. Fuck them. Fuck them all.

CHAPTER THIRTY

GRIFFIN LAZARUS

Griffin drove into work on Monday with Lilo in his car and parked in the underground garage of the Cardinal Copy newsroom.

She allowed him to open her door. It made a subtle warmth expand in his chest. He offered a hand and she accepted, just like she had all weekend and the routine of this action had settled deep. It cleared his greedy slate and calmed him to the core. As men would often say, he felt as though he'd been walking on clouds and had almost forgotten the yearning pressure greed left behind.

That was until they entered his office and she let go of his hand.

Sin ebbed like a lazy ocean, oozing back into his pores.

When she kissed him, he tugged her close and inhaled her soft natural scent to drown out the waves.

"You don't wear perfume anymore. Or chew blueberry gum," he noted, with a rumble of appreciation.

She smiled. "You caught that, huh? I stopped when I heard it bothered you."

"I never told you that."

"Grace did a while ago."

He stared for a while, unsure what to say. "No one has ever cared enough about me to change their scent. Usually my family like to push and test me. Our way has always been to keep each other strong. It's all we've known."

"Well, that's between you and them. For us, we can handle things our own way."

"Thank you," he whispered and captured her mouth in a searing kiss. The tingling in his teeth drilled into his brain, but he had to do it. He was drawn to her like a magnet. One last kiss before she went to her desk because he wouldn't see her for the rest of the day, and already the thought of her absence niggled at him. He wanted the sense of her to last.

Over the weekend, the more time he spent with her, the more her calming effect lasted. And when they spent any time apart, he would crave her touch like never before. She only went to the grocers for an hour, but when she'd come back, he'd been unable to help himself from stripping her naked the instant she got home. For a minute, he considered locking his office door and taking her on the desk. He considered just having the day off to go home with her, despite the fact he'd never played hooky in his life.

She moaned and rubbed her hands over his arms. "I like that you let me be affectionate in public."

It was an odd thing to say, and he was about to mention it, but she kept talking.

"Never-mind. It's nothing. So," she stated brightly. "I will see you at lunch. Here at twelve? I made that zucchini slice, remember?"

"Sounds delicious."

She preened from his approval with a slight blush. "Oh, and do you want donuts when I bring them around?"

"No, but—" he pulled a fifty out of his wallet. "You're always paying. Let me."

"I don't mind."

He arched a brow. "Let me pay."

"Fine," she conceded and took the money. "But I'll bring some by."

"I'll keep you updated if I have to leave the office."

She went to leave, but he'd almost forgotten.

"Wait," he said, stopping her. "I'll bring you coffee at morning break time. Same time?"

"Ten? If I can wait that long. No wait, nine-thirty. No. Ten. I need to cut down."

He walked to his desk, lowered his heavy backpack, and then cut a look to her as he sat in his chair. "Ten it is."

After she left, it took him a moment to acclimatize to being at work again. He regretted to admit he hadn't spared a thought for the place the entire weekend, or for Doppenger, who was his primary target now. This was his last secret from Lilo, and he had no idea how to broach the subject. She had been intimately involved with this man, and with so much bad blood between her and her family already, he didn't want to add more pain to her life.

After training on Sunday, Parker outlined the current situation with the imposter. Doppenger had stayed in his building for most of the weekend, most likely recovering from what Griffin had done to him in the warehouse, but they were all on standby, hence the backpack full of his combat uniform and battle gear Griffin had brought in.

It had been decided that all the seven would take their uniforms wherever they went. Crime happened during the day, as well as night, and with the Syndicate in town, they had to be vigilant.

Until then, he would assume his day-to-day duties at the Copy.

He spent the next few hours going over the data he'd gathered the previous week and working out which staff members he'd yet to assess before his nine-thirty with Fred the editor. Eager to have the meeting done with so he could get to Lilo, Griffin went to Fred's office early with his notes.

Cresting the hallway corner, he sensed two greed signatures within Fred's office and stopped just in time before walking in uninvited. The door was open. Inside there were two men having a discussion at Fred's desk. One man was obviously Fred, but the other man… Griffin's heart stopped at the sight of him. The immediate snapshot of this stranger had the blood roaring in Griffin's ears. Maybe it was because of his idyllic weekend, or maybe it was his recent confession trudging up old memories, but the man looked exactly like his fallen comrade—the one he'd killed.

James.

Impossible.

The same red hair, the same square profile, and the same broad shoulders. Sensing his arrival, the stranger turned his head, and Griffin held his breath.

Not him.

He exhaled.

Of course it wasn't him. James was dead.

"Griffin," Fred said, surprised. He checked his watch. "You're not due for another ten minutes."

"My apologies," Griffin replied, and glanced at the face of the stranger, one last time to be sure. "I'll come back later."

Heart pounding, he stepped back into the hall and out of view of the men in the office. He stood with his back to the wall and processed what happened.

He checked his wrist tattoo. Still balanced. So why was his internal chemistry going haywire? He closed his eyes and took deep, lungfuls of air, slowly blowing out through his teeth.

Why?

He kept repeating the question in his mind.

Why now?

James was dead. Griffin was paying his debt. He was in control.

But the panic was real.

No… he wasn't alive. It wasn't James.

His throat closed up as he realized how much of himself relied on Lilo now. Already he'd forgotten his balance protocol, leaving everything up to fate and the proximity to his soulmate. Forgetting his past could have devastating consequences. One snap from an ill timed comment could mean the difference between life and death for anyone around him.

A new level of anxiety seized him. Could this mean Lilo too? Could she be the one he irrationally lashed out on?

No. She wasn't at risk. Her very nature prohibited him from reaching that level of insanity… he hoped.

He needed to see Lilo with an urgency that had his eyes watering, so he strode immediately to her desk. She wasn't there.

It's fine. She's probably out at the bakery.

Forcing his insecurities away, he went to the break room and made their coffees, all the while counting in his head. When he'd sufficiently calmed his nerves, he returned to her desk station.

Still empty.

No.

A chill ran up his spine with the force of an avalanche. Why wouldn't she be there? He put the steaming mugs on her desk and surveyed the room. Everyone else seemed to be at their desks. Her bag hung on the back of her chair. *Not at the bakery then.* She wouldn't leave without her bag. Her computer was on the lock screen meaning she'd been gone long enough for her account to lapse.

Bev lifted her head to watched him curiously.

"Good morning, Bev," he said. "Do you know where Lilo has gone?"

The woman glanced at the mugs and back up to him. "Well, aren't you a darling."

"Lilo?"

"She's gone to meet Donnie. Shouldn't be long." She sat and returned to her screen as though her words hadn't pierced a hole in Griffin's heart.

Everything inside him roared.

His power magnified and surged, escalating and filling

him to the brink until it he almost exploded. Metal in the room rattled, computer screens blanked. He looked around wildly, just in case Bev was wrong and Lilo was somewhere close, but the walls closed in. More computers blanked. The lights above their heads flickered.

Focus, Griffin. Don't lose it. Not yet.

"How long ago did she leave?" he asked through a dry throat.

"About half an hour." Bev turned back around. "Is everything okay?"

"Did she say where she was meeting him?"

"No. What's happened?"

He didn't respond. He was gone, back to his office where he scooped up his backpack and then jogged to Doppenger's office for a glance inside. Empty.

Griffin went to the ground floor and stopped at the security room. Two white-uniformed men were sitting in chairs, lazily watching the wall of monitors in front of them. Littered on their desks were half empty packets of food and greasy fingerprint covered soda cans.

He banged on the doorframe. "I need you to look up some specific footage from the Cardinal Copy."

The men turned his way, frowning. The younger one had a mustache. His name badge said *P.Evernty.* Evernty the Everlong Mustache. The second man was olive skinned, had a body mass index of about twenty-eight, and nibbled a donut. Griffin couldn't read his name badge because a smear of chocolate icing covered it. This one lifted an eyebrow at Griffin's interruption.

"Uh. Buddy," the overweight man said. "I don't know

what workplace you're used to, but we don't just let any old Tom, Dick or Harry barge in here to—"

"We don't have time," Griffin cut him off. "A woman has gone missing." And if they'd been doing their job, they might have seen something.

They stared back at him with vacant expressions.

Anger surged through his veins, and the monitors flickered in the room. The disruption was enough to snap the men out of their stupor. Evernty waved him over, but the closer Griffin got to the monitors, the more they flickered and blanked out. He had to step back.

"What floor?" Evernty asked, tapping his monitor until the flickering stopped.

"Fourth floor," he answered. "Search the area of the office space for the journalists. Rewind to about half an hour ago. Her desk is the second on the right next to the break room. Lilo Likeke. Tall with brown hair."

"Miss Likeke's gone missing?" the overweight man said, looking devastated. "She was just in here an hour ago, giving us the donuts."

"So, Doppenger got to her between then and half an hour ago."

"You mean Donnie?" the overweight man asked, face going pale. "He wouldn't do anything to hurt her."

"Are you quite certain of that? Do you know the man personally?"

"Well, no, but… it's Donnie."

"Got it," Evernty said, pointing to footage of Lilo at her desk. "Here she is returning from the bakery."

"Fast forward until she gets a phone call and leaves."

The video footage was black and white and a little grainy, but with every minute, every second of watching, a sense of rising dread gripped his heart. And when she took a phone call and her lips pursed, Griffin knew that was the one. Within seconds she stood and said something to her office-neighbor, then left. He checked the time stamp and his watch. Thirty-nine minutes ago.

Tick-tock.

"She left her bag which meant she probably didn't think she had to travel far to meet him. Do you have street front cameras?" Griffin added urgently.

The young man flicked to another monitor, typed in some directives on his keyboard, and brought up the front of the building. There was Lilo meeting Doppenger at the front, and there he was looking haggard and feral-eyed as he grabbed her arm and forced her down the road with something pressed into her back. Most likely a gun.

Tick-tock.

Griffin slammed his hand on the security desk, rattling the foundations. Damn him for keeping Doppenger's real identity from her. If she knew the extent of his psychopathic tendencies, she would never have agreed to meet him.

His phone rang. Parker.

"You're late," Griffin growled down the handset.

A few seconds of silence and then Parker spoke. "Well, I'm calling you now."

"Now is too late. He's got Lilo. You promised me that wouldn't happen." Griffin stormed out of the security office, ignoring Evernty asking whether they should notify the police. "You said you were watching him."

Griffin kept walking until he got to the elevator and stopped. Up to the roof, or down to the basement?

"Shit," Parker said. "I was calling to tell you to suit up because we got him moving to a location on the south-end of the Quadrant."

"The footage on the CCTV cameras had him going north. Are you sure you had him going south? Check again."

The phone sputtered and crackled.

"Parker?" he called. No answer. He checked the handset, and it had blanked out. His damned power prevented him from using it. Dead. The phone was dead. He let an almighty growl of frustration out and then threw the phone against the metal elevator doors. How was he going to find her now?

Think, Griffin think.

Relax. Focus.

Remember your training.

Tick-tock.

Panic caught in his throat. He was running out of time. Statistically, the longer a kidnapping victim was taken, the harder it was to find them. Worse. Seventy-four percent of kidnapping victims were at risk of being murdered if not located within the first few hours. If something happened to her...

He forced the thoughts away and shut out all noise and sensation and focused on his breathing. In. Out. In. Out.

Roof. He was going to the roof.

Being masked would give him the freedom to fight unhindered, and with his industrial grappling hooks and bo-staff, traveling via rooftop could be more expedient than running through traffic. He punched the up button on the elevator and traveled to the highest level, then took the stairwell up to the roof, two steps at a time. When he breached the building, he discovered he was on a flat roof with air vents, large antennas and no one else but a flock of pigeons he disturbed. He was alone.

Quickly, he dressed into his combat gear and released his metal baton to extend to its full length. He stashed his backpack behind a vent, crouched low at the lip of the roof, and concentrated on the city. He would never feel Lilo, but Doppenger—he was another story. His greed was astronomical, and if Griffin focused enough, hard enough, he would find him.

And he would make him pay.

The city sounds blared in his ears.

Traffic. Car horns. Wind.

A man shouted angrily somewhere.

Pigeons gobbled.

All of it, he drove down and shut out until the only things he sensed were the cool breeze tickling his skin, the sun warming his face, and the eternal greed belonging to a city of millions.

Tick-tock.

CHAPTER THIRTY-ONE

LILO LIKEKE

The hard butt of a metal gun dug into Lilo's shivering back as she was herded along the busy street, away from the Cardinal Copy, and away from Griffin. She hadn't brought her coat. Only thought she was popping out to the street for a minute. Never believed Donnie would do this.

It was fine. Whatever was happening, it would be over in a minute. She knew it. Still…

"Why are you doing this, Donnie?" Lilo hissed, almost tripping over a dislodged slab of pavement on the pathway.

"Shut up and keep moving, princess." He put the heel of his palm into her back and pushed. "Unless you want to end everything right now."

She bit her lip to stop herself saying something she'd regret. They continued along the street. She tried to come up with an escape plan, but her brain wasn't working. It was locked on the hard object digging into her back, and the sad fear that of course this was happening—she'd only just found happiness with someone she could have a future with —of course it was being ripped away from her.

This is what happens when you want things for yourself.

She should never have agreed to meet Donnie outside the building. Damn her for being so trusting. He'd lured her out by saying he had something he needed to return, but hadn't wanted to do it inside the office. It was such a Donnie thing to do that she never questioned it, and she was keen to put that part of her life behind her. The instant she got out of the building, he pulled a gun from his pocket—just long enough for her to see it was there—then took her arm and jammed the blunt edge into her spine.

Did she have a sign plastered to her forehead saying, *Easy to kidnap?* This was the third time this week! First was Griffin dressed as Greed, then the Irish gangsters, now Donnie. God, she felt foolish. All that training in Krav Maga and nothing could prepare her for having a gun shoved at her temple or back.

Hopelessness seeped in.

They'd been walking for at least twenty-five minutes, and she wasn't wearing shoes for walking. Not since she's been able to catch a ride with Griffin. Oh, God. What would be going through his mind by now? He'd have turned up with her coffee. He was so reliable like that. Tears burned her eyes and her throat closed up as she imagined him standing at her empty desk, wondering how long to wait before sounding the alarm.

"Where are you taking me," she tried again.

He didn't answer, leaving Lilo to stew a little longer. She hadn't missed the bruises on his tired face. He hadn't been to work for the latter part of the previous week. Something was going on with him. The arguments and the fight with Griffin weren't the only sign. It was the desperation in his eyes every time he missed out on a news story.

"Dammit, Donnie. You're scaring me. I don't know what the hell you are hoping to achieve, but people will know I'm missing soon."

She was jerked around to see his face twisted into something ugly.

"Like who?" he asked, eyes blazing. "That uptight cocksucker, Lazarus?"

"Hey! We're no longer dating and haven't been for months. You have no right to—"

Pain burst at her cheekbone from his backhand.

Her eyes watered, her ears rang, and for a breath she couldn't see. When she gathered her senses, she registered not one passerby cared to intervene. She wasn't sure if anyone had even taken the time to turn their head.

Right. If she wanted to get out of this, she'd have to help herself. Having a gun shoved at her temple was hard to weasel out of, but she'd been trained in other ways to relieve a gun. She just had to wait.

"You think he's going to miss you?" Donald hissed. "He won't care if you're missing, Lilo."

"Yes he will." She knew he would.

"No, he won't. Because you're not worth it. You're just the daughter of a failed criminal who can't even hold on to her story without someone else writing it properly for her."

His hurtful words crushed her.

"Keep going." He jammed his gun into her and shoved.

She winced from the sting and stumbled forward.

Bide your time. Wait for an opportunity. Stall.

"What do you want, Donnie?" she asked. "Maybe I can help you get it."

Donnie wasn't taking the bait. With a one track mind, he pushed her onwards until they came to an intersection where a monorail passed overhead, and an exit to the subway beckoned. Maybe if she screamed, created a diversion, she could escape down there. Then again, maybe that bank on the corner would help. Surely there would be security guards inside.

Donnie halted her. "Stop here. Don't do anything stupid."

He was silent for a while as he gauged the street action. There were people rushing about, as you would expect for a Monday in the city. So many people, and he had a look on his face that she didn't like. He scrutinized the walkers by and kept darting a glance to the monorail and then to the bank. He was up to something.

With both of them standing still, she had time to assess him. He wore a long black trench coat with God knew what hidden inside, and he had an erratic aura about him. The black backpack slung over his shoulder contained something bulky. He hadn't shaved in days, and she wasn't even sure he'd washed. The man was about to snap—or already had.

"You know what I want?" he said, surveying the street, eying it like a hawk.

Lilo shrugged, eyeing his gun. "I give up. What do you want? Obviously me for something."

"I had a lot of time to think this weekend while I recovered from what your asshole did to me."

She barely contained the surprise on her face. What had Griffin done to him? He'd been with her most of the time. Except... except the night he left her after the kidnapping situation. It still wasn't adding up.

"I don't know what you mean, Donnie."

"Oh, come on, Lilo. You call yourself an investigative reporter," he scoffed. "You're not that blind, are you?"

"Spell it out for me."

"Your new man is one of them."

She pressed her lips tight. Damn him if he thought she'd give away anything. Instead, she bided her time, always vigilant, waiting for him to step into a position where she could relieve him of his weapon.

"Fine." Donnie rounded on her, waving the gun in the air. "Don't admit it, but you were there. You saw what they did to me."

"What they did to you?"

"Jesus, Lilo. I'm the new Greed. The new hero this city needs. The kind of hero who could get the job done. I was doing it better than them, until he came along and fucked with it all."

Her heart stopped. Donnie was the one who shot those people in cold blood? He shot Nathanial in front of her face... he shot Griffin.

Donnie called murdering getting the job done.

"Why?" she gasped.

But he didn't answer her, not directly. A red mottled rage covered his expression, and he spilled it all out: "They wanted Lazarus, not me. I'll always be the second choice for them, just like I was with my parents. No matter how hard I tried to be the better option, I was never enough. Well, fuck them. Fuck them all. I don't give a rat's ass what they want. This is about what I want."

He slipped his hand behind Lilo's neck. The fury in his eyes softened as he locked onto her, as though he really did have a soft spot for her. It made her skin crawl, and she tried not to show it. This man before her was nothing like the one she'd dated months ago. Okay, maybe a little. It was Lilo who'd changed. Lilo who'd garnered a little self-respect.

"You see, Lilo. I've been going about this all wrong," he said, eyes darting over her face. "I never thought about it until he came on his high horse to assess our productivity." He choked on a laugh. "Ironic isn't it? He was the one who made me realize that all this time they were getting all the attention, not me. All that effort we spend chasing a story, only to have our names printed in the teeny-tiny byline. Such little words compared to the big headline, don't you think?"

Lilo didn't like where this was going.

"That's what I want, Lilo. The headline. And if I can't have the fame, then I'll have the infamy and the fortune."

Donnie slammed his lips on hers, and she tried to pull away, tried to struggle, but damn him, he was so much stronger than her.

He jerked away, eyes showing way too much white. "I'm just going to take what I want from now on. You included. So keep going. To the bank."

Lilo juddered forward, a real sense of panic clawing at

her lungs because Donnie began to mumble like a crazy man. She'd missed her chance to grab the weapon, it had returned to its spot, jammed into her back.

"I'll show them sin," he mumbled.

"Who, Donnie? Show who?"

"They wanted him. They wanted me to ruin them, but I want them to see my face. I'm done hiding behind a mask. Stop here."

She had no choice, he jerked her to a halt. "You know what I never understood? You had everything growing up, Lilo. Your parents gave you anything you wanted."

"It was blood money. You know that."

"Who gives a fuck where the money comes from if you're rich. Money buys power, and soon, I'm going to be very powerful. You'd do well to remember that." He leaned in close to her ear. "Be a good little mafia girl and do as you're told. Just like you always have."

She flinched. In a way, he was right. He always knew that about her. From the time she lived under her parents' roof, doing as she was told, to the time she was with him. She loved hard, and she fell hard under their spell. Would it be the same with Griffin? Would there be something unseen in the future that dragged her down? Giving all of herself to her loved ones was her weakness, and she knew, that deep down, it all stemmed from a feeling of unworthiness. She wasn't enough for her parents. They had to lie and cheat and steal to fill their lives with *things*. And when she called them on it, threatened to leave… they let her go. She was never enough. All of her fight slowly bled away.

"Yes," he crooned. "You see it, don't you? You don't

have the guts to stand on your own. You're only worth as much as the person telling you what to do, what decisions to make, so I'm telling you now. See that armored vehicle?"

Lilo's gaze traveled across the street to the bank and to where an armored van was parked. Two black uniformed guards stood watch while a bank employee carried bags— seemingly of money—to the van's open back.

"We're going to steal that."

"Stop, Donnie."

He chuckled. "No. I planned for this. For everything."

He pulled something from his pocket. It wasn't a gun, but a syringe. What the hell? He jammed the needle into his neck and depressed, pushing the contents into his veins. Within seconds, he contorted and the tendons in his neck protruded. Bloodshot eyes widened, and he hissed, growled, sounding as wild as an animal trapped in human skin. He sucked in a deep breath and then exhaled slowly, eyes fluttering as whatever was in the syringe hit his nervous system. He pumped his fists. "Fuck, yeah."

She should run. Run right now while he was occupied, but that little voice inside her kept whispering… maybe he's right.

Too late. He pulled out his gun, and she almost lost control of her bladder, but he didn't turn it on her. He sighted the black uniformed guards and fired. A precise bullet to each heart. The loud cracking sound echoed, bounced off the buildings and ricocheted. People screamed and scattered. Lilo caught the flash of a mother and child almost being trampled in the rush to get away. When she turned back to Donnie, he'd gone insane. It wasn't a man peeking out from behind those eyes, it was a beast.

She found it hard enough to fight him when he was a man. Now this?

Donnie slung his backpack toward the footing of the monorail and then grabbed her hand and ran across the street toward the armored vehicle. Traffic beeped, and brakes suddenly engaged, tires squealing on the road. But a path had been cleared. Nothing was between them and the van except a few yards of street. Donnie almost ripped her arm out of its socket as he yanked her along. Before they got to the car, something long and narrow slammed into the ground in front of them, cutting them off. A long shuddering pole had implanted right into the asphalt.

"Let her go," came a low modified voice Lilo recognized.

Both she and Donnie whirled around. Griffin was perched up on the monorail, dressed as Greed and ready to fight. Elation lifted her spirits as she took in the blue face-scarf and hard eyes aimed with predatory focus at her captor.

His gaze flicked to Lilo. "It's going to be fine."

His words reached into her heart and banished all her self-doubt. He was here. For her. Why would he do that if he didn't think she was worth it? God, she wanted to smack herself over the head. She wasn't this afraid, timid person she used to be. Maybe loving hard had been her weakness, but now, it was her strength.

Screw Donnie. She wasn't going down without a fight.

Run! Her instincts screamed at her.

But his fingers were like an iron manacle around her

wrist, and the more she yanked and resisted, the harder he pulled her forward, running. When she resisted again, he didn't shoot her, he shot at Griffin. "Get in the car, Lilo."

Griffin raised a palm, and the bullet halted mid-air, as if stuck in invisible jelly. Then he slipped from the rail to land below, fist to the ground to steady himself. But Lilo couldn't see more, she was being shoved into the passenger side of the van, and pushed across the seats to the driver side.

"Start the car!" Donnie shouted, still shooting out the open window—keeping Griffin busy.

"No!" She tried opening her door to escape the other side, but Donnie grabbed her hair and yanked her back. Pain spiked at her scalp as he held her.

"Do it." He pulled her back and jammed his gun into her temple. "Now."

She trembled with fear, but she wasn't going to let him control her anymore. "No!"

"For fuck's sake, Lilo. Do I have to do everything for you?" He turned on the ignition. She shoved her elbow in his face, snapping his head back.

When he came back up, blood dripped from his nose, but before he could say a word, Griffin was there—standing before the van, looking at Donald with menacing eyes.

"I thought you learned your lesson, Doppenger. You're no match for me."

"You're right, I did learn my lesson," Donnie said. He aimed his gun out the window. "It just wasn't the one you think."

He swung his aim to point at his backpack left by the

monorail. *Bomb?* The train would be coming soon. It came every nine minutes. There were innocents on board.

"Bomb!" she shouted.

Griffin must have yanked on the gun with his power, because it suddenly seemed as though Donnie grappled the air for control of his pistol. But, instead of being worried, Donnie turned to Lilo with a grin. He pulled something from his other pocket. A remote detonator.

"This is the infamy part." Donnie's thumb pressed down on the red button.

CHAPTER THIRTY-TWO

GRIFFIN LAZARUS

Griffin had been standing only meters away from the monorail sub-structure when the bomb went off, exploding into him. On instinct, his hands went up to protect himself, and he rolled, letting his leather take the full impact of the blast. The kinetic clash launched him backward and slid him across the asphalt. For a moment, he lay face down, feeling the heat while his ears rang.

Arms good.

Legs can move.

Not on fire. Not dead.

His magnetic power must have taken the brunt of the blast. His skin was scorched in patches through his leather, but he was okay.

Alive. And seriously pissed.

He rolled his limber body to land swiftly on his feet and stared at the armored vehicle. Doppenger had his gun pointed at a frightened Lilo, and when he noticed Griffin unscathed, he became infuriated. Griffin reached out with his power to grasp the car, intending to bring it closer, but a loud creaking sound drew his attention over his shoulder. The steel metal structure holding the monorail began to buckle. The rail track snapped in two, and the steel column fell hard, bringing the track with it. Griffin let go of the van and moved his power to grip the monolith framework, but he got to it too late. With a deafening crash, the rail collapsed, throwing cloud and debris everywhere.

It was then Griffin heard the telltale sound of screeching metal-on-metal as the approaching Nine-Train grew closer.

He tapped his earpiece to open up the communication channel. "Where are you?" he shouted. "The rail has collapsed."

"We're almost there," came Parker's voice through his earpiece. "Hold on."

Griffin widened his stance, pushed his force out and readied himself for the train's impact. He had to save the people inside.

Had to save Lilo.

But the train.

He roared in frustration, knowing he had no choice, despite the wants of his heart. Protecting a train load of innocents was his first priority. He would kill Doppenger if he hurt Lilo. Kill him. The darkness of his past had nothing on the depths of his heart. The screeching grew louder. He only hoped he had enough force to hold the heavy train as it approached the end of the line. He'd never stopped anything that powerful before.

"The train is almost here," he bit out. "I don't know if I'll be enough to stop it derailing. Someone needs to get through to the driver. We may need emergency assistance."

The closer the heavy object came, the less faith he had. Almost there. Get ready. He braced, heart racing every second the screech of the train tracks escalated.

Impact!

He staggered as his power caught the force of the train speeding toward him. Metal wailed, rails screeched and, through it all, he heard the distinct sound of tires spinning as the armored van took off behind him, taking Lilo away.

His defiance surged and all he could think was that he couldn't let them get away, he couldn't let Doppenger take her from him. He needed her. He had to protect her.

Protect them both.

The magnetic force inside him pumped, and, like flexing a metaphysical muscle, he strained for more force to generate. Steady, steady. Soon he was filled to the brink with power. He took one hand from the train, now almost teetering at the edge of the broken rail line, and caught hold of the armored vehicle, halting its tracks. The van's tires spun, burning rubber.

Griffin trembled, but smiled, then... pain sliced through him and he roared in agony as the severe demand on his resources strained. It felt like his muscles were ripping apart, like his eyes were bleeding, and he heard Parker's voice from a distance: "*Greed*. You're tearing yourself apart. It's too much. Let go of the van. Stop, Greed, stop!"

But he couldn't stop. If he did, then Lilo would go, or the train would fall.

"Let go of the van, Greed. Let go."

"NO!" he bellowed, about to snap. "I won't let her go."

I need her.

His throat closed up. No. No. He couldn't but—the train. People screamed as his hold loosened and it tipped past the broken edge, coming toward him. He let go of the van and transferred his power to the train, pushing back on its nose. Slowly it edged backward, creaking and cracking, and shrieking at him, but it was nothing compared to the sound of his heart breaking as the van began to drive away.

LILO LIKEKE

"DRIVE, LILO. DRIVE!" Donnie shoved the gun at her temple.

"I'm trying, I'm trying." She planted her foot on the gas, but made the van bunny hop in her haste.

Donnie growled.

"I'm sorry!" she cried. "I rarely drive. I-I've forgotten."

"I know what you're fucking doing, Lilo. You're stalling. It won't work."

He placed his hand over hers and crunched the gearshift. It grated but then she felt it slot into place. *Shit.*

"I don't know why you're doing this," she said, trying another tactic. "You said you wanted infamy, but no one can see your face in this car. No one knows this was all because of you!"

"Shut up!"

Like hell she was going to shut up. Being quiet was never her thing.

"You said you planned this well, except you haven't. You haven't accounted for the fact that you won't get a mention, let alone the headline. Not if I have anything to do with it."

He growled and shoved his leg onto her side of the van, squashing her foot and hitting the gas. When the van jerked forward, Lilo caught the rear van doors swinging in the side-mirror. Her stomach flipped as she realized another of his mistakes. He'd forgotten to shut the doors. Earlier, he said money was power… and if anything, Donnie was a greedy man—she knew what to do.

"Unless you want your brains all over the window, you'll drive, Lilo," Donnie snapped.

"Fine, but you need your seatbelt on," she said, clipping hers on.

"Fuck that, go!"

Don't say I didn't warn you.

She pushed on the gas and sped off, heading toward the brick wall of the butcher shop across the road. If she could just crash into that, the bags of cash would go flying out the back and spill over the road. It might be enough to distract Donnie. She pushed harder on the gas, lurching them forward.

"What are you—"

But she didn't get to the wall. The van hit the box curb and became airborne. For a moment it felt like they were flying. Her stomach dropped like a stone, the van tilted, random items inside the cab floated and then they crashed, hard, glass shattering. White airbags compressed and a powder stench filled the air. The wind knocked out of her. Her head hit the window on the side. The seatbelt burn in her shoulder stopped her from getting far, but Donnie's body ricocheted around the cab as they tumbled around. One second he sandwiched her into the driver window, the next he bounced back to hit the passenger side.

The van stopped moving and every cell in her body ached. She was the right way up. A warm steady trickle ran along her cheek. The chemical stench of burned tires filtered through the broken windows, or maybe it was something else. Something related to the accident. Oh, God. The instant she registered the trail of blood on her face, pain exploded at her temple and she cried out in pain. Everything around her blurred. With trembling hands she tested her head and landed on a sore wet bump, but was too afraid to explore the wound further.

I'm okay. I'm alive.

Gasping for air, she checked Donnie.

He lay forward on the dash, moaning.

Damn it, he was gathering consciousness.

Quick. Escape. Now.

Before it was too late.

Survival orders snapped in her brain, urging her into action. Go. Go. Get out of there. Those trembling hands shifted to the clasp on her seatbelt. It took her three goes, and great big gulps of air before she got herself unbuckled, but then Donnie was sitting up. His eyes were glazed and adjusting focus. Blood streamed down to his face in dark rivulets.

"You bitch," he rasped incredulously, blood spitting from his mouth. "I trusted you. I wanted you with me. You bitch!"

Lilo went for the handle on the van door and opened, but he shoved her back into her seat with a forearm to her neck, choking her. "You're not going anywhere."

"Screw you, Donnie." She locked onto the gun, fallen in the gap between the car seat and the center console. If she could just reach it. She'd—

A glimpse of something moving in the rearview mirror. It was the money from the van. Bags had indeed fallen from the back as they flipped. Cash went everywhere, flying, twirling and floating in the air like an expensive tornado. And like clockwork, the greedy citizens of Cardinal City came out of the woodwork to capitalize on the accident.

"They're stealing your money, Donnie," she rasped through his chokehold. "Money is power, right? If you don't get it, you'll be weak. You're done for."

It was all she needed to say and his eyes flashed wide, his pupils were tiny pinpoints of rage, and then he howled. "NO!"

He let go of her and fumbled in his jacket pockets to pull out a leather compendium which he unzipped. Three syringes filled with a substance similar to what he'd already injected himself. Wide-eyed and erratic, he darted a glance outside to where Griffin helped secure the train, to the approaching two dark figures—Griffin's deadly back-up—and then back to the people thieving his money.

"I need more. I have to use it all," he murmured and began to inject himself with haste.

All she could think was to get the gun. It was protection.

Get it. Get it. She reached in the gap, but the weapon was wedged hard, caught on the under wire of the seat. Her fingers couldn't get a stronghold. The gun kept slipping, falling deeper under the seat.

The growl that ripped from him as he breathed through his pain wasn't entirely human, and when he depressed the third and final syringe into his neck, Lilo watched, petrified, as an animalistic transformation came over him. That monster peeking out from behind his eyes became real.

Veins in his head, neck and hands bulged. His shoulder muscles expanded, stretching his coat, creaking and groaning until the seams split. He grunted and snorted like a bull at a red flag, and when he finally faced her, she saw nothing human left. His eyes were vacant.

"Mine," he grunted and reached for her, but his new larger frame took some getting used to and he knocked his head on the rearview mirror. He shook, dazed.

She abandoned her efforts with the gun, snapped open the car door, and tumbled into the street.

An almighty beastly roar reverberated in the cabin of the van, shaking its foundations.

Adrenaline scorched Lilo's body. She crawled as fast as she could, heedless of the asphalt scraping her knees and hands. When she looked over her shoulder, Doppenger tore the roof off the van from the inside, and burst out to land adeptly. He spied the thieves stealing his money, and he spied Lilo on the floor escaping him. He roared and it thundered through the air.

CHAPTER THIRTY-THREE

GRIFFIN LAZARUS

Griffin strained, his power at the brink. The amount he'd expended on holding the van at the same time as the train had seriously taxed him. Now he took too long pushing the train car back on the rail. Parker was inside the train, helping passengers move to the rear of the cabin in case Griffin's power collapsed and he lost his hold. Once evacuated, they could disconnect the front car from the rest of the train and let it fall. Then Griffin could help Lilo. God, he needed her. Every ache in his bones cried out for her soothing touch. *Just a few more minutes. Just a few more.* Until everyone was out of the train. *Hold. Hold.*

Dressed as Envy, Evan jogged up, arriving at the scene. "What the fuck is that?"

Dragging with lethargy, Griffin turned around and wished he hadn't. The scene behind him was chaos. The twisted and deformed features of a man too big for his clothes—too beastly to be human—swatted bystanders as they tried to collect the fallen cash bags. It was Doppenger turned monster. He had the same horrific aura of greed, but now had a face to match his sin. That was the darkness inside made real.

Could that have been Griffin once?

Was that a future without Lilo?

Bodies went flying through the air as though they were soccer balls, and then the beast turned—caught sight of Lilo crawling away—and bellowed in outrage.

Griffin's throat closed up. He stepped toward her, but the train came with him. Passengers screamed.

"Hold steady, Griffin." A voice through his ear comms.

Lilo.

The beast made a grab for her ankle, snarling and growling. He missed, but then swiped again, this time catching and dragging her toward him. She screamed.

"Lilo!" Griffin shouted and his hold wobbled. He turned to Evan. "Help her!"

"Shit. Fuck!" Evan swore. "I can't electrocute him while he's holding her. It'll pass into her."

Evan pulled *shuriken* from his belt and threw them at the beast's head, but the metal throwing stars glanced off as though made of plastic.

Thousands of screams overhead snapped his attention back to the teetering train. Griffin was tired. So tired. If he didn't let go soon, he'd break. And people were in danger. But he had to save Lilo. He would die before he let that happen.

"Power me up," he ordered Evan.

"He's like a fucking ape. King Kong. Jeezus."

"EVAN. Focus here. I need a boost. Just like we spoke

about at training. Give me a boost."

Evan turned on Griffin, noticing for the first time his dangerous strain. "But Parker said it was risky. You could die."

"I don't care!" he shouted, one eye on Lilo struggling against the beast. "There's no time. Do it."

Evan frowned, but acted immediately. He placed his hands on Griffin and electricity surged into his nervous system. Griffin seized in agony as the power threatened to rip his atoms apart, but with each millisecond of charge, his magnetism boosted and he grew the strength to push the train back on the rails until it reached safety. The instant it had, Griffin twisted out of Evan's grip because the subatomic manipulation was excruciating. His vision blurred. He tasted metal. Gasping, he dropped to his knees, not only cramping from the recent surge, but the deadly greed hitting him from the beastly version of Doppenger now gathering Lilo in his large claw-like hands.

Lilo.

He had to keep going. Had to get up. Had to go hard.

Trembling, Griffin lifted a knee and then pushed himself upright, reaching for his metal bo-staff still wedged in the asphalt. It trembled and shook until it dislodged and soared through the air to his awaiting hand. Biting through his pain, he ran toward her, legs pumping. Two meters out, he leaped and swung his staff toward the beast's head. When the force of the rod hit the monster, vibrations rang along Griffin's arms and he went flying backward from the transfer of energy.

When he landed, he rolled and returned to an attack

position, staff poised to his side for balance.

Doppenger had let go of Lilo and was crouched, shaking his head for focus.

He shouldn't be able to withstand that sort of blow. It would have caved any normal person's skull in. For the first time since arriving, Griffin's battle confidence disintegrated. This was no normal foe. Nothing liked they'd faced before. He was bigger than them, stronger than them, but not smarter than them.

"Lilo." Griffin dashed for her and lifted her to her feet, guiding her swiftly away. "Are you okay?"

Blood oozed from a wound at her temple, and her brown hair was covered in white dust, but she held her head high. She barely had a chance to nod before a deafening growl filled the street, rumbling the ground: *"Mine!"*

The grating sound froze Griffin for a good moment before his instincts kicked in. He turned to see the Doppenger beast approach with murder in his eyes. "Give me!"

Tiny in comparison, Evan launched onto Doppenger's back and gripped him around the neck. What the hell happened to make Doppenger that way? What had the Syndicate fed him?

Evan loosed his power. White and blue light sparked at his fingertips, sizzling into the giant whose eyes rolled back in his head.

"What happened to Doppenger?" Griffin asked, hand on Lilo's shoulder, still guiding her toward the safety and shelter of a building.

"He injected himself with something," she said,

breathing hard. "Triple the dose he was meant to have. No wait. Four times the dose."

"Do you know what it was?" Parker came up behind them, dressed as Pride—full leather combat gear, purple mouth mask, dark hood shadowing his eyes.

Lilo shook her head, then winced, hand moving to her bruised and bloody cheek. "Only that it doesn't last long, that's why he took more doses."

"Must be what gave him the power of Greed," Griffin said. "And it's twisted him into something else."

Sirens blared in the distance.

"Shit," Parker said. "Cops will be here soon. We gotta wrap this up."

The passengers must be safe. All that was left to do was secure Doppenger for the authorities to deal with. Or perhaps it would be better to take him back to HQ for investigation.

The instant the thought formed in Griffin's head, Doppenger rallied and resisted the electrical charge pumping into him. His eyes stopped rolling, they refocused on Griffin with his hand on Lilo and broke free from his constraint like a raging bull. He threw Evan from his body and charged.

"Get back, Lilo." Griffin pushed her away. "Get to safety."

Griffin wasn't sure if it was pride or stupidity, but Parker charged at Doppenger first.

"Pin him down like you did with those guys in the alley," Lilo said to Griffin. "Then all you need to do is wait until the serum wears off."

"Good idea," he said and scoured the area for something suitable. He was still searching when he noticed Lilo hadn't moved.

"Go!"

She got two steps, but hesitated and turned back. "I won't go far. I have to be close so I can report the truth."

She must have seen the fear in his eyes. What if he blacked out? What if he killed everyone, including her? He was running perilously close to the bottom of his reserves, and he didn't want to know what he'd do if he was pushed to the limits, but it might take a monster to beat a monster.

"You need to be as far away from me as you can," he ground out. "I can't have you hurt. Parker and Evan won't hold him for long."

"Griff." She saw right through him. "Don't hold back. You got this."

He shook his head, denying it.

She limped back to him, gripped the base of his neck and forced him to look at her. She took his bare fingers, letting her touch soak into him.

"I know you're holding back. You're afraid I'll get hurt. You're afraid of losing control. But you need to do this, Griffin. I trust you. You have to give it your all. He could hurt everyone here, not just me." She touched her forehead to his, her silent proclamation of solidarity, and two-seconds later, she was gone, back to a group of bystanders under the butcher shop awning, asking around for a camera phone.

Give it your all.

Her words rang in his ears and he knew she was right. He wasn't the same man he was back then. He'd trained, he'd taught himself to manage his sin, and now thanks to her, he was balanced. She just gave him an extra boost with her touch. It was time.

Griffin turned back to his brothers and assessed. Parker had just been hit and stumbled. Evan whipped out his Katanas, now going for the deadly option. He rotated them by his side as he studied the beast, circling him.

Pushing off with burning thighs, Griffin bolted forward. As he got within a few meters, he used his staff to vault feet first at Doppenger's chest—kicking him in the center. The ground quaked as the beast crash landed, sliding backward until he hit the box-curb on the other side of the street.

"Envy, pin him," Griffin ordered. "I'll help."

"With pleasure." Evan stabbed through Doppenger's shoulders with his swords, driving through with all his might until the metal went through soft skin, flesh and maybe bone. Griffin used his power to continue the Katanas' momentum and slammed them through to the asphalt, embedding them deep. When Evan let go, the blades were almost buried to the hilts.

Doppenger's whine of pain shook the sky, and he thrashed about on the ground, back arching ineffectively. Froth foamed at his mouth. Griffin clenched his teeth as he held on with his power. "Pride and Envy, reinforce the Katanas. I'll find something else to pin him with."

For once, Parker took the order and joined his brother in holding a fist to each Katana handle, keeping the beast pinned like a mounted scientific specimen. Griffin dropped his bo-staff, and with his power, ripped a gutter pipe from a side building. Water sprayed, dripping as the metal pipe levitated closer. Griffin slammed it lengthwise over Doppenger's thick legs, stapling him into the asphalt, locking his ankles in place.

"Get another two for his wrists," Parker added.

When he had done the same for Doppenger's hands, they all stood back, gingerly taking their hands from the beast's body.

Heedless of the swords in his shoulders, Doppenger writhed and snarled, gnashing his teeth, spitting foam. "She's mine!" he kept repeating.

"She's not yours." Griffin's words solidified something he'd been contemplating. He wanted Lilo to be his. Committed forever.

He shot a look in her direction and found her filming the entire thing. Tension loosened in his shoulders. She was safe. The police were coming. It was over.

A thousand voices in his head screamed for him to stay put, but he needed to be with her. He took a few steps. Lilo lowered her camera, their eyes met, perhaps thinking the same thing. She stepped away from her group, and into the street, hesitant. It was as though his magnetic power pulled her straight to him. She took another step.

A steady grip landed on Griffin's shoulder.

"Not now. People are watching." Parker's gruff computerized voice rumbled. "You can't be associated like that. You've already shown her too much attention. More will put her in danger."

Damn him. He was right. Evan had already skated up the damaged gutter pipe brackets and headed for the rooftop like a shadow's afterthought. Headed home.

The police arrived, getting out of their vehicles further down the road blocked with traffic. Red and blue lights flashed, reflecting off the city buildings.

"You know I'm right," Parker added as though reading his thoughts. "Let's go before the—"

Greed flared.

A colossal weight landed between Griffin's shoulders, slamming him face first into the ground. His forehead smashed on the rocky surface and everything jarred in pain. Warm, wet liquid ran over his face. He barely caught the beastly *"Mine"* before the weight lifted from his back.

In horrifying slow motion, Griffin understood— Doppenger had broken free from his constraints, had torpedoed into him and used him as a stepping stone to get to Lilo. The beast lunged with lethal speed, but he wasn't fast enough. Griffin's hand snapped out and caught the meaty ankle as it soared over his head, tugging them both back to the ground. Beast and man grappled and scrambled to their feet, but with Lilo's blurred face in the distance, Griffin's determination turned rock hard.

I trust you.

Give it your all.

Time to end this.

A calming sense of peace settled over him. He threw out his hand, calling his bo-staff through the air. The cold metal surface hit his palm, and he swung the pole around Doppenger's body, using it for a chokehold. He pulled tight across the larynx, blocking the beast's airways, using his power to boost his strength and pull the metal bar closer.

Choke.

The injured beast struggled and Griffin wasn't sure if the serum wore off, or it was his irrational need to protect his mate, but Doppenger choked out within minutes, slowly going limp within Griffin's arms until his massive body slumped to the ground unconscious. Heaving air into his burning lungs, Griffin refused to remove his eyes or fists from the beast, now slowly shrinking to become the man once more.

The serum. It wore off. He was vulnerable again.

Parker tapped him on the shoulder. "He's done. We need to go."

But Griffin kept the pressure on.

"Greed," Parker warned.

Choke.

"Greed!"

Griffin let go.

Gathered behind them were city cops, pistols out warily, unsure who to point them at. He couldn't see Liza among them. *Shit*. Had they stepped out of the frying pan, only to land in the fire?

Someone shouted, "They saved us."

The police slowly lowered their weapons.

"I have a recording," Lilo said to the closest officer, stepping toward him. "I'll show you everything."

While she distracted with her camera-phone, she shot Griffin a meaningful look full of urgency. *Get out of here while you can*, she seemed to say. *I've got your back*.

And in that moment, Griffin knew she would. Always.

Taking advantage of the confusion, he turned and followed Parker swiftly and expertly to make their escape.

CHAPTER THIRTY-FOUR

WYATT LAZARUS

Straddling his idle Ducati, Wyatt Lazarus watched the aftermath of the monorail disaster unfold. His vantage point from the hilltop street leading to the City Bank gave him a full view of the cluster-fuck incorporated. Cops swarmed over the place like a pack of drunk bees. Obviously no one knew what the hell was going on because bystanders contaminated the scene, same as the dumbass police officers. All they needed now was for—*fuck it.* There they were. The press scooted into the cordoned off area with their cameras.

His fists squeezed his motorcycle's handlebars until metal creaked and his knuckles went white.

It should have been him down there helping his family put that beast to bed, but instead he'd been stuck up there, paralyzed and watching from the sidelines like some pre-schooler afraid of his own shadow. But Wyatt wasn't afraid. He was angry. Pissed. Furious.

Blissfully consumed with wrath.

He had been for months, ever since… he bit his tongue,

unable to voice her name, even in his thoughts. A metallic bitterness burst through his mouth as he drew blood, shedding light on his emotional state. He couldn't remember the last time he wasn't filled with wrath, but he didn't give a shit. Hell, it gave him something to focus on.

The longer he watched the scene, the more his anger simmered. He was angry at Sara for betraying him. Angry at his brother Evan for not speaking out loud enough. Angry at the rest of them for taking the bait, too. Angry at the world for making him what he was today because it was their failing humanity that prompted the Syndicate to create the Deadly Seven in the first place. He didn't ask for this shit.

But most of all, he was angry at himself; he should have seen it coming.

A fierce longing tightened his chest. All he ever wanted was a normal life, a normal family, and a woman who called bullshit on his false pretensions. But instead, he got the colossal mess that was Wyatt-fucking-Lazarus.

He revved the engine and cast one last glance at the milling mess, trying to pick up the pieces of something he had yet to fully understand. Part of him wanted to go back to the family, to rejoin the fight, and he fucking hated it. If he wasn't fighting to keep the peace, then he was working against it, but he was so sick with fury that he couldn't see straight. After everything, a part of him still wanted to be back with the family who weren't strong enough to save him from that humiliation, but the other part… the bigger and louder one said they didn't need him. They were doing fine on their own.

Two of them had now found their fated soulmates.

Wyatt would have to be blind to miss the way Griffin had fought to save his girl, or the way she ran to him like he was her world... and he knew that he'd never have that. He laughed bitterly at the irony. For the past few years he'd accused Evan of deadly envy, but it was now Wyatt feeling the everlasting burn of that sin.

Still, even if he miraculously found his soulmate, he'd never be able to commit. He'd never find true peace. As if to remind him of the fact, the scar at his throat twinged and cramped until he rubbed his finger along the thick, ropey disfigurement. He smoothed the tension away. It had been months since he'd lost the use of his voice and all he'd managed to speak was a whispered rasp. Forget Heaven, he'd never work in any prestigious restaurant again. Say goodbye to the point of his fucking hard earned Michelin Star. He couldn't shout orders to save his life. As if anyone would hear his chicken scratch voice above the din of the kitchen. *Fuck it.* He was done. He kicked the asphalt, rocking the bike.

Probably got what he deserved for having faith in a woman who not only twisted the knife in his heart, but sliced it across his throat.

When the uncomfortable ache in his neck subsided, he plucked the tracker chip from the undercarriage of the Ducati and held the tiny bug-like device. He'd always known it was there. It was hard not to miss the green glow in the dark, but he hadn't been quite ready to make a clean break from his family... until now—now the loved up family was multiplying in his absence. He dropped the tracker-bug and crushed it beneath his boot. That life was over for him.

He'd never be able to trust another woman again, and the thought of being surrounded by their happiness made him sick to the stomach.

He snapped his visor down, revved the Ducati engine to its monstrous capacity, scaring the shit out of a little old biddy walking past with her grocery shopping, and then he took off in the opposite direction, not looking back.

It was time to leave Cardinal City for good.

CHAPTER THIRTY-FIVE

GRIFFIN LAZARUS

Along with his two brothers, Griffin strode into the basement headquarters of Lazarus House, still wearing his full combat gear. He went straight for the central operations room where Flint and Sloan sat behind their laptops at the briefing table, and Mary paced the floor beside them, repeatedly flipping a dagger in her hands.

Griffin tugged his hood from his head and plucked the face mask off. Parker and Evan did the same, slowly shedding their second skin. Flint had a headset on and was listening intently to something. Sloan's gaze was locked on her screen.

While Evan pulled out his phone, no doubt to contact Grace, Parker moved to stand behind Flint and Sloan for a better look.

"Have you heard anything?" Griffin asked them.

Flint held up his finger in a way that meant he'd be with him soon. Sloan, on the other hand, completely ignored him. And when Parker rolled his eyes dismissively and walked away, Griffin took a peek at her computer. The rage that surged and bubbled under his skin was so severe that the computers flickered, blanking out.

"Ah, bras! What was that for?" Sloan scowled at him.

"You're playing a game," he shot back. Unbelievable.

"That's because there's nothing else to do. Jeez. Take a chill pill."

Nothing else to do. Did she mean…

"Yes. She's fine. Liza has her and will bring her in shortly."

He exhaled in pure relief.

Mary gave him a small smile and offered her knife. "I find keeping my hands occupied helps."

She'd always had his back, even when he thought she didn't. He'd been so wrong to take it out on her.

"Thank you, mama." He tugged her in for a crushing hug, riding out the waves of sensation because he knew she missed it.

"You did good, Griff," she murmured, then pulled away. "You saved about forty people on that train. And that was only the car in danger of coming off. If you weren't there, and the entire train derailed, the death toll could have been in the hundreds."

The gravity of the situation made the room feel smaller. He needed to see Lilo. It was an aching sensation that went beyond his muscles lethargy. He wouldn't be settled until she stood before him, safe and sound in his arms. And the second he had her, he wasn't letting go.

Mary pressed her knife into his hand. "It helps to keep your hands occupied."

He turned the blade in his hands. She might be right.

She gently patted him on the arm and surveyed the dried blood on his face. "Are you badly injured?"

He nodded, then shook his head. It was sore, but nothing he couldn't handle. "I'm good."

She went to stand beside her husband, rubbing his shoulders with affection. Seeing their love only made him long for Lilo again, and his power surged, blanking out every screen in the room.

"Yeah, we need to keep you away from the tech," Flint said and waved in the opposite direction. "Shoo. You're disrupting the feed, and I'm listening to scanners to make sure nothing else happened."

Parker gripped his shoulder and tugged him back. "This ability of yours is going to affect your new suit. Damn it, I'll have to insulate it to keep the tech functional. In fact, I'll have to insulate all of them. Come. Distract your mind while you wait."

For the first time, Griffin noticed a dark figure inside a glass display cabinet at the corner of the room. It was a mannequin wearing a new version of their combat gear— gray, not black, and made from a slick fabric that looked both mat and glossy, depending on the angle approached from. The hood was a familiar shape. A face guard covered the nose and mouth. It was streamlined and without seams.

That made Griffin extremely happy. The seams on his outfit sometimes irritated and rubbed the wrong way. But… if there were no seams…

"How do you get it on?" he asked.

"I'll go into the details when everyone is here," Parker replied. "Where is Tony, by the way?" he asked Mary.

Her gaze darkened with disapproval. "Sleeping off a hangover."

"It's after lunch," Parker scoffed. "I was hoping to discuss our progress with the Syndicate."

"More like lack of progress, don't you mean?" Sloan muttered, without taking her eyes from her game.

Parker stormed to Sloan and slammed her laptop lid closed, almost catching her fingers on the keyboard. "Exactly!"

"You asshole. I was in the middle of a battle."

"You should be focused on *this* battle. The one where you can actually lose your life."

Sloan screwed up her nose and slumped in her seat. But she didn't say a word because she knew Parker was right.

"The Syndicate is dangerous, and they're up to something," Griffin said, trying to divert their hate filled attention from each other. "We've learned that they can grow clones and give them enhanced abilities. They can now, by the flick of a syringe, alter someone's DNA and give them enhanced abilities instantly."

"We also know that their clones—or replicates as they called them—expired after a few months of being awake." Parker went to the central bench which also doubled as a computer screen, cleared the surface and wrote with an erasable marker: 2 *month life expectancy*. "And the serum was instant, but the effects were temporary. What else do we know?" He looked at them.

"They want samples of our blood," Griffin offered and Parker wrote it down.

"Why?" Mary asked. "Can they use your blood to clone you?"

"No. Not the way they've taken the samples."

"But if they got more blood, fresh from the vein?"

Parker shrugged. "It's possible. Scientists in Japan have successfully cloned mice from a drop of blood."

"Jesus," Flint cursed from his corner and met Mary's worried eyes.

"But I don't think that's what they're doing." Parker tapped the pen on the bench. "I think they don't have enough information yet."

"Why do you say that?" Evan walked over to join Griffin and Parker at the bench.

"Because they wanted Griffin's blood. It seems like Evan's one sample wasn't enough. They could go after Evan, but they've stopped. They went after Griffin the instant they discovered he had powers. It's like they're collecting new information when they can get it."

"They've been unable to replicate the initial experiment. Your biological mother did something to your DNA," Mary said. "Maybe the Syndicate need all of you to complete the puzzle."

An ominous thread drew all the evidence together, leaving an unanswered question hanging in the air. *What would the Syndicate do if it completed the puzzle?*

Parker answered: "If they get all the information they need, they could create an army of instant, powered soldiers."

All of this talk was not helping Griffin's nerves. Lilo was late. It was almost night. He decided to try for the knife flip option and resumed pacing the room. But instead of catching the knife, he focused his power on the metal object to raise and lower it, then spun it, and honed the finer precision part of his skill to aim the knife.

When a figure burst into the room, he dropped the knife, almost stabbing his toe through the boot.

But it was Grace, still in her green scrubs. She lowered her medical bag and wildly surveyed the room until her gaze snagged on the man she needed. Evan was poking his fingers on Sloan's reopened keyboard, much to her chagrin. Evan looked up to catch Grace rushing toward him, barely bracing in time for her leap into his arms. He caught her legs around his waist and hugged her tight. The passionate kiss they shared was enough to make everyone in the room blush.

Behind a smirk, Parker cleared his throat loudly.

"Get a room," Sloan mumbled, trying to angle away because Evan was still next to her.

"Thanks. Don't mind if we do." Evan grinned back, and carried Grace toward the exit, but she wriggled out of his hold.

"Wait," she said. "Are you hurt?"

"Nah, Doc, I'm good."

"That's because Griff did most of the work," Parker stated, eyebrow raised.

Nevertheless, she checked Evan with her hands, deftly searching his body for signs of injury. She turned to Griffin and her eyes widened.

"My goodness, Griff. Your face!"

Griffin's fingers went to his sore forehead where it came back tacky and stained with red. It was fine.

"Come here, let me check you."

He shook his head. "It's not bleeding anymore. I'm fine."

"Oh, dammit. You're all a bunch of stupid heads— standing around casually looking like you've gone through an apocalypse. Just let me check you." Grace stormed to collect her medical bag and came over to him. "Over there on the stool."

"Go on and sit. Don't be a stupid head, Griff," Evan joked, giving him serious eyes.

"Fine." It would keep him occupied until Lilo got there. Griffin moved to meet Grace at the central table and perched on a stool. He supposed his forehead was a bit sore. Perhaps that had been the crunch when Doppenger pushed him along on the street.

Grace squinted and poked and prodded around his head. "I think you fractured it," she murmured, then said over her shoulder, "Hon, can you do me a favor and wet this?"

She handed Evan some gauze.

"Call me hon again, and I'll do anything you want." He gave her sultry eyes.

She snorted and refocused on Griffin, checking his pulse and shining a light in his eyes, testing for concussion. A few seconds later, Evan came back with the gauze. Grace used the damp cloth to pat and wipe down Griffin's face.

"While you're doing that," Parker said, coming up to stand behind Sloan. "It might be a good idea to talk about a certain someone's tracker being disabled."

"Wyatt?" Mary asked, tone hardening.

Parker ran his hand over his head. "He's gone dark."

A frustrated rumble came from the base of Evan's throat. "I don't like that. Not at all."

"None of us do, Evan." Parker shot him a derisive look. "But we're not making any decisions without the whole family here."

Griffin winced at Grace's dab to his forehead.

"Sorry," she said. "Just testing. The swelling is mostly down. With your healing, you should be fine in no time."

"That's what I said," he replied curtly.

Evan shoved Griffin on the shoulder. "She's just looking out for you, bro."

"I apologize, Grace."

"And what about these?" she continued, unperturbed as she poked through the holes in his fighting leathers. "The skin looks grazed, but closed over and healing. You're all damned lucky you have this fast healing skill. Still… maybe a course of antibiotics will help with a possible infection."

"We don't get infections."

"Oh. That's right." She straightened and packed her things back into her kit. "You're all good, then. Just eat and get some rest. Now, what about you Parker?"

He arched a challenging eyebrow at her.

Grace pursed her lips. "Have it your way. I won't check you." She checked her watch. "I should probably get back to the hospital. I just came to see if you were all okay."

"You can't stay?" Evan whined and reached for her.

She smiled softly. "I'll be back in a few hours. Just a small appendectomy today."

He tugged her in for another kiss. "Dinner?"

"You bet ya! Oh," Grace said. "I almost forgot." She went back to her medical kit and pulled out a folded up piece of paper, holding it out to Evan. "You should probably show everyone this."

"Shit, yeah. Thanks Doc. I forgot." Evan showed a sketch of Wyatt working in an unfamiliar restaurant. He held it out and rotated around the room so they could all take a look. "Does anyone recognize any of the other people?"

"I do."

Griffin's heart seized at the sound of Lilo's voice, and he whirled around.

She stood in the doorway. Ruffled hair spilled around her weathered face. Small stitches lined her temple, but when her eyes landed on Griffin, she beamed. His breath hitched.

"What you talking about? What's that?" Liza sidestepped Lilo and came into the room, commanding attention as she peered at Evan's paper. She gave an unimpressed expression and then held up a syringe. "I'll bet mine is better. Empty syringe from the whack-job. We can test the contents."

"Is Doppenger awake?" Parker asked.

"Hate to be the bearer of good news, but the asshole died. Burned his insides out with this shit." Liza threw the empty syringe vial to Parker who plucked it effortlessly out of the air.

Griffin couldn't care less about their exchange. He wanted Lilo, and his power swelled with unchecked emotions, impatiently. More screens blacked out as he crossed the room.

"Out there," Parker ordered Griffin, pointing to the door.

"Don't come back until you're in control. I don't want my equipment ruined."

Fine with him. Griffin strode toward Lilo with laser sharp focus. He didn't even notice Evan stepping between until he was upon them.

"You know who this is?" Evan held up the sketch to Lilo.

Griffin slammed to a halt. His mind spluttered at the man standing between him and his mate. What the hell? It took a moment to process the sudden intrusion blocking his reunion, but then the muscles rolled under his skin, tensing and tweaking, ready to let loose. With as much restraint as he could muster, he carefully placed a hand on Evan's shoulder.

"Out. Of. My. Way," he ground out.

Evan glanced at Griffin and must have seen murder in his eyes because he stepped back.

"Sorry." He made an awkward face, still retreating. "I get it, bro. I'll ask later. My bad."

Griffin's mouth twisted with frustration, scooped Lilo up and kept walking with only one thought replaying in his mind. He needed to be one with her.

Lilo giggled and slipped her hands around Griffin's neck. "I missed you, too," she murmured, then shouted back to Evan, "It's Misha Minski's family restaurant."

Then they were along the corridor and at the lift. Griffin hit the up button to get to his apartment. "You can talk more later. Right now, we have more important things to do."

CHAPTER THIRTY-SIX

LILO LIKEKE

With absolutely no idea where she was being carried, Lilo kissed Griffin passionately. She was dirty; he was filthy; they were both sore and worse for wear, but she didn't care. She had wanted to touch him for hours, to make sure he was okay, and there he was—carrying her in his powerful arms. Arms that saved so many lives today.

"Lilo," he muttered against her lips. "I'm taking you to my room."

She went in for another kiss, but he moved his face to look away. It was then she noticed they stood before the elevator that went up to the apartments, but Griffin couldn't get the button to work. He shifted to free his hand and stabbed again. No luck. It blinked and flickered.

"Damn power," he burst out.

"What's wrong?" She was already dragging his jacket zipper lower, trying to get inside. She wanted to touch him, to feel his heart beat steadily against her palm. To reassure herself he was okay, that he was there.

"When I'm around you like this," he said, squeezing her rear pointedly. "I can't concentrate. The magnetism inside me goes haywire and disrupts electrical signals."

A smile tugged at her lips. She made him like this. Her. She slipped her hand inside his jacket, and under the collar of his undershirt. The skin on skin contact made him close his eyes with a throaty groan.

"Keep touching me and I might drop you."

"You won't do that." She leaned into kiss his neck and a guttural sound ripped from him.

"Fuck it," he bit out. "I'm taking the stairs."

She laughed, loving his urgency. She didn't think she'd ever heard him say the F-word. But... "Aren't you exhausted? You should put me down."

"I think I'm having a second wind."

Lilo squealed as he shoved through the stairwell door and took steps two at a time. She didn't try to argue and held on for the ride. Before she knew it, they'd traveled up four flights—maybe five—of stairs, burst through his apartment door, through the living room, bedroom, and onto his bed. He was breathing hard, but he never slowed once.

She landed on her back, bouncing on the mattress and bedding, blinking as she came to her senses. The big hero loomed over her with a look of such concentration and longing on his face that she couldn't breathe from the intensity.

"I'm sorry." He put his hands on his hips while he caught his breath. "I should have told you about Doppenger earlier. If I had, he'd never have had the chance to take you."

"You knew?" For a moment, her desire plummeted. Her world came crashing down. She propped herself up on her elbows, frowning at him. "Why didn't you tell me?"

"I knew what he meant to you once, and I didn't want to hurt your feelings. I wanted to keep you separate from that, and safe."

"When did you find out?"

He paused, still panting. "I suspected when he punched me in the office, drawing blood. He's working for the Syndicate. The same people who experimented on us when we were children."

Her heart broke a little. As children. Those bastards, the same ones who fed Donnie that sick serum. Anger boiled through her and she gripped the sheets. Those assholes had been getting away with their horrible experiments for decades. It shouldn't be allowed. Resolve hardened in her gut as a new goal took shape. "They're my new unicorn, Griffin. I'm going to find out who they are and reveal them to the world."

Silence.

She looked up to his surprised face.

"You're not angry at me?"

She thought about it. "No. I mean, I wish you had trusted me enough to tell me earlier, but... I understand. This was an extreme situation. I wouldn't want you anywhere near them if the situation was reversed."

Suddenly, she had a face full of angry Griffin. "Don't ever keep something like that from me. I don't want you in danger."

"Deal, but…" She put two palms to his chest and pushed him back. "Don't lie to me again. You can trust me."

"Deal." Desire flared in his eyes and he hastily peeled off his jacket. "Enough talking. I have to have you now. I'm so hard, it's like steel. I'm sorry, but I can't wait for a shower."

Her brain short circuited when he tugged his undershirt off, and her eyes dipped appreciatively to the bulge straining the pants that had no give. But then… a shower? She glanced at her body. God, she was covered in dust, dirt and scrapes. So was he. They would dirty the sheets. But as she turned back to his shirtless frame, all ropey cords and tight muscles, she realized he wasn't waiting for that kind of permission, but for something else. The last few times they'd been together, she'd insisted on being in control. She had been afraid of being hurt again.

No way would this man ever hurt her.

He'd fought a beast for her.

He'd die for her.

She leaned back on the bed and dragged her skirt up, revealing her legs until the fabric bunched at her thighs, all the while holding his smoldering gaze. "It's okay. I need you too."

His composure broke. He unzipped his leather pants to pull his erection free.

Yep. Steel. Rock hard. So many other stupid metaphors blubbered in her mind while she watched him pump with his fist, trying to relieve his ache. Desire bloomed in her body, making her nipples hard enough that his eager eyes went straight to where they strained through the fabric of her top.

"Lift your blouse," he demanded. "Let me see you."

She pulled it off, bra as well, and sat there with his heavy-lidded gaze drinking her in. His naked desire made her squirm under his attention. When her own fingers got tired of waiting, she squeezed her sensitive breasts. He made a desperate sound, took two strides to the bedside table, found a condom, ripped the packet, and rolled it on. Gripping Lilo's ankles, he dragged her toward him and spread her legs. He shoved her panties aside to drag a finger through her wetness.

She writhed at his intimate touch, clenching deliciously as he teased and tested her.

"You're ready for me," he rasped, a pained expression flitting across his face.

"Yes." She arched into him, body aching to join with him. Urgency made her voice tight. "Now, Griffin. Don't make me wait. I need you too." No truer words had ever been spoken. She needed him more than air. She needed to feel his strong arms around her, holding her, making her feel good. Making love. She needed to know he felt the same way.

But he simply stared at her, eyes roaming her body.

"No more waiting," she begged, eyes tearing up—all the adrenaline of the day finally coming down, crashing through her system. *Don't make me beg.*

He gently touched a finger to her trembling cheek, right underneath the stitches at her temple. Darkness shrouded his expression as he took in the injury, but when she shuddered, he brought his gaze back to hers and he softened. Slowly, he lowered himself until his large body consumed hers while he braced beside her head. He was so close. Lips hovering over lips. Breath heating between them. So real and present.

Fuck Donnie. Fuck him and his wicked words, saying that Griffin didn't care about her, that she wasn't worth his time. She squeezed her burning eyes shut and drew in a ragged breath.

"Shh," Griffin crooned near her ear, stroking her cheek. "It's okay. I'm here." And then he thrust his length in, all the way to the hilt.

She cried out as he filled her completely, eyes rolling while blissful heat crawled up her spine. He buried his face into her neck and moaned against her skin, adjusting to the sensation of being inside her, whispering sweet words into her flesh—how much he needed her. How much he wanted her. How he couldn't live without her. Everything her heart felt for him—all the while holding himself firm, unforgiving steel inside her.

Soon, ragged breaths replaced his words and he rocked his hips, moving slowly at first, and then fast and unrelenting. With each thrust, he took himself to the hilt, hitting her most sensitive spot, sparking heat throughout her body.

"I could have lost you." It was almost an accusation coming from his lips. His fingers speared into her hair, grasping until he bared her face to him, to see the naked fear in his eyes.

"I could have lost *you*." Tears broke free, and she clawed his back, trying to hold his hard and sweaty back. "You could have died. I love you, Griffin. Don't ever leave me."

"Never."

"Faster. Harder," she demanded, gripping him tight.

At her plea, his movement took on a kind of desperation —a soul-splitting drive to get closer to her—and she met him with each savage stroke.

He captured her mouth in a relentless, teeth-knocking, ruthless kiss that only ended when everything tightened, when her body seized with sweet tingling pleasure and her climax crashed so hard that she had to gasp for air. After he joined her in release, they remained together and he rolled them to the side, breathing hard as they hugged, faces buried into each other's necks.

After a while, she blurted, "I love you, Griffin." Because maybe he didn't hear her the first time.

His arms tightened around her, but he said nothing.

Did he not… was she… was he going to say it back?

She drew back to look in his vibrant blue eyes. "Aren't you going to say something?"

He frowned. "I don't love you."

Her heart stopped. "Wh-what?"

"It's more than that. Love is too small a word for how you make me feel, Lilo."

"Okay." Okay. What did that mean? What does too small mean? Not enough? A four letter word? Oh, God. Already a million things were running through her head. Was he just not that into her? Because, um, hello, that was amazing sex, and…

He lifted her chin to meet his eyes again.

"Lilo."

"Yes."

His lips curved smugly. "Marry me."

"What?"

"You heard me. Marry me. That's how much I love you. I don't ever want to be apart."

"I…" She bit her lip. "Oh fuck."

"You don't want to?"

"It's not that. I love you, Griffin. I'll say it a million times if I need to. You've made me feel like no one else ever has. I'm so confident around you. I feel loved. I feel… worthy. Happy." Tears sprung to her eyes. Damned tears. Would they never leave? "But I don't want a big wedding. I have no money, and these things cost a lot. You know I've seen how these big family weddings go in the magazines. Sometimes there are ice sculptures and bands, and… you belong to a prominent family—"

"I'll pay for it."

"That's not the point. Besides, I don't have a family to invite. My dad's in prison. My mom is God knows where—"

"I'm your family."

"—and all that wedding excess reminds me of my mother. I don't want to become her."

That was it. Her real fear. The money, the extravagance…

Griffin's finger traced patterns on the back of her neck. The small touch calmed her.

"So we have a civil ceremony," he said. "We elope. Just you and me. No money. No extravagance."

"Really? You'd do that for me?"

"I want to be with you. I don't care about anything else."

She drew his lips to hers. "Then yes, Griffin Lazarus. Yes, I'll marry you."

He grinned, perfect white teeth flashing, blue eyes crin-
kling. And it was the most majestic sight she'd ever seen,
better than any treasure a human—or mythical beast—could
possess.

CHAPTER THIRTY-SEVEN

TWO WEEKS LATER

GRIFFIN LAZARUS

Griffin held onto Lilo's hand tightly as they entered the visiting quarters of the prison just outside Cardinal City. The room was cold and concrete. Tables and chairs were bolted to the ground, and a menacing guard watched from the corner of the room, making sure his presence was known. Cameras also kept a close eye on inmates. Lovers, parents, reluctant children all filled the room, visiting with their misguided family members.

Because of his guilty plea and cooperation in investigations, Lilo's father was kept out of the maximum security prison. Griffin would have preferred he'd stayed at the super-max, but he couldn't deny the fact Lilo's father had little greed in his soul. He was a man driven to extremes for the misplaced love of a materialistic woman.

"You ready?" he asked Lilo as they were shown to a vacant round table in the corner of the room.

She glanced at him, but tightened her grip. "Yes. Thank you for coming."

"I wouldn't leave you to do something like this alone. We're family now."

Her eyes glistened, and she lifted her left hand to look at her wedding band. It was a plain platinum band. No diamond engagement ring. She hadn't wanted anything, but he'd convinced her a simple ring was something they could both share. He wanted the world to know she was his. He had a matching one on his own hand.

The security door leading to the prison buzzed open, and a guard came in with Lilo's father—Haulani Liota. Griffin tracked the shackled man as he was led by the elbow across the room. Dressed in a jumpsuit, the man had a shaved head and appeared to have lost a little weight, but he was happy. The grin on his face as he took in his daughter could not be dimmed.

"Hi Dad," Lilo said as he took his seat.

"Pumpkin, I'm so glad you came." Haulani met Griffin's eyes. "And you must be Griffin. Thank you for taking care of my daughter."

Griffin gave a curt nod but said nothing.

"I can take care of myself," Lilo said, affronted. "You know that, Dad. But yes, this gorgeous man here is my husband."

Haulani's eyebrows winged up. "Husband?"

"Yes." Lilo's voice rose in pitch and she opened her bag to retrieve a small picture album. Her fingers shook with nerves, but she opened the album and showed it to him. "We were married at the courthouse yesterday."

There weren't many pictures taken, but Griffin had insisted there were some. Mary and Renata had come to act as witnesses. Lilo wore a basic white dress that she insisted on purchasing herself, and Griffin wore a plain tailored suit.

"I wish I could have been there," Haulani said, a melancholy tone creeping in.

"Me too," Lilo replied. Griffin knew family meant a lot to Lilo, and having this reunion with her father, no matter how troubled, was a step in the right direction for her. He also knew that he would do everything in his power to let her know she was cared for and loved, even if she shied away from the attention sometimes. She *was* loved.

He may have let her have her way with the wedding, but he'd make it his mission to show her all the ways she was important to not only him, but the rest of the people in her life.

Her father oohed and aahed appropriately at the pictures until they got to the end of the album which was a good segue for Lilo to discuss the pictures they found in his safe.

"Why did you have them, Dad?"

His eyes darted to Griffin in such a way that suggested Haulani had taken a good look at the pictures and knew exactly who Griffin was. When he turned his gaze back to his daughter, he said, "I was approached by a woman to gather irrefutable evidence as to the real identities of the vigilantes. Paid a lot of money for it. At the time I was under pressure to increase my income."

"For mom, you mean."

Haulani stared at his daughter knowingly, but remained tight-lipped.

"I don't know why you keep trying to protect her, dad. We know she was the one who drove you to such extremes."

"I have to accept responsibility, pumpkin. I could have said no. Love makes us do strange things, I suppose. Have you heard from your mother?"

Lilo shared a resigned look with Griffin. "We looked into it, but after your assets were frozen, it became difficult to track her. We think she was sighted in Jamaica."

Her father sighed deeply. "Good."

"Good?" Lilo was outraged. "How can that be good?"

He shrugged. "Love makes us do strange things. I just want her to be safe."

"Dad. She encouraged you to do bad things, and now she's leaving you to rot in here while she's gallivanting around the globe. For the record, I'm not happy about that." She reached across the bench and took her father's hand, despite the stern rebuke from the guard in the corner. "And for the record, I'm glad you've taken responsibility for your part."

Griffin cleared his throat. "And regarding that part, what can you tell us about the woman who paid you for the surveillance pictures of my family?"

Haulani thought about it. "She was tall, beautiful, had long white hair."

Falcon.

"She was hard to say no to. She knew exactly what I hoped to get out of the arrangement—the money and… yeah. She knew the darkest fear of my heart so she could capitalize on it."

"Do you have her contact details?" Lilo asked.

"No. She called me from an unregistered number."

"And why didn't you pass the pictures on?" Griffin asked.

"Because I read my daughter's article about the vigilante turned superhero. I knew how much these heroes meant to her, and… I just couldn't do it. Couldn't break her heart again. I made sure that she was the only one who could gain access to the safe. I knew Lilo would do the right thing if something happened to me." He met his daughter's eyes. "I'm sorry, pumpkin. I should have done the right thing a long time ago."

Lilo sniffed. "I believe you."

The guard came up to the table. "Time's up, Liota."

"You'll come again?" he asked his daughter.

She nodded and it brought tears to her father's eyes.

When he was gone, Griffin took his wife's hand. "Come on. I'll buy you lunch."

***

GRIFFIN GUIDED Lilo into the front entrance of Heaven. He'd called ahead to make sure arrangements were in place, and everyone was where they were supposed to be. Lilo didn't know it yet, but his mission to make her feel loved had already started. Before he opened the door to the restaurant, he stopped and took her by the shoulders.

"I need to tell you something," he said.

A worried tone washed over her expression. "Is everything okay?"

Nerves churned his stomach and for a split second of

doubt, he considered taking her to another restaurant. But…
No. He needed to do this for her.

"I lied. We're not here to have lunch."

"We're not? I'm hungry."

He laughed. "Well, there is food there, but…" His hand slid along her arm to grip her hand, and then he pushed open the door. "We're here to celebrate."

"CONGRATULATIONS." A thousand voices shouted in unison.

Lilo's palms flew to her cheeks. "What?"

The entire restaurant had been hired out and filled with wedding reception decorations and family. His family were all there, plus her family and friends. Renata, Misha Minksi and her family, Bev, Candy, Fred the Editor. Anyone whose life Lilo had touched had come to bless her union with Griffin, and to wish her well.

She turned to him with tears in her eyes and for a moment, his heart clenched. Would she be angry?

"It's nothing fancy," he whispered, leaning into her. "No ice sculptures."

She burst out laughing and wiped her nose. "Thank you, Griffin. I never imagined something like this in my life. Especially not after the morning we had."

"I once asked you what impressed you. Do you remember what you said?"

She frowned and shook her head.

"You said you were an actions speak louder than dollars kind of girl. So I thought this… all this is something I could do to show that you are loved, that you are worthy and that you have family. So… Always, and forever. I'm here." Griffin took her hand and looked around the filled room. "We're all here."

THE END.

Thank you for reading *Greed*. I hope you enjoyed Lilo's and Griffin's story. Next up is Wrath. Read on for an excerpt, or order your copy of Wrath Now.

WRATH

WRATH EXCERPT

WYATT LAZARUS

It was pitch black when Wyatt woke in his borrowed bed. His lids snapped open as he lay there, all senses straining because something was off. The wind knocked the windows from the outside. He pushed his sixth sense out to feel for the sin of wrath, but his sin wasn't like envy or greed— wrath mainly reared its ugly head when shit got real. He sensed nothing but the breeze, his heartbeat, and his ragged breath.

Then he registered the temperature. Hot, but it wasn't a hot night. It was *he* who felt sweaty. Feverish. His skin prickled and warmed as though he'd come down with the flu. Maybe that was why he woke... but he never got sick. None of his siblings did. They were born with resilient immune systems and regenerating cells that healed exponentially, making recovery time short.

So why was he awake?

He held his breath, slowed his heart and listened.

Seconds ticked by.

Then a woman's moan hit his ears and everything went on red alert.

What the actual fuck?

A shuffle. Something dropped.

"Where's the goddamn light?" she hissed through the dark.

Wyatt tensed. Either he was having a weird dream, or there was a woman in the room with him. Two thunks reverberated on the cheap floating floorboards. Boots? Sliding and scuffling followed. Why would a female be searching his room, and—another soft thud as something fell to the floor —*Christ,* she was getting undressed!

Who would be getting undressed? Must be the daughter who used to live there. *There* being the semi-detached apartment above their suburban home garage. It was only one room, a bathroom and a tiny kitchenette. One bed. Sliding doors opened onto the garage roof that doubled as a balcony with external steps leading down to ground level.

It had to be her. What was her name, again?

Movement as his bed dipped and another moan, as though she wasn't feeling too good.

He swallowed, mouth dry.

"Ahh," she sighed, landing ungracefully, face first onto the pillow beside him, sending a waft of feminine perfume and alcohol into his lungs. "Home at last."

She's drunk.

Her hand arced out, perhaps to stroke the sheet beside her, but hit his ribs instead. She patted around to test the odd shape her bed had taken. Her soft palm hit his face, his hair… down his naked chest. Wyatt winced and froze, holding his breath as if it would turn him invisible.

What should he say? He couldn't say anything! He couldn't speak.

She was going to freak.

But she didn't. She made an appreciative sound while her hand headed south, bumping low over the ridges of his abdomen, slick with sweat.

An electric shock sparked between them and they both jackknifed up.

Fifteen years of martial arts and combat training had him springing to land deftly on his feet, while she stumbled and grabbed her head with a pained groan.

"Stop spinning, room," she muttered.

He turned his side-lamp on but, when his thumb went to depress the switch, he pushed right through it. The damned thing crumbled in his hand like a cookie. *Shit*.

She switched her lamp on and the room illuminated.

Wyatt lost all train of thought as his eyes locked onto her body—pure, lush feminine curves, toned in all the right places—naked except for a dark crop-top and panties. It was the kind of body men would give their left nut to see in the flesh. Blond hair stuck up in a disarray of curls around her head. Wide blue eyes blinked but, where he expected fear, he found desire burning back at him.

Aw, hell no.

He scrambled back, hands out, and shook his head. He wanted none of this. No fucking way. He didn't care how cute she looked, or how many of his atoms were clambering to touch and taste her like—he shook his head to dispel his derailing thoughts. What the hell was wrong with him? *No.*

"I like this dream," she purred and seductively crawled over the mattress toward him.

He refused to speak, and she made a girly growl of appreciation that shot straight to his groin like an aphrodisiac. He thickened immediately, and she noticed. She licked her lips, eyeing him at the crotch. When he didn't move, she glanced up, confused. "You're so quiet… like a *koteczek.* Come to Misksha…" She couldn't say that last word properly and repeated it a few times, then she broke out laughing. "Miscop. Mishko. Mizzzz." She giggled again. "I'll get it right at some point. *Koteczek,* come to Misha."

She tripped over her knees, collapsed and rolled off the bed, calling out for her *koteczek* to come out and play. He didn't know what the fuck she rambled about, only that he'd better take control of the situation. The last thing he needed was for her father to think he took advantage of her, especially when they were already disagreeing about most other things.

He should kick her drunk ass out. Surely there was room for her at the main house. It would teach her a lesson for turning up unannounced. But Vooyek would be pissed. He was a good man. Alek was a good kid. In fact, the entire family was decent, even that chatty older sister. He shouldn't give a shit about the way they ran the restaurant. He should just fix Betty and get the hell out of there, but he couldn't help inserting his expertize, especially when it came to meal prep. For Christ's sake, they used instant potato in their kopitka. There was no way in hell, he'd serve that in his restaurant. He'd skin any chef alive if they tried that shit with him. *Seriously, fucking Betty Crocker instant potatoes.* If it was his—

It's not your restaurant, an insidious voice clipped from the back of his mind. *You're only there to earn enough dough to fix Betty, and then you're out.*

He growled at himself.

"Ooh *koteczek* has a growl." Still on the floor, she rolled to her knees then rested her head on the mattress, as if it was too heavy to keep upright. She muffled half-heartedly into the bed: "Like a tiger. Rwoarr!"

When she quieted, and her breathing evened, Wyatt gently helped her back onto the bed and settled her on pillows where she promptly tunneled into, moaning about the delicious smell he'd left behind. When he put the blanket over her, she kicked it off until she was bare. He tried one more time, but after she dislodged the blanket again, he left it and went to stand on the other side of the room until he figured out what the hell he was going to do.

But instead, all he could do was watch her, mesmerized. He stood there for minutes, perhaps hours with the aware-ness of her presence tingling down his skin. As he stared, conflicting emotions encircled him. Eerily at peace but incredibly aroused at the same time. Every inch of skin felt hot and clammy to touch, not to mention the fucking shame boner that wouldn't go away. This was wrong.

Light from the lamp made her skin sparkle with glitter. Curious woman. With her every breath, new parts of her body came to his attention. Delicate collarbone. Firm thighs and calves. Breasts swelling over her barely there top. She had the kind of body you worked for. Not muscular, but trim, taut and voluptuous at the same time. This woman wasn't a slacker, by any means. She worked hard, and from the sound of her drunken talk earlier, she played hard. The thought sent an unruly thrill through him, shattering the calm, and with each passing second, his heart rate picked up, his breathing escalated. He was stuck—enraptured.

Traitorous fingers twitched to touch her. When he held his palms in front of his face, the sight of his Yin-Yang tattoo on his left inner wrist had the wild beating of his heart stumbling to a halt. He blinked and rubbed his eyes. He rubbed his thumb over the ink, but it was still there, equal parts black and white for the first time in years. Completely in balance.

Bullshit. Fucking bullshit.

It was a coincidence, nothing more.

But the room began to spin as the truth punched him hard. Why else would he feel feverish? Sweat still prickled his scalp, and he itched all over. It was a biological response. There was only one reason for this… she was his mate.

No.

Sara had been.

The fiancée who'd betrayed him, not this drunken woman in his bed. But the tattoo was never perfectly balanced with Sara. It was close, but not perfect.

All the anger and self-loathing he'd felt over the past few months came flooding to the surface, threatening to choke him. It filled his veins with napalm. It trembled through his muscles. It tightened his face until he tasted blood on his tongue.

This Misha wasn't his soulmate, the one who would bring inner harmony to his turmoil, because if she was, then he'd had no right to be angry at his brother. No right to run from his family. Every ounce of righteousness he'd thrown up as protection was unfounded.

No.

With an almighty roar of defiance, Wyatt stormed to the bed and tipped the mattress, rolling Misha effortlessly to the ground. She landed with a thud on the other side. Before she had a chance to rouse and respond, he threw open the door and left in only his boxer shorts, breaking into a barefoot run down the suburban street dusted with dawn. It wasn't until he was halfway down the road that he noticed the broken door knob crumbling in his hand.

FIND out what happens next in WRATH. Get it on Amazon.

JOIN LANA'S VIPS

Subscribe to Lana's newsletter and receive a free box set, first dibs on giveaways, special printable freebies and more. You won't want to miss out.

subscribe.lanapecherczyk.com

On Facebook? Join Lana's Angels Reader Group https://www.facebook.com/groups/lanasangels

CHARACTERS & GLOSSARY

The Deadly Seven

(Appearance in order of age from youngest to eldest)

ENVY: Evan Lazarus
SLOTH: Sloan Lazarus
GLUTTONY: Tony Lazarus
GREED: Griffin Lazarus
LUST: Liza Lazarus
WRATH: Wyatt Lazarus
PRIDE: Parker Lazarus

Mary Lazarus: Adoptive Mother of the Deadly Seven and ex assassin for the Hildegard Sisterhood
Flint Lazarus: Adoptive Father of the Deadly Seven

Other Characters:

Dr. Grace Go: Surgeon at Cardinal City General Hospital. Mate to Evan Lazarus.

Lilo Likeke: Investigative reporter at the Cardinal Copy. Mate to Griffin Lazarus.

The Syndicate

The Syndicate is a secret organization who believe the only way to save the world from its own harmful self is to eradicate all sinners, even if that means destroying half the world.

THE BOSS: Julius Allcott

SARA MADDEN: Ex-girlfriend of Wyatt Lazarus

FALCON: Enforcer for the Syndicate

The Hildegard Sisterhood

The Hildegard Sisterhood are nuns with a history reaching back to medieval times when the original Sister Hildegard struggled against a male dominated clergy. Now the world know her as the founder of scientific history in Germany, but back then, her opinions were disregarded until she claimed to have visions from God himself. Belittling herself as a woman in order to be heard was only the beginning of the humiliation the woman faced.

So she started her own abbey filled with women. That same abbey exists today and is a place where women are celebrated and their education encouraged—minus the male influence. Records at the Sisterhood archives reveal they had a hand in the rise of many women over history from *Joan of Arc* to *Indira Gandhi*. From *Catherine the Great* to *Margaret Thatcher*.

Under the surface of the auspicious abbey lays the secret mission that no woman will ever suffer the same struggle as Hildegard and they condition a select few "Sinners" to enforce this mission. These Sinners are trained as assassins for the cause: Sinners like Mary Lazarus. A necessary evil.

In the prequel novella, *Sinner*, Mary Lazarus escaped the Sisterhood who wanted to use the children for their own gain, much like the Syndicate who created them. To this day, she is still on the run.

ALSO BY LANA PECHERCZYK

The Deadly Seven

(Paranormal/Sci-Fi Romance)

The Deadly Seven Box Set Books 1-3

Sinner

Envy

Greed

Wrath

Sloth

Gluttony

Lust

Pride

Despair

Fae Guardians

(Fantasy/Paranormal Romance)

Season of the Wolf Trilogy

The Longing of Lone Wolves

The Solace of Sharp Claws

Of Kisses & Wishes Novella (free for subscribers)

The Dreams of Broken Kings

Season of the Vampire Trilogy

The Secrets in Shadow and Blood

A Labyrinth of Fangs and Thorns

A Symphony of Savage Hearts

Game of Gods

(Romantic Urban Fantasy)

Soul Thing

The Devil Inside

Playing God

Game Over

Game of Gods Box Set

ABOUT THE AUTHOR

OMG! How do you say my name?

Lana (straight forward enough - Lah-nah) **Pecherczyk** (this is where it gets tricky - Pe-her-chick).

I've been called Lana Price-Check, Lana Pera-Chick-ywack, Lana Pressed-Chicken, Lana Pech...*that girl!* You name it, they said it. So if it's so hard to spell, why on earth would I use this name instead of an easy pen name?

To put it simply, it belonged to my mother. And she was my dream champion.

For most of my life, I've been good at one thing – art. The world around me saw my work, and said I should do more of it, so I did.

But when at the age of eight, I said I wanted to write stories, and even though we were poor, my mother came home with a blank notebook and a pencil saying I should follow my dreams, no matter where they take me for they will make me happy. I wasn't very good at it, but it didn't matter because I had her support and I liked it.

She died when I was thirteen, and left her four daughters orphaned. Suddenly, I had lost my dream champion, I was split from my youngest two sisters and had no one to talk to about the challenge of life.

So, I wrote in secret. I poured my heart out daily to a diary and sometimes imagined that she would listen. At the end of the day, even if she couldn't hear, writing kept that dream alive.

Eventually, after having my own children (two fire-crackers in the guise of little boys) and ignoring my inner voice for too long, I decided to lead by example. How could I teach my children to follow their dreams if I wasn't? I became my own dream champion and the rest is history, here I am.

When I'm not writing the next great action-packed romantic novel, or wrangling the rug rats, or rescuing GI Joe from the jaws of my Kelpie, I fight evil by moonlight, win love by daylight and never run from a real fight.

I live in Australia, but I'm up for a chat anytime online. Come and find me.

Subscribe & Follow
subscribe.lanapecherczyk.com
lp@lanapecherczyk.com

facebook.com/lanapecherczykauthor

instagram.com/lana_p_author

amazon.com/-/e/B00V2TP0HG

bookbub.com/profile/lana-pecherczyk

Made in the USA
Las Vegas, NV
05 October 2022

56588697R00240